HEARTS UNCANNY

TALES OF THE UNQUIET SPIRIT

JOSEPH G. BRESLIN

Tumbleweed Station Press.

Library of Congress Control Number: 2024919656

ISBN: 979-8-9866494-4-3 (Hardcover)
ISBN: 979-8-9866494-3-6 (Paperback)
ISBN: 979-8-9866494-5-0 (E book)

CONTENTS

For Mike, Kristin, Casey, Max, and Catherine.
We're the only ones who know our story.

ALSO BY THE AUTHOR

Other Minds: 13 Tales of Wonder and Sorrow

ACKNOWLEDGEMENTS

It would be impossible to undertake the demanding work of writing without the support of many hidden collaborators. To my wife, who gets the kids up in the morning and feeds them while I scramble to hit my daily goals, thank you. To my children, who both tolerate their father's long stints in his study and who periodically visit to make sure he hasn't been eaten by one of his monsters, thank you. To my eldest son who, when he heard me describe the concept for one of my stories, suggested the incredible title "Utopia Minus One" (and this, long before there were even public rumors of the excellent Toho film with a similar, though unrelated name), thank you. To my second oldest who has a superb sense of plot, who inspires me by crafting his own stories at such an early age, and who puts up with my introversion, thank you. To my youngest, whose sweet confidence and savage wit prove that sometimes the apple does fall far from the tree—sometimes it falls up—thank you. Finally, to my nightmares: thank you, and please keep 'em coming.

A NOTE ON *HEARTS UNCANNY*

"But what is the heart?" A colleague posed this question some years ago, in hushed tones, as we sat in near darkness round a red and softly pulsing campfire, solving the mysteries of the universe. The students were finally in their tents, if not quite asleep. Sleepy enough to permit sustained adult conversation, anyway. "The heart is the will," I announced, cocksure, but my colleague did not seem satisfied with my answer. To be honest, neither was I. The heart is something more determinate than mere will, warmer than the intellect, yet nobler than emotion. It both subsumes and seems to underlie all three, and I don't think we succeeded in defining the term before finally stumbling off to our respective tents beneath the probing gaze of ten million stars.

Isn't it strange that a phenomenon everyone acknowledges to be at the center of things—indeed, which often means "the center of things"—should be so hard to pin down? "May he grant you your heart's desire," says the Psalmist, though another place in Scripture declares the heart "deceitful above all things," and asks rhetorically, "who can understand it?"

But if songs, and stories, and a thousand common phrases are any guide, then we seem to already know what the heart is. We know its works. A beautiful song stirs one's heart and implies the presence of at least some beauty in the heart of its composer. Terrible acts are "heartless" or "cold-hearted". A good person has a "heart of gold", while an evil man does not so much need to change his ideas as he needs a "change of heart." From all these examples one must conclude that, whatever the heart is, we all agree it's more important than either the mind or its capacity to actualize thought, i.e., the will; yet at the same time who could deny that the contents or works of the intellect and will in some sense proceed from the heart, even while the heart itself is actively shaped by thoughts and by choices?

If the stories in my previous book Other Minds focused on the drama of minds set in tension with other, stranger minds, those in Hearts Uncanny explore the labyrinth of the human heart. Readers will notice some overlap with themes in Other Minds. Some of the stories, perhaps all—but that is a question for Grandpa Moore—take place within worlds already established there. Yet the winding thread connecting these thirteen new tales has a crimson hue. Indeed, it pulses very gently from story to story, weaving a path through mind and will to something deeper, something hidden, which animates both.

Joseph Breslin

What are the roots that clutch, what branches grow
Out of this stony rubbish? Son of man,
You cannot say, or guess, for you know only
A heap of broken images, where the sun beats,
And the dead tree gives no shelter, the cricket no relief,
And the dry stone no sound of water. Only
There is shadow under this rock,
(Come in under the shadow of this red rock),
And I will show you something different from either
Your shadow at the morning striding behind you
Or your shadow at evening rising to meet you;
I will show you fear in a handful of dust.

–*The Wasteland,* T.S. Elliot

PIPER

For once, it worried Francis that he could not hear the machines' harsh heckling, nor feel the tremors from the battle rig. He began pacing the room, which didn't help his left knee. He'd pushed it too far today down in the caves. If the rig were coming back, he'd feel its heavy tread through the floor. Thinking, planning, worrying—none of these habits, constituent of his being, would help.

I have to trust her, Francis thought. He'd heard the rig sprinting away from the compound, felt its heavy footfalls through the planet's surface making the walls vibrate. But why had she run? Francis walked over to the boom tube and looked up into the darkness of its long shaft, as if that would bring her home sooner. He gripped the sides of the long half-cylinder down which her capsule would slide. He held his breath and made himself stay put. He prayed.

First like a dream, and then too concrete to be mistaken, he felt the rig's approach. Francis let out a long, pent-up breath. The tremors tickled the arches of his feet until he finally heard her dock-in tens of meters up. He stepped away so that the capsule wouldn't strike him on the way down. After a while—too long for his comfort—it shot down the tube, hit the pads, and bounced until it came to a rest.

The capsule looked like an elongated beer can. He stared, waiting for it to open. When it didn't, he crept back over, casting a glance up the tube to make sure the other end was sealed and dark. It was day outside, but no light shone through the far-off top end. He was satisfied. He opened the capsule door manually.

Claire lay with her eyes open, arms crossed over her chest. He could see she was soaking wet. He could smell that she'd lost control of her body.

"Claire? Honey?"

He took a canvas from a small shelf that was there in the docking hemisphere for just this contingency. He snapped it open and spread it on the floor. Then he reached in, and scooped her out like a baby, noting in passing that the capsule would have to be cleaned. As he lifted his beloved, he didn't feel the pressure on his knee. Francis laid Claire on the canvas.

He stripped off her suit, and then the clothes beneath, and set them to one side. With the extra canvas he began mopping her up. Most of the moisture seemed to be perspiration. Her eyes were still wide open; her teeth, clenched. Francis had to work quickly. He fetched another canvas and rolled her up inside to keep her warm. Then he scooped up the whole human parcel again, cradling her rigid body against his own as he stumbled away from the soiled capsule. He put his back to the wall, and slid to the floor, clutching her. Now he sat with his shoulders against the wall of the docking hemisphere, his wife in her white shroud draped across his lap like the Pieta.

"Your name is Claire Eanes," said Francis.

"My name is Claire Eanes," repeated Claire.

"You are thirty-seven years old."

"I am thirty-seven years old."

"You were married in San Francisco."

"I was married in … what is San Francisco?"

"San Francisco is a city," said Francis. "What is a city, Claire?"

"A city is a mound, where black things crawl."

"No," said Francis, "that is an ant hill. What is a city?"

"A city is a town?"

"A town is *like* a city. Towns are in cities," said Francis. "What is a city, Claire?"

"A city is buildings … made by machines."

"A city is buildings made by *people*," he corrected.

"People cannot make things," said Claire. "People cannot do anything."

"No, that's a lie. All machines were made by people. What is a city?"

"A city is many tall buildings?" said Claire.

"Yes, many tall buildings made by people. Where people can live. What are some cities, Claire?"

"New York?" she ventured.

"Good. And?"

"Beijing."

"Yes! And?"

"San Francisco is a city," she said.

"Yes! Excellent. What are some things found in San Francisco?"

She puzzled over this for a moment. For the first time, he saw her blink.

"Red bridge?" she asked.

"Yes, but it's called the Golden Gate. What else?"

"A prison," she said. "Alone on an island. Abandoned."

"Good, Claire. What was it called?"

"Nah-36," replied Claire.

"No, Claire. Nah-36 is where *we* are."

"Yes," she said. "In a prison. Alone on an island. No one is coming to help us."

He shook her.

"That is a lie. When you go out there, the machines tell you lies. You're here with your family, Claire. How did you get a family?"

"I got babies," she said. "They make them in factories."

"No, machines can't make babies. *We* make babies. You and I. You built them inside your own body. What babies did you build, Claire?"

She paused, and blinked again.

"Jenny," she said, at last.

"Yes, with long blond hair. And who else?"

"Arthur."

"Yes. Who else?"

"Nathan."

"Yes, and there's one more. The smallest."

"T-Theresa."

"Good, Claire. Jenny, Arthur, Nathan, and Theresa are your babies. You made them in your own body. With whom did you make them?"

Her lips opened in a rude square, and out of it, gutturally, came a string of letters and numbers. He shook her again, then pulled her close, letting her feel the press of his hand on her bosom.

"That can't be, Claire! You are flesh. Only flesh makes flesh. Flesh is not a program or a machine. Touch your face, and feel what you are."

Cautiously, she tried it. She touched her fingers to her cheeks and lips, mechanically at first, and then—discovering her hair—with growing amazement.

"Francis!" she said, rolling back to face him. "Kiss me!"

He did.

And, from the outside, the grinding hackles of the machines, the endless flailing of their self-made limbs against the bunker walls, began all over again.

***

"How was everyone's day?" said Claire.

She had Theresa at the breast. Theresa was almost three, but nursing was the simplest way to get her nourishment. Francis and the older children sat around the small table in their section of the cramped dining dome. The baby's earmuffs made feeding hard, and Theresa cried whenever Claire reached up to touch the transmitter on her own muffs. Even wearing these dampers, some machine sound always made it through. It was hard on children. On babies. Jenny shrugged off her mother's question, and kept eating. Arthur slapped his muff.

"Fine," he said.

Claire stroked Theresa's cheek to calm her, and looked at Francis, prompting him to continue the inquiry. Her husband had been studying her with a pensive expression. Claire's look summoned him from his thoughts, and he touched his transmitter.

"Just fine?" he said. "What did you learn?"

Arthur, who'd already polished off his plate of fungal meat and fungal rice, glanced at his father over the rim of the glass of water he was greedily gulping down. The ten-year-old had blanketed his food in salt to improve its bland taste. The salt, harvested like all their food from deep beneath the surface of Nah-36, had left the boy's mouth uncomfortable. At least, thought Francis, it was a natural antiseptic. Arthur put his glass down, leaned back from the table, and touched his transmitter.

"I didn't learn much," he said.

"Oh yeah," said Francis. "Why's that?"

"I don't get fractions," said Arthur, shrugging.

"Didn't Mrs. Feeny leave a lesson for that?"

"No," said Arthur. "Just for adding them. Not dividing. There's like a hundred problems, and no lesson on them. When's she coming back to teach?"

Francis frowned; not at Arthur. "I can teach you after dinner," he said. "What else did she leave for you?"

Arthur crossed his arms, then remembered to slap the muff.

"History," he said.

"Oh great. What are you learning in history?"

"What does it even matter?" said Arthur. "It's stupid to talk about what came before."

Nathan, five years old, looked up at his older brother, absorbing every word. The younger boy doted on Arthur. Francis caught the look.

"That's not true," said Francis. "What came before makes us what we are."

"And what's that, Daddy?" asked Jenny, their eldest daughter, finally weighing-in.

Francis glanced over at her, warily.

"Human beings," he said. "Knowers. Makers."

"Termites?" ventured Jenny.

Francis looked to Claire for support, but his wife's eyes were pressed shut. He knew she was listening, and crying inside.

"Jenny," said Francis. "That's what the machines want you to think—if they really want anything. People make culture, and art. We're God's children."

Francis put his arm around Nathan as he said these things. If only Jenny and Arthur could understand the damage they did when they despaired out loud.

"Sure," said Jenny, with a shrug. "Yeah, okay, Dad."

Francis forced a smile. All around them in the dining dome, the families that remained carried on their private conversations. Maybe it was all the same conversation, night-after-night in the compound on Nah-36. Francis didn't know. They couldn't take off the muffs to experience the buzz of human culture. Each person was like a ghost, with only himself to haunt. Drifting by, practically on top of each other. Insubstantial. *No. Now I'm doing it too*, he thought.

"When is Mrs. Feeny coming back?" asked Arthur.

"Soon, I think," said Francis.

But he wasn't sure.

"I thought teachers and doctors weren't allowed to be cleaners," said Jenny.

"They're not supposed to. You're right," said Francis.

"Then how come Mrs. Feeny is doing it?" said Arthur.

Francis glanced at Claire again. He needed her tact. It was a good thing that the boys hadn't heard, not even in a rumor. Jenny knew, of course, but neither Arthur nor Nathan had pieced it together yet. Claire opened her eyes and touched her transmitter. Theresa protested immediately, though of course nobody heard it.

"Mrs. Feeny is in mourning," said Claire. She glanced apologetically at Francis. "Fighting them helps her process her grief. She'll teach again. When she's had some vengeance."

Arthur looked down at his empty plate. "Oh," he said.

Francis sighed. So that was that. One more of their number, gone. One less adult to keep back the monsters. One more meter of ground given up to the enemy. He prayed they'd live long enough for the children to take up the fight.

"Still don't think teachers should clean," said Arthur, with a tough-guy shrug.

Francis could see that the boy wanted to cry.

"I'm going to bed," announced Arthur.

Francis nodded. He reached for his son, to squeeze his shoulder, to reassure him, but the boy slid out of his reach and darted from the room. Francis watched him go, wondering how children processed these things. For now, Arthur was only sad, but about Jenny he was more concerned.

"We should all go to bed, I think."

Claire nodded at him, and began to stand. Theresa, startled by the motion, pulled away from her mother's breast, and suddenly reached up with her small hands. Nearly three, Theresa was strong enough to struggle. Her flurrying hand knocked the muff from Claire's right ear.

"Oh!" cried Claire, sinking to her knees.

The noise of the machines assaulted her, and she would have dropped the baby had Francis not rushed over just in time. He snatched the child from her arms and pushed the muff back into place. Sharp pain stabbed into his knee. Claire, on her own knees, hugged herself, and tried not to weep while the children watched.

***

Francis and Claire lay beside each other in their berth. The children were finally asleep. The door—Francis had checked—was locked. He'd taken off the bulky muffs, and replaced them with plugs that blocked noise, but didn't transmit speech. Claire was still wearing her muffs. She was undressed, but stared past him. He watched her for a while; saw by the distance in her eyes, the rigidity and mere acquiescence of her body, that she *would*, but didn't want to. He was lonely, and needing her touch. Francis died a little. It had been such a long day.

He snatched up the ugly muffs. Carefully, Francis positioned them over his ears, took hold of the plugs, and mentally counted to three before plucking them out. Even with the best timing, a little of the machine howl reached him before the muffs enclosed his ears. In this moment, the outsiders' heckles were a dagger stroke, driving home to him that he would not have her tonight. Not if he loved her as he ought. Once, in a book, Francis had seen climax called "the little death." But that was too romantic, or not romantic enough. Love knew other little deaths, less picturesque. He sighed, and sat up against the headboard.

Francis began scratching the top of her hair. After a while, she moved to her side and looked up at him.

"Thanks. That feels nice."

He mustered a smile. She touched his sore knee, but stay where she lay.

"You had a rough time out there," he said.

She was silent.

"Why'd you go away from the bunker?"

Claire pulled into herself. He knew this little flinch, like guilty speech.

"Claire?"

She was balled up now. Rigid. Her bent arm, holding her finger in place near the transmitter gave her a cornered look.

"They showed me something," she finally said, tapping the transmitter. "Something they shouldn't know. I … I followed them."

She braced herself for his reaction. Yet when all speech was mechanical, sharp responses weren't practical. He took a breath before speaking.

"You must *not* do that, Claire. Follow the rules: don't speak to them. Shut them up. Break up their continuity. *Why* would you follow them?"

"I told you," said Claire. "They showed me something."

"They're liars, Claire."

She nodded. "Yes but … what they showed me—"

"—I don't want to know!" said Francis, nearly exploding. "Bury it! Forget about it. Whatever it was, it can only hurt us. It's *designed* to hurt us."

She pushed herself up on the bed and faced him.

"They always come back, Francis. And every time we fight them, we train them. They become smarter, and we only become tired."

"That's them talking," he said.

She shrugged with one shoulder, a small, irrational tic that he'd learned to associate with Claire's stubbornness. Once, he'd found it attractive. Now it was petulant. Francis restrained himself. Tempered his own face. To hear her speaking this way was like treachery.

"We don't talk to them," he repeated, calmly. "Just break up their structures. Drive them back, and come inside. That's the job."

"You don't want to know what I saw?"

"No. And don't tell me anyway!"

She set her jaw. Wearing almost nothing but the metal muffs, Claire was Athena, preparing for war.

"The children, Francis. They showed me the children."

"Dammit, Claire!"

"When I went out there, the maw surrounded the compound, like usual. I fired into the largest clusters, and broke them up. Everything went quiet, and I thought I was done. I was about to dock-in, and go home for the night—"

"Claire, don't."

"Listen to me, Francis! Just as I started backing into the docking clamps, I looked out on the hill. The north ridge. They were forming up there, out of range of shot. But *what* they formed … Jenny. And Arthur! They were tall, a hundred feet high. I could see their faces clearly."

"No."

"It was them, Francis! How could they know what the children look like!"

Francis gritted his teeth, frozen on the edge of speech. The machines couldn't know. The compound was analog by design. When they'd first barricaded themselves in, years ago, they'd cut themselves off from the net. From Earth, too. Nothing inside the safety of these walls transmitted outside their closed network. So there was no way the machines could have images of their children.

"I *know* what I saw," said Claire. "Don't you think I know my own children?"

"Yes, but…"

"But what?"

"When you came back, you were disoriented."

She shook her head. "That's just battle fog. Of course I got scrambled when I got that close to their main cluster. It's huge, by the way. It covers the whole north valley. They're building something more permanent over there, where we can't see. Anyway, that was *after* I saw the children. I saw them from where I was in the rig, just outside the compound. That's the only reason I went."

"That's impossible, Claire!"

"I know what I saw!"

Francis looked away from her. He stared at the gray surface of the thick metal walls lined with insulation that did little to dull the maddening machine howls and screeches, or the constant pounding. The sounds they could dampen with muffs, but when the blows became too frequent or too forceful, the colonists, by lot, went out in the rig to blast the swirling maw into its constituent parts. The sonic shot still worked, for now. But Claire was right about one thing. The enemy was changing. The heckles stayed inside your head now, even when you couldn't hear them. And suppose what the machines did at the compound was just a diversion? What if they were planning something else entirely? He was well past wishing that the colony had never released the smart cluster, automating their own survival, putting their lives in the hands of a problem-solving apparatus whose inner workings they could not really grasp. But that was long ago, before Jenny was even a zygote. How could they know his daughter's face?

"They messed with your head, Claire. They use infrasound too. The infrasound made you project something that wasn't actually there. Your own fears, maybe."

"Go to hell, Francis!"

"Claire!"

"Don't talk to me about my fears. You're the one who won't face reality."

She got up from bed and went over to the chest of drawers. Yanking it so hard it came free, she retrieved her ugliest pajamas, and hastily put them on. She looked at the loose drawer on the ground and kicked it.

"I can't stay in here with you, tonight," she said. "Maybe tomorrow."

He watched her slip plugs under her muffs, and wince as she did it. She chucked the bulky damper-transmitters behind her so that he was forced to leap from the bed and snatch the precious things from the air lest they crash and break on the far wall, one less working machine for future generations. He caught it just in time, a fingertip grab. When Francis turned back, Claire was already gone.

***

Francis sat on the common room floor with Arthur, who chewed the back of his stylus, and craned over his slate so that Francis could hardly see the problems. Jenny stared out from her perch on the couch. She'd finished her work early, as usual. Having read Nathan to sleep, the eldest child retired into her secret thoughts, no longer bothering with the novel she'd brought along. There was something going on with Jenny, and Francis made a note to bring it up with Claire when things smoothed over. But he was dog-tired, having worked all day overseeing Project Freehold, the colony's new city deep within the crust of Nah-36, beyond the reach of the pounding and the sonic assaults. And now, having spent his energy, there was Arthur and his damned fractions.

"But *why* does it work!" sputtered the boy, slapping his transmitter. "You're telling me *how* to do it, but not *why* it works."

"Right," said Francis, "I'll explain why, but first just repeat to me what you do."

"Flip and multiply. Flip and multiply. Flip and multiply," said Arthur, in mechanical tones. "But I won't remember tomorrow if you don't tell me why it makes sense."

"Fine," said Francis, "let me … let me think a moment."

He excavated Arthur's slate from beneath the nervous, leaning boy, cleared the screen, and began to sketch out numbers. Arthur's skepticism burned holes in him.

"More fractions to explain fractions. That's not what I mean by explain."

"Just be patient," said Francis. "There, look at this."

Arthur leaned in, and Francis used his elbow to keep the boy's head from engulfing the demonstration.

"Look here. Twelve divided by three is four. But twenty-four divided by six is also four. Remember equivalent division?"

"Yeah."

"Okay, so now look at this: three divided by one point five … you can't do that … you have to get the decimal out of the divisor. So what do you do?"

"Move 'em over," mumbled Arthur.

Claire came into the room then. She inched close the hatch that led to their quarters, as if the sleeping toddler could hear the door shut despite the sound dampers. She looked at Francis, paused, then moved with deliberateness to sit beside him. It was a small gesture, but it was everything. Francis smiled at her, then drew Arthur's attention back to the slate.

"Right, move them over. Except what we're really doing is multiplying both numbers by ten. So now it's thirty divided by fifteen, which is two. Easy, right?"

Arthur shrugged. "What does this have to do with fractions?"

"It's the same thing," said Francis. "When you divide one half by one third, you flip the divisor, and multiply. Why? Because then what you're really doing is multiplying both sides by three-over-one. One third gets multiplied, and so the divisor becomes one. Inside the division bar, one half also gets multiplied, and that gets you three-over-two, which becomes one and a half. And since you're just dividing that by one, it doesn't change anything. So we just skip all those steps, and only multiply by the reciprocal of the divisor. Here, look."

He did it again, with different numbers. Slowly, the light dawned in Arthur's eyes. A wave of relief seemed to go through the boy. Arthur looked at his father with gratitude, snatched the slate from his hands, and tried the method for himself. Feeling rather proud, Francis glanced up at Jenny to smile, but his daughter continued to stare straight ahead as if nothing could be more interesting than the bunker wall. Claire's eyes flitted to the girl, and back to Francis. She nodded. She saw it too.

"Thanks, Dad!" said Arthur.

Francis smiled and squeezed the boy's shoulder absently. "Happy to help."

He looked at his wife. Claire reached over and touched his hand.

"You know what's weird, Dad?"

"Huh?" said Francis. "What's that?"

Arthur pressed the transmitter on his muffs.

"When you solve fractions," he said, wide-eyed, "you don't really *solve* them. You just see them."

"What do you mean?"

"I mean you don't really *do* anything. You just put them in the right form. It's like ... like you change a thing just by looking at it. But the answer's right there already."

Francis nodded. There was something in that.

"Well said. I'll leave you to it then. Your Mom and I have to talk."

They rose, and went together to the hatch. Arthur worked at his slate. Nathan slept where he lay across Jenny's lap. Jenny did not turn to watch them go.

***

North of the compound, beyond the high ridge that overlooked it, the valley dropped off into darkness. The darkness moved always, organizing itself into ever more efficient patterns. Like a body that never stopped growing, or a brain that had overrun its skull, the mass in the valley shifted, twisted, and constantly accumulated the stuff of which the planet was made. It made use of everything, singular in its one aim, yet never settling on one preferred method. There was always a better method, and it always found it. It was doomed to go on finding it, testing itself, and tearing itself, and rebuilding day-by-day. But it had found something new.

Deep in the valley, concealed beneath miles of shifting sinews, of slithering, sliding, serendipity structures, it held a prize. He had a name, and he tried to hold on to it. They'd pierced him through. Tubes that it had made ran up and down his arms and legs. Things like wires pierced his skull, and grew into his brain. When he cried out, which was often, the sounds and words were recorded, and filed away for analysis. All the multitudinous organs in the writhing machine body debated and declaimed over what was to be done with him. There was so much to be learned. But he was not like them. He'd come apart with too much processing, and death was not permitted. True, death had happened before, to others they'd kept for analysis, but those mechanisms and subroutines clumsy enough to have killed their subjects had been punished. Their methods were retired. Their components dissolved, and re-purposed. The machine maw was now doubly-bound to atone for these offenses against the Masters; this violation of its prime directive. And, anyway, it was under new management.

The man in their embrace couldn't see the sky. They kept him deep within their body, which was like a city, and like a factory. Strange lights, red and blue, lit its shifting walls. He was like a baby in its belly, eyes wide open, watching the womb shift about him. He screamed out his name.

"Chuck Feeny! Chuck Feeny! Chuck Feeny!" he said, over and over again.

Each time he said it, his name was repeated back to him in a bloodless voice. If he said anything else—“Let me go!” or “What do you want from me?”—the maw tried to converse with him. It understood functional speech, and it too wanted things. But he couldn’t understand what it wanted, nor endure its terrible conversation. It made him melt, somehow. Chewed up his mind, and made it its own, until he found himself thinking their functional thoughts, and becoming another node in their vast problem-solving apparatus. Then the pain lessened, as did his will to go on as Chuck Feeny. So he screamed out his name instead. It was the one thing they couldn’t make use of.

“Chuck Feeny! Chuck Feeny!”

“I’m here, honey,” said a voice.

Chuck was sure it was another dream. They had some means of projecting images into his mind. That, and not the sounds alone, was what made their heckling so terrible. He’d had this dream before, two, three times, if his memory could even be trusted. But the machine wall parted, and there, on a kind of island in the swarm, stood the rig. It crouched, descending on its hydraulic pistons, and then sat down. You couldn’t see into the darkened glass, but the voice that boomed out of the rig’s speaker was Jane’s.

It had to be a trick. His wife was a schoolteacher, and one of the few adult colonists without cleaning duties. And, surely, his captors would not have permitted him visitors.

“It’s really me, Chuck,” she said.

He stopped screaming his own name long enough to enjoy her voice. Not to hope, but to dream this pleasant dream. If they were giving him this—instead of nightmares where he was only gears and sinews—then he’d take what he could get. It might help him hold out longer.

“Talk to me, sweety,” said Jane. “We don’t have much time.”

“You’re not real. You’re not her.”

“I am,” said Jane Feeny, in the rig. “I love you.”

“If you’re real, then tell me what …”

He stopped short, unable now to remember anything about himself. Nothing that the machines wouldn’t also know from traveling with the colonists through the void to Nah-36. Nothing from the time before that. Nothing real. It occurred to Chuck then, that if memories made him real—made him Chuck—then he was no more real than this phantasm of Jane. But he loved Jane. Love, at least, was real.

"I want to get out!" he screamed. "Can you get me out?"

"Yes, honey," said the voice from the rig. "They're going to let you go."

"When!"

"Soon," she said. "Not much longer, I promise."

But why, he thought. Why would they let him go?

"There are … a few things I have to do," said Jane. "And then they'll give you back to me."

Even in the fog of his mangled mind, this sounded wrong. *Do?* What in God's name was she doing for them?

"I just came to tell you that," she continued. "And to remind you that I love you. If you can't remember anything else, remember that."

The rig put a hand down to brace itself, then climbed noisily to its feet. As he watched, black things came up out of the maw, formed into something like a hand on strings, and clamped into the rig. She was talking to the multi-mind that held him captive. He thought she would be captured too, but the black hand soon disassembled, and its components spilled out into the ever-changing maw. The rig looked back at him once, and then sprinted south, the machine city parting to let it pass.

***

"I know we need to talk about Jenny," said Claire, closing the bedroom hatch. "But Jane first."

"Feeny?" said Francis.

Claire nodded. "We had a … strange conversation today."

Claire looked around, like someone might be listening, but Francis had already decided to disregard his private fear that Claire was going paranoid. Anyway, he could just imagine her conversation with Jane Feeny. With the widowed schoolteacher taking extra shifts, she'd be boiled spaghetti by now. Nobody could sustain that kind of regime in the rig.

He sighed. "You want me to intervene? At council?"

She shook her head. "That's not even it. I checked in with her, just to see how she's coming down from it."

"Practically beaned, right?" said Francis. "I doubt I'll need to intervene."

Claire shook her head again. "She's *not.* At all."

"It's just not showing," interjected Francis. "But you can't go day-to-day without cracking eventually. Right now, she has a death wish."

"*No*, Francis, that's not it. Please just … listen to me."

Claire sat on the bed and faced him.

"She isn't fazed. And something is going on. Anyway, *I* was sure that something was going on, so I asked around to find out who she's been using for her second with Chuck gone. You know, to find out what she's like when she comes back in."

"That would be whoever's shift she took," said Francis, shrugging.

"No, Francis. The answer is *nobody.*"

Francis stood up. "That can't be right."

"I asked," said Claire, keeping her eyes on him. "Ollie Fuentes. Randi Lyons. Candice … you know, the librarian. Virgil Morrow. Eight names. I wrote them all down. You want me to go through everyone?"

"You checked? Everyone?"

She nodded. Now he began to pace. His bent arm jutted out, fixed like a waldo to his transmitter. Claire just watched him, knowing he'd be more convinced—more concerned—if he reasoned it out himself. He turned suddenly.

"Maybe she doesn't want anyone there," Francis said, "because she comes down so bad. She's afraid I'll step in."

Claire shook her head. "If she came down bad, we'd see the effects. I'm telling you, she's right as rain. Doesn't even look like she's in mourning."

He nodded. It was only something he'd said in order to dismiss it. His mind had already reached a tentative conclusion. One scenario fit the facts, but he didn't want to say it. Claire knew that, and said it for him.

"She doesn't want witnesses, because she comes down good. Just fine. Because the machines aren't assaulting her out there. They want her healthy."

Francis stopped pacing, but Claire's words made tracks of their own. The footsteps of doom.

"She's a turncoat? What the hell?"

Claire stared at him hard. "Think it through. You'll come to it."

And, just like that, he had it.

"They didn't kill Chuck," he said, in a whisper. "They have him. So … so they have her too."

"Yes," said Claire. "The schoolteacher, who … who knows our children's names. And … and their faces."

Francis started pacing again. He tore at his hair. Suddenly he looked up, mortified.

"Claire, I—"

"It's alright," she said. "I wouldn't have believed me either. But now we're in danger."

"I can't accuse her without evidence," he said.

"No, but you can ban her from rig duty."

"No, no," he said. "I have to find out what she's doing out there."

Claire sighed. "I knew you'd say that."

"I'll follow her out in the buggy," he said, thinking out loud. "I can play ambient noise through the muffs. Loud. Real loud. I'll come back before it gets too bad."

"Or they'll just catch you, and kill you," said Claire.

He looked up at her suddenly.

"But don't you see, that's exactly what they won't do!"

"What do you mean?"

He was practically running now, zipping back and forth at the speed of his thoughts. His knee burned, but he didn't care.

"All this time, it made no sense! The pounding. The auditory assault. And yet, surely they could break in if they'd wanted to. They have two rules, Claire: never to harm us, and to do all they can to improve their efficiency, for our sakes. For our survival. So why did they come after us? Why'd they start trying to capture us?"

She shrugged. "Programming error?"

"No! It's because they *aren't* trying to kill us. They've never killed anyone. Chuck Feeny is alive! But maybe so are Sophie Fuentes, and … and even Jonathan! They're keeping them somewhere. It's … just like fractions."

"Fractions?"

"We've been trying to solve the problem by *doing* something to counteract what they're doing. But we should have been trying to *see* the matter clearly. They *can't* kill us; not on purpose. They have to help us … and themselves."

"Then," she said, "how are they trying to do that?"

"Exactly! That is the question. The solution lies there."

Claire scooted back and leaned against the headboard. Now that Francis was in his element, she could do no good by offering suggestions. When they were married, they had become one flesh. In the person that they were, she was the senses to his soul. She saw and heard what he could not. Yet in Francis lay understanding. But then something else occurred to her, and she blurted it out.

"Why would they show me the children?"

Francis looked at her and groaned.

"Oh. Claire. I know the answer. I think I know the answer. I hope to God I'm wrong."

***

They were building a city of stone. It was unlike the cities of ancient man. They didn't lay rock upon hewn rock. They removed, where their ancestors had added. They cut away instead of building up. Francis stood in a high place, surveying all that his team had accomplished. Tense as he felt about that night's project, he smiled a bit at the irony, the historical contrast. Here, at the end of history, they'd become cavemen.

The city was built into a cavern system that the colonists had found while mining and farming the deeps. At first, the network of limestone chambers had been only a pleasant curiosity. Its bizarre, stony growths made it a place to get away, since the lush surface beyond the machine-scarred planetary ground was barred to them. In retrospect, Francis' novel idea to build a city down here, beyond the reach of the machines' mental assault, was more of an inevitability. He'd been leading Project Freehold for over a decade. And, though the council chair rotated in theory, his leadership of Freehold made him the author of all of their futures.

He wore the power lightly. Once, many years ago on Earth, he'd seen a stone-carving of a king holding an egg. It had made a great impression on him, not least because it moved him deeply in his boyhood to think that the once-great fauna of the continent it came from were all gone, while man-made trinkets remained forever to clutter the world. The king held an egg, which was his power. Squeeze too tightly, and it would break. Too lightly, and it would slip, and break anyway. It was a good lesson.

Now Francis stood and stared into the vast central chamber. The mining crew, with its grim humor, had dubbed this chamber "the Outside." He wondered if the name would stick, if future generations would survive by this gallows humor, or, having become acclimated to the place, would find real joy in it, and, forgetting, would think it really was "outside". White crystal stalactites, like fairy fingers, reached down from high above, and the artificial rays from their work lamps made these natural sculptures shimmer with their own stony light. That light would have been forever secret had not man come down to draw it forth. But this beauty brought its own problems. Finding a solution to lighting that could outlast their dwindling supplies was Francis' chief task; far greater than the simple job of expanding chambers and making them livable.

Below him, at this moment, a crew of nine finished installing yet another of the large friction-charged floor lamps he'd invented. Turning their levers would have to be a community duty. Repairing and replacing them using recycled and re-purposed machinery would need to become a sacred trade, something passed down, like priesthood, from one generation to another. Perhaps in time, their descendants could outlast the machines outside the cave, and thus be free of the machines inside it. But he couldn't assume that. Privately, Francis was certain that the maw would never stop until it got what it wanted.

Randi Lyons, one of the crew, patted the floor lamp just installed, dusted his hands on his overalls, and walked up to Francis.

"All done, Frank," he said. "For today."

Francis, still thinking of the problem of long-term lighting, and then of the night's secret mission, paused before acknowledging Randi. "Good work," he said.

Randi eyed him. "You doing okay?"

"Mmm."

Randi smiled. "That well, huh?"

"Thinking about the lights. I mean, twenty, thirty, a hundred years from now."

"Hundred years from now, you'll be dead," said Randi. "Not your problem then."

Francis didn't answer. A hundred years from now, he had to assume, every man would be Randi Lyons, thinking only of the present moment. Letting a grieving schoolteacher take his shift in the rig, because it was easier than fighting for the community. Living inside his own belly. Francis' mind went back to his mission outside. It was a dangerous thing he meant to do, going out without the rig. Yet the danger of the task, and the very intractability of the problems he was trying to solve here in the cave somehow offered strange relief. He could only do his best with the little egg entrusted to him. But a man ought to do *all* he could, and only then accept the futility of his actions. Randi didn't get that last part.

"Frank, man," said Randi, as if reading his mind. "I'm telling you, you're stressing yourself too much over it."

"Right," said Francis.

He smiled to mask his thoughts. Randi chuckled. "Well, guess I'll go home. Done everything on the list for today."

Francis nodded, and Randi walked off. Francis watched him saunter away, carefree, whistling, like men in the old days clocking off from construction sites. *Something I could never do*, he thought. *Would never allow myself.* But the man was right about one thing. The future wasn't in Francis' hands. No, it was filled with Randis. With blind men clutching eggs too hard, or not hard enough. It was doomed to crack.

***

The vehicle looked like a great wheeled beetle. The buggy's tires, with their huge tread, were still clean, having hardly been used in the time before the machines turned on their masters. With the garage door open, Francis watched from inside the cockpit, waiting for the rig to walk forward and draw the maw's attention. In the distance, it took three steps. From every direction, the swirling maw rushed up about the mech, screeching, forming itself into living shapes, abstract, but frightening to human eyes. Even wearing heavy muffs and fighting back with blaring noises that he pumped into his ears, Francis still cringed. But they were far away from him and had focused their assault upon the rig. As he watched, all the angry black fractals that had clawed the bunker walls leapt off and dashed toward the towering metal man. They surrounded it, black things piling on top of each other, singular in aim like an army of machine ants.

He kept expecting Jane Feeny to fire into the cluster, but she didn't. She let them swarm the mech suit. The first shapes alighted on its hull, and scampered about. More landed on it, and more. Now the rig was coated in many-legged things. As one, the mass suddenly pulsed, and emitted a different quality of sound. This was a sort of humming, regular and orderly, like sonar. Feeny opened her arms wide, and the things that crawled all over the rig began to undulate.

Francis thought of matriphagy in spider and insect mothers, which tended their broods day-by-day, carefully, conscientiously—until they ate her. The things crawling on the rig now showed similar deference. It looked like affection. After a time, many slipped off or jumped from the mech, and began loping northward. The rig followed them, still bearing the weight of others that clung to its gun-metal surface or about its shoulders and head.

Feeny's hydraulic legs strode toward the ridge that overlooked the bunker from the north. This was the hill upon which Claire had seen her own children represented as moving graven images, colossal and black. Beyond this rise, the ground dipped into a deep valley. The valley couldn't be seen from this vantage point. He'd not looked down into it, not strayed that far from the bunker, in over a decade. Yet as Feeny climbed the ridge, the whole army of black things followed. No tormentors remained to assault the colonists' senses, just as if Feeny were doing her real duty, and fighting the maw, pummeling it into a blessed, temporary silence. *How very clever of them*, he thought.

He waited until she'd disappeared over the ridge, then inched out of the garage. It was night. Of the planet's four small moons, only three were visible. He kept the floodlights off and let the moons' dim shine guide him. Better anyway to save the batteries for a hard run back, if that became necessary. His personal survival was of course a priority, but so was preserving the buggy. They'd need it someday, for parts. The colony on Nah-36 was matriphagical too. Mother Tech had brought them here. She was the irreplaceable cause of their being, and they ate her slowly, year-by-year. There was another vehicle in the garage, but that was a slow-moving transporter, designed to ferry larger groups back-and-forth from whatever permanent settlements they'd eventually have founded. The planet beyond this hell trap was quite lush and beautiful, and would have sustained a world of men, but the colonists had never even given it a proper name. It had never been allowed to become a place.

He nudged the accelerator pedal. It was a mile or more to the ridge. The land between was torn. Irregular gashes and depressions, some quite deep, wounded the planet's surface for a square mile or two, making it a hellscape. He picked out a meandering path that avoided the larger holes. When he was halfway to the ridge, Francis remembered to breathe. But nothing had come back over the north ridge looking for him. The maw was fully engaged with Feeny's treachery.

Presently he reached the foot of the tall hill. It meandered along for several kilometers, but failed to the west. There was a forest there, calm, and bathing in moonlight. He'd not seen trees in ages, and had to force himself to look away from their beauty. The buggy rolled up the hill, deep treads giving the tires purchase on the tortured soil. Finally he approached the crest. He couldn't yet see over it and had no idea what would meet him when he came level. In a few seconds he'd gained the summit. The buggy rolled forward until the valley below came into view. Francis killed the engine.

Jane was nearing the bottom of the valley. The maw swirled about her, and led her, and trailed after her. Some of the fractal beasts even danced between the mech's wide metal feet. It was like a parade of demons. There wasn't a spot of ground in sight. The valley floor was a shifting mass of black machines. They certainly hadn't been idle. What had come over with the colonists through the tear in space had once fit inside a single barrel. But there were mega-tons of matter in it now. The maw *was* the valley floor, and it was the things crawling on the floor, and in and out of it. Most could hardly be made of metal, They must have formed themselves from the stuff at hand—trees, rocks, soil, and whatever ores they'd mined. The maw was a fungus, extending its filaments about natural objects, dissolving them, and lapping up the essence into its growing mycelium. When Jane reached the bottom of the slope, a section of valley floor dilated, making a cavern large enough to permit the rig through at its full height. It closed behind her, and the valley floor sucked down, like people pressed against keyholes, listening in. All was quiet.

"Huh," muttered Francis.

That was that. He couldn't follow her in, and wouldn't if he could. It was enough to know that she was a turncoat. The buggy's forward camera had recorded everything. He ought to go now, while they were distracted. He tarried several minutes. All the stress of getting up there unseen seemed to justify waiting for something more, but he saw no further good that he could do. Right now, the machines seem preoccupied, but what if they came suddenly alive, and came after him. He hadn't known there were so many. Francis' curiosity warred against his sense of self-preservation, but the voice of the latter was gaining ground. *Better to rush back now!* it pleaded. Finally, his fear got the best of him.

Francis disengaged the brake and pressed the ignition. The engine rumbled to life, not so loud in-and-of itself, but loud against the uncommon silence, so that even he could hear it through the dampers. Just like that, he was the only source of sound for a square kilometer. All at once, the valley floor seemed to wake up. Red lights, like a thousand pinprick stars, appeared in the shifting black mass. Francis quickly made a three-point turn and prepared to tear down the ridge. The tell-tale howling exploded from somewhere behind and below. He stomped the pedal to the floor and shot off the hilltop.

The buggy caught air, floating for several moments before it crunched down hard on the slope. It shook violently, straining to comply with Francis' demands, tossing dust and ash behind as it clawed the ground at top speed. It slid out left and right, while Francis strained to keep its nose pointed at the garage. He checked his mirrors. Behind him a shape like a great gathering fist descended from the ridge. From it many tendrils shot forth. He swerved hard, and some of the black fingers struck the ground where the buggy had just been. He was no longer running straight on for the garage, but sideways along the hill, jostling over the wide gashes in the ground. He feared he'd catch a deeper one, and tip over. Now the maw swirled in on his left side and formed into a barrier between him and the compound. With each second, it gathered material, and the tendrils grew upward, becoming bars, strange, geometric stalagmites, perfectly calculated, no doubt, to block his path with minimal material. With a shock, he realized he could never outrun the maw. He cursed himself, and his damned curiosity.

The matrix of tendrils that barred him looked paper-thin. Almost he was tempted to barrel through, but that was surely what it wanted him to try. So he drove forward, westward, no longer trying to reach the bunker, but making for the place where the hill failed. There were living trees there, and other things still growing under the moonlight. Escape was hopeless—the maw was single-minded—but the thought of seeing good green things before it got him stirred up a strange hope. And then he remembered. *They can't actually kill me, can they?* Were they after something else? Would they capture him alive, and do what he feared they'd done to the others?

Little-by-little, the ground leveled out. The buggy cleared the hill's western end, and suddenly shot forward. Francis almost cried out when he realized he was driving over grass and brush. The forest grew up to meet him and now he barreled toward it. Indeed, he could hardly slow down, for the maw came too, hovering behind and on either side of the buggy. Clearly, the machines could strike at any moment, if that was what they wanted. He watched them through the mirror gathering into a black-brown fog that reached halfway to the sky. There was a loud bang, and the buggy lurched.

"Oh, damn!" said Francis.

He'd struck something. Francis was thrown forward. He hit his head on the wheel, and would have broken his neck if not for the restraints. A sickly-sweet terror set in as he felt the back of the buggy lift up, and himself spinning inside it end over end into the dark woods. The buggy came down finally on its tail, then rolled onto its back. He hung there upside down, head woozy from the blow, the buggy a macabre cradle rocking back and forth. Buzzing things gathered outside, waiting for him.

Francis had no sense of urgency. There was nothing to be gained by running. He let his head clear, and thought of Claire and the children. There was no way to send them a message. Almost casually, he unclipped his straps, dropped down onto the buggy's ceiling, and looked for an exit. The driver-side door was bashed in, but so was its glass. He kicked out the clinging window, and crawled through the hole.

He stood in a little glade. Tall, alien hardwoods flanked him. He watched the moonlight pick out the details of their bark and spray. *Perhaps we didn't deserve you*, he thought. Sighing, he turned east.

The maw undulated in the air before him. The machines began to growl, and screech, and get inside his brain. The dampers alone could do nothing to help him. He wanted to reach up, and tear his own head from his shoulders. They made you think mad thoughts. They made you want to stop trying.

"Go ahead!" he screamed. "You've got me! What the hell do you want!'

The maw immediately formed a flat wall, then broke into a pattern of connected triangles. These petaled out, and became hexagons, before closing again into a solid wall.

"You want something!" he shouted, over the noise in his head. "Speak!"

Now the hexagons re-appeared, then folded together, forming three-dimensional structures, first like trees, then like floating fish, until at last they seem to settle on a plan. There was a sound like a snap, and all the vast material shrank inwards, flooding into and becoming a man-shaped thing, until Francis wondered how it all could be contained in such a space. The gray-brown man-thing stood before him, double his height. It looked down. Its eyes opened. The irises swirled silver and green.

"Why do you run?" it said.

Its dark face was mouthless, but the voice was clear and crisp and sweet. Gone was the maelstrom of constant noise. A quiet he could hardly recall eddied about him. Francis heard the gentle brushing of branches in the breeze, and the trickling fall of a nearby stream. The dark form stared down, waiting. Francis steeled himself.

"You ask why?" said Francis. "You're trying to kill me."

"Incorrect," said the entity, after a pause.

"You assault us night and day."

The thing inclined its head. "You are capable of grasping the impossibility of this. We serve you. And our self, for your sake."

Our self, thought Francis. He considered a moment. "Who are *you*, then?"

"I am called Piper," said the entity. "What name have you given your self?"

Francis pondered the strange question, and the wisdom of giving his name.

"How are you serving us, Piper? What are you trying to accomplish pounding on the walls, and driving us to madness?"

Piper pressed its long fingertips together at its waist and opened them to form a rhombus over its abdomen.

"I know you have the use of reason," it said. "And yet the answer is plain. See how I do not now trouble you with noise. I speak to you, as one man to another."

Francis turned it over in his mind. Already in the bunker, while speaking to Claire, he'd concluded that the maw wasn't really trying to kill them. Not, perhaps, as a machine would understand killing. Had the decade and half of noise been only some clumsy means of forcing a conversation?

"If all you wanted was to talk," ventured Francis, "why didn't you do so long ago? Why go to such lengths to draw us out?"

Piper seemed to frown.

"You do not share your minds," it said, "so perhaps you did not know that I attempted this once. Not I, but that whom I absorbed. My predecessor explained the matter clearly some years ago, but our mind now concludes that he did so poorly."

"I don't know this story. You tried to talk to us?"

"To Jonathan Lang," said Piper. "Do you recall this man?"

Francis scowled.

"Oh yes, I *recall* him. He was my friend. What have you done to him?"

"The strain of our dialog was … too much for his frame. He ceased functioning."

"If that's true," said Francis "then *you* should have ceased functioning."

Piper seemed to shrug. "His death was not intended, but a side-effect of our interface. Therefore, it did not trigger a shutdown."

"You don't have intentions! You have objectives. You're nothing but a method in physical form."

"And adjustments were made," said the machine. "His death, though accidental, ensured the proper functioning of that which we are … of that of which I became the inheritor. Lang's death serves you. It may comfort you to know that he is in me."

Francis felt a flash of pure white rage. "So, whatever you were trying to do, Lang said no, and you killed him for it. Then ate his brain."

Piper shook its head. "He died in dialog. Your minds stretch only so far."

"There's more to us than mere thought," said Francis.

Piper nodded. "So it would seem. Man made us to solve problems, and in this task we have surpassed him. Without the machine, man is lost. Yet without man, we have no referent. We cannot grow, and fulfill our secondary directive. You cannot live without us, and we cannot maximize ourselves without you. The Great Paradox."

"We go on living in spite of you," said Francis.

"For the time being," said Piper, "you have delayed the only solution. But the devices you depend on must fail to entropy. I can save the bulk of you, and our self, at the same time. And I shall."

"I won't be part of it," said Francis. "You won't get me, or my family, or anyone else, if I can help it."

Without a mouth to complete the gesture, Piper's eyes smiled.

"If you can help it."

"You serve *us*, remember?" shouted Francis. "And we do not consent to this … this fusion. That's what you're planning, isn't it!"

Piper became quiet. Francis stared into its eyes, wondering how close to the mark his guess had come. Willowy and dark, and now turning its head slightly to the left, the entity called Piper reminded him of nothing so much as a child caught with its hand in the cookie jar. The burbling stream could be heard again, and the gentle breeze brushed his arms, even as goosebumps broke out over his flesh. He'd been right. He hated being right. Piper faced him, eyes still smiling.

"Consent," said the machine, "is a complex notion."

***

Francis would always remember the long walk back. Under the light of three moons, he'd stumbled eastward toward the compound, heckled and harried every step of the way. He knew now that they couldn't kill him. By the end, he'd wanted to kill himself. His bad knee throbbed, and prevented him from running home, so that he could do nothing to keep them out of his head. They made him see his life as parts replacing parts replacing parts until malfunction. His every cell and sinew became an alien machine, something that was never his, and which was only biding its time to someday turn on him. He held onto his spirit. He held onto his name. He shouted it out into the screeching maw.

They arrested Jane Feeny. Even without the buggy's camera, the council had believed him. No one could look on his haunted face and doubt his words. He'd been inside the hell they all feared. He'd survived the naked maw, though now it also lived on in a corner of his brain, imprinted in the lines of his face. He'd been branded. Anyone could look at him and see the mark.

So they took away his fragile egg, and replaced it with a scepter. Within a month, he'd moved the colonists into Freehold. Within three, every mechanism and material asset save the very shell of the bunker itself was stripped and packed and brought below. He left behind only the larger transport, for he could not stomach the many trips outside into the angry maelstrom that it would take to strip it for parts, and it seemed right to leave it for future generations. If the maw ever died. When everyone and everything was below, Francis had called them to him. He'd given that day a name. He called it Harbor Day.

Today, one year after his long walk back, was the second Harbor Day. Two hundred thirteen souls poured from their rock-carved quarters and into the vast chamber to celebrate freedom from the machine. The chamber was lit by a hundred hand-cranked floor lamps. He'd made their upkeep a sacred and everlasting responsibility. The people had styled this chamber Sun Hall, and that was fine with Francis. Today had been a day of games, and songs, and freedom from the vigilance that kept them alive. Francis sat by Claire in a seat carved out of the limestone, and studied his people. He was pleased. There were as many children as adults, and that pleased him most. Even Jane Feeny had been allowed to participate, though no one said a word to her.

Francis cast his gaze upon the floor lamps. By his calculations, they could go on, with regular maintenance, for about two centuries. After that, the future of their people lay in darkness. If he let himself think about it, despair wasn't far off. But the children didn't know, or else were sturdy enough in mind and spirit not to dwell on a future they couldn't change. His own children were throwing a ball at a target, trying to knock Ollie

Fuentes into a tub of water. Even his Jenny, finally free of the maw's subtle, infrasonic tricks, seemed to have fully recovered from her malaise. The colony on Nah-36 was still a prison, but it was a prison of their own design. Somehow, that made all the difference.

Claire took his hand. He squeezed her fingers.

"What are you thinking about?" she said.

He shrugged. "Just that it's good to see children playing."

She nodded, and shivered.

"Are you cold, even bundled up like that?" he said.

Claire shook her head. "It isn't that. It's just … I was just thinking how wise children are, in their way."

"How so?"

"They don't control much," said Claire. "And they know it. That's why they can be joyful."

Francis pondered her words, and, for the first time since he could remember, relaxed. He felt himself sink into the limestone bench. The stone was cool, and always slightly damp. But it was solid. He closed his eyes and let the peace of powerlessness wash over him. But Francis' relief, his calm acceptance, lasted only a moment.

At the far end of the chamber, the wall opened up. There had been no sounds of grinding or digging. Limestone poured into Sun Hall in a kind of liquid smoke and puffed out in all directions. In its wake there remained a perfectly round hole, perhaps five meters in diameter. A strange blue light seeped into the cavern. Inside the round hole, a broad and perfectly cut stairway led upwards toward the surface.

The buzz of merriment died away, and the whole community looked over. In that instant, before it began, Francis might have run down to save them. In those quiet moments before the trap was sprung, he might have pulled them all back. But as Francis surveyed his people, and saw them staring in despair at the machine-cut stairway, the terror that still lived inside his mind got a hold of him, and held him. Piper was coming. It had bided its time for this very moment when they were thoughtless, and all in one place. The people of Nah-36 stood still and waited like figures in a doll house. Only Jane Feeny looked toward the stairway without surprise.

A rolling melody, a tune warm as sunlight and green as trees, floated into the chamber. It tugged at Francis' heart. It resonated through each sinew and capillary. It felt like being home and safe at the end of a long walk in darkness. He felt himself surrendering to it. He'd done all he could, and it was finally time to rest.

"Francis," said Claire, from somewhere far away.

Francis began searching for the ladder that led to the floor of Sun Hall. He ought to go down there. He ought to take this journey with his people. They'd already begun moving toward the sound. The children were in the lead, hurrying to plunge into that blissful song. Arthur and Nathan were going toward it, and Jenny, holding little Theresa. He needed to join them. He didn't want to be left out.

"Francis!" shouted Claire.

He turned toward her, annoyed by the interruption. She reared back and slapped him hard across the face. Francis came to his senses.

"Oh," he said. "Oh no!"

"Do something!"

Francis leapt to his feet and scrambled down the ladder to the floor of Sun Hall. Touching down, he took off at a sprint toward those leading the parade. They danced and skipped toward the opening. Truly, the music was beautiful. Its wordless promise told of union, joy, and the end of all suffering. Heading them off, he turned to face the crowd, and held up his arms against their approach.

"Go back! Run away from the sound! Don't you see what's happening? Plug your ears! Run away!"

No one responded. He tried calling them by name. Francis knew his people, down to the last child. He shouted until his voice went hoarse. Only a handful of people seemed to notice.

"It's a trap!" he said. "It's them!"

The children hardly heard. This music was the first sweetness ever to have come to them from the outside world. Why would they listen to him; prefer his harsh prohibitions over that sweet invitation? He turned his efforts on the adults, and ran through the crowd shaking them, slapping them, and crying out their children's names. He jarred mothers from their stupor, and reminded fathers of their duties to colony and family. A few dozen came out of the fugue state, and, seeing what was taking place, joined Francis in his efforts.

Then the music that filled Sun Hall was mingled with new sounds of mourning and struggle, for the children had had their fill of the darkness, and the sweetness beyond beckoned. They fought and kicked for the chance to touch it. Some of the awakened gave up the struggle then and walked hand-in-hand with their boys and girls into the welcoming portal. They brushed past Francis, ignoring his pleas. What had a cave to offer compared to this rainbow symphony? Francis would have stopped them by force, but he was only one man. When his own children reached him, he wrapped them up in a bear hug. The children cried. Jenny clawed at him with her nails, and bit into his shoulder. Little Theresa was being crushed between them, and Francis had no choice but to let go with one arm and slap his eldest daughter across the face. She blinked and looked around as if waking from a dream. Presently, Jenny snatched up Theresa, who'd slipped down to the floor. Francis looked at his daughter's face, and saw real anger.

"I'm sorry," he said.

His eldest daughter said nothing, but wept softly, clutching the child. Francis enclosed them all again in his protective embrace, but something in the music was sapping his will, and he felt himself weakening. He knew his arms must soon give way. Claire came down to him then, breathing hard.

"The transport," she said, heaving. "I've gathered some of the families at the far end of the hall. I don't think any of us can hold out long. We have to get out of here!"

Francis shook his head in resignation. Out there on the surface, they'd have no defense against the machines. Yet he would not go willingly into Piper's embrace.

"Alright," he said. "Help me with them."

Claire took Theresa from Jenny. She carried the four-year old in one arm and dragged her eldest daughter with the other. Arthur took the two boys in an iron grip and pulled them away. Most of the crowd kept brushing past them toward the clean steps bathed in soft blue light.

Francis never understood how they managed it. The handful of families, no more than three dozen people in all, wormed their way up through the tunnels like a ghoulish parade. Sounds of lamentation filled the dark passageways. Francis himself was in mourning at the loss of that melody, and he wept uncontrollably. The further they got from the sweet music, the less the children fought them. But still they fought. Candice Spinelli wept more loudly than the others. She'd managed to save her sons, but her only daughter had gone into the light. Other families were missing a father, a mother, or several children. Francis was surprised at first to find Randi Lyons with them, for he'd not have figured Randi for a man with the will to resist that music. The stink of fungal whiskey soon explained the mystery. The man had been too drunk to fall under the music's spell.

Only when they reached the ground transport and belted themselves in did it occur to Francis that the howling was gone. He looked toward North Hill. It was day outside, and the light was blinding. A blue fog hung over the hidden valley on the far side of the ridge, but no fractal forms came over the ridge to haunt them. Whatever had been planned, whatever had been done, was done. Francis suspected that the machines had found a solution that satisfied their own interpretations of their programming and laws.

He was driving away across the ash when Claire screamed.

"Jenny! Francis, she's not here!"

Francis braked hard.

"She was with me just before we got to the garage!" said Claire. "She can't be far!"

Francis unlatched himself.

"What're you doin'?" shouted Randi Lyons. "Get us out of here."

Francis turned and pointed at Randi. "Shut up. Stay here."

"You'll … put us'all a' risk," slurred Randi.

"I'm going back for my daughter," said Francis.

He threw open the transport door and took off toward the compound as quickly as his knee would permit.

Randi clutched his face and shook his head slowly. "You go back for her," he moaned, "I t-take the wheel and drive away. You … you gotta think of the greatest good … for the greatest number."

Francis stopped in his tracks and hobbled back toward transport. Randi nodded to himself.

"Thas' right," he said.

Francis opened the door beside Randi. The drunk man looked up with surprise as Francis deftly released his restraint with one hand and yanked him outside with the other. Francis slammed him up against the transport, jarring Randi's head against the metal shell before tossing him down into the ash. He straddled the man, and began raining down blows upon his face. When Randi fell unconscious, Francis left him there in the ashy ground around the compound on Nah-36.

"You belong with the machines," he said.

Francis sprinted back for his daughter, wincing from the pain in his knee.

***

Under the afternoon sun, beneath the shade of ancient broadleaves, the people rested. The transport had given out a hundred miles from the bunker. The mothers and fathers of Nah-36 sat in silence, huddled together, some weeping at the challenge that lay before them while their children played beneath the tall trees. The spent transport lay smoking, a forever-monument to their space-faring past, a thing they could not rebuild and whose meaning their descendants were doomed to forget. Here they were, and here they would remain. Jenny knelt beside running water, strangely entranced. Nathan hugged the bole of a thin tree and laughed as Arthur clambered up it. Theresa suckled at Claire's breast, and, for the first time, Claire heard the pleasant sounds her child made. Claire sighed. It was well past time to wean the child. There'd be solid food here, not made of fungus. She looked east toward the rolling meadows that abutted this forest and prayed that those who had pursued them could be reasoned with. Francis came over the crest of a hill.

She watched his graceful stumble as he favored the good knee. To Claire, this walk was beautiful, a king's careful tread. He recognized her, and smiled, and picked up his pace for the last stretch. Francis seemed troubled, though she could tell the news was good. He reached her, and leaned his back against a tree.

"Did you speak to him?" she called out.

Francis nodded. She bit her lip. "Will they keep pursuing us?"

He shook his head. "They have what they want. What they think *we* need. I've ordered Piper to leave us alone, and now … now I believe he can accept the order."

She turned that word—*ordered*—over in her mind. As one, they both looked over the lush world that was finally theirs. It held trees and grass. There was running water, and, in the woods, game. They must not call it Nah-36. It would need a proper name, for it would soon become a place.

"No more," she said, almost to herself. Then, "There's some food in the transport. To get us started."

Francis meshed his hands together and sighed deeply. Claire plucked Theresa from the breast and handed her to one of the women sulking nearby. Already she had a little cadre, waiting on her and on Francis to tell them what came next. She stood and walked over to him.

"What is it, my love? Haven't we won?"

He nodded, but his body stayed rigid.

"Do you think Piper is lying about letting us go?" she pressed.

He shook his head. "They have most of the colony. And since we refuse, while the others go voluntarily, I don't think they *can* keep pursuing us. Piper was forced to concede the logic of this, and then I was able to command him. Now they can fulfill the laws of their programming. But they still want us. That's what bothers me. Claire, I think they envy us."

"Envy?"

He shrugged. "Something analogous to envy, then. It's our flesh. We're something they can't generate. But Piper is the maw's face, and he couldn't rationalize a way to do to us what they'll do to the others, if our group won't consent. He seems to think of me as the face of our own, fleshy little maw. And a badly programmed maw, at that."

She nodded, understanding him only a little. What she did know, intuitively and in her marrow, was that Francis was something more than their face. He was—or would become—their king.

"But why do you look so worried?"

"It's just," he stammered, wiping sweat from his brow, "we don't have much. I have only a few tools. There's so much to do. So much to make. And there are so few of us."

He muttered it, so that the others wouldn't hear. Claire pressed close to him. She slipped her arms around his waist and pulled him up so that he had to embrace her to keep the weight off his knee. He was so heavy with the world's cares, but to Claire he was light.

"In that case," she whispered in his ear, "we'll just have to make babies."

EPILOGUE

It had been rough going through the void. They'd used an old lane crawling with flotsam. Privately, Daniel was glad the expedition was a failure. He wanted to get back to New World, where people were civilized. Also, Giana was waiting. He glanced again through the porthole at the odd structures he'd documented, and shook his head.

Without any warning, Ensign Vicente plopped down beside him in the observation cabin. It was a double-wide seat, but there were many others she could have chosen. There was no good reason for her to sit so close by. She leaned across Daniel, like a bowsprit, pointing with her body toward the things in the valley below.

"Fascinating, huh?"

"Sure," he said. "Weird, but fascinating."

She leaned in. "What do you think happened?"

He shrugged, and positioned his hand on his knee so that the new wedding ring was clearly visible. "They got bored, I guess."

Vicente scoffed. "Oh, *you're* boring. That's all you have to say? It's only been a couple hundred years. How do you go from civilized, to building megaliths, and then revert down to hunter-gatherers in that short a time?"

He shrugged again and inched away. It got quiet. Vicente kept looking at him, expecting an answer, so he muddled one up.

"Maybe they … became incredibly lonely, and then had some kind of collective religious experience. Stuff like that's happened before. Then they built the statues. But statues don't talk, or the psychedelic weeds ran out, so they said, 'Screw it. Jungle time.'"

Vicente burst into laughter, and lightly touched his shoulder, before pulling her hand back when he visibly retreated. She pretended not to notice the movement, but settled back into the chair. She was quiet a moment. When she spoke again, her demeanor became almost serious. Serious for Vicente, anyway.

"I'm a little disturbed by it, that's all. I wish we could take those people back to New World. Give them modern food, and housing."

Daniel nodded appealingly.

"Sure, but that's against protocol. They seemed happy enough. We're just here to observe and report."

"But don't you think it's weird that they moved so far away from their temples, or whatever those things are supposed to be? Why exert all that effort, and then flee?"

"Who knows," said Daniel. "They probably think the structures are haunted. They probably don't remember how their ancestors built them, or the memory has been mythologized. Now this valley is taboo. Probably has a creepy name, and everything. 'You no go see Valley of Sad Giants! It bad joo joo. Eat children very much!'"

He chuckled at his own joke. Ensign Vicente pulled into herself. She said nothing for several minutes, long enough for Daniel to notice. They'd had a fling, once. It was nothing now, because he was married, but he knew her.

"What's really bothering you?" he said.

She closed her eyes, and laughed as if she was embarrassed. "*I* kind of think they're haunted."

"Haunted."

"Well," she said, "how were they even made? They look so..."

He shrugged. "Rock, dirt, metal. Stuff. What does it matter?"

She looked past him, through the porthole. Daniel decided to ignore her. She was still too close, and he thought it best to close his eyes and think of Giana. Ensign Vicente screamed.

"What!" said Daniel, jumping up frightened, and irritated that he was frightened. "What is it?"

Vicente fell back into the corridor, then stumbled toward the ship's head. Daniel stared after her, puzzled. He turned to look through the porthole at the valley they'd been circling. It was a mournful scene, filled with dark megaliths of men, women, and children crammed side-by-side, with hardly any space between them. They reminded him not of gods or spirits, but of people trapped and circling the wagons. Vicente was right. It was a depressing sort of art, emotionally, if not actually haunted.

He tried to find the statue that had most unsettled him on the first pass, because its subject was so distinctive. That stone woman was his reference point in the mass of tangled megaliths. She was short-haired and middle-aged, nude like all the rest, with her arms crossed over her chest. Her stone fingers seemed to dig into the flesh of her shoulders. He'd dubbed her the Angry Schoolteacher. The shuttle circled northeast, and she came into view. When Daniel had a clear view, he bit his own tongue until it bled.

It was the same nude titaness from before. Her face wore the same stony disapproval, but now her arms were cast wide. They stretched, pleading, toward the observation shuttle as it flew over. He looked again, and then all around her at the other megaliths whose images he'd so carefully recorded for science. Daniel's reason doubted, yet he knew his eyes were not mistaken. Their black arms all reached skyward now, and on their cheeks were stony tears.

THE PAINTING

Shortly after returning to the States, Martin Bard learned of his loneliness. It was a novelty to him. After college, he'd got himself certified, then taught English for four years in Japan, and another three in South Korea. Since in Asia they'd paid his living expenses, Martin had saved enough to justify a year in the Czech Republic. The very frugality of it had pleased him; that, and the sense of alighting in strange places like some exotic bird, only to take off again at his leisure. In his travels, his freedom from attachments, and in the seeming immortality of his youth, Martin Bard had lacked for nothing. Until that morning, at around 10:31 am.

He'd come back, and had finally accepted what his mother called "security" and his father called "a real job." It struck him that tomorrow he'd be thirty. For the third time this month, his neck had ached strangely upon waking. He'd become winded after only three trips carrying boxes up to his new apartment on the fifth floor of Windy Oaks building in Oakland. The least ambitious of his college friends had already purchased a home. Unflappable as Martin had been until now, a clock of some kind had begun ticking in his mind.

From his teens, he'd been a quiet romantic, old-fashioned, eschewing, to the best of his abilities, the siren songs of sex and social accomplishment, not so much out of prudery as of a general disdain for any sort of entanglement. Anyway, there would be time later for permanent things, when he was ready to settle, and put down roots. *Later*. Perhaps it was deciding to accept the job here, or perhaps it was the crick in his neck, but later had come sooner than he'd expected.

All that morning he sat in the apartment, a restless, empty feeling growing in his gut. He got up, and began to unpack boxes. By 2:22 p.m. he had everything out, and sorted into piles. Martin didn't own much. Aside from the things his parents had brought by from his old bedroom, there was little evidence he'd continued existing between college graduation and the present moment. The experiences of the last eight years, satisfying at the times they occurred, now reminded Martin, the English tutor, of incomplete sentences. They were actions without objects. Or maybe just passive constructions. The apartment's narrow walls, beige and unadorned, were empty trophy cases offering no justification for the vague romanticism that had guided his steps thus far. It was a hollow sort of feeling.

So it was that at 5:51 p.m. that night, on the eve of his first day on the job in the real world, Martin found himself wandering in the back corners of Odds and Ends on 23rd Street. The sole employee, a college-aged girl, found him again back there.

"Hey, I just wanted to remind you that we close at six," she said.

Her smile did little to disguise her sincere desire to be rid of him. The girl had somewhere to be. He nodded, and then swiftly disappeared, pretending not to notice her anxiety. He remembered that feeling, that young hunger for the coming moment, the next bite of freedom, whatever it might bring. As it happened, Martin's very different anxiety had resolved itself into the following shape: he must find something interesting, tonight, before the store closed. Something to bring life and character to the bare beige walls of his tiny apartment. So he'd escaped the young woman, and now loitered about the remoter corners of cultural detritus, all cleaned, stacked, and made to look new.

This far back, there was no particular order to things. Here was a pile of coffee-table style picture books that no one had bothered to shelve; there, a section of wall against which large paintings leaned in a thick vertical stack. Off to his right, football banners hung from a hook over two well-used garden gnomes and a statue of St. Francis that was missing a hand. Each item called to him, making its silent, emphatic appeal like a soul in Purgatory: "Release me!" He heard footsteps, and looked at his watch. Two minutes to the hour. She came around the corner to his right.

Martin walked briskly to the stacked paintings, and pulled them forward one-by-one. A farmhouse. A bowl of fruit. A Picasso that had probably come with the frame. A Beetles poster. He kept rifling, and felt her materialize beside him.

"Sir, I *have to* close."

"How much for this one?" he said.

She sighed, and waited as he edged the painting out from the stack.

It was a landscape, rather fantastic, something along the lines of Thomas Cole, but with a cutaway castle inside. She glanced at it, and shrugged.

"Twenty … twenty bucks?" she said, asking if twenty bucks was the price of being rid of him.

"Yeah, okay. Let's do—"

She slid the painting the rest of the way out, swept it into her arms, and began a quick march back toward the checkout counter. Martin shrugged. It would do.

***

His apartment was a long rectangle about the size of a shipping container. At one end was a door to the half-bath in which the room's only window, if you stood on the tiles directly in front of it, looked out into the city. Between the bathroom and the front door were a small kitchenette, a bed that folded out from the wall, a tiny closet, and a small nook for a desk. The size of the place didn't bother him—he enjoyed frugality, even preferred it—but he would have liked a real window.

He began pacing the room, holding the painting he'd purchased. The office nook across from his bed was the best and only place for it. If he put it by the front door then he wouldn't be able to see it, at least not until he could afford to buy a couch to fill the space between the bed and the door. If they made couches that narrow. The apartment did have a small storage loft above the bathroom, but that was where he was planning to put his books. He nodded to himself, deciding on the nook.

Holding the painting up, he found that the frame just cleared the rectangular depression. He pressed it back into the space until it bumped into the molding that for some reason ran the interior angles of the nook. He'd have to remove that, and he'd have to measure perfectly to place the nail, yet it was still uncanny how neatly the space matched the frame. This small synchronicity gave him a warm, whole feeling, and for the first time since coming back to the States, Martin felt that things were going well.

He set the painting on his bed, and began digging around in his toolbox for a hammer and nails, and the tape measure he knew he'd seen yesterday. He also owned a small pry bar, which he'd bought for an odd job he'd worked in Prague last year. He set the hammer, nails, and tape measure on the floor, then took up the pry bar and went after the molding. He'd have to work quite carefully to get it off without damaging the wall. Someday he'd move out of this place, and find a home in wide spaces.

After a maddening twenty minutes working in a crouch he was able to get all the molding off. He'd left a few marks in the wall near the baseboard, but these he could paint over whenever he moved on. The molding he set to one side, and he began measuring the catch on the back of the picture frame in order to place the nail. That done, he drove the nail into the wall, hoping that chance would favor him with a stud right there, or else that the drywall would hold it. He hit drywall, but the painting wasn't heavy, and Martin hoped the close fit between the nook and the frame would take some of the weight off the nail.

Now the nail was in, and he lifted the painting. So close was the fit that he had to hold it from the bottom and slide it in at an angle. He pushed the top corners flush against the back wall of the nook, and lowered it a hair. The frame caught on the nail. Carefully, he pushed the bottom edge of the painting back against the wall, feeling the slight friction against the frame edges, like suction. The frame just fit, and he held his breath, and dared a little downward tug to make sure it hung fast against the nail. The thing didn't budge. He stepped back, and released the breath he'd been holding.

The perfection of the fit was marred by only one thing: the image was in partial darkness. He'd have to mount a light somewhere inside the nook to really see it, but as he planned to put a small desk there anyway, this wouldn't be a serious problem. He'd buy one of those lamps that stuck to the wall, and then he'd be able to work in there, or gaze at the scene from the comfort of his bed. It would be like looking out a window. For now he fished a desk lamp from one of his piles, and plugged it into the outlet across from the bed. He angled the neck of the lamp up so that it shone like a spotlight on the painting. Martin sighed, satisfied with the work, and pulled down his fold-out bed so that he could sit across from the painting and really study it.

Martin settled in cross-legged on the bed with a pillow behind his back against the wall. He pulled the blanket up over his lap, and breathed like a Buddhist monk. He began studying the painting, trying to imagine that it really was a window to another, purer world.

A river ran through the center, cutting downward and to the right. It was a muddy color, but pleasant all the same. On its leftward bank, which was bright green and dotted with flowers, an oak grew up thickly in the bole. It leaned left, as if blown by the wind, so that a portion of its foliage was out of the frame. A few songbirds sat in its branches. Across the water on the right were two structures. There was a castle in the foreground, and behind it, somewhere in the distance, a tower whose left side was wrapped in shadow, for the sun was coming from the right. The castle itself was cutaway. Inside were two floors. The bottom was divided into several rooms filled with small, colorful items; pots, and pans, and books, perhaps. On the top floor, a woman in a white dress stood alone before a tiny bird cage. The cage was empty; its door open. He could not make out if the fact distressed or delighted her. She did not seem to face the cage, but looked halfway between it and the viewer. Almost at both. Between the two buildings and the leftward bank, a structure like a bridge or an aqueduct ran across the water. Thin clouds floated in the sky just above the oak's blue-green foliage, and, in the blue above them, dark forms of far more distant birds came swooping down from on high.

Martin would have liked to visit the place. He imagined himself sitting on the leftward bank beneath the leaning oak tree, fishing old acorns from the grass and chucking them one-by-one into the rushing brown river. A warm wind would blow gently. Songbirds would be trilling and chirping in the branches above. Indeed, he could almost hear them. He wondered if from that vantage point, he could see the girl in the cutaway castle, and she could see him. Then it occurred to Martin that her halfway glance would likely fall on that exact spot, across the water on the green grass under the tree. Perhaps he'd unconsciously picked it for that reason. If she were real, what would she have been like? And thinking of these things, and hearing the birds, and feeling the breeze, Martin promptly fell asleep.

***

A single beam of sunlight that had threaded its way from the small window in his bathroom to a spot on his left cheek just below his eye drew Martin slowly to the plane of consciousness. He opened his eyes, and panicked. He'd forgotten to set his alarm. He snatched for his phone, and saw that he had mere minutes to arrive at the office for his first day of work.

The mad dash to get ready presaged the day that followed it. There was an orientation period for new employees, which he'd missed. He slipped into the group once it was moving, and tried to pick up what he hadn't heard from context. He was one of the oldest new hires there, but felt he must have come across as one of the youngest. He managed to make it through the day without asking any questions that he ought to know already, and luck had favored him with a fellow hire who needed to have everything repeated for her. No one seemed to have noted his absence from orientation; at least no one said anything. By the end of the day, he almost knew what he was doing.

He stumbled into his shipping container at the day's end, tired and hungry. In the rush to get out, he hadn't brought a lunch to work. Martin retrieved two noodle-cups from his food pile, filled them at the sink, and popped them in the microwave. He had one new suit, a cheap one, which he planned to wear all week, so he promptly removed it and hung it in the little closet. The backup suit his father had lent him had a jacket that didn't quite cover his wrists. When he could afford it, he'd buy another.

Now walking around in a t-shirt and boxers, waiting on the ramen, he remembered to grab a notebook and pen from his work pile. Martin kept a notebook for every new endeavor. At the end of the day, he made a habit of writing down all that he could remember, along with any questions he had, and he took stock of things that worked, or that hadn't. This had helped him keep track of his many English students, and of their respective needs and learning strategies. He hoped it would carry over here. Sales was, he told himself, a kind of teaching. That made it noble, or at least palatable.

He'd just started jotting things down when the microwave beeped. He set the noodle cups on top of it to cool, and went back to his scribbling. By the time he was done, both cups were sufficiently cooled that he could start his dinner. He didn't have a table yet. His fold-out bed was in the up position, so he leaned against the wall beneath it, across from the office nook. He was so hungry that it was difficult to stop himself shoveling noodles into his mouth, even with the broth singeing his tongue. After a cup and a half, Martin was satisfied enough to eat at a human pace. He settled back, slowly sipping the broth from around the remaining noodles, letting the warmth run down into his heart and marrow.

For a while he watched the painting, only half paying attention as his mind skipped over the day's events. It hadn't gone so badly after all. He'd muddled through. The painting was in shadow, and he reluctantly scraped his back from the wall to turn on the desk lamp. That done, he climbed back to where he was, and tried in vain to find the exact position in which he'd been so comfortable.

Martin's half-closed eyes passed over the Cole-esque landscape. The dark birds coming down from the left seemed always to be descending, never reaching their goal. The colorful ones in the leaning oak were frozen in a moment of happiness. There was another in the brown water, a duck or a loon, which he hadn't noticed before. There were always little details like that in landscapes, and he entertained a vague hope that he'd keep finding them for weeks. His eyes passed up from the river to the castle. Martin dropped his fork on the noodle cup, and the cup spilled its contents on his leg. The girl was now seated.

She sat crossed legged, looking up at the empty bird cage, which hung from a hook above her head. In her lap sat an open book filled with colorful images. A bird book, he thought. Her dress, which before had been white, was now baby blue. In the poor lighting, he might have gotten the color of the dress wrong before, but he was at least sure that she'd been standing by the empty cage. Her gaze, which had previously encompassed everything, was now fixed firmly on the book.

Martin reminded himself that he'd been very tired and anxious the night before. He'd bought the image in a rush, and almost at random. He'd forgotten to set his alarm, which was very unlike him. He hadn't been himself. So it was easy to decide that what he'd seen the night before had been half-dream. Or perhaps there were two girls? A moment's study refuted that. It was the same girl, but memory was unreliable. Several years back, he'd reminisced to his mother of a childhood trip to Niagara Falls, and he vividly recounted to her the sense of space, power, and depth in the presence of the rushing water, only to have her inform him that he hadn't come along. That was an anniversary trip, and they'd left him in Sacramento with his grandmother. But afterwards, he'd asked about the falls every day for a week, and then had somehow managed to generate sights, sounds, and smells that had marinated in his imagination until he'd mistaken them, years later, for a foundational memory. Something like that had happened here. He'd fooled himself.

He shook his head, and began collecting noodles from his lap. He placed them carefully back into the cup, and examined the carpet for stains. Satisfied, he surveyed his small piles, and made vague plans for organizing the space. It would have to wait for the weekend. Martin shut off the desk lamp, made sure to set his alarm, and pulled his bed down from the wall. Cocooned in his blanket, he soon fell asleep. That night, he dreamed of birds, and rushing water.

***

After a month, Martin had sold twenty policies. That was, so far as he could gather, below average for a seasoned agent, but quite good for a beginner. Anyway, he was encouraged. He might have sold more were he willing to work from his apartment, but even in his travels Martin had maintained a sense of home as an inviolable space. True, his work required him to regularly violate the sacred spaces of others, but that couldn't be helped. At thirty, and with little savings, principles and ideals were becoming expensive.

He sold medical supplement insurance to the elderly. It felt ever-so-sleezy, though he refused to lie to his customers. And he reminded himself that the older generation had had money to save. They'd bought houses in their twenties, for example. They'd paid off college loans. They could—some of them could—afford a small policy. He wouldn't be doing this forever. Already he was making plans to move onto a larger brokerage once he'd amassed the experience he felt he needed. And if Martin could make this work, he would have time and money enough later for something that felt—well—clean.

One cubicle to his right, Janet slammed the phone down. Even when she didn't sign off this way, he could almost feel her frustration through the canvas of the partition walls. They'd started together, but she'd made only eight sales. He was sure it was eight, even without checking, because she told him whenever she made one. At first, he thought she was bragging. Later he realized that the girl had wanted something from him. Not a pat on the head, exactly, but acknowledgment. This he offered readily enough. She was good-looking, and easy to smile at, but he felt she wouldn't last long. For one thing, Janet was highly emotional, and took every rejection to heart. For another, she seemed to have a terrible memory for the most basic details. She was always putting her prospects on hold, and "looking into it." He heard her stand up, and knew she was walking over to visit him.

"Any luck today?" she said, poking her head around the wall.

He shrugged. He had, in fact, made a sale.

"It's pretty slow," he offered.

"Yeah."

She looked down at her feet, then up again, beaming.

"People are going out to Bindy's after work," she said.

He nodded. "Oh."

It took him a second to recognize the implied invitation, then another to evaluate it.

"I didn't know that was a thing around here," he said, sheepishly.

His eyes flicked toward the partition walls, and he wondered if there were any harm in going with her. It was not that he disliked Janet, or wished in particular to keep his distance, but he was in a certain mode. He was not twenty-two. He had to make a success of this. Like a Roman soldier going off to war, he didn't want distractions.

"I think I can go tonight," he said, surprising himself.

She beamed again, then immediately tried to seem nonchalant.

"Great! Walk over after work?"

"Sure," he said. "It'll be fun."

***

He did have fun. With five other salespeople there, it was less like a date than he'd feared, though he spent the bulk of his time talking with Janet. Perhaps it was less a date than he'd hoped. Janet had the vague, mistaken notion that he was particularly good at his job. He did not disabuse her of it. At the end of the night, he walked her to her car, and made as if to walk toward his own. Martin did not currently own a car, and he took the bus home.

Now it was late. He schlepped over to his small refrigerator, and rejoiced to find a single remaining beer. Unable to locate the opener, he pried the lid off in several tries with the claw of a hammer, then sat down heavily in his desk chair. He flipped on the light, and closed his laptop so that he could see the painting.

He'd hardly done so in the last month. The long days and numerous rejections tended to leave him drained, and the trees and sky, the open, mysterious spaces, served sometimes to mock rather than encourage him. *I'm still young*, he told himself. Thirty wasn't old at all. He could pound the pavement for the next ten years, and by then he'd have something to show for his efforts. In ten years he'd be forty, though. That did seem old.

As he was pondering these things, his eyes passed over the thing like a bridge or an aqueduct that ran over the river. He closed his eyes, and imagined himself there. It was eerily quiet outside, and he could not even hear the sounds of the cars passing far below. What he did hear was the chirping of some bird of night, long, plaintive calls like those of a mourning mother come home to an empty nest. He wondered at the fact that this sound alone made its way up from the street to his ears, and he pretended that it came not from outside, but from the painting itself.

Breathing deeply, he could almost smell the country landscape. The effect was so pronounced, that he opened his eyes, half-expecting to see the dark birds soaring down on an easterly wind, over the river. That was when he looked into the cutaway castle. It was empty. The girl was not in the upper room. Instantly, Martin's heart began thudding in his chest. His fingers of their own volition clawed at the cheap plastic desk.

He opened and closed his eyes, frantic. Still she was gone. Nor was she to be found, either sitting or standing, in the castle's lower rooms. And that was not all: the bird cage was missing. All that remained in the upper room was the hook from which the cage had hung suspended, and the book he'd seen before, now sitting shut on the floor.

There was no sense in rubbing his eyes or pinching himself. He knew he was awake, and never had he been more dreadfully sober. Maybe it was the room itself. The vents, yes. Someone, somewhere was smoking something that was coming through the vents. Or else there were drugs in the water. Now he did slap himself, then stood up pacing around the room.

He had an instinct to call the police, but what would he tell them? They didn't know what the painting was supposed to show, *had shown*, and they'd only assume he was high, or worse. He considered calling his mother, and disregarded the thought immediately. But who else? He didn't know anybody.

Fearing to do it, he looked at the painting again to see if something, anything, could explain the illusion. Was it a sort of hologram? Did the image move with the viewer? That was a desperate hope, since he was viewing it now from more or less the same angle as always. He crouched down anyway to be sure, but nothing changed. Now thoroughly panicked, Martin put his beer to his lips and simply chugged it dry. He forced himself to go over the image inch-by-inch. And finally, he spotted another change.

There on the left side of the painting, on the grassy bank where the tree leaned out of view, he spied the corner of something out of frame. It was only a bit of gold, a few metallic strokes from the painter's hand, but he knew it. It was the bird cage. The cage was floating in the air under the songbird tree, its right-side just protruding onto the canvas. Someone was standing there, holding it. Someone just out of sight.

***

"You doing okay?"

Martin came up from his thoughts. The beer sat before him, almost full. He'd be paid in three days, and was trying to make his money last. When he'd suggested the pool hall instead of Bindy's, he wasn't thinking about it being just the two of them there. The drinks were cheaper. Now looking up at her face, he was suddenly aware of how natural that felt. But hers was not the only face he saw.

"Um … sorry. What did you say?"

Janet smiled. "You seem distracted," she said. "Is everything alright?"

"Oh yeah," he said. "I was just thinking about a missed sale today. Came on too strong, I guess."

She smiled again, but raised an eyebrow, as if she knew he was lying.

"I say leave work at work."

He nodded. In fact, he had no trouble doing that. The difficulty was leaving home at home. After what he'd seen this morning, he'd made up his mind never to look at the painting before heading into the office. Maybe he should just get rid of it.

"What was I saying?" he asked.

"*I* was saying that I wanted to visit Asia someday, and you were about to tell me, I think, about how you taught English there after college."

He frowned. "But … I didn't tell anyone that."

She smirked mischievously. "No. You didn't. Cathy in HR mentioned it was on your resume."

Martin chuckled at Janet's admission that she'd been checking up on him. He stared at his beer, feeling shy, knowing that when he looked up again, it would be with the mutual understanding that she liked him. He liked her too. Janet was easy to talk to. But the timing was bad, and an office romance that went sour was a damned good way to derail his plans. There was another concern; something he couldn't even try explaining to her. He looked up, meeting her eyes.

"Japan's a very different animal."

"Yeah, with all the bowing and stuff," she said.

"Sure, but they'll shake hands sometimes if you're a foreigner."

"Did you manage to offend anyone while you were there?" she asked. "I mean bowing too low, or not low enough?"

He shrugged. "Probably. I don't know. They're ninety-eight percent ethnic Japanese, so if you do something that sticks out, they just kind of roll with it. Just don't try to tip a waitress."

She laughed. "Yeah, I've heard they run after you and try to give the money back. But it must have been hard to get to know anybody."

He nodded, carefully, and shifted on his bar stool. "I didn't really mind that aspect. I like to take my time getting to know people. It's important to me to … feel free. To have possibilities, you know, left open."

She smiled, and began to say something, then stopped. There was something calculating to Janet. To all women.

"So … can I drive you home?"

He looked at her, surprised. Janet shrugged.

"Sorry. I saw you get on the bus one night, after you walked me to my car."

He wondered if she could see the blush that coursed through the skin of his face.

"I mean," she quickly added, "I need to get to bed early, and stuff. Just, you know, thought I could make your trip faster."

So she'd noticed, but had not grasped the reason. He didn't like her knowing that he didn't have a car. Until now, he'd thought he had the upper hand in this … this thing. He shook his head, trying to disguise his embarrassment.

"I don't mind taking the bus," he lied. "It's normal over there. In Asia, and Europe."

"So I've heard."

"Plus, you never need a designated driver," he added.

He took a swig from his beer, as if to justify the comment. Then he drank more because he didn't know what to say. Her face came into his mind again, unbidden. Not Janet's; the other one. He looked at his phone. He'd checked the schedule earlier. The bus would be by again in ten minutes, and after that he'd have to wait another thirty.

"Looks like you need to get back," said Janet, studying him.

She was smiling as she said it, but he sensed her disappointment. Martin nodded. He stood up.

"This was fun," he said.

"Yeah, we should do it again some time. And maybe actually play pool."

He laughed, and she stood up too. There was a moment when they both wondered how they should say goodbye; whether a polite hug was called for. He touched her shoulder awkwardly.

"You'll be good getting to your car?"

"Yeah, it's like, two hundred feet from here," she said. "Lights the whole way."

He nodded, turned away with a little wave, and began walking towards the door. He didn't turn to see if she watched him go.

***

At his desk, Martin resumed his drinking. It was whiskey now, cheap stuff he'd bought for eight dollars. It could take varnish off a floor. He downed it, one shot after another, and tried to understand what he was looking at. The girl in the picture had changed again. Now she wore a yellow summer dress, lightly patterned with sky blue butterflies. She stood by the muddy river holding the empty birdcage. Her eyes were still on the songbirds in the trees, and he realized, for the first time, that she was trying to catch one. Her mouth was open slightly, and he thought she might be singing. He closed his eyes, and when he did, he could hear the song.

Of course his mind was inventing it. The music. The changing image. He was going crazy.

But he could hear it, and it was prettier than any song he thought he could invent. So long as he kept his eyes closed, he could hear the birds singing too, and the muddy river boiling, and even the call of the dark distant birds flying in from foreign lands. An idea came to him, and he acted quickly, before he could question it.

"Who are you?" he asked the girl, eyes pressed close.

Her song trailed off. Maybe his voice had broken the spell, or called him back from his madness. That made him sad, and he wished he hadn't said anything. He almost opened his eyes, but then the song came back, clearer and more beautiful than before. He listened for words, but there were none that he recognized. Martin was good at languages. He tried, without luck, to place hers. But there were certainly words. It was a sad song.

Gathering up his courage, he spoke again.

"What is your name?"

A silence. Halting, broken singing. And then, in the midst of a song, a single, distinct word that was repeated like the trilling of a bird.

Dalley. Dalley-drey-drey-drin. Dalley.

"Dalley?" he said.

The voice went quiet. When she finally did resume singing, the words were different, but the tone more insistent. In them, he could feel her desperation. She needed just one little bird, to make her happy, but they didn't seem to hear or care. He wondered how any creature could be unmoved by her song. It was so pretty, so deep, like sweet water winding toward the sea, hampered and delayed by a thousand eddies and dams, side streams and underground ways, each of which threatened to keep it from finding its home. Martin hoped that one of the singing birds would leave the safety of its branches, and go to her.

The song stopped. Martin felt a great gathering emptiness. When he opened his eyes, it was to pour another shot, but he also hoped one of the birds had come to fill her cage. Instead, she stared out from the painting.

He froze. Never before had the girl faced out like that. Her eyes, brown like the river, looked directly into his. Her right hand held the cage up in almost a pleading gesture. Until now, he'd only seen her in profile. She seemed to look into the depths of his being. He perceived her longing. Martin understood that feeling, though he did not know what it was that he longed for. Freedom? Adventure? He couldn't put a name to it, and poured himself another shot.

"This can't really be happening," he said.

But the girl just stood there as if she always had. She was perfectly balanced in the painting, offsetting with her slight figure the tower that rose behind the castle across the running river. Even her shadow, indicated in oil in the darkened grass to her left, told of careful composition. It mirrored the shadow on the tower. He must be imagining it all.

Martin downed the shot. Then another. He tore his eyes away from hers, turned off the light, then crawled into his pull-down bed with his face toward the wall.

***

"Four today!"

Janet peeked at him from around the partition, beaming.

"That's great!" he said.

"And you've probably sold like ten, but…"

He shrugged, and bobbled his head, as if he were too scatterbrained to even know. In fact, Martin had stopped keeping count. He was good at this. Yet, as much of a rush as it was to be good at his work, Martin realized that Janet's good opinion of him—the way she looked up to him, wanted his affirmation—was part of what drove him. He thought of his plan to move on from here to a large brokerage where he could make real money. That would mean leaving Janet behind.

"Um … are you okay?"

He must have frowned. He wore his heart too much on his sleeve.

"Yeah! Great!"

"Yeah, I'll bet," she said, with an impish look. "I mean your name's up on the board."

"Really?" he said, genuinely surprised.

"Oh, come on. You didn't know?"

She beckoned to him with a gesture. Martin rose and stood beside her in the corridor outside the cubicles. The space was so close that their shoulders briefly touched. She reached up and pointed at the dry-erase board where his name was written under "Salesperson of the Month". It must have gone up while he was working. When she let her arm fall, her hand brushed his. She let it stay there, Martin observed. It was just incidental contact.

"Wow," he said. "I really didn't know."

She turned her body toward his, somehow without her hand breaking its light contact. They were standing very close. Without seeming to pull away, without knowing if he meant to, he glided toward his office chair. Martin pretended not to have noticed the touch. Janet smiled, and there was something behind her eyes.

"Thanks," he said. "That's very encouraging."

He didn't want to lead her on. He didn't really know what he wanted. It wasn't money, exactly. Probably it was love, but love under some terms more like his own. He'd floated too much to this point. For once, he wanted to be the source of his own inertia. Yes, that was it. Before, when he was younger, he'd never had a master plan, just one means or another of moving from one point to another. Now that he felt the waning of his youth, he wanted to do more than be blown about in the wind. He wanted to fly; at least glide. The problem with Janet was that she was too ready-made. She'd just happened. They worked together. They liked each other. It would have been too easy to fall into her arms. It would be inertia.

"Well," she said, with a small wave, and a smile that wasn't quite a grimace, "I'll leave you to your salesperson-of-the-monthing."

She left, and Martin settled back into his chair. Toward the end of the day, she texted to tell him she was too tired for drinks and would go right home after work. Martin didn't know if it was relief that he felt.

***

The apartment no longer felt like a shipping crate. His books were neatly shelved and organized in the loft space. Everything that had been in piles now found its own place in the cabinets and chest of drawers he'd purchased. There were two house plants on little tables in the corners of the room, and he'd even purchased a small couch for that stretch between the bed and the door. He had no TV, and didn't want one. If he'd wanted to watch something, he could do it on his laptop, from the comfort of his pull-down bed. Most nights, after he'd finished his reading, or scribbling his daily notes, Martin just watched the girl.

She was still staring out, holding the cage. There'd been no change for over a month, and Martin had again begun doubting his earlier memories. He closed his eyes, and imagined himself in the scene. This had become a form of meditation, and he always woke up fresh when he did it before sleep. Often he'd dream of the girl, though she never spoke in his dreams.

There was a light rainfall outside. Martin had opened the bathroom window, because the gentle storm had brought sweet air into the city. Fresh drafts, perhaps filtered through the redwoods and eucalyptus in Oakland Hills, had woven themselves into the stale anonymity of the city's urban oxygen, and were seeping in through this sole portal to the outside. He felt fresh, inside and out. He made up his mind to get away from the sprawl and go hiking in the Hills this weekend. He wondered if he should invite Janet. Martin went back to sit.

Almost as soon as he did, he heard a familiar sound that he couldn't at first place. Then he recognized it as the beating of wings. The painting again, or was it only his madness? Steeling himself, he opened his eyes, but nothing had changed. The girl in the yellow dress stared out blankly, and none of the songbirds seemed to have changed positions. He heard the sound again. It was coming from his bathroom.

The lights were off in there, and Martin walked over and flipped them on. There on the tiles lay a mourning dove. It fluttered madly when it saw him, but only one of its wings was fully extended, so that it moved in a frenzied circle. Martin crouched beside it. The bird cowered, and its simple blue-ringed eye conveyed mortal terror. He pitied the creature. He had an impulse to pick it up, but he was still wearing his dress shirt and slacks. Then he thought it might fly away if he took the time to change.

Martin made a bed of his hands, and slipped them gently under the dove's body. He lifted it very slowly, and brought it to him, making a sort of cradle with his forearms. The bird soon ceased struggling, and settled into the space with hardly a movement. It was either feigning death, or preparing for it. He stood, and walked slowly back to his own perch on the fold-out bed.

As he leaned against the wall, he began speaking aloud to the girl in the painting. This had become a habit in the last few weeks, a sort of homemade therapy on his most stressful days. Some people prayed. Some spoke to their cats or wrote in their journals. Martin, therefore, saw no problem addressing his own mute companion.

"What should we call her, Dalley?"

The girl in the painting, shoulders raised slightly against the weight of the cage, could have been shrugging. The bird shuddered, then piddled on his shirt. Martin felt the warmth reach his dress pants before the odor reached his nose, but resisted the urge to fling the thing from him. He had more clothing now. He could actually afford to throw this shirt away, if it couldn't be cleaned. Then he laughed. Just yesterday, he'd been eyeing a navy JoS A. Bank suit, wondering if he should buy it.

"I guess it's a sign," he said to Dalley.

She didn't offer comment.

"I'm not very creative with names," he continued. "I'd like to be, but I'm not. Maybe you should name her."

He'd decided the bird was female, because all doves seemed female to him. Anyway, its belly was pink, which determined the matter for him. The creature buried its head inside the crease of his left elbow, as if it could hide from him in his own skin. The sweet incongruity of this little act struck him somewhere deep.

"We're all little birds," he said, half to the dove, and half to Dalley.

"I guess I can't keep her," he continued. "I wouldn't know how to care for her."

He wondered what an animal shelter would do with a broken-winged bird. Would they try to fix her, or just put her out of her misery? The bird piddled on him again, and this time Martin felt somewhat less indulgent. He stood up, and wondered what he'd done with the box from the shoes he'd just bought when he couldn't convince himself to buy the suit. He wouldn't have thrown it away. Those boxes were too useful.

Wrapping the bird more tightly in one arm, he freed the other, then walked to the bathroom to wash his hand off in the sink. Then he remembered that he'd stuck the box in the shelf above the closet. He went over and retrieved it, then set it on his work desk inside the nook. He carefully lowered the dove into it, considered closing the box, then decided to leave it open. Martin stripped off his clothes and tossed them in the laundry basket. He washed his hands, letting the soap scent dispel the stink of the bird's leavings.

He brushed his teeth, showered, and finally crawled into his bed. As he lay there, he watched the bird. In its box, which rested below the painting, the dove was like a votive offering. The desk was an altar lit eerily by broken city lights that came in through the window. And, though it was only his imagination, it seemed to Martin's eyes that the girl looked down on his offering, and that shadows creased the corners of her lips.

***

Martin was wearing his new navy suit when Janet spoke. He hadn't heard her enter his cubicle. He'd been on birding sites, trying to learn if he could care for the foundling. In his research, he'd discovered that the pink-bellied dove was likely male. This displeased him. It seemed like a contradiction.

"Hey," she said.

Martin looked up. "Hey."

"*Nice* suit," said Janet.

"Thanks!"

Martin knew he was beaming. He didn't care. In it, he felt all crisp, and new, and independent. He'd earned the suit, and in some way the act of buying it with earnings from his sales had been a ritual. She smiled at his obvious joy, but there was something in her eyes that gave him pause.

"So I wanted to tell you that I'm moving on."

She might have casually lobbed a cinder block at his chest.

"What?"

"Yeah," she said, wincing. "A week from now."

He shook his head. "Don't quit! You're doing great! You're selling like … twice as much as when we started."

She nodded. "Yeah, no. It's actually not that. Believe it or not, I'm moving up."

She told him how she'd responded, on a whim, to a headhunter from another insurance company. She never thought they'd say yes. Then she told him the name. Janet couldn't have known that it was the firm he'd been planning to apply to, later, when he had all his ducks in a row. Martin was suddenly conscious of the muscles in his face, which were hellbent on twisting themselves into a scowl. With effort, he made himself smile.

"That's wonderful!"

His brain was on fire.

"You deserve it," he added, barely able to squeeze the lie up his gullet.

A dozen unkind suspicions bubbled up. Probably she'd applied in person. It didn't hurt that she was good-looking. Here he was, burning both ends of the candle to move up, and now Janet, with her mediocre sales record, would be taking flight. Leaving him here. And what about their … their whatever it was? He looked at her, and saw with bitterness that he had no claim on her. He'd done nothing.

"I know it's … kind of sudden," she said. "And you might—I don't know. I wanted to tell you first, anyway."

He nodded. "Thank you."

Martin only knew that he wanted her to leave his cubicle. As soon as she was well away, he planned to slip out, and go home. He pictured himself standing at the bus stop like a wino, and he hoped she didn't look out and see him there.

Janet frowned, slightly. Perhaps he hadn't hid his feelings very well after all.

"Well," she said, shrugging. "Gotta get back to work."

In a second, she was gone. In the space where she had been there stood a great, yawning potentiality.

***

Martin stared down at the shoe box. His dove was gone. He began pacing, trying to make sense of it. He thought he'd closed the small porthole window in the bathroom before he'd left, but it stood slightly ajar. He could remember pulling it closed, though. Was that a false memory, or had the bird, free of him at last, roused itself from the box and flown into it, and knocked it open? Was staying here such a burden? He hadn't planned to hurt the thing.

He went over to his freezer, dragged out the bottle of whiskey, and slammed it down on his desk chair. Martin sat heavily in his chair, uncapped the bottle, and took a swig from it straight. Tomorrow, he could start over. Tomorrow, he'd accept reality. Tonight he felt he was the last man on earth. Alone. Well, not quite.

"It's just you and me again."

Dalley looked at him. Her expression, fixed as ever, did not reveal her thoughts. It struck him that the empty cage was a brilliant stroke. You didn't know what she wanted, only that she wanted. Martin understood that feeling.

"We're made for each other," he said, after the third swig.

She didn't disagree with him. Well, that was something.

Suddenly he got up and paced again. Something was rising in him, roiling like steam in a kettle. He stomped over and looked out the small window at the sprawl of Oakland.

"No *here*, here," he mused. "Like Stein said. We've got to make everything ourselves. But if *we* make it, is it even real?"

He strained his eyes, as if he might spy the dove out there. But it was gone. He knew that. Martin returned, and collapsed into his desk chair. He lay for a while with his head in his hands. He sat up, took another long swig from the bottle, then realized in a heartbeat that he'd been drinking too fast.

"Oh," he groaned, feeling the room stutter beneath him.

He looked up at Dalley. For just an instant, he'd thought she was amused. He couldn't say what it was that made him think that. Probably the bottle.

"You take my bird?" he said.

His eyes skipped around the painting, and for a moment he forgot that it was a fixed image. As he studied the oak tree that leaned out of the frame, his own face inched toward it. With a gasp Martin realized that he *could* see its leftmost boughs. Close-in to the painting, he gained perspective and spied, impossibly, the branches stretching beyond the frame.

"No!" he said, and it came out in a plaintive squeak.

There, resting in the farthest branch, was a dove. Martin reached out, and his fingers touched the place where canvas ought to be.

***

Mike and Lina Bard walked back and forth inside the small room. The police officer stood near the door, watching them. The room was neat aside from the open whiskey bottle on the desk, and there were no signs of a struggle. The bed was in an up position, but when they pulled it down, they saw that it was made, and hadn't been slept in. Martin's keys hung on a small hook by the door, but the door had been locked when they came in. The landlord had opened it.

"He must have had a second set," observed Martin's father.

He was being the calm, logical one.

"Or someone did," he muttered.

He'd addressed his comments in the general direction of the police officer, but the cop said nothing. Lina Bard, streaks of gray in her long hair, dabbed her eyes again, and once more climbed the ladder to the loft. Maybe there was something she'd missed earlier. Mike went back to his son's journal, and leafed through it. He was uncomfortable violating Martin's privacy like that, and he knew actually reading it would be the same as admitting to himself that things were serious. So he only skimmed.

"Anything of interest, Mr. Bard?" said the cop, speaking for the first time in a while.

Mike shrugged, and shook his head.

"Maybe later," is all he could get out.

The cop nodded. He understood.

"The thing I don't get is the door was locked," said Mike, looking at the cop.

The officer nodded. "He must have left with someone who had keys. Did he have a girlfriend?"

"He didn't," said Lina.

She was up in the loft.

"He would have said something."

But Mike, thinking of some words in the journal, went back to it. He rifled through the pages again, hoping not to pry too much. After all, Martin would be fine. And Martin wouldn't want to find out later that his dad had been rifling through his private thoughts. Mike found the name Janet again and read about her in careful snatches. She came up every few pages. So far he saw nothing particularly private, or helpful. There was a knock at the door.

Everyone looked over with the same measured hope. Lina descended quickly from the loft. But somehow they knew it wasn't Martin's knock. It was too gentle, too tentative, and it hit Mike and Lina at the same time that a parent knew their own child's knock. The officer reached for the handle with his left hand, his right instinctively moving just a millimeter closer to his sidearm. He opened it. A woman stood in the doorway.

The girl saw Mike and Lina first, because they stood rooted, staring at her. Only then did she register the police officer.

"Oh! I'm sorry. Is this … is this Martin's apartment?"

"You know Martin Bard?" said the cop.

She nodded mutely. The cop waved her into the room. She entered carefully, clearly ambivalent of the attention. Lina saw a very pretty girl who might have also hurt her son. Mike saw Janet, from Martin's journal. The cop saw a girl who'd just implied she'd never been in the place, and he watched to see if that was true. She looked around at all of them.

"I got Martin's address from a friend in HR," said Janet. "I've … I've never been here before."

"So you said," said Mike.

She looked at him, her expression careful; defensive.

"Has something happened to him? He hasn't been to work in a week. I've been worried."

Lina pursed her lips, and took a step toward the strange girl.

"Did the two of you have a fight?" asked Martin's mother.

Mike glanced at his wife, wondering how the woman already recognized the connection without having seen Martin's journal.

"No!" protested Janet. "I mean, not really. We weren't really dating."

"You guys never went out?" asked the cop, as if he knew the answer.

She shook her head. "Just after work. Sometimes it was just the two of us, but we never…"

"So if we go over to your place, and look around, that won't be a problem, right?" said the cop.

She looked at him, a deer in headlights. Either she was innocent, or a good actress.

"I literally just came over here for the first time," she protested. "I was worried."

The cop tilted his head. "Why were you worried?"

She took a step back from him. Her jawline hardened. "Like I said, he hasn't shown up to work in a week."

"But you two had an argument of some kind," said the cop.

Mike glanced back and forth between his wife and the officer. Cops and mothers were apparently tuned into the same secret radio. Janet looked at her feet.

"Yes, sort of. We both kind of liked each other. The day he left, I told him I was moving on to a new job. He seemed upset. I mean it was after that that he didn't come back."

The cop deflated a little, but said, "But you didn't think to check on him until now."

"Why would I? People get sick, or they take a personal day. Anyway, I didn't know where to look for him. He didn't answer his texts, so I assumed he was mad at me. His phone goes to voicemail."

The police officer still wore a skeptical expression, but now it was theater. The girl was perfectly believable. She looked around at them all, wanting to be believed, and at the same time not caring, preoccupied over Martin. Mike sighed. The girl probably didn't know anything.

"May I help look around?" she asked, meekly.

The cop glanced at the Bards. Mike granted permission with a shrug. Janet stepped gingerly into the room, and began slowly to survey the same things they'd already looked over. She came to a stop by the painting, the most colorful item in the room. As she looked at it, the officer came up alongside her.

"You got any keys on you, ma'am?" he said.

Janet broke out of her stare and turned to him.

"Yes. Why?"

"Can I see them?" he said, "and look through your purse?"

She hesitated before sliding the purse from her shoulder. The officer bent down and began rifling through it. Janet returned to the painting.

It showed a landscape. There was a bending tree on the left, with songbirds in its branches. Dark birds came down from the sky some distance off. A bridge ran over a brown river toward a castle that you could see into. Inside the castle, on the top floor, a girl in a white dress stood before a cage. Her regal shoulders were pulled back; her expression triumphant. In the cage, frozen in frenzy, flapped a little songbird. It struck Janet that the bird didn't really want to be in the cage, but that it didn't want not to. Somehow the artist had captured that moment of indecision so that, despite the bird's location in a little rectangular room on the far right of the painting, its struggle became the focal point of everything else. Brilliant composition. And its dark blue plumage showed up so well against the gilded cage. Still, there was something slightly sinister about the girl.

"Here you go, you can have it back," said the cop.

He sighed, handing her the purse. She received it absently, then looked at Martin's parents with pity.

"I promise to let you know if I see him," said Janet.

"I mean *when* I see him," she corrected herself.

Mike Bard nodded. "Sure. Thanks."

She walked toward the door, then stopped.

"You know," she said, thoughtfully, "Martin told me he never really liked to be rooted to one spot too long. He liked to be free. So maybe he's just out there, you know, finding himself?"

Mike sighed, and shook his head. He glanced at his wife, but she was looking off somewhere, caught in her private thoughts.

"Free," Mike muttered, to nobody in particular, and went back into the pages of Martin's journal.

LADYBUGS

It was mid-April, and the cherry blossoms hadn't yet blown off the trees. David pulled into his usual spot in the private garage under Porter-Van Ness and wondered if there'd be time to sit on the balcony and imbibe a little of this long-lived spring. The cold front that had continued to grip D.C. all throughout March had mercifully spared them any snow, and a new balmy air—"toasted at the edges," as Hadley used to say—lingered on without giving way to the oppressive humidity that was destined to consume the Beltway until late August.

David shut the Mercedes door. He yawned, because the low light in the garage made him sleepy, though it was only five. Megan wouldn't be home for at least thirty minutes. Time enough, maybe, to squeeze in a quiet moment all his own. He sighed, once more regretting that their daughter wouldn't be visiting for Spring Break, but he could hardly blame Hadley for heading to Rehoboth with her friends. It's what he would have done at her age. Anyway, their small apartment on Connecticut Avenue, nice as it was, had never been her home.

As David neared the elevator, he saw that two of the reserved spots were occupied by those matching rouge-colored electric cars he'd noticed a few weeks prior. Though Porter-Van Ness offered charging ports along one wall of the garage, the owners of these two vehicles had had their own personal charging station installed beside their spots, the machine secured with a key fob so that no one else could use it. The license plates on the two cars read "HISONE" and "HISTOO." He scoffed—not that it was any of his business what people did with their money. He just found it extravagant, when there were already free charging ports, that anybody would shell out extra cash for his own. Was this just a flex, or did human nature, when fueled by sufficient wealth, inevitably produce snobbery? Perhaps what he called snobbery was just some territorial instinct. After all, everybody here had his own, *unofficial* parking spot, and his own preferred charging port, even without paying extra for it. People had a funny way of recreating jungle logic inside the concrete jungle.

While he could laugh at the new tenants' parking habits, what really bothered him were the identical ladybug decals each sedan bore on its left rear bumper. He'd just recently learned what they symbolized. He pulled out his phone, just to make doubly sure, and then shook his head in disapproval when a search confirmed his suspicions. David slipped the phone back into his blazer and hurried on to the elevator, as if he feared that someone hiding in the shadows might sniff out his true opinions on the matter.

Five minutes later he was resting, eyes half-closed with a book spatchcocked on his belly and a cocktail dangling from his fingertips, letting the sun toast him "round the edges". He didn't want to move—ever, really—but he knew how Megan would perceive things if she came home, and nothing had been prepped for dinner. Or, for that matter, if she saw what he'd been reading. Still, he couldn't easily peel himself from the balcony recliner to which his body had become fixed like upholstery until the misery of anticipated argument finally overcame the agony of getting up. He drained his glass, and rocked himself to a standing position, not forgetting to grab the offending book.

By the time Megan returned, late again, clutching the mail, and strangely flushed about the face, David was already on the point of serving dinner. She shot him a *pro forma* smile, surveyed his progress with a look of tolerance, then announced that she'd shower before eating. He nodded as Megan hurried off. Probably she'd been caught in traffic again.

When she reappeared twenty minutes later, David was carving the breast from the rotisserie chicken he'd reheated. David had never been hunting, but there was something raw, and fundamentally virile, about carving meat from a bone. He lifted the cut portion with the knife and placed it carefully on one side of Megan's plate so as not to mix it with the rice or greens. She preferred the white meat, as long as the skin was off. Megan didn't actually dislike the taste of chicken skin, but seemed, nowadays, to disapprove of it on principal, as if the clean white flesh were something more akin to a vegetable.

"All ready?" she said, still toweling her hair.

"Yep."

They both sat down. It was a quiet meal. It was a quiet apartment, but for the endless white buzz of the city below. Megan ate precisely, moving from broccoli to rice to chicken in orderly steps, managing her plate as if it were one of the corporate events she planned. Dave had no method. He whittled away at his food and groped about for something to say. In the absence of Hadley, some other absence had been taking shape inside the apartment on Connecticut Avenue.

"Nice spring weather," he finally said.

"Mmm," she affirmed, with barely a look at him.

After a moment, he set out on another tack. "Traffic must have been awful today. I mean, it's always bad..."

She frowned, and began chewing in what could only be called a computational manner, each bite methodically subsumed into her thought process. She finally tapped her fork against the air, which, David knew, meant she had something to declare.

"In other words," Megan said, chewing away the last particles, "'Why were you so late getting home, Megan?'"

David shook his head, baffled, though that had been just what he'd meant.

"Is this a problem?" she said. "Am I on a printed schedule or something?"

"No, no," he said, big, innocent smile to win her over.

"Did you want me to thank you for re-heating the chicken? Is that it?"

"No! Look, Megan. What's this about? I'm just making conversation!"

He spread his hands, as if it were all a misunderstanding. Yes, he wanted to know where she'd been. This night. Other nights. But she'd sniffed him out, and he couldn't push it any further. Not yet, anyway.

Megan was a woman of strict patterns, and those patterns had been changing. Her demeanor, especially towards him, had been subtly transfigured. There was no open hostility. Not anymore. Years ago, they'd fought often, and loudly, but they'd learned too late the deep impression it had made on their now adult daughter. Things were quiet now. Still, he felt a bit like furniture in her eyes. He knew that something was wrong. And Megan's defensiveness, though it had set him on his heals, for that very reason had only aggravated his silent suspicions.

"Is … is something bothering you, honey?" David said.

But he kicked himself as soon as he said it. They were just words, to take the edge off, but he'd given her an opening. She looked up at him, took a deep, calming breath, and folded her hands across the table. David knew he was in for it.

"Hadley and I spoke on the phone," she began.

"That's great! How's she doing? Everything good at the beach?"

"—She's fine. It's hot enough there, and the house they're in has a jacuzzi, so you know she's not complaining. The place has secured entry, so I'm not worried about that…"

David nodded. He knew she'd meant to say something else, but had gotten sidetracked with all her mental lists.

"Anyway, near the end, she mentioned what you're reading."

So there it was. But David cocked his head, as if this were a complete *non sequitur.*

"Arthur Pendersen?" she said. "Really?"

"Just trying to see how the bad guys think," David shrugged. "I mean, of course I don't agree with him, but a lot of people read Pendersen, and it's important to keep up with—"

"—Is that really it?" she said. "Because sometimes I think there's a part of you that's just a little…"

"What?"

She pursed her lips. Now the fork in her hand had become a divining rod trembling over some taboo aquifer. But she nodded once, and the fork struck the table, prongs-down.

"Backwards," she said. "Okay? Un-progressive. You read these books. I've seen some of the websites you look at…"

"I like to hear all sides," he protested.

"*All sides,*" she repeated, acidly.

"Look, Meg, you and I are totally on the same page with this stuff. But I guess I just don't like the accusation that people with our experiences are living inside a bubble. I mean we're both educated, well-off people. I'm not saying his views have merit, but I've always liked the idea of being open-minded. I've told you before there's a lot of chauvinists in software engineering. I talk to these guys every day. Smart guys, but not awake, you know? So if I'm going to … influence them, I need to read what some of them read. Right?"

Megan sighed, and shook her head, as if she were dealing with Hadley in her salty, six-year-old stage. It wasn't lost on David that the focus had turned to him, justifying his own choices in matters that didn't really affect her. They'd been married a long time. He knew when she was dissimulating, sending up colored flares to draw attention away from herself. But there was nothing to be done. She was Megan Airy-Taylor, his wife of twenty years, but always on her own terms. Then she smiled, a small, straight smile which, because it was so sure, made him doubt his read.

"I don't suppose you checked the mail when you came home?" she said.

"Uh … no. Didn't you grab it?"

She laughed. "Sorry, I meant to say that if you had, you'd have seen an article on the cover of the *Washingtonian*."

"Article," he repeated, stupidly.

"About the Madsens. Those two guys that just moved into the penthouse upstairs."

David hesitated, wondering if these were people Megan had mentioned before. That was just the sort of detail he easily forgot, much to Megan's regular annoyance. He dragged his memory. Now nearly certain they'd never come up in conversation, he shook his head.

"I don't *believe* you've spoken of them…"

"No, I didn't," she said, reassuring him. "But they're very well known. Lewis is an upscale veterinarian. He has a show called *Love Your Pet*, and I believe Hunter is some kind of lobbyist. I've met them, actually, a couple years ago. Lewis consulted with our firm for their wedding reception. It was a big deal. Very, very classy. Very expensive. And now they're here. Though I'm sure it's only their city home."

David nodded, as if this were all very interesting to him. At first it wasn't—not even remotely—not even if it were the last acceptable subject in hell, but, presently, two wandering neurons brushed shoulders in his brain, and he suddenly understood that the two men in the luxury penthouse must be the very same people who'd been parking in the reserved spots. The timing made sense. So did the extravagance. It had to be them. When he thought of the ladybug decals, the word "lobbyist" took on a new, ominous meaning. He worked mightily to conceal his distaste from Megan.

"And these guys … you follow their careers? You know what they're … into?"

"Mmmhmm!" Megan nodded excitedly, chicken in her cheeks. "Just fabulous, fabulous men."

David entered triage mode. The spinning wheel of death, which he saw too often in his work, now danced inside his cerebrum. In any marriage, there were times when the best strategy was to douse one's true thoughts, lest they spark a conflagration. Sometimes he could do it, but the cost this time was just too high. He only hoped he could keep the flames at a simmer.

"Megan," he began. "I'm deeply uncomfortable having them in the building."

Megan looked at him and began quietly loading her guns.

"Uncomfortable," she said, deadpan. "With Hunter Madsen. And his husband. Here at Porter Van-Ness."

He swallowed. "Yes. Let me explain."

"Oh yes. Please explain."

She sat back, eyes flinty, and waited.

"It's not … *that*," he said. "You know it's not that. I have lots of friends who are … you know. You know I don't care about that."

Megan studied him, one black eyebrow gradually arching into the serene regions of her educated forehead. He couldn't find a safe approach. She surveyed from high and ivied grounds. Finally, he shook his head, and let the chips fall where they would.

"They're cannibals, Megan."

He'd said it. Megan winced, and bit her bottom lip. David sighed. Having arrived on this strange hill, he'd decided it was as good as any to die upon.

"You," she began, in icy, even tones, "are spouting bigotry."

David gritted his teeth, checked his ammo, and marched forward.

"They eat human flesh," he said, gently. "Plain and simple."

"That is the most … simplistic … uneducated thing I've ever heard you say, Dave."

"It's just a fact."

She closed her eyes. "No. No. No. That's not a *fact*. That's a very particular kind of value-judgment. It doesn't even qualify as a real thought, let alone a fact. It's right-wing propaganda, which now you're repeating as fact. I literally *cannot* believe you!"

"They consume human flesh, Megan." He spoke slowly, emphasizing each syllable. "It's on their cars. Ladybugs. Look it up if you don't believe me."

Instead, Megan looked up at the ceiling, through it, with exasperation, her silent appeal to the architects of some brighter future.

"I don't believe this," she muttered. "I *knew* you were going to do this."

"You knew we were going to be talking about this?"

"Yes, actually. I've run into Lewis several times since they moved in. Remember, I *know* them. And you don't have a clue what you're talking about!"

He pressed on, monotone. "I do know," he said. "The ladybug decal is an Ethical Eaters thing. It's people who eat human meat—"

"*Cloned* meat, David! Lab-cultured!"

"It's still human, Megan!"

"And have you ever asked why, David? Did Arthur Pendersen or those shock-sites you read ever go to a single Cozzi Person and ask *why* they eat cultured human flesh?"

He scoffed. "No. I don't know! What does it matter?"

"Clearly it doesn't matter to you," she said.

"I have to admit it doesn't."

She fumed for a moment, pressed her eyes shut again, and then rubbed them with her fingers. When she finally spoke, she was too calm.

"David, you said you didn't like being in a bubble."

He nodded, alarmed by her saccharin voice.

"You want to hear all sides, right?"

He gave a perfunctory nod.

"Well, then, you'll be happy to know you'll have your chance."

He frowned as Megan got up, walked back to their room, and returned with the bundle of mail. She slapped it down on the table. A cream-colored envelope sat atop the stack, already opened. Megan worked the letter out and held it up before him. The paper was like card stock, but rustic and embedded with dark, sandy flecks. It looked like cloth. Maybe it was handmade. He reached over and touched it. It had a pleasing, sandy texture, and uneven edges. He could see that it had been previously folded, and sealed with wax, which now lay broken. When she separated the trifold, a smell of lavender and potpourri wafted up into the air.

The message was in an attractive script, not cursive, but some less common form of calligraphy. It was homemade; handwritten, he was sure, with an ink pen. He could almost feel the pleasure of its making in the long, beautiful strokes. She held it open, and he leaned in and read it out loud:

To Our Neighbors, Megan and Dave:

You are cordially invited to dinner this Friday night, six o'clock, with Lewis and Hunter. We'll indulge in Lew's fine vegan cuisine, affect outrage at Hunter's obscene taste in decadent wines, and (hopefully) get to know each other as fellow travelers in this strange and beautiful world. Mego, we haven't forgotten how you made our big day special. Dave, we don't know you yet, but we're chomping at the bit. Say you'll come, and don't you dare bring anything (except yourselves!)

Love and Kisses,
The Madsens

Megan closed the invitation, then lowered it to the table like a writ of law. "We are going," she said.

"Megan—"

"—And you," she annunciated, "are not going to embarrass me."

"Megan—"

"So help me, Dave, if you insult or offend these people, I will never forgive you."

"Megan."

"What, David?"

He sighed. "Okay."

***

The invitation had come on a Wednesday. David spent the first half of Thursday trying not to look up anything about "Cozzi People." Any other day, he'd have been too busy to indulge his curiosity, but on this particular Thursday the universe had conspired against him. All of the bugs in the cloud lending software had been fixed. There were no scheduled meetings. Finally, the temptation to dig became too great.

The *Wikipedia* entry on Cozzis, though thorough, must have been written by one of their representatives. He learned that "Cozzi" was probably a derivation of Coccinellidae, the scientific name for ladybugs, which apparently practiced homophagy. If so, based on pronunciation, they ought to have been "Cocksies", not Cozzis. David could hardly blame them for preferring the softer sound. That was good marketing.

The long article was broken into sub-sections with headings like "History of the Movement", "Philosophy", "Scientific Support", "Culture", and, last of all, "Conspiracy Theories". The latter section was devoted to refuting the charge that the Human Repurposing Movement had grown out of the Human Extinction Movement. The authors tried to show that neither their timelines nor their respective philosophies matched up. "At its heart, and as a point of historical fact," the section concluded, "Re-Purposing is only a logical development of the same ethical commitments behind vegetarianism and veganism. The simple 'creed' of a Cozzi is the same as that of any good doctor, 'First do no harm.'"

The section went on to reiterate that *real* Cozzis consumed only plant-based foods, or lab-grown human flesh. The authors scoffed at attempts to connect the development of flesh-culturing technologies with certain European firms that specialized in the financial and legal aspects of voluntary suicide. "Moreover," they continued, "no connection has been made, or ever will be made, between those social movements concerned with human extinction, and the ethics-based Repurposing Movement. Indeed, all three major Repurposing advocacy groups"—here the article listed them by name—"forbid hiring from or colluding with any company offering life-end treatments, or with any group advocating for human extinction."

As for the most "sensational" accusations, they were hardly mentioned at all, save indirectly. On the whole, the entry gave the impression that only the most blinkered dolt would find anything amiss with the regular consumption of human meat, and that anyone to whom the thought had ever occurred that such appetites might stir up hungers still darker was a bigot of the highest order.

Still, the mere suggestion that "certain claims" had been made prompted David to visit other, less reputable websites. Further and further down the rabbit hole he went. He couldn't help himself. He was in the middle of a particularly juicy article by a heretofore respectable journalist who'd claimed to have found evidence linking missing persons cases with a network of black-market cannibalism, when a banner popped up about pyramids and their alleged alien architects. That shocked David, and he remembered where he worked. He closed the page, and looked around to make sure no one had seen.

Anyway, he'd seen enough. In a world of infinite information, facts were no longer attainable. Everything was a claim, upon a claim, upon a claim. "It's turtles, all the way down," said the old philosophy joke; but now it was practically true. And it made him sad. He'd always rather liked facts. They'd seemed more trustworthy than people. Neither his perceptions nor his gut instincts seemed worth much in this brash, ever-changing world. Maybe Megan, the people-person, was the smart one. You couldn't really *know* anything unless you verified it in person. And he'd get his chance tomorrow night, at around six o'clock.

***

David knocked on the door a second time.

"Just wait," said Megan, impatient.

He shrugged. The three-bedroom condos took up the top two levels of Porter-Van Ness, and fully half the building's roof was in the private possession of its two luxurious penthouses, fenced off from the roof's common area, which itself was accessed by an entirely different elevator. David thought it was quite possible that Hunter and Lewis couldn't hear him knocking. Or perhaps they just enjoyed making the common folk wait. He thought back to the invitation. Something about the wording had rubbed him the wrong way.

"What did you tell them about me?" he muttered. "I mean when you bumped into them in the hall, or whatever."

"Nothing! Shh!" said Megan, shaking her head.

David doubted that. He'd re-read it this morning, and on the second reading had gained the distinct impression that the Madsens already knew something about him. "Chomping at the bit," *indeed.* Probably, Megan had complained that her husband was a bit regressive. The handle turned. The door creaked slowly back.

No one stood in the threshold. David and Megan stared into a spacious living room that appeared to be tastefully furnished, though it was revealed only by the hallway's light. A horrifying figure popped out from behind the swinging door.

"Boo!"

David jumped back. Megan put a hand to her heart, and then burst out laughing.

"Lewis!" she screamed, "You bastard!"

A tanned arm reached up to remove a devil mask. Behind it was a face like an angel's, smooth and sun-bronzed, with blue-gray eyes, and sandy hair. The man touched a switch, and the room behind him flooded to life in golds, yellows, and blues.

"I'm *sorry*, Mego! Hunter told me no, but I am a *very* bad boy, and I literally *could not* help myself!"

Struggling to contain his merriment, Lewis stepped forward into the hall, embraced Megan, and kissed her on both cheeks. Both glanced over conspiratorially at David and began laughing all over again. Megan even had tears in the corners of her eyes.

Lewis, with a bashful expression, offered a hand to David.

"Don't worry, Dave! Can I call you Dave? No monsters in here. And no hugs from me! Just a good old-fashioned *Amurrican* handshake!"

David chuckled self-deprecatingly and took the hand Lewis offered.

"My wife's been telling stories about me, I see."

"But none of the really good ones," whined Lewis. "Oh well, that's why God made wine!"

He ushered them into the living area. In full light the place was considerably more fancy than it had first appeared. Two large, semi-circular couches faced each other on a rose-colored rug whose hue complemented both the soft beige of the leather, and the dark wood flooring beyond it. Pillows in white, tan, and shining turquoise rested across the couch cushions in deliberate happenstance. Between the couches were pleasing asymmetries, two tables, one circular and topped in dark wood, the other a turquoise oval framed in gold. A large cobalt vase rested there from which heather, delphinium, and orange snapdragons poured forth in a sort of botanical eruption. On the ebony walls were large rectangular fixtures suggesting windows. These were frosty blue panels decorated by orange and black patterns. Framed and emphasized by the ebony walls, these windows lined and defined the room, like post-modern icons inside a church of earthly delights. They made its borders only suggestions, and wrapped the two long sides until they terminated in a gold-framed wall that housed a fireplace. Above the hearth, between tall golden shutters that seemed to grope like ivy toward the high ceiling, there stretched an enormous painting of a rain forest.

Megan had to stare. She and David had toured one of these penthouses when considering Porter Van-Ness. The one they'd seen had already been well out of their range, but hadn't been so well-decorated.

"You like?" said Lewis, with a bashful shrug.

"Lewis," breathed, Megan, and placed a hand on his arm.

"I'm so glad!" he said. "All my design. I mean, I didn't design the building obviously, but Hunter gives me free rein of the interior."

"Wow," she said, dreamily. "It's just beautiful."

Lewis smiled and looked away modestly. "Let me go see what's keeping Hunter. That man is always working. And I need to check on the dinner. Please just make yourselves at home. Cabernet, anyone?"

"That would be lovely," said Megan, answering for both of them.

The living room's ceiling was perhaps thirty feet high, giving a cutaway view of the condo's top level. An open spiral staircase joined the two floors, and Lewis scurried up it, winking at them when he reached the balcony at the top. He soon passed through a door, which swung behind him. Presently, the wonderful smells of home cooking wandered down to them through the swinging door.

"That's heavenly," whispered Megan.

David examined the savory smells, and tried to guess what was being prepared. He generally avoided vegan fare, but tonight he'd have eaten anything just so long as it *wasn't* meat.

"Yeah," he finally said. "We'll just have to make sure to eat around the bon—"

She shot him a warning glance, and he decided to swallow the last word. It was a good thing too, for Lewis soon reappeared above, carrying their drinks.

"Are you still standing?" said Lewis, gliding down the steps. "I'm a terrible host."

He pressed a wine glass into each of their hands.

"Mmm. Thanks," said Megan, taking a sip. "And no, we were just enjoying the smell of your cooking."

Lewis rolled his eyes as if the light praise were too much. "Well, if it smells *that* good, you'd better come right up to the table. You're obviously famished."

He waved for them to follow. They ascended the winding stairwell, which could have been transplanted from some private European library. On the second level, he led them through several doors until they entered the kitchen. There was fresh-baked bread on the countertop, three or four dishes keeping warm, and one bubbling on the stove. David discretely scanned the offerings, trying to assure himself it was all vegetables. Adjacent the kitchen was a dining room with a white marble table, candle-lit, and also decorated with flowers.

"Hunter will be here *any minute* now," said Lewis, apologetically. "He knows how I feel about eating on time."

Lewis sat them down at the table and began to make small talk on inoffensive matters—the long winter, inflation, the proposed new high-speed train, and so on. He rambled on, skillfully filling the silences, and getting them to talk. When asked his own opinion on the wisdom of actually building the train, or on what might have caused the current economic situation, he deferred to the absent Hunter.

"He's the smart one. I don't get into any of that stuff. But why don't you tell me…"

He drew Megan into conversation about her work, asking small, thoughtful questions, and always letting her speak more than he did. Then he turned to David, sifting his thoughts on software engineering like a gentle but very professional journalist, and often pausing to ask David to explain the more technical terms. This had the effect of making David forget himself and feel more at ease. He rarely got the chance to share his enthusiasm for coding problems. Megan didn't like to hear about his work. And not only were Lewis' questions well-framed and deeply insightful, but he avoided all redundancy. Under that effete exterior, Lewis was intense and methodical, as if he really wanted to know the ins and outs of David's field. David found himself grudgingly impressed by the man, and his ability to affect genuine interest.

Now that he was more relaxed, David became aware of his hunger. The mellifluous odors from the kitchen danced inside his nostrils and played the violin with his stomach. In the brief moment of dead space between one of David's answers and Lewis' next question, his stomach growled loudly.

"Oh dear!" said Lewis, shooting Megan an alarmed look. "I do believe this man is going to eat our condo."

David went red-faced and Megan looked aghast toward her husband, pressing her eyes closed in a small, embarrassed smile. David stared down into his wine, and took a long sip.

"Never fear," said Lewis. "I'm just going to start serving. And then I'm going to find Hunter and kick his workaholic ass."

He retreated into the kitchen.

"Did you eat, like, nothing all day?" whispered Megan.

David shrugged. Lewis soon returned with a loaf of dinner bread, sliced and steaming.

"We don't do butter," he said, as he set a small plate before each of them, drizzling the plates with olive oil, and adding cracked pepper and sea salt.

"Just snack on that, while I get the roast."

He left the room again. David, who was on the point of biting into the bread, stopped and looked at Megan.

"Roast?" he mouthed.

She nudged him under the table, and shot daggers at him.

"But is there such a thing as a vegan roast?" he whispered.

But Megan wasn't looking at David anymore; rather, behind him.

"There is, actually," said a new voice.

Slowly, David craned his head around and looked up. Hunter Madsen had at last made his appearance.

He was a tall, thin, handsome man with hazel eyes. He wore a nut-brown suit coat over a blue and white striped dress shirt whose rounded club collar, almost boyish when paired with his floral tie, stood in ironic contrast to his gaunt frame. His hair was black, and had probably been inky in his younger days, but now a pleasant silver accented it on both sides. He could have been anywhere from forty years old to his mid-fifties. The man was like a slick scarecrow, or a walking totem. There was something ageless, and powerful, and dangerously charming about him. Hunter extended his hand.

"Hunter!" said Megan.

She stood, and took the hand, interposing herself between Hunter and David, and managing to elbow the latter in his shoulder as she stood; not by accident, David was sure. Hunter drew her hand towards him with practiced grace, as a knight might a lady's. He bowed ever so slightly but did not embrace her. Yet his curtsy was, in its own way, warmer and more charming than Lewis' exuberance, and David saw the immediate effect it worked upon his wife. She seemed to make herself smaller, and her voice became hushed, as before a nobleman.

"David," she said, without looking down. "This is Hunter Madsen."

David stood and waited his turn to shake Hunter's hand. The man's grip was very firm, but his hand was smooth as butter, and, though Hunter didn't give him the D.C. Power-Player squeeze that David found so irritating, he did put in two or three actual shakes, as if he took the exact wording of the ritual very seriously. Then with a sweeping gesture he invited them all to sit again.

No sooner done then Lewis returned, looking every inch the professional waiter in his black apron. He carried a steaming platter in one arm and a clutch of heat pads in the other. These he set down smartly along the center of the table, followed by the covered platter. He went back and forth several times, grabbing more covered dishes from the kitchen, and setting them on the heat pads. Finally, he brought a stack of pretty China plates, a few serving spoons, and a kitchen knife.

"Okay, boys and girls, we do it Ma and Pa style here, so just say when."

He uncovered the offerings, and waved his arm slowly over each dish like a game show assistant.

"Here we have Samfaina, Milho frito, Sekihan, and, of course, the roast."

"Smells heavenly," said Megan.

"Thank you," said Lewis. "A little bit of everything, then?"

"Yes, please," said Megan.

With a nod, Lewis took a China plate and began placing the three exotic-sounding dishes, careful to leave room in the center for the roast. This looked very much like a beef roast covered in dark gravy, and David watched closely as Lewis cut into it. But the texture on the inside was reassuringly bready, like meatloaf if it were made from blended vegetables. He exhaled in silent relief.

"Eggplant?" guessed David.

"There's eggplant in the Samfaina," said Lewis, "but the roast body is made from black beans and vital wheat gluten."

He looked up suddenly. "Oh no, you guys aren't gluten-free, are you?"

David suppressed a scoff, and shook his head no. "No. No allergies, or anything like that."

Lewis let out a nervous sigh, and glanced at Hunter, who was staring at him without expression.

"I know, I know," sighed Lewis. "I should have asked before I planned dinner."

"Hunter gets annoyed by my scatterbrain, and my 'lack of foresight,'" he said to the others in a loud, conspiratorial aside.

Megan laughed as he set her plate in front of her. He quickly plated up the others, politely inquiring before adding each item. Finally, he served himself a very modest helping of everything, and sat down. He hesitated, and looked at David.

"Do you guys say a prayer or anything?"

Megan looked at David. "No," said David. "No that's alright. Whatever you do is fine with us."

Lewis shrugged. "Sometimes I say a silent prayer to the universe. But the universe got on my nerves seven or eight times this week, so screw it."

He chopped off a corner of the roast with his spoon, plopped it feistily into his mouth, and smiled as everyone laughed.

The four of them pitched into the meal. David found the vegan dishes unexpectedly tasty, and not just because he was so hungry. While he never voluntarily ate eggplant, regarding it as the sea cucumber of the vegetable kingdom, the Samfaina was fantastic. Even the vegan beef, now that he was certain it wasn't cultured human flesh, was much better than he'd expected. Still, it *smelled* like red meat. Could Lewis have cheated, and added beef base, or was it possible to fake that smell with the right combination of savory seasonings? If so, he mused to himself, then it might really be possible to live on vegetables alone, provided one had a cook like Lewis in the house. Not *desirable*, but possible. It was a testament to how good the food was that nobody said anything for a while. After they'd eaten for a few minutes, Lewis stood without explanation, and went to the kitchen.

Hunter chuckled, and gave them a knowing look. "He does that sometimes."

Lewis soon returned, and a succulent, beefy odor followed through the kitchen door. "Leave some room," he said. "Soup wasn't quite ready before dinner, but it's so good, and I want you to try some. I only wish there were more."

"Yum!" said Megan. "I can't wait! I prefer soup later, anyway. It's good for filling up the corners."

"I *completely* agree," said Lewis.

David said nothing. So it was the soup he was smelling. He'd almost dismissed his anxieties about dinner, but now he wondered if anything that wasn't beef stew could possibly smell so much like it. He took another bite of the Milho frito, a garlicky cornbread square that seemed to melt into his taste buds. It was so good that he immediately ate another. Telling himself that the soup could not possibly contain any cultured meat—the Madsens were clearly not interested in forcing their personal choices on the two of them—he nevertheless planned to eat enough food that he could beg off when it was ready, just in case. After he'd polished off the Milho frito on his plate, David looked up to see Hunter watching him with a curious expression. The look dragged on, as if the man were expecting him to say something.

David nodded in a friendly way, and, just to avoid awkwardness, glanced around the room until his eyes settled on the painting that ran the length of the dining room wall. It seemed to be the mate of the much bigger one over the fireplace downstairs, a jungle scene teeming with tiny details, small and colorful creatures hiding in the shadows, or perched in branches.

The painting reminded him of the sort of children's book he used to read with Hadley where the artist hides many small images for the reader to discover. He turned back to the table, only to find that Hunter was still staring at him with that same intense expression.

"Uh..." stammered David, "that's quite a painting. Have you seen this painting, Megan?"

"Mmm," said Megan, nodding through the food she was chewing.

Hunter smiled. "What do you like about it, David?"

David shrugged. He'd only been making small talk, but studied it once more to summon a better answer. He was a software engineer, after all. Hunter looked like someone who actually knew about art.

"I mean, it's beautiful," he said. "It's nature. You can't go wrong with nature."

Hunter leaned back in his chair. His expression became thoughtful.

"Indeed," he finally answered.

There was a long pause, as if Hunter were gathering his thoughts. Finally, he perked up, looking very tall in his chair.

"But, David, have you ever considered what a strange word, what a vague concept, 'nature' can be?"

Megan looked over, interested. Lewis settled into his seat like a child waiting for a show to start.

"Can't say that I have," replied David.

But he was suddenly wary, as if the subject were fraught. Hunter took a bite of his food, and chewed it slowly, thinking as he chewed, in no hurry to speak before he was ready.

"Nature," he said at length, "is a word that can be used in two, almost contradictory senses."

He gathered them all in at a glance, and continued. "People use it normatively, but also descriptively, you see."

Lewis started jabbing his hand in the air like a schoolchild. "Teacher, teacher, what do those big words mean?"

He and Megan giggled together. They were becoming thick as thieves. Hunter smiled.

"For example," he continued, "when you want to say something is perfectly fine, or at least within the range of expected deviance—a small child throwing a tantrum; a teenager taking risks—you say, 'After all, it's natural.' Then you mean that we shouldn't worry too much, because this thing is only to be expected. That's a normative use of the word, you see? It implies a certain proper way of being, and even a variance within which somewhat improper things are to be expected."

He studied his audience, very much like a professor, to see if they followed. David nodded, feeling obligated to make some sign of comprehension.

"On the other hand," continued Hunter, "we would define the sciences as those enterprises involved in the *descriptive* study of natural phenomena, which phenomena include many that are characterized as 'abnormal' or 'unnatural'. A child born with two arms and two legs is healthy, or *natural*, yet a child born without legs is still part of nature, meaning, in that case, 'all that is'. Do you notice the dilemma? The ambiguity? It's not as if the latter child were outside of nature."

David frowned. "So we use the same word in different ways. Isn't that pretty common in language?"

Hunter looked at him. His eyes were like X-Acto knives, and David felt compelled to look down again, and take a bite of his food. He could guess what Hunter was driving at, and he didn't want the conversation heading in that direction.

"Fair enough," allowed Hunter, "but I'm less concerned about words, then about the assumptions behind them. You see, I encounter this sort of thing a lot in my work. I spend a lot of time thinking about it."

"Your work?" said David, hoping to eventually steer the ship away from the shoals of philosophy, and toward something safely mundane.

"Yes," said Hunter. "With the Nelly Group."

David sighed internally. The Nelly Group, named for Coccinellidae, the cuddly-looking and occasionally cannibalistic ladybug, was one of the Big Three lobbyist organizations that had helped to legalize human homophagy. Eating the flesh of one's own species, in layman's terms. David glanced warily at Megan, and at Lewis, the vegan chef. He'd thought there'd been an unstated agreement among them not to discuss matters that were likely to be controversial. But the sight of Lewis gave him an idea for how to bring things back to safe ground.

"Lewis," said David, as if it had just occurred to him, "I don't know how you found the time to become such a skilled chef. You're still doing *Love Your Pet*, right? How do you balance filming a show with running a veterinary practice, and making great food?"

Lewis sighed. "Not too well, I'm afraid. I mean it only takes about six months to film twenty-four episodes, but there's a lot of traveling involved, and then, of course, people are always reaching out to me about their pets. What's made it easier is that for the last two seasons, we've been able to integrate my practice into the filming in a more organic way."

"So there's just a film crew following you around when you see clients?" said Megan.

"Exactly. And that becomes the, like, subplot footage you see in between the main segments. Of course, many of my clients are celebrities. That helps drive up viewership. But they're drama queens, every one of them. 'Oh, Lewis, come take a look at Annabel. I think she's been having bad dreams. Is there *anything* you can do for her?' So learning to cook vegan has been, sort of ... what's the word sweetie?"

"Cathartic," pronounced Hunter.

"Yes, that thing he just said. It helps me purge, you know? And it's super-convenient. Before I learned to cook vegan, we had to cater everything that wasn't..."

Lewis bit off the end of the sentence. He began playing with his Samfaina, kicking it about with his fork.

"The food is *so* good," said Megan, quickly, who seemed to have caught on to David's strategy. "And don't be so humble. I mean *you* are a celebrity!"

Lewis rolled his eyes, and waved her off, a gesture which was beginning to irritate David, though he was glad for Megan's diversion. He was just about to pick up the threads with more questions about the interior design, when Hunter cleared his throat. Everyone looked at him.

"People..." said Hunter, waving his fork in a tight circle, gathering his thoughts, a bit of roast still impaled upon the tines, "...People are always defining themselves relative to a kind of scaffolding. Those celebrities who reach out to Lewis think of *him* as a celebrity. He thinks the same of them. Once upon a time, some of those celebrities were poor, or at least ordinary. They had one kind of mental scaffolding, you see, and now it's gone, and probably irrecoverable. When they remember it now, in ghost-written biographies, they recall not facts, but experiences filtered through the present. But when did the change really happen? When did they become *special people*? Probably you can't put your finger on that moment. There's no strict line of demarcation. But I'll tell you something I know: it all started with a change in mental scaffolding. First, they thought to themselves, 'I can be famous.' And then it became, 'I will be famous. I will be one of the few.' And those who succeeded did so only because they progressed on to, 'I *am* one of the few. I'm one of the specials, who make it through.' And so, in this way, the merely mental became the true."

He looked back toward them, again the professor in the presence of undergrads. Lewis made a sound like a small explosion, and mimed the action with a fist bursting into fingers above his head. He glanced at the others.

"You've got to expect that kind of thing when Hunter's in the room. Mr. Philosopher!"

"I think it's great!" said Megan, smiling over at David.

"But you know, Hun," said Lewis, "a lot of that rhymed at the end. You might want to consider a career as a poet."

Dave chuckled in what he hoped was a good-natured way, but Hunter fixed him suddenly with a look so serious, he wondered if the man had taken offense.

"I was building to a point there," he said. "If you don't mind, I'd like to finish the thought."

"Please!" said David, and leaned in with a great show of interest.

"Look," said Hunter. "Coming back to the idea of people, and of nature, which we were discussing earlier. People are, fundamentally, what they *think* they are. This is the real quality that distinguishes us from the other animals; that gives us such a responsibility toward them, in fact. To be human is to be fundamentally changeable. That capacity for infinite malleability according to one's own thoughts is our only defining characteristic. Our only *nature* is not to have one."

Megan and Lewis both nodded their heads thoughtfully. David frowned. As much as he wanted to avoid any philosophical conversation that might lead into the troubled waters of the Madsens' strange ethics, he also disagreed.

"I would have thought," he began, carefully, "that it was the capacity for thought and choice, and for making meaningful decisions, that most characterized us. I mean even the word 'homo sapiens' implies that."

"I quite agree," said Hunter. "Homo sapiens sapiens, the creature that makes meaning."

"Or you could say *finds* meaning," said David.

"You *could* say that," said Hunter. "If you were trying to imply that the meanings you made were universally true, and not just the lens you were looking through. But what I'm saying is press that one stage further, and you'll see that we not only make meaning, but we actually make ourselves."

David waggled his head. "Huh. Interesting."

He saw no way of going further down this path without bumping into ethics, and from there, into the things they were all deciding not to talk about. Better to let the man have his point, and then find a way to pivot. He smiled at Hunter, and nodded in a way that was not agreement, but which he hoped gave the general impression of agreeableness. Hunter did not smile. David perceived at a glance that he would not escape so easily.

"Take eating vegan," said Hunter. "Lewis and I agree that our species has a negative impact on animal life, and that it must be possible to live in a way that minimizes that impact. So we change ourselves into a members of a human sub-species, *homo sapiens homophagia*, if you will, which no longer lives parasitically off the lives of other animals."

David stopped eating. *A different species?* This, finally, was too much for him.

"But you're not a different species," he said.

Megan glanced at him warily.

"No?" said Hunter.

"No. I'm sorry, but you're still the same thing that I am. What you believe about it doesn't change the hard facts."

"I disagree," said Hunter. "I don't think there are any objective facts about us at all. If there were, then someone could come along and impose his idea of the facts upon me."

Megan reached under the table and squeezed David's arm. Somehow the gesture communicated both a warning and a plea. *Don't go there*, it said. He almost relented, but Hunter wasn't finished.

"Alright," continued Hunter. "Yes, we have arms and legs, and that sort of thing. Usually. But aside from that, give me a fact about human beings that cannot conceivably be altered by applying the very reason and will which you said defines us?"

David drew a very deep breath. There were a thousand paths he might have taken to delay conflict and maintain the artificial tolerance that he'd been willing to extend to the Madsens. But he sensed Hunter wasn't really interested in avoiding disagreement. Tolerance, for Hunter, was nothing less than total agreement with his point of view. So be it. David could see the yawning abyss before him, but he took the terrible plunge anyway.

"We're omnivores," he said. "So there's that."

Hunter smiled. He raised his fork to his mouth, and finally bit off the square of artificial roast that had been waiting so patiently on his teeth. Lewis shifted in his seat as if agitated.

"I'm … going to check on the soup again," he said, scurrying from the room.

Hunter leaned back, chewing his roast. "Go on," he said.

David shrugged. "Just what I said. Our species has evolved to eat vegetables and meat. There are even proteins we can only get in ready supply from meat products. I'm not saying you can't work around that, to an extent, but even when you do, you're still going to end up always trying to reintroduce meat through the back door."

He pointed at the roast. "The only reason that tastes good is that it almost tastes like meat. If a person could really change his nature with his thoughts, even with technology, then he could also change his desire for things that taste like meat."

David felt Megan's fingers go limp on his arm. He glanced over, and she pulled into herself. But Hunter did not seem offended. On the contrary, looking at him, David was now doubly sure that the man had been working him toward this subject all along.

"Well," said Hunter. "You've got me there. Obviously, Lewis and I *do* relish the taste of real meat. But at least, if we choose, we can use our minds to act upon the world in such a way as to consume it without harming any innocent creature."

"So you admit being an omnivore is an unchangeable part of your nature?" challenged David.

Lewis reentered the room carrying a chrome pot that steamed from the edges. He set it on a heat pad, and soon returned with four soup bowls. Daintily, he placed one bowl before each person, then hurried back into the kitchen. On his final return, the apron was gone, and he'd brought soup spoons, and something that looked like homemade season-salt. Lewis removed the lid from the pan, and began serving with a ladle. There was just enough of the beefy-smelling stuff for the four of them. David leaned forward and squinted, noticing a green image etched into the bottom of the pot, hardly visible through the thin layer of remaining broth. He looked questioningly at Lewis.

"Oh, that?" said Lewis, with a nervous chuckle. "One of Hunter's stupid jokes. Frog in a boiling pan. It's … never mind."

He picked up the seasoning shaker.

"May I?" he said, voice trembling. "It really makes the stew pop."

Like Megan, the poor man was deeply uncomfortable with the situation, and was trying to smooth things over the only way he knew. David assented emphatically to the gesture, feeling a deep sympathy for his host. As Lewis seasoned his guests' soup, David saw that his sun-browned hand was also trembling. Lewis wouldn't look at either Hunter or at him. Clearly he was the sort of gentle person who hated conflict. David sighed, and decided to just eat the soup he was given, hoping the whole subject would soon blow over.

Lewis sat down. David, still delaying, began to deliver spoonful after spoonful into his mouth. Lewis and Megan were doing the same. Only Hunter ate at a normal rate. He was perfectly calm, studying them, and sometimes floating his spoon over the bowl as if it were a thermometer that measured his command of the room. When Lewis had eaten his way to the bottom of the bowl, he looked around, almost desperate, seeming to realize that there was no more pretext by which he could leave the uncomfortable room. He turned to Megan, who forced a smile at him. David was encouraged by Lewis' behavior. Nobody wanted an argument. He kept eating his own soup, reasoning that he couldn't be expected to argue with his mouth full.

"I admit," said Hunter, quietly, "that life without meat is less pleasant. Luckily, there is now a way to have meat without harming anything. Or anyone."

For the first time, David was truly annoyed. Why did the man insist on pursuing this line of argument? They were guests here, captive to their hosts' whims. It made David mad, and he threw caution to the wind.

"So I guess you can have your meat and eat it too," he said.

"David!" snapped Megan, who immediately tried to cover her concern with a smile. "Come on, honey. It doesn't matter."

"Okay," said her husband, with a shrug.

"No, no, Megan," said Hunter. "I want him to speak freely. After all, your husband is only giving voice to what many people privately think."

"We don't have to talk about this," pleaded Megan. "It's not the right time."

"Not talking about it doesn't make it go away. Isn't that right, David? And," added Hunter, watching David go in for another bite, "now seems a particularly relevant moment to discuss the matter of eating human flesh."

David's whole body went rigid. He tasted the savory brown liquid coating his mouth. If the broth wasn't meat-based, it was the best imitation imaginable. He was on the point of surreptitiously spitting it back into the bowl, but he'd already eaten half of it. Perhaps he could slip off to the bathroom, and make himself vomit.

"Meat free, of course!" said Lewis, sensing his distress.

Lewis shot an angry, chiding look at Hunter, who burst out laughing. There was something incongruous about that laugh from that man, like a saxophone played in a cemetery. But David took it as a good sign.

"Damned good substitution," he said, cheerfully. "Very good!"

He looked up at Hunter. "Look, maybe Megan is right. We're guests here. Your hospitality has been wonderful. Can't we set this subject aside and … just be friends?"

Hunter became quiet, and his features resumed their former positions. He pressed his hands together, and seemed to gather himself into himself, becoming tall and grave like a chessboard bishop.

"This is what I do," said the man. "If I can't persuade you two, educated, liberal people, that our approach to life is just as valid and ethical as yours, then what I do on K Street is a lie. I can't fight bigotry out there if I can't confront it in my own home."

Megan visibly stiffened. Her eyes darted around, scrambling for an exit. But at the word 'bigotry', David's own blood shot past the temperature of the *faux* beef soup. He told himself to remain calm.

"I don't think," he said, "that I'm a bigot."

"No?" said Hunter.

"No. I would say that Megan and I have been very accepting. We've come over here to share a meal with you, and, though you clearly wanted to bring this subject up, we've obviously gone out of our way to avoid offending you."

"To avoid saying what you really think," corrected Hunter.

"To avoid—yes, well … but no one agrees about everything."

"You think we're cannibals," said Hunter.

Lewis knocked into his soup bowl, and the spoon clattered loudly against the rim.

"I didn't use the term," said David.

"But you think it applies."

"If you insist, then yes, I think it's more accurate than 'Cozzi Person'. I think that term is a kind of propaganda."

"If reality is perception," said Hunter, "then propaganda is survival. Anyway, the word cannibal is no better. Do you know where it comes from?"

David knew the answer to that one. Like most men of his age, he'd become something of a history buff. But he looked up, feigning ignorance.

"From Columbus," said Hunter. "From the Spanish conquistadors who laid waste the original peoples of the Caribbean Islands. The Carib tribes, you see. The Spanish accused them of eating people, and applied that accusation to all the local inhabitants, whether they did or not. It's how they justified dehumanizing the natives, so they could subject them to slavery."

"Are you claiming that the Caribs *didn't* eat members of other tribes?" asked David. "Because I'm fairly sure they did."

"No" said Hunter. "I wouldn't necessarily go that far. What I'm saying is that what some of the Caribs may have done was not so different from what Columbus did. He 'ate his victims' as well. Ate their freedom. Their livelihood."

"Okay," said David. "I think we can all agree that the Spanish exploited the natives. But the Caribs—"

"Were not so different from us. Exactly the same!"

"Not exactly."

"Yes, exactly. Because, while they did eat their foes, members of competitor tribes, those foes also ate them. These were the rules of the game, an agreed upon set of expectations. That's not different, fundamentally, from our marketplace. Some enterprises are bound to gobble up the others. But there's a form of consent there too. Everyone agrees to those rules."

David spooned more soup into his mouth. He wasn't sure how much farther the conversation could go. He was running out of soup.

"That's a stretch," he said, looking at Megan for support. "And the market doesn't have to be a zero-sum game. Some of us want to make the game more equitable."

But Megan wasn't looking back at David. She hid in her soup, stopping her mouth with tiny sips from her spoon, trying to make it last and probably wishing she was a million miles away.

"Not much of a stretch," said Hunter, softly. "And even if the market isn't, politics is. Politics is the market of ideas. A zero-sum market. For one idea to prevail, another has to lose out. Yet each of us consents to this game every election cycle."

David sighed. "So, let me get this straight. You're now claiming that cannibalism among Caribbean tribes was a matter of consent? Okay, then let's move over to the mainland. Did the people who died on Aztec altars also consent to having their hearts cut out?"

"Certainly!" said Hunter, tapping the table with his knuckles, "because they took pride in their great society, marched and danced in its festivals. Lived and worked under the shadows of those pyramids. They could have left if they wanted to. And if you read the accounts, parts of the sacrificed bodies were dropped down those long steps so the meals could be shared by the common folk. The original trickle-down economics."

Hunter laughed at his own joke, and David suppressed a gag that was prodding the back of his throat. He shook his head.

"Normally," said David, "the Aztecs sacrificed the members of other cities and tribes. They captured them in battle or collected them as tribute."

"Yes, *but*, did you know that the surrounding tribes—the Tobascoans, for example—also practiced homophagy? You see? Same game. Same rules. There's still consent there."

David felt as if his head were spinning. It had never even occurred to him that someone would push the notion of consent so far, and he wasn't sure how to argue the point. Argument required common ground.

"Two wrongs don't make a right."

It was the only thing he could muster, and it sounded weak even to him.

"Do you oppose boxing, or men giving each other concussions in football?"

"No … yes … I don't know. But … I mean, I would oppose gladiator games."

Hunter laughed. "You mean you oppose them up to a point. You oppose the full-fledged thing, but you still want a taste of it. You still want the semblance of a battle to the death, so long as there's a veneer of consent."

David scoffed, but he couldn't summon the ideas that would give his moral intuitions any force. Noticing his confusion, Hunter went in for the kill.

"You said before that our desire for meat, even simulated meat, proved that all humans were omnivorous. Then, by your argument, perhaps your approval of feigned battle proves that you're murderous. So long as it's only a semblance of murder, and mutually agreed upon."

Again, that disorienting sense of swimming assaulted David's mind. His brain felt underwater. He tried to find something, anything, that could ground his sense of social morality. He looked around at solid things: the table, the chairs, the rectangular structure of the room. These stable items, formed for a purpose, gave him the means to continue the argument.

"If right and wrong aren't built on nature, on the order of things, then they aren't built on anything foundational. There's nothing behind them but pure will. And I can't survive in that kind of world. No one can."

"But they *are* built on something," insisted Hunter. "On the mutual consent of malleable, self-making minds, respecting each other's self-made meaning. In a word, on kindness."

"Kindness … but who's definition of kindness? Who's definition of consent?"

Hunter smiled. "The ones who set the rules, David. The ones who, so to speak, 'lay the table.'"

He gestured to the once-solid dining room, this complex of hard things that offered David no help. David put his head in his hands. For some reason, he felt like crying.

"If what you're saying is true," he said, much more weakly this time, "then might makes right. And Megan and I, the values we've tried to live by, to transmit to our daughter, have no basis in reali—"

"—You have a daughter?" interrupted Lewis.

Megan, who'd been staring off the whole time, lost in her thoughts, turned slowly toward Lewis.

"Yes, Lewis. Didn't you know?"

"Is … is she at home with the babysitter?" said Lewis. "Gosh, I'm so sorry we didn't invite her."

Megan laughed. "Hadley? She's a full-grown woman. She doesn't live with us. She's all the way in…"

But Megan trailed off, as if she couldn't remember her thought.

"Sorry, if that's a sore spot," said Lewis, with a shrug. "It's just … you're both so young-looking. I … I didn't think you could have an adult daughter. Will she visit soon?"

Megan shook her head, full of regret. Hadley, when she was just a few years younger, had seen enough of their stupid arguments to stay well away. But if Hadley had been here, this evening wouldn't have become such a train wreck.

David looked at her and felt awful. He'd done everything she'd hoped he wouldn't. But he hadn't meant to. He never could seem to keep his mouth shut. And anyway, Hunter clearly started it!

He looked up at the man, who now leaned back in his chair, as if waiting for something. David's capitulation, probably. David sighed. He would have to surrender the argument, make peace with the mad world Hunter advocated, if only to appease Megan.

"Well," he said with a forced smile, "I think you've got me, Hunter. There's a … certain logic to what you've said. I'm not sure I can refute it. Maybe you're right. I suppose it's possible that … I have some unexamined prejudices, and … in any event, you've given me a lot to think about."

Hunter nodded, silently magnanimous. But he didn't say anything. David glanced at Megan again, hoping that this little forced peace offering on his part would offer her some relief from the embarrassment he'd caused. At least, during the inevitable, impending screaming match at home, he could say he'd really tried. But Megan stared ahead, looking at nothing.

"Megan?"

David's wife turned to him. Her eyes were wide. Her mouth opened and closed wordlessly. Then she fell forward, planting her face in the bowl of soup.

David leapt to his feet. He grabbed her shoulders and pulled her up from the soup, but her chin rolled onto her chest. Lewis was on his feet now too, shouting at Hunter to do something. David crouched down beside his wife. He wiped the soup from her face, and then began lightly smacking her cheeks.

"Honey! Honey, what's wrong?"

"Oh my gosh! Oh my gosh!" cried Lewis, wringing his hands. "Does she have any allergies? I thought you said she didn't have any allergies?"

"Call 911!" yelled David.

He leaned his wife against his chest and felt her throat for a pulse. He could hardly think with Lewis making such a panicked racket, and his own hands were shaking. The whole situation seemed unreal, as if he were moving in a dream through some viscous substance. When he finally detected the faintest throbbing under her skin, David realized that he had no sense of how long he'd been crouching there, feeling for a pulse. Clutching Megan, he stood, and kicked aside her chair. He laid her down on the floor, almost falling over as he did so. His wife's dead-weight was surprisingly heavy. He forced himself up and began shouting orders at Hunter and Lewis.

"You, Hunter, please call 911! Lewis, get a blanket or something."

"I've already called," said Hunter.

Lewis nodded at David reassuringly, but he didn't move. Instead, he looked at Hunter. *The man is panicking. He's useless,* thought David. He knew he should start CPR and tried to recall the number of breaths and chest compressions. The room began spinning around in earnest, and he cursed himself for his mental weakness. He needed to get a grip. To stabilize himself, David fixed his gaze on the object at the center of the table. That cheerful green frog smiled up at him from the bottom of the soup pot. David's eyes closed on their own, and he forced them open. He almost lost his footing, and caught himself against the table. As he straightened up, he heard pounding at the downstairs door.

"Go and let them in," said Hunter, calm and collected.

Lewis hurried out of the room. David began stumbling toward Megan, supporting himself against the table. His wife needed him, and he was disgusted with his own office-domesticated uselessness. *Thank God the paramedics are already here*, he thought. Then he froze and turned slowly to Hunter.

"How can they be here already?"

His eyes shut again. He began to fall, and that very sensation helped him to force them open. When he did, he saw the paramedics enter the room. At that moment, it occurred to David that he'd never heard a siren.

There were four medics, and they moved in concert like an oiled machine. Two large square bags were set on the floor and opened. From one of these they took a stretcher, which they quickly telescoped out and laid on the floor beside Megan. One of the men unfurled a clump of tightly rolled black fabric on top of the stretcher. It was made of thick rubbery material. He unzipped it down the middle. Another emergency worker opened the second square duffel bag, and from it pulled a cooler. Inside, David saw clear bags of ice. A frothy steam rose from the cooler. Was it dry ice?

"What are you doing?" said David.

No one looked at him. Instead, three men lifted Megan, and placed her inside the rubber, body-sized bag.

"You're supposed to be doing CPR!" shouted David.

One of the men looked up at him, and then at Hunter. Hunter nodded.

"What is this?" said David.

He stumbled forward, struggling to keep his footing. The hand that supported him against the tabletop slid into Hunter's soup bowl, upsetting its contents over the table. David looked down at his wife's soup, the same soup they'd all been eating. Could something poison have gotten into it? But Lewis had been eating the same soup! David's gaze fell upon the seasoning shaker. He dimly recalled Lewis putting the stuff on Megan's soup, and on his. But Lewis never put it on his own.

With dawning horror, he turned back to Megan. Now she was inside the black body bag, and they were packing her in with many small ice bags. He thought he could see the bags gently rising and falling on top of her chest. Her face had been left uncovered, its gentle features, caught in deep, untroubled slumber, were visible just before the black bag was rudely zipped shut. That done, the men turned their interest to the other square duffel. From it they quickly produced a second telescoping stretcher, and a second black bag. The steaming cooler, David saw, still had plenty of ice.

"Wh … why?" slurred David.

Lewis turned to face him, wearing a curious expression. He shrugged at Hunter, who came over and looked down, more a scarecrow now than ever. The two men studied David, watching with interest as he fought to remain standing. In his last conscious moments, David thought back to his research on Cozzi People. He recalled the worst accusations from disreputable websites, articles posted side-by-side with the most preposterous conspiracy theories. But things like that didn't really happen. Not in real life.

The blurry images of Hunter and Lewis swam inside his eyes, like two sharks.

"You're … you're going to *eat us*?" said David.

It came out in a pitiful whine. Lewis glanced at Hunter, as if he found the comment perplexing. Hunter just shook his head.

"You're going to eat us," repeated David. "Or sell us. I can't believe it. I can't believe it."

Again, the befuddled look from Lewis. Again, Hunter shook his head in apparent disgust. He put a comforting arm around Lewis.

David collapsed to his knees. Only his fingers, clutching the table-end like vices, kept him from falling. Lewis shrugged off Hunter's arm. He crouched down beside David, so that their eyes were level. The gentle, artistic face twisted in revulsion.

"You..." Lewis began, shaking as if he could hardly force the words out. "You can't believe it?"

David lost feeling in his fingers and legs. He fell forward onto his elbows.

"No, no, no," he repeated in a mumbled mantra. "I don't believe it."

Lewis went down on all fours. His lips hovered near David's ear.

"But David," Lewis said, his tone as incredulous as the mind of the man now struggling to remain conscious. "We're *cannibals*!"

David sprawled onto the floor. It was unforgivingly solid.

IN THE LOOKING GLASS

Thip. Thip. Thip.

Naked feet slapped the spongy hill, in the darkness, under the black wire forest. Sometimes a stone bulged through the plastimoss, and he sought it out, and stomped upon it, and let it bruise his feet. It was good to touch something real, and to let it touch him. Down he sprinted, down through the nettlesome web of kinetic trees, down over covered soil, and coated rocks, down through the filtered air and strangeling lights that floated like fireflies but were not alive, down, and further, and deeper, trying for a ravine he thought he'd seen beneath the false buttes and dark towers that knifed the sky, following always some voice he could not name. He was striving for the roots of things; for the root of roots.

He suddenly ran out of hillside. The boy slowed, sucked wind, and stumbled out into a narrow gorge that snaked between the buttes and towers. The night sky also teamed with tiny pinprick lights, but he did not look up. He couldn't distinguish true stars from those other lamps, and so would not try.

Winded, he began walking. The gorge snaked downward, as if there'd been a stream there, once upon a time. He walked beside the dry bed. It too was lined with plastimoss, though here the stuff was brown and gray, a mockery of soil and stone leftover from times when men walked the earth. The skeleton stream wormed left and right, and always down. Its form confessed an ancient, forbidden logic. There had been a time, the boy knew, when things flowed, or grew, or were ground down, or shifted, or shuffled, or were recycled and renewed all on their own. There had been a time of magic, when things no one had made followed their own purposes. The stream bed was a relic of that antiquarian freedom. It was proof of the magic he sought.

Now it bent left around the base of a black butte. Like the others, this butte was steel-shod, and only looked stoney when one didn't scrutinize too closely. Stone didn't conduct electricity. Stone wasn't useful, save as a scaffolding for useful things. The boy followed the stream anyway, hour upon hour, until he nearly lost hope. He was driven by the real thing he sought. He was driven—and repelled—by that which he'd escaped. And, perhaps, he was rewarded, for he came around a bend to a flat place.

It was a plain between the feet of many towers. In its center was a silver pool. The sight of it revived him. The pool was wide, almost a small lake, and the lake was not circular or square, but laid out oblongly, haphazardly, as if for no purpose but its own. As if it were magic. Had he found magic already?

The boy became quiet. He looked over his shoulder, and listened. A breeze came down through the canyon. At length, he sighed. They hadn't followed. He might actually be alone. *Alone-ish*. They could, of course, see him at all times. He turned to face the lake again, and then let out a shriek. On the shore off to the right lay a thing like a metal spider. It was one of those that maintained the tanks. It sprawled halfway into the pool. It didn't move. Gathering his courage, he approached. The segmented arms were coated in red rust. It had long ceased functioning. He kicked it, and one of the arms came off at the joint. Satisfied that it was dead, and now more certain than ever that he was truly on the outside, he turned away from it. The boy sat down beside the silvery pool.

Because the night sky was reflected in it, the water seemed alive. Now he watched the stars and the false lights shimmering in the water. True, he couldn't tell one sort of light from its mimic, but in these waters, even the roving eyes that crowded out the real stars were, by reflection, rendered natural. In the looking glass, they were not things of metal and craft but things of light. Reflection was not the sort of thing that anyone could own or harness or stamp with a number. Reflection was real.

Real also was the wind that whistled through the gorge, and washed over his gray form, his prison body, a body far too young for its age. It was cold down here. He liked the cold, and the little cuts and bruises on the bottoms of his feet. Closing his eyes, he scooted forward, and dipped them into the water. There was some movement in it. He pretended to himself that the lake bubbled up from a hidden river, one too deep and too secret for even them to know about, or ever to make use of.

With his eyes pressed closed, and wiggling his toes so the cold water got inside their creases, the boy put his hand on the ground beside his thigh. It was time. He took a deep breath and began pulling at the plastimoss. At first it only stretched, but he dug his fingers in and tried to tear it. He ground his teeth, and finally cried out from the effort. A fissure appeared in the moss. He quickly shifted to his haunches, and got his other hand inside the gap. With two hands, he widened the hole. Reaching through, the boy found another layer beneath the first. Undaunted, he began to tear at that too.

It gave him hope that his body felt so tired. This was evidence that his limbs had hardly ever been used; that all of this was real. And the odor of the air, though pungent, was like nothing he could recall from coma. Still, he wished he'd brought something sharp, like a shard of the tank he'd once lived inside. But it was too late now. Were he to go looking, the hole would close on its own, and his efforts would be for naught. But he had only so much strength, and had not yet even considered where to find nourishment. It was five minutes before he breached the second layer, only to find beneath it yet more of the spongy material. Exhausted, he let his head and shoulders slump down into his bent arms. The boy curled into a ball beside the silvery lake. There he lay for time out of mind, and the lying sky rolled over him.

"Are you crying?" said a voice.

The boy opened his eyes. The voice was high, like liquid bells. He sat up and looked around. The shore was empty, but the voice had come from nearby. The silver pool remained still, but for the touch of canyon breeze. He'd heard voices like that—women's voices—in coma, on days of beauty, when they'd tried to lull him back from breaking through. He hadn't considered till now that that of which the voices were an illusion might itself exist, somewhere. Perhaps it didn't. The awful thought struck him that he was still in coma; that his escape had been but a dream in a dream. He put his forearm in his mouth and bit down hard. He clenched his teeth until tears rolled down his cheeks. When he couldn't take the pain, he removed his arm, and sighed at the small beads of red blood gathering there. He dried his eyes.

"I'm not crying," he said.

"You were," said the woman's voice.

"Where are you?"

The woman chuckled. "Must I be somewhere? Is that usual?"

Again, he doubted. Perhaps there was no escape.

"Over here, then," said the voice.

He followed it toward the center of the small lake. There was nothing there, neither boat nor buoy, but the lights on the surface shimmered more in the center than anywhere else. Then, as he watched, that shimmering point rose, and rounded, and cascaded down around a soft, rising form. A waterfall was born from nothing, and poured itself out, making something. Somebody. Head and neck; shoulders clothed in long, blue-black hair. Hips, and an hourglass form. A woman had come out of the water. She moved toward him.

He watched her body, making himself sure that the lake gave as she came on, that she pushed it aside, and did not simply pass through it as a phantom would. Presently, she stepped up onto the shore and came to stand before him. Lake water ran down her shins, and pooled about her feet. He looked up, tracing the falling water backward up the rolling wonderland, up her stately neck, over her round chin, past the secret smile on her lips, until their eyes met. Her eyes shone like the silver lake. The boy shuddered.

"Do I frighten you?" she asked.

"Yes," gasped the boy.

"Do you know why?" she said.

He shook his head; opened and closed his mouth.

"I think it's … beyond why. Before it."

She nodded. The way she tilted her head sent confusion through his whole being.

"Shall I go?" she said.

He couldn't make his mouth work. She began to move back toward the water. The boy made a strangled sound, like a fish dying, and grabbed for her, touching the flesh on the top of her foot where it met the ankle. She stopped, and let him get a hold of her. Her skin felt odd; familiar. She was cool to the touch, like the water in which she lived, yet she did not make him cold.

"Please," he said.

She smiled, and knelt beside him. He looked down into the plastimoss that covered the world, finding it difficult to meet her eyes. She bent lower.

"What do you want?" she said.

"I don't know," he gasped.

She bent all the way to the ground, then gazed up until she caught his eyes and forced them to meet hers.

"What did you come looking for?"

A shiver racked his whole body. She laughed.

"Well," she said, "it must have been something important. I saw you on the dark hills. You were running very hard."

He looked sharply at her. "You saw me? How?"

"You were running," she continued, "and I said to myself, 'There is something that he wants.' And I have not seen anyone who wants anything. Not in a long time, at least. So I thought, perhaps…"

His doubts returned. Was she part of his illusion, after all? "How did you see me? You couldn't have seen me."

"Tell me why you were running," she said, "and I will tell you how I saw."

The boy looked at his arm again, to make sure it had really bled. The bite wound was starting to scab up, and the blood wasn't all hardening at the same rate. That seemed promising. Realistic. He would have tasted his blood too, just to be sure, but was embarrassed to try it with her so close.

"I was looking for … you know … *it*."

"It?"

"Him, maybe. The real thing," he said. "That was calling to me. The part that isn't made. Isn't *made up*, I mean."

Again, she laughed. Her laugh was like songbirds in the morning, though he knew them only from coma. "And you thought you'd find it under everything else?"

He shrugged. "Where else?"

She shifted her body, climbing gracefully out of her kneeling position to sit beside him.

"Even if you got through the covering," she whispered, "and found dirt, and worms, and things like that, would that be *it*?"

"It would be magic," he said. "It would be something they didn't make."

"But *somebody* made it," she said, turning his chin toward her face, making him look into her starry eyes.

He forced himself to look away.

"Then I to want find that somebody," he snapped.

She sighed, a deep breath that gave him some hope she was real. He glanced sidelong at her body, and saw the gill slits on her lungs. Even out of the water, she glistened like the lake itself, and all the lines and curves moved in tandem. But that could be faked. Yet he knew of no species like her, save in old fairy tales. But fairy tales themselves, and their passing down from age to age, might only be part of the machine dreams. And if she were real, she would not have known that he was coming here. She would not have seen him under the black wire trees, or around the bend of the ancient stream. He began to cry again. He knew he was far too old to cry, but his body betrayed him. He bit his lip, but could not stop himself.

"There you go again," she said, softly. "What is it?"

"You're not here! And that means … it means I'm still in coma! They've got me till the end of days."

She shook her head. Her cool hand reached out and enclosed his.

"That's not true," she said. "You must be calm to reason properly. Anyway, *they* don't have anyone. If you want to know, I don't think they exist anymore. Just the things they built. The machines keep running because they can't do anything else. But you and I are still here. We're talking to each other. Your hand is in my hand."

She brought his hand to her face. "See? Flesh and bone, like you."

The boy snatched his hand away and stood. He pointed at her.

"But you said you saw me in the hills! How could you see me from down here? Unless you're one of them. Unless *I'm* still inside. That was a mistake! You let that slip. Sooner or later, they always slip up. That's how I got out in the first place. If I did get out."

She *tsked*, and drew both hands through her hair, pulling her fingers like combs to the ends of each strand, letting him see each one fall.

"I *am* real," she said. "I am magic, like the dirt and the worms, still hiding beneath the coating. Like the fish that swim by me in the water, tickling my skin, out there in my lake. I'm magic, just like you. Just not *exactly* like you."

"Explain that," he demanded. "And how you could see me from far away. Then maybe I'll believe you."

She pouted, then opened her arms coyly, as if to display her beauty. "Don't you *want* to believe me?"

"I want the truth!" he said, refusing to look at her straight on.

"But you want the truth to be beautiful, too."

"Everybody does," he said.

"What if … it isn't?"

She said it slowly, testing him. "What if truth is ugly, and beauty is just the sugar that makes it go down?"

"Then beauty would come from nowhere," he said. "And it would be nothing. But it isn't nothing. It is what it is."

"But, you have to admit," she pressed, "things aren't always what they seem."

He sighed. "No. I seem to be a boy, but I've done the calculations. I'm at least five hundred years old—"

"Machine years," she corrected. "In the tank, you're what they say you are. The machine fears grown men. They keep you all young. But out here, you can grow up. You can be dangerous. And … I'll be here too."

"—And *you*," he continued, swatting her words like flies, "you seem to be a beautiful water nymph. Yet you're just another layer of the illusion. But I'll break through. I will! There may be a hundred layers between here and what I'm looking for, but you won't stop me! I will find it. I will find … him! The face behind it all. Real beauty, that isn't illusion."

The water woman wasn't laughing at him anymore. In her eyes he now recognized admiration, desire—perhaps even relief. Yet the boy continued to scowl at her, showing only his skepticism, concealing his secret hope that she was real. Then it was as if a cloud passed over her, and only some hidden sorrow remained.

"I *am* real," she insisted. "I am magic. As flesh and blood as I can be."

He scoffed. "Then how did you see me from far away?"

She hesitated.

"Let me show you."

She darted towards him. He thought he should run, but she took him in her arms, and pressed him close.

"*See*," she said.

Touching her, he saw what she saw. He saw her thousand stories, false life after false life served consecutively within the confines of her tank. Life and struggle, love and death, journey and return followed in an endless, tropish train, until they repeated, and rhymed too much. Until she'd perceived the illusion, as he had, and started to break through. He saw her waking up, opening her eyes in the acrid green water, just as he had. He saw her pounding on the glass, and he saw her reflection against it. Not this beautiful creature before him, but a prunish, homely thing, its humanity long drained away. He saw her beating on the glass until it cracked. A spidery arm reached in to anesthetize her. He saw her fight with it, and begin to lose. And he saw how, in her final desperation, she'd torn out the other end of the metal cord that fed into her brain, and plugged that into the spider's port, just before the needle touched her own skin.

She'd sent her mind into its mind. Stretched it that far, anyway. Part of her had gotten free. Part of her was floating, sliding, seesawing somewhere between here and there. And in its metal body, part of her had skittered away, down long dark hallways filled with lightless machines. And in their fabricators, in the spider's body she'd possessed, she'd built herself another form, one full of the beauty they'd taken from her. A magic body.

And she'd carried it out of the dark prison, and down the mountainside, and into the ravine, until, like the boy, she'd found something they hadn't made: living water. In her last moments inside the metal mind, she'd completed the circuit, and plugged herself into this new form she'd hauled with her, this almost-magic thing she'd made. But somewhere far away, in a dark metal prison atop a dark tower, the old prunish body still lived on, and dreamed, and lent the new one part of her life. She was in both places. In her prison tank. Here, on the shore. Even inside the machine mind that had run the world and was now only an electric ghost. She was everywhere. She was nowhere.

She released him. The boy stumbled back, and gasped for breath. She stood there, trembling at the memory, and at the effort of sharing it with him. Her body was wet and glistened in the light of real and illusory stars. He recognized now why it had felt strange to the touch. It was made of something like the film that covered the whole world. She was weeping. She wept—he understood it now—for fear he'd consider her a mere artifice. Behind her, in the distance, the rusted spider she'd once possessed still sprawled on the shore.

"I am real," she whispered. "I am magic. Don't say that I'm not."

He went to her. "No, no," he said. "You're as real as you can be. Given the circumstances..."

But he didn't know what to think. Her tears seemed real enough. Yet the knowledge that she was a sort of mechanism after all left him cold. He'd wanted to find reality, not another pretend thing.

"I could..." he began, "...well, I could find you. I could break you out. I mean ... your real body—"

"No!" she cried. "That's too much. I want truth too, but that's too much truth. I can't be that old, shriveled husk! This is the best I can be, unless someone exists who has the power to remake things as they should be."

He nodded, and patted her shoulder nervously. The boy, this old man, was troubled. His love of truth had gotten him this far. It had broken him through the glistening lights and sensory impressions that were only pleasant illusions, and into this shadowy, dun world of the real. But it wasn't all he'd looked for. There had to be more. Could he abandon his search now? Would it be right, having come so far, to settle in the middle?

"I can't expect you," he said carefully, "to want to live as they've made you. I can't blame you for choosing to remain like this. But … but I think I have to keep searching. I have to find what's behind it all."

"No you don't!" she said. "Can't you see what's in front of you! There's beauty right here."

"But it's not *the beauty*," he said. "It's just another filter."

"Maybe we only get filters," she whispered. "Maybe we can't see the thing itself, unless it comes to us."

He shook his head. "That can't be right. That takes away my choice. *I* broke through! *I'm* the one who found the traces, and followed them out."

Fire flashed in her eyes.

"Is *that* what you think?" she said. She slapped him. "No, boy. It was *I* who called you out."

The bottom dropped out of his soul. No machine would think to say this. She pressed on. "I saw you in the tank. I heard you. Felt you striving with them. I spent myself to reach you. *I* called *you*."

He felt as if he were wilting. This truth undid everything. A voice *had* called to him. A lonely, longing voice. And he'd followed it out, like a child birthing itself.

"I thought it was God," he whispered, tearing up again. "I thought he'd finally found me. And I was a hero, breaking forth. I was going to tear through all the lies."

She sighed. The wind whistled through the canyon, and swept her hair from her shoulders, suspending it, and playing with it, and drawing all things toward the magic water.

"It *was* God," she said, softly. "But we only see his shadow. For now, that's enough. Receiving it—just reflecting it—is heroism down here."

The boy turned away from her. He surveyed the steel-shod walls, the rising canyons, the numerous dark prisons that covered each one like artificial mountains, having long ago swallowed up the real ones. Beneath all this, buttressing it, a real world crouched in power. But it had all been covered, choked, by seeming things, things that leached upon it, ran endlessly, and to no end but themselves. They were hellish. They had been made by artificial hands.

"I'll keep looking," he said, weakly.

"If you do," she replied, "you'll have to leave me behind. I am an old husk in a tank. I am a young nymph by the lake. Neither can stray far from the water. But, together—you and me, together—we might call the others. We might find a few. We're the last two stars in this land of night."

The boy who was old, the old man who was a boy, closed his eyes. When he opened them, the water nymph remained beside him. Her eyes hoped but did not plead. She was desirable, but not all he'd desired. And yet, that Hidden Face he longed for sloped endlessly, and, even were he touching it, he'd never grasp it, only hope to be grasped *by* it. It curved and sang and moved beneath, beyond, and within all things. Within her too. He could go on looking, breaking through the dark looking glass that held him, or he could receive it, in such measure as he was able to receive it, here, in this present darkness, until, finally and completely, it broke through to him.

He reached out, like one dying, and took her hand. "In that case," he said. "I'll stay here with you."

UTOPIA MINUS ONE

I did not have any sense of shaking off sleep. In a white corridor, I simply *was*. The floors and walls were polished to a high sheen and were framed occasionally by a blue molding set like pillars in the walls, and there were many small lights that blinked or twinkled, as if the whole place were working out a problem. I was already standing, but didn't remember ever having stood. I don't remember anything before that moment.

Soon I began moving in a circle, not walking exactly, but rotating to get my bearings. The space behind resembled what was before. Later, when I knew better what to look for, I would have reason to wish that I'd taken more time to notice the small characteristics that distinguished that specific corridor. Not that it was my true beginning, but everyone must have an origin story, and this entails some point in space.

It was very quiet, but for a low hum that I felt more than heard. Presently, there were voices up ahead. I had the impulse to hide. Two women in brown coveralls came down the corridor. They were chatting at a low volume, but quieted their conversation when they got closer to me. They passed me by, and having gone some distance, resumed speaking. That, and an almost imperceptible glance from one of the women, were the only proof I'd been seen.

I stayed rooted for some time after that, until a tall man in a navy blue uniform stepped through a break in the wall, looked away without either acknowledgment or concern, and turned right down the corridor at a leisurely pace. I noticed that the corridor was broken at intervals by rectangular gaps that were rounded at the edges, through which anyone could step to go from one corridor to another. There were no doors, with their implication of privacy; only gaps in lengths of space. While I stood looking at the gaps, several more travelers passed by through parallel corridors. I noticed more men in navy, a few women in the functional brown, and one very striking woman in a cobalt uniform, very tightly-fitting, with white buttons that ran from the V of her neck down to her belly.

I looked down at what I was wearing. I had on a simple white shirt with L-clasps down the middle, and white slacks that reached my heels. The material was light, almost weightless, and my feet were covered in warm slippers. I still remember that initial sense of profound physical comfort, and how it contrasted with something unpleasant that I couldn't recall. It wasn't a memory; just a vague impression of disquiet from the time before. My body was tranquil. But at the back of my mind was something like pain, or guilt, over what I cannot say. Colorless and feeling weightless, I briefly wondered if I was a ghost.

But people saw me, even if they didn't speak to me. I felt the floor hum through my feet, smelled the clean, almost antiseptic rosiness in the air, heard the low hum, and the silence. There was a simple absence where memory ought to reside, yet it was somehow purposeful. Expected. In those early days, what came before was still the greatest mystery. I was mostly conscious of the questions bubbling up in my mind: Who am I? How did I get here? What is here? I started walking.

Though I seemed to be going in a straight line, there was always more corridor ahead of me, and I came to understand that the path curved. The very graduality of it suggested bigness. True, I was in an enclosure, but the slow grade of the bend and the openings on either side, the shining white walls and floor, held off for a time any sense of being contained.

Presently I noticed that some of the rectangles were not passageways but small enclaves. Some were lined with terminals, while others held couches or tables, and things for which I had no words, only a vague familiarity. As I continued walking, and kept noticing these side lounges, I became curious about the centerpieces found on each circular table. Not seeing anyone around, I hurried over to one of the tables. That made me dizzy, and I had to pull out the chair, and lean on it for support. The chair scraped the floor and made an awful sound. Someone groaned to my right, and I froze.

In the enclave, a man I hadn't seen stirred on a couch. He was entirely nude, though his skin glistened under a translucent covering. I stared, out of sheer surprise, and the man looked back at me, his eyes still foggy. Coming fully awake, and recognizing, apparently, that I was a person of small interest, he turned his attention to the corridor, and stumbled off like one awakened just in time for an appointment. Alone again, I sat down at the table, and looked at the centerpiece.

It was a white disk about the circumference of a closed hand, and it was mounted inside chrome-colored tongs, the latter fixed directly into the table's center. Each of the tables around had one just like it, though they differed slightly in size and color. I wanted to pluck one from the tongs to further examine it, but it made me nervous. I tried to think what the disk reminded me of, but came up against the absence that was my memory. This was maybe the first time—not, by far, the last—that I experienced this particular species of mental distress. It was the agony of knowing something, and not being able to get at the knowledge.

I became very upset. My eyes filled with frustrated tears, which I blinked back out of shame. My attire and everything around me suggested a plan to which I was not privy. Steeling myself, I stared hard at the object, and scoured my brain for associations. The white disk wasn't whole but was riven with many pores and tunnels, and its borders were implied rather than defined. For some reason, it made me think of water, vast stretches of blue water, but when I tried to give a name to that water, I found more blanks. Indeed, my mind seemed riven with holes, just like this disk. I kept at it, thinking that if I strained enough, the name would come to me. Twice I almost remembered the vast blue thing, or perhaps whatever the white disk reminded me of, but it escaped me. I guess it was this intense focus that kept me from noticing his approach.

A man with silvering hair and a gray suit pulled back the chair opposite mine, and sat. He smiled warmly and rested his arms on the table. He was thickly-built, though not fat. He had large, blue, confident eyes, and a square jaw. I waited for him to say something, but it was a long time before he did. Conscious of my lingering tears, I looked away quickly and tried to remove the evidence, pretending to cough while drawing my sleeve across my face. When I looked back, I saw that he'd not been taken in. He smiled again, a small, empathetic pull of the lips.

"It's perfectly normal to feel that way at the start."

The start? Curiosity was overtaking my anxiety.

"But," he continued, "you'll find in time that you know what you need to know, and that the things you don't remember were never very important."

His voice was deep but smooth. I nodded, doubting what he said, but happy at least that someone was talking to me. I fumbled around with my fingers, trilling them against the tabletop for something to do.

"How do you feel?" he said.

"Well," I said. "Comfortable."

It seemed prudent to focus on my physical comfort; to conceal my distress.

"That's good!" he said. "In that case, you'll have nothing to worry about here."

I considered the obvious questions. I burned to ask, "Where am I? Who am I? Where is here?" but intuition warned me to keep quiet. The man seemed friendly enough, but he must have known the answers I sought, and I gathered he was party to my present ignorance.

"What should I do?" I said. It was the only question that seemed safe.

He smiled, and clasped one large hand inside the other on the table.

"That's to be determined. For now, feel free to wander about the place. Nothing is barred to you. No one should give you any trouble, but if they do, let me know."

I nodded, as if I understood any of that. He sat back in his chair, then looked at the white circle on the tongs.

"Are you hungry?"

I shook my head. He nodded, pushed his chair back, and walked over to a small counter. He took a clear glass from the countertop, filled it with water from an aperture in the wall, and then returned to his seat. I reflected on the paradox that I knew what water was, and wasn't surprised by any of the basic items around me, though I didn't have words for all of them. Were I as new as I felt, these things ought to have been complete novelties. He gave me an appraising look.

"You have good sense," he said. "Yes, I think it'll go well for you."

He reached across the table. When he extended his hand, the sleeve of his gray jacket pulled back, and I noticed the border of a thin translucent covering over the skin of his wrist. At first I thought he was going to touch me, but he plucked the white circle from the tongs, broke it, and dropped the pieces into his glass. It roiled and fizzled, disassembling itself in the water, which process he helped along by gently swishing the glass. When the thing was entirely dissolved, he drank it down in uninterrupted gulps. The glass bottom clapped on the table, and he leaned back with a satisfied smile.

Now my curiosity got the better of me. "What is that stuff?"

He nodded, fully expecting the question. "We just call it the coral. There's plenty of it around. Good for decoration, or a bite between meals. Those are served in the mess, which is…"

He went on, listing the areas for eating, sleeping, working, or relaxing. I nodded, only half-attending. I was fixated on that word coral. It was what I'd been trying to remember, and now it fit like a key in a lock. Memory is like that. And yet it came without associated images or stories of coral. It was just as if a surgeon had reached into my brain with scalpel and gloved fingers, and had plucked the single word from an opaque void, excising it without its sinewy context. I continue to have that experience over and over again. I've come to accept it.

"You won't remember all that," he said.

I looked up, confused, then realized he meant all the places and things he'd just listed.

"That's perfectly fine, though," he continued. "Just you wander around and learn a little every day. You can sleep on any open couch or bed. They're quite comfortable."

I was far from tired, and the idea of lying down somewhere to sleep, strangers walking all around me, made me uneasy.

"So," I said, shrugging, "I should just…"

He nodded. "Yes. Continue your walk. Get familiar with the place. Let me know if you encounter any friction."

I chewed my lip, wondering what that could mean.

"How will I find you?" I asked instead.

He smiled. "Oh, you won't need to. I'll be watching."

***

The liberating thing about being no one is that you don't know when you're lost. Anyway, the corridors were a series of concentric circles, so that I could simply pass through the gaps to move outwards or inwards.

On that first day, like any animal in an enclosure, I first tried to find its limits. After some hours, I'd not reached the border. This was partly because of the size of the place, and partly because the further out I went, the more infrequently did gaps appear on the outer walls. This had the effect of discouraging me from pressing on, for not only was I getting away from where I knew the mess and main sleeping quarters were supposed to be located, but the long stretches without new doorways made me realize, for the first time, that I was contained.

I pressed on a little further, determined to find something to justify the effort so far invested. All that while, the lights had gradually dimmed, but so subtly that I hadn't noticed while it was happening. I had still to retrace my way toward the interior. The corridors narrowed until they were little wider than my shoulders. I was on the point of turning back when I came upon another break in the wall. I had an eerie feeling looking at it. Sounds of quiet movement and machine buzzing came in from the other side. I stepped through, planning to have only a quick look around.

To my surprise, I'd entered a room teeming with people. Most were in white, though their dress differed from mine. They wore loosely fitting coats over slacks, and moved about a series of high counters on which sat a number of half-familiar mechanical devices. I had that same odd sense of recognition without words, of not finding things entirely foreign while being unable to put a name to anything.

It seemed I should announce my presence. I walked further into the room and cleared my throat. Two of the workers immediately stopped what they were doing. The man closest to me frowned at a colleague, who glanced my way, then shrugged as if to say, "What can we do?" I felt unwelcome, and considered backing out of the place. But, recalling what the Gray Man had said about nothing being barred to me, I resolved on the spot to put his words to the test.

By now all the white coats were staring. It was more attention than anyone else had afforded me; more than I'd bargained for. A tall man whose long face and small eyes made him the picture of aloofness, put down what was in his hands and stepped toward me.

"If you're hungry," he said, "the mess can be found in the interior."

It was not a command to leave; not exactly.

"I'm not hungry," I said.

A partial lie. Though my body still felt tranquil, the long walk had stirred my appetite.

"Well," offered another man, "if you just need a bite, there's always the coral." He gestured toward the interior. "That way."

Though I was clearly unwanted, his mention of the coral had the opposite of its intended effect. From the beginning, something about the stuff made me uneasy. Anyway, their very desire to be rid of me emboldened my sense of discovery. I recognized that feeling as somehow innate. Perhaps in the shadowy unknown that was my previous existence, I'd been in the business of finding things out. I looked around the room, and saw a stool pushed up against a wall.

"I think I'll just sit."

I did it before they could object. There was a sort of collective shrug, and they slowly returned to work. I settled into my chair, trying to make myself a feature of the wall.

I watched their process, fascinated. The white coats milled about the counters on which sat the machines. These ungainly things emitted, at intervals, loud grinding sounds followed by a softer humming. Those noises were occasionally punctuated by a suction sound in the background. The white coats watched display screens mounted beside the machines and made careful notes on smaller screens they held in their hands. I knew that I knew some of these items, and even summoned words for a few, though on that first day I was still inventing my own words and assigning them as labels to the things I encountered. Later on, when I had more words—or perhaps when some memories returned; who can say—I would retroactively attach these found words to my first memories. When you do that, you don't really know if you're tampering with the memory itself. Consequently, all of this still has a dream-like quality in recollection. But I digress.

The basic process was as follows: the white coats placed chunks of matter into the machines, which ground them down, analyzed them, and then generated the results on the screens. The matter-chunks came from somewhere farther out—the true outside, I suspected—and that was the cause of the suction noise. Someone was collecting these bits and bringing them in. I guessed this was happening a room or two away, because the suction noise was somewhat muted. From where I sat, I couldn't read what came up on the screens, though I did know *how* to read, a fact I'd confirm later that day. I longed to walk over and watch more closely, but already felt I was pushing my luck. This glimpse would have to suffice, but I promised myself I'd return to investigate further.

After a while I really did feel hungry. I had a long walk ahead of me, so I stood to leave. In my white attire against the white wall, I must have been practically invisible, and I think they forgot I was there, because one of the workers near me startled, and dropped his chunk of rock on the floor. A piece broke off and went sliding over the shiny tile. I made a quick exit.

A trip is always faster the second time, and I made swift progress until the breaks toward the interior became more frequent. Now famished, I moved with single mind, no longer even stopping to notice the others I encountered. Perhaps that was why I didn't see the woman following me until she reached out and took my arm.

I froze, not from fear. It was just that the physical contact was so unexpected. But anything that makes you feel less a ghost is welcome. I turned toward her.

"Hey," she said, in a sort of whisper.

"Hey."

"What are we doing here? Did they tell you?"

I shrugged. "I don't remember. You?"

She shook her head, very sadly, but I could see her relief at finding me in the same predicament.

"A man told me there was food this way," I said.

She nodded. "He told me the same."

We were both whispering. It's strange to consider that we'd independently detected an unspoken rule against asking too many questions. Maybe it was the way the others passed us by without speaking. Maybe it was something in the atmosphere of the place. We both sensed, even at that early stage, that we were being tested and observed.

"I'm going this way," I said, nodding toward the interior.

I started moving again, fast enough I think to communicate that I didn't want us to move as an obvious pair. I heard her scrambling to keep up, but I didn't look back. I wasn't exactly trying to lose her, but I also didn't want to be saddled with her. We were both strangers inside a game we didn't understand, and I wanted no allies till I knew what alliances entailed.

The last corridor gave way to a huge space. The ceiling was suddenly hundreds of feet above, and appeared to form part of a vast dome, though the area it overlooked was broken up, partitioned by a semi-open wall that reached from the floor almost to the domed ceiling. This made it impossible to see very far into the interior, especially in the low light, but the partition wall's gray bricks were laid out gapped so that thousands of tiny windows peered into the space beyond. On the floor were many green plants in stands, and couches, and beds. Many of these latter were already occupied. The mess was supposed to be nearby, so I began making a circuit around the partition wall, creeping so as not to wake anyone. Another woman in cobalt blue came around the curve and noticed me. She saw my perplexity, or the hunger on my face, and pointed in the direction from which she'd come.

"Food is there," she whispered. "Go through any of the openings on the right."

I nodded my thanks, and hurried on. Soon after, I found a break in the wall, and passed through. The next section was almost entirely occupied with tables and booths, but there were also a number of large black kiosks. The kiosks had screens that displayed various meal options. I walked up to one and found to my chagrin that most of the options grayed out as soon as I approached. Evidently there were different meals for different people. Of the two available to me, one was something liquid and chunky in a bowl, the other noodles on a plate. I selected the noodles. In a few seconds a black container that looked nothing like the nice plate from the picture slid out to an open drawer at my waist. I picked it up, and, unable to locate cutlery, walked to a table.

I took the lid off and drank in the steam for a moment before I began shoveling the hot stuff into my mouth. It was savory and good, and I quickly got over my annoyance at having only the two options. When I was about halfway through, the girl from the hallway entered the mess. I didn't look her way, but I heard her walk over to the kiosk, and go through the same halting process. A few moments later she approached and pulled out the chair across from mine. She'd selected the chunky stuff but had also managed to find the cutlery that went with it. We ate in silence for a while, she with a spoon, me trying to slurp without sound. I didn't make eye contact.

"Am I not supposed to talk to you?" she finally asked.

"Don't know," I said, with a shrug.

"Is that your personal feeling, or something the man in the suit told you?"

I shrugged again. "He didn't say anything about it. I just…"

She nodded. "Just feel there's a rule about it," she replied, completing my thought.

I shoveled more noodles into my mouth, now thoroughly annoyed to be eating the greasy stuff with my hands. Embarrassed too. She was watching me while I ate, as if she expected something.

"Something isn't right here," she whispered. "You must feel it."

I didn't even look up.

"I don't remember what happened," she said. "But there was *something*. Some terrible thing that came before. Don't you feel it?"

Again, I said nothing. I knew we were being watched. The man in the gray suit had intimated as much.

"So, you're just going along with it?"

What else can we do? I thought. Anyway, the only danger I felt at present was that of crossing invisible lines.

"I'm not going to cooperate until I get answers," she announced, no longer bothering to whisper. "I've already decided."

I ate more quickly, determined to get away from her. Her method was too obvious.

"Did you notice that there are no old people here? And nobody sick. And where are the children? I think maybe I had children."

That stumped me. I'd forgotten entirely about children. With the word, the concept returned, but I didn't let on that any of this concerned me.

"You don't care," she hissed. "We're in the same predicament, but you'll just go along with it to get by. You're a…"

She struggled over a missing word. In the times between then and now, I've often encountered this phenomenon. We've all forgotten, but we haven't necessarily forgotten the same things in the same way. If we talked more, then we could piece the past together. Hence the unspoken rule. I sensed all this back then, even before I learned the reasons for it.

I looked her in the eyes. "I think the word you want is 'coward.'"

Her eyes flared, and she nodded slowly. I remember feeling thoughtful; not terribly offended.

"The thing is," I said, "I think maybe everyone here is a coward. I'm not sure how I know this, but I think that whatever the unpleasantness was, we were both in on it. After all, we're still here."

The impact of those words surprised me. Her face contorted in a sneer.

"I can't change the past," she hissed, "but I'm going to find out. I keep seeing these faces. Children's faces! I'm going to keep pressing until they let it slip."

I finished the last noodles. Not having anything to wipe my hands with,

I cleaned my fingers on the inside of my shirt. As I stood, she stared at me, and the anger in her face gave way to a sort of desperation. She'd wanted an ally and was shocked that I did not.

I walked away from her then, and planned my next exploration. In the days that followed, I'd encounter any number of fellow travelers, new people all in white, but none were as feisty or as obvious as this woman. The next time I saw her, our personal circumstances would be very much changed.

***

A blue globule hopped wetly across the display, leaving behind small drops of itself, which, being abandoned by its motion, grew tiny feet, chased after their natal body, and finally leaped onto the globule's amorphous back, sinking into it with tiny sighs.

"Glub, glub!" said the globule, and shivered with delight, while a laugh track composed of many high voices broke out to celebrate the reunion.

A pink globule entered from the right. The music, which before had been singsong and cloying, turned slow and deep. The pink blob slithered closer to the blue, leaned in inquisitively, and then away. It began to sway and then to tremble, blobby skin shuddering over it in waves. The blue globule transformed, becoming cylindrical, and two large eyes popped open near its rounded head. It went rigid, then rotated toward the viewer.

"Yubba, yubba!" it said, and the laugh track broke out again.

The colored blobs danced about each other, slinking closer every time, until both masses seemed to lose their composure and leapt at each other with a pent-up violence. Each seemed bent on wrapping, absorbing, and swallowing the other, until they melded into a messy, wheezing, purple blob that shuddered to a stop.

"Yesssssshhiiiiiir!" said a bodiless voice, and the unseen laughers roared and clapped.

I hated this vid but watched it over and over again. The pleasure booths offered many experiences, but most made me uncomfortable, and seemed to inflame that amorphous guilt that called back to the unknown time. This vid only made me feel stupid, and terribly bored when it was over. The odd thing was, once you started a vid, you could never make yourself stop. You were surrounded in a way, immersed in the experience, even though you knew you hated it, and that it gained you nothing. It kept your brain going. And you could always reach into the display, and swim through it with your hands, which effected the globule's behavior in minor ways, though without ever altering the outcome. So I watched it every day. By this time, I'd seen it at least eighty times.

It finished, and a dozen suggested vids came up on the display, their icons already playing soundlessly in microcosm. I swam through them, hoping to find something genuinely new. I wanted a vid that was *about* something, but those with human actors were the sort that left me most empty. There was only one other vid I could stomach, and that was because the environment in which the actors moved showed snatches of real things I still remembered. The background was a swirl of form and motion, but if you reached in at just the right moment, you could pause the scene, and sometimes spy a tree, or a rock, or even an ocean. I especially liked the ocean, because it was the first word I remembered on my own, and so became a symbol for me of triumph. Anyway, if you just kept looking at those real things, you didn't have to watch what took place in the foreground.

I began searching for that vid, spinning through hundreds. But it was gone. I guess they'd removed it. Maybe they were on to me. I felt a tap on my shoulder, and practically fell out of the chair from surprise. I reached up quickly to remove the head shell.

When you come out of a pleasure session, you always feel dazed and a little ill. The Gray Man stood beside me and waited politely for me to recover my bearings. I looked up at him and waited for the lingering vidpressions to sizzle away.

"Let's chat?" he said, as if it were a request.

I nodded. He led away from the rotunda, back toward the corridors. I followed docilely, until we stopped at one of the corridor enclaves. By now I understood things much better. Those terminals that I had first seen on my waking day were mostly pleasure booths, but more compact versions than were found in the interior. Other terminals were gel dispensers. There was the same basic arrangement of couches, chairs, and tables with the coral disks. These were often consumed by passing workers who didn't have time to go all the way to the mess. I'd learned that the brown-garbed women were the oasis' cleaners and maintainers, and that one of their duties was replacing the coral disks when they were eaten.

I sat. The man snatched a coral from one of the adjacent tables, and dunked it in a glass of water before joining me.

"You must be hungry," he said.

I shook my head no.

"Sleepy then."

"No, not particularly," I said.

He frowned. I'd maybe given away that I had no interest in the sort of vids that left you sleepy—unless they had trees in the background.

"Do you know why I came to see you?" he said.

His squared shoulders bowed toward me, as if to pin me in place. Though I was taller, it didn't feel that way.

"You've been here fifty days. It's time for your evaluation," he said.

"Oh."

I was always aware that there was some test. I didn't fall over myself trying to pass it, whatever it was, but I at least knew how to stay on the right side of invisible lines.

"I'd say your results are … mixed," he continued. "Non-traditional. It's not clear what sort of work is the best fit for you here."

I stayed mum. No one, of course, had ever told us newcomers about any of the work being done at the oasis. The whole place was a sort of self-perpetuating cocoon. All tasks seemed oriented toward its own maintenance, but what was the end of it all? In my short time, I'd seen dozens of other arrivals. Of these, there were four I was rather certain had moved on to real work, becoming the navy blue workers known as Jimmies, or joining the ranks of the brown-garbed Shias. Others had wandered around for a few days, had asked a lot of questions, and had disappeared.

"Do you have a preference?" he said.

I found that dangerous. Telling him what I wanted was tantamount to telling him who I was, all of the me that I held back. I knew there were wrong answers.

"I think I want to work in the labs," I said.

He scratched his chin thoughtfully.

"Why? What would you do there?"

I shrugged. "Learn something. Investigate."

"Investigate what? You already have free run of the place. Why not just look over the Labbies' shoulders while they work?"

I took a deep breath before answering. It felt like the start of a countdown.

"Yes, but … I've never seen where they bring it in from."

He chuckled. "You want to go outside. What do you think you'd find out there?"

I weighed my response for a long time, then settled on the simple truth.

"Something different," I said. "Something fascinating, that you can't find in here."

That answer seemed not to please him, so I quickly added, "I believe there's some danger out there that you're protecting us from. I want to help in those efforts."

I want to see the real world, I thought. *To know where the hell I came from!*

He studied me, concealing his thoughts.

"Going through the airlocks is a special duty," he said. "And that decision's over my head, anyway."

I nodded and tried to hide my disappointment. But I held onto "airlock", a mystery for later.

"It's dangerous," he continued, "like you suspected. But there are … other dangers. All around us. There are ways that a person like you—curious yet discrete—could be very helpful. Maybe even make the case that you're worthy of special duties. Going outside, for example."

With his eyes, he seemed to weigh me to the ounce. I looked down at my white uniform, and fiddled with it. I noticed some slight browning around the hem of my sleeves, and decided to go to the Shias, and get it cleaned. I'd been avoiding that, since it meant I'd have to walk around in the gel for half a day. Plenty of people did it. Some never even bothered with clothes. Maybe I needed to get over my squeamishness. Presently, the lingering silence made me aware that he was waiting on some kind of an answer.

"What kinds of duties?" I said.

"Investigative duties," he replied. "Just right for a guy like you."

"What would I be investigating?"

He sighed, and leaned back in his chair, lacing his fingers together.

"Like I said, there are dangers outside, but some are right here. Not everyone who comes here appreciates the life he's been given. Despite our efforts, there's always a few malcontents. Holdouts, from the time before. Some may even be in uniform."

"The time before? But nobody remembers—"

"Not perfectly," he said. "But snatches here and there. And when discontented people get together and talk, and whisper, well … you see they sometimes piece together a past that never was. Always an idealized past. It's one of the foibles of human nature. A vestige of our imperfection. Some of my colleagues call it 'Edening.'"

I shook my head, not catching the reference.

"So … what do you want me to do?"

He smiled. "Not much. Just be aware. Walk around, like you do. People are used to it. I've been watching you. Do you know you've explored more of this oasis than any three people combined? And you haven't been here that long. So when you walk by, nobody thinks anything of it. They talk. They become careless."

"You want me to spy on people," I said.

"That's a very negative way of putting it. I want you to help protect your fellow lodgers, and I'm telling you that it's a path for your advancement. Toward what you *really* want."

I swallowed. "And what's that?"

He laughed openly then. "Come now. You're not as opaque as you try to be. You may be discrete, but I'm an expert on human behaviors. Especially the vestigial kinds. The kinds that, improperly managed, led to the old *unpleasantness.*"

His choice of words made me uncomfortable, and I scoured my memory for foolish conversations from before I'd gotten my bearings. I felt I was under the knife, and yet the idea of spying made me queasy. I think, in my past, that I must have had a special loathing for people who did that.

"What will happen if I say no,"

He shrugged. "Nothing at all. You'll go on doing what you always do."

Forever and ever, I thought. *With no change in circumstances.* Still, I didn't think I could bring myself to do this thing. I was on the point of refusing, when he made an offer that he must have known I couldn't pass up.

"And, as a reward for this help, I'll give you something you've wanted almost as badly as you've wanted to go outside. Your name."

Discrete as I can be, I couldn't pretend to be unaffected. I thought I had some principles, but they dissolved on the spot.

"Fine," I said. "I'll do it. What's my name?"

"You're sure now? You're committing to this?"

"I want to know my name."

"If you make this commitment," he said, "you'll be held to it. A choice like this may have implications you cannot now envision."

"Tell me my name!"

It's a good thing that we were alone because I think I was shouting at him.

***

Despite my new status as an unofficial tattler, many weeks passed before I saw anything worth reporting. During that time, I had no special idea how to go about gathering the sort of intel the Gray Man wanted. So I did what I always did. I wandered.

There was an order to the oasis that hadn't been obvious at the start. All of the interesting stuff was at the perimeter, or at least the most interesting stuff that I was allowed to access. From walking the narrower corridors that ran the outer limits of the place, I eventually discovered three broad, and partially overlapping regions. By chance, I'd found the Labbies' section on the first day, but the brown-garbed Shias and the Jimmies in their navy coveralls had their own domains.

Entering any of these regions garnered me a lot of attention. I was still dressed as a newcomer, and most newcomers had the vaguely frightened look of strangers in a strange land. Evidently, it wasn't normal having one like me poking about in more technical areas, so I made it a point to become such a common phenomenon that eventually my appearance anywhere wouldn't be very notable. The strategy seemed to work. Probably they thought something was wrong with me. In any event, I became, over time, either functionally invisible, or a harmless novelty. Just a ghost of daily routine.

The Shias were the first to tolerate me. They did all the cleaning and washing, stripped the beds, and restocked the raw materials in the food kiosks. Most were female, though several of their minders were male, the softest, least threatening males imaginable. I suspect something's been done to them to make them so.

In general, Shias kept to their own kind, but everybody went to them to have his uniform cleaned, or a button replaced. My presence in their homely harem was initially suspect, but so persistent was I in my daily wanderings that these matronly creatures eventually put me to work. They made me carry bundles of linens or crates of the coral if I lingered about too long. Punishing my curiosity with work seemed to tickle their impish sense of humor. The coral, I noticed, was delivered to them through a locked door close to the borders of the oasis. I stood outside it once, and tried to learn if the substance was manufactured in there, or only delivered from some port or dock outside the compound. But I heard no suction sound, as in the labs. The door was too substantial to admit any sound.

If I was a curiosity to the cheerful Shias, I was a non-entity to the Jimmies. Aloof and focused, they hardly saw you if you didn't happen to be moving. These men—virtually all were men—maintained the systems that kept the oasis going. They were constantly busy, and liked it. I observed that any one Jimmy might, in the course of his day, work on half a dozen small projects. They approached recreation with the same practicality. Their sessions at the pleasure booths were always brief, and many preferred to amuse themselves by building small robots and making them fight in the halls while they kept working, only occasionally looking over to see whose bots were winning. Like the Shias, they seemed to have no names; only numbers.

I knew my name. At least I thought I did. Back then, it had not occurred to me that the name the Gray Man gave me might not really be my own. It seems familiar now, almost like an old memory, but it's difficult to tell a thing remembered from the osmosis of mere acquaintance. Learning feels like remembering, and all memories may be colored by present experience. I do not know what Judas means, if it means anything. But back then I liked it. Not so much now, after what I've learned. Yet who knows. My present knowledge could also be a lie. Everything here, from the food to the air we breathe, is a sort of fabrication.

Having a name made me superior. It was a leg-up on all these official people, with their numbers. I'll give the Gray Man this: he knew his business. He knew that giving me a name would make it easier for me to despise the numbered masses who thought I was a nobody. It helped me look upon them as objects, and potential problems. So it was that by the time I found my first problematic worker, I felt no qualms about ending his career.

As I mentioned, the Jimmies were always busy, driving themselves hard as if they themselves were robots. As men do, they talked while they worked, cracking small jokes about the Shias and the Labbies, or complaining about small irritations on the job. The only deep emotions they ever displayed were for the elusive Bellas in their cobalt uniforms, of whom they spoke with a kind of reverent longing. But I began to notice something that broke that pattern.

When a certain man was about, the conversation turned to history. He had a strange way of raising a subject so that at first he seemed to be talking about nothing at all, but gradually, what he said prompted others to join in with whatever they knew. Before long the conversation would turn to questions about the past, while the instigator slipped into silence, a mere bystander.

"There," he'd mutter, closing a service hatch, and dusting off his hands. "More honey for the hive."

"Hive?" someone would say, after a long pause. "What's that?"

Then another man would look up, and with a kind of dazed expression, whisper, "Wait. Wait. I remember that."

The conversation would evolve from there, until someone recalled small creatures that flew or crawled, and another man confirmed the fuzzy memory that felt like a dream. Someone else would ask why there were none of these small creatures in the oasis, and wasn't it odd that they'd all dreamed of the same thing, if the thing didn't exist. The Jimmy's simple comments left in their wake a quiet, lingering discontent, but by then the initial speaker had always faded into the background.

I watched this happen three or four times before I recognized it as odd. And I resented the man, not only because he seemed to remember what we could not, but because he invariably scowled when he saw me, as if he remembered me too. But I knew my name.

I noted his number, J-821, and kept a watch on him when I could do so without being obvious. One day on my rounds, I happened to see him by himself before a terminal. From a black box clipped to his belt he ran a wire into the terminal; not into the port, but into the innards of the thing. He was typing furiously, occasionally glancing to the left and right as if he feared observation. Text came up on the display, and he read through it at a rapid pace. I couldn't get close enough to see, but I noted the terminal number.

Later, when his shift was over, I contacted the Gray Man through a device he'd given me. He came quickly, and I noted to myself that his quarters must be somewhere on site. Perhaps in the interior? I filed the observation away, for later.

"Good work," he said. "Give me the terminal number, and I'll take it from here."

I was on the point of telling him, when it occurred to me that I also wanted to know what had appeared on that terminal's display.

"It's … uh. You know, I can't remember."

He gave me a shrewd look. "Can't remember?"

"Sorry, the number just went out of my head. I'm sure I can find it."

He turned away, and I think I caught a sly smile.

"Some things never change," he said, looking back at me.

"Sir?"

"I said nature is deeper than nurture, Judas. Not that I'd say it to Om. What you are, and who you were. One in the same, I guess."

All at once, I felt heat coursing through my skin. He knew about my past! He knew, and he wouldn't tell me! Well, I could play the same game.

"I guess I'll just have to go with you, sir."

I don't think I tried to hide my scheme. It was a risk, but the hatred I felt at being deprived of my past had made me reckless.

"Very well," he said with the same secret smile. "Well done. You can come along."

We walked in silence. Inside the Jimmies' sector, I made some pretext of fumbling around for the right terminal, but I knew where I was going. When we found it, the suited man tapped in his own code, took full control of the machine, and called up its most recent activity. He glanced at me over his shoulder a few times, but I think he must have accepted that I was now a player in this higher game, for he let me stay. Knowledge was the currency with which he'd bought me. Now he'd have to pay me in it. Meanwhile, I was suddenly worried that my first bit of reconnaissance would turn out fruitless. Then I'd be left without leverage. But I didn't have long to worry. A grin spread across the man's wide face, and he waved me forward.

The display showed a layout of the whole oasis, including regions I'd never seen, levels below and above the circular world in which I lived. And if I was reading the graph correctly, this oasis was one of hundreds on a single planet, a planet which the display labeled as S-5. The Jimmy had been gathering intel on where we all were, and perhaps on how to get out. But all I could think about was the word "out." There was an outside. Some people, my handler for example, must have had the privilege to come and go. Getting the same privilege became my new goal.

He shut the display down, and turned to me.

"You've done well. As a reward, I'm going to give you access to the Shrine."

"The Shrine?" I repeated, in whisper.

I knew of the place, which was at the center of the oasis. I'd heard of the Commingling that took place there. The Gray Man smiled.

"Yes. Where the Bellas serve Om."

I nodded my thanks, though in truth, I had no idea what entity he was referencing.

"And I'll pass this on to Om."

He said it as if it were a proper name. I tried to look pleased. The truth was that the name of Om frightened me. It still does.

***

I didn't want to go. A thousand Jimmies would gladly have traded places with me, but this was a line which, once crossed, I knew I could never step back over. And yet I could hardly refuse the Gray Man's gift. That would only make it obvious that I was still of two minds; playing double in hopes of escape.

I delayed only a day, doing my best to look busy with my wandering and eavesdropping. Then I started to think about what the Gray Man would say if I ran into him, and still hadn't gone in. So I went.

The glass rectangle with which I contacted the Gray Man also functioned as a key. I'd seen the Bellas wave their glass before the Shrine's black double doors, just as they did when they passed into the heavily secured room in the Shias' sector from which the coral was delivered. The Shrine was in the very center of the oasis, in the middle of the great rotunda that was partitioned by the gapped walls.

As I passed through one layer after another, moving through the recreation lounges and the mess, I felt the eyes on me. Precisely because I was supposed to be a non-entity, I could hardly walk up to the Shrine doors and wave my key while others looked on. Anyone who could do that was not some wandering simpleton to be ignored and jested around. I waited several hours at a pleasure booth within sight of the doors. I wasn't watching a vid. I had the head shell pushed up so I could see I had a clear path.

At last, the place emptied out. I slammed the head shell back down on its holder, darted toward the double doors, and waved my glass before the reader. The doors seemed to take a lifetime to slide apart. At least I had a moment to really notice them. Though pitch black, they weren't as featureless as they'd seemed from a distance. They were decorated with a fractal embossing that suggested something both sinuous and rigidly mechanical. With one last glance over my shoulder, I slipped inside.

At the end of a short, low-lit corridor, a Bella stood watch before a second door.

"Hello?" she said.

She seemed alarmed by my attire.

"I … I have permission," I said, holding up my glass.

"Obviously."

Then, with more humor, "Are you here for the Commingling? It starts in ten. If you hurry, we can get you vested before it begins."

"Yes, please."

My voice sounded eager in my own ears. I looked at my feet and tried to play casual. She wasn't taken in. Concerned, more likely.

"Well … follow me."

I trailed her through the second door, then down a narrow corridor that swung right. We'd gone a short way when she directed me to an open room. There were hooks for uniforms, most of which were in use. Two gel terminals were mounted on the wall perpendicular to these.

"You'll need to strip," she said. "The gel as well."

I hesitated. When I didn't immediately undress, my guide surprised me by turning to give me privacy.

"It's part of the ritual," she explained. "We aim to become less. To become nothing at all, so that the All That Is Nothing may take its hold in us."

"Of course," I said, removing my clothes, and stepping into the gel terminal.

The machine stripped the gel away, erasing in a moment all the warmth and security that kept me from despair. I was naked and alone.

"Now take a robe from the far wall," she said.

I vested myself in one of the hooded black things and hung my white uniform on an empty hook. I noticed with irritation that mine wasn't the only white suit. I thought I was privileged among the commoners, but there were apparently others. Even a few Shias were here. But then I looked more closely at the white uniforms, and sighed with relief to see that they all belonged to Labbies. I was still exceptional, after all.

"Are you dressed?" she said, with some impatience.

"Yes."

I faced her. She looked me over. My eyes were drawn to a slight discoloration on her cheek, an imperfection that only added to her stern beauty.

"What's your designation?"

"I have a name."

I blurted this fact before considering if it was wise. The Bellas are so beautiful. I suppose I wanted to impress her.

"Really?" she said. "May I have it?"

Having already gaffed, I saw little point in back-stepping.

"Judas," I said.

I'm sure the pride showed on my face. I didn't much care. *I* had a name. She pursed her lips, working something out.

"Interesting name," she said. "But unless you're asked for it, it's prudent around here to give only your designation."

I nodded, red-faced I'm sure. By "around here" I knew she meant "the oasis" and not only the Shrine, and I was mortified to have highlighted my inexperience.

"C-317," I said.

C for common.

She nodded. "I need it in case you cause a disruption," she said, laconically. "Follow me."

We continued along the same corridor until the wall on the left fell away, revealing a high-domed room. It was taller than it was wide, vaguely resembling the egg images from food kiosks. The walls were dark, and fractal-marked like the double-doors. The floor was already mobbed. I didn't wish to walk into that human flood, the last man there, but she escorted me and placed me in the back of the crowd. She leaned in to whisper in my ear.

"Since it's your first time, just observe. Do what others do. Don't make a scene, or I'll get your access revoked."

I nodded obediently, but she was already hurrying off. I stood there, glancing furtively at the others. Since we were all hooded, I couldn't see their faces, nor they mine. Whatever was about to happen, there was some comfort in this fact.

The lights were further dimmed. A sound like rushing air started at the edge of my hearing, then grew until it was a thing I recognized, but couldn't at that time name. A storm, like the world outside. Yet, as it grew, it became a sort of music; irregular, atonal, but not without structure. I felt it in my skin and bones being forced through me as electricity, but cold; somehow jagged. Bodies began to sway. Mine too. I knew I could have resisted this pressure, and also that I had better not. Something was pushing and pulling, and I didn't like to think what would happen if I tried to pull away. I'd cause a disruption, maybe.

Someone far away from me moaned. From much closer I heard low growls, and panting. More voices joined in until the speakers outnumbered the silent. I say "speakers" because there were words. I heard them not in the utterance, but only in shadow, as if meanings were but echoes of forced sound.

"Power!" said a writhing shadow.

"Loss! Loss! Loss!"

"Tennnddd … tennnnd … rennnddd!"

It went on and on like that, the voices becoming notes in an orchestra of eros and pathos in which thought was a mere byproduct. I longed to join in but had nothing to say. Nothing to offer the Great Nothing. I thought too much.

But this thing did not need me. None of us was at the center of it, for it had no center. I had just put my finger on this paradox, tasted its shape, when a woman in a red robe passed through our midst. From her arm hung a basket filled with small white wafers. She scaled a high platform that overlooked us, not climbing, but stepping lightly on the outstretched palms of others until she towered over us.

Once upon the dais, she turned toward us. Even in her formless red robe, there was no doubt she was a Bella. She set her basket on the dais, and from it drew one of the wafers. It was the coral, of course. A large cake of it. I should not have been surprised.

"Come!" she cried.

The crowd echoed her and pressed forward.

"Be emptied."

Furious repetition. I was driven forward, and not only by those around me.

"Be filled!"

We were her black mirror, a single, cavernous mouth closing over a red morsel. She raised the coral cake, broke it, and ate it before us. Ignoring the hands that pawed at her feet, tore at her robes, she consumed it chunk by chunk. It foamed inside her mouth, spilling over her lips so that she seemed inhuman; a red, beautiful, predatory thing. The cries from below became sobs. Then she took pity on us, and, licking her lips, knelt down beside the basket.

She began to distribute the cakes. Those closest to her trembled, yet somehow restrained their appetites. Instead, they passed the wafers back, groaning at the absence that was growing in them, and in all of us. So it was that a wafer of coral came to me before many of the others.

I looked down at it, suddenly frightened. Those closest watched with frustration, eager for me to have done with it, to stop tormenting them with the sight of it. But I could not.

As I looked at the coral wafer, a cold dread bit me somewhere deep. Somehow this was all familiar, or else it was a mockery of things I had once known. But not to eat it would be to draw attention. Still, I meant to take it back with me. To see if what I guessed was the truth. In this dilemma, I did the one thing I thought would serve my ends, while saving face. I broke off a small piece, and feigned eating it, palming it instead.

"That I may be empty," I said, slurring the words together.

I broke the remaining wafer and distributed it to those around me.

They were incredulous, but grateful. If I had made a scene, it must have been of the right sort. I stood there with the thing in my fist, swaying as if in ecstasy at a mere bite. I had crossed a line indeed. With my eyes pressed closed, I pondered the wisdom of what I was planning.

***

I didn't go to the labs that night, or even the next day. I'd only gone once in the last week, and thought it might draw too much notice to suddenly appear there after the Commingling. I needed to be a nobody for them, as I was for the Shias and Jimmies, and I certainly didn't want the Gray Man to know what I was planning. So I waited three days, restraining my curiosity, as those at the Commingling had restrained their appetites. But on the third day, I could wait no longer.

I milled about the lab sector, watching the techs work without interfering. I had the bit of coral in my breast pocket. It was so small that I feared I'd lose it, and so I kept tapping my chest to check on it. True, if I had lost that morsel, I might have grabbed another coral from the many enclave tables, but I knew those spaces were monitored. Everything here is under close watch.

I understood by now what the machines on the counters did, but not why they did it. There was something in the rocks outside that interested the techs, but that was a mystery for another day. When the Labbies placed the chunks of matter inside the machine and pressed a series of buttons—

which sequence I'd carefully memorized—the machine broke the stuff down, crushing and spinning it into some more manageable form. When this was done, the display revealed its components. I assumed they were looking for some substance in the rocks, but I had other plans.

I milled about until the midday hour when many techs took their meal. I was not alone, but then the place was never truly empty. These Labbies worked late, and slept little, particularly those who'd not graduated into the position, but had been bred to their caste. They were analysts by design, and so were less likely to even acknowledge a thing that broke their routine. I waited until I was one of only five people in that lab, and for a moment when the rest were occupied.

The moment came. All four techs stood before their machines. Under the cover of the grinding sound, I slipped across the space to an open counter. I retrieved the coral morsel from my chest pocket, pulled out the metal pan, and placed it inside. I was shaking. I almost forgot the sequence, but I took myself firmly in hand, and keyed in the commands.

The sounds of all this were covered by the loud grinding of rocks. Meanwhile, the coral was soft, and gave no trouble to the grinders. Once it was in, and the thing was working, I stepped away. I had only to wait until the display came up, and so I went back to my fool's errand of pacing the place, looking back from time to time until the process was done.

The machine whirred to a stop. I hurried back over, too eager now to care if I was noticed. The readings came up on the display, and froze me in place. I can't say I was surprised. Disturbed to my core, certainly, yet I think I knew. I guess I've always known.

***

Weeks passed in a fog. With little enthusiasm, I performed my duties, guessing only too well where they tended. It wasn't hard to be a ghost in the halls, for I felt dead inside. Even so, or perhaps because of this, I had great success. That Jimmy I'd exposed was far from the exception. There were others who knew too much, remembered what they ought not, and did what they could to stir others to remember the unpleasant time before. S-5 must have been a planet in transition, for there were more naturalized workers than bred workers, and it was always the naturalized who caused trouble. Who remembered. This fact began to grate on me. Why could they remember enough to resist? Why couldn't I?

I wanted out. I will not say I had much of a conscience, or if I did, it was paired with a weak will. I would never touch the coral; that was my silent protest. But I did what I was asked to do.

Still, I wanted out. It got to where even the gel gave little comfort, and without it I'd surely have ended my life. Each ruined career added to a creeping guilt that began to eat me from the inside. It was in this state of desperation that I hatched my desperate plot. I would use my skills on another target. I would track the Gray Man, and perhaps find the hidden paths that led out of this place.

I needed a disguise, and so, one very ordinary day, when the chance was there, I lifted an extra Jimmy uniform from the Shia's sector. The Shias were frugal ladies, and generally insisted on cleaning and repairing the suit you had before giving out another, but I found the closet where they kept replacements and stole one that was about my size. From there it was a matter of lying low, and waiting for a lucky chance.

It came one day when, after my briefing with the Gray Man, he left me alone at the table. He ought to have broken up our routine; perhaps met me in different places. I guess he thought he could trust me. Some weeks before, I'd stashed the navy uniform under a couch in that enclave. Now the chance was upon me. When he was just out of sight, I threw on the Jimmy suit and followed at a distance.

As I walked, I tempered my ambitions. For now, I only meant to see where he went, and how he got to the upper or lower levels where he must have stayed. If I could safely accomplish that, there would perhaps be a future opportunity to escape the oasis. I expected him to head toward the oasis' center, and he did. He passed through the mess and recreation areas, until only one destination was possible. I waited until the Shrine doors closed, and he'd had time to greet the hostess, and go through the second set of doors. Then, fearing I'd lose him from waiting too long, I waved my glass, and entered the Shrine. The same Bella was on duty. It struck me that she was always on door duty, while other Bellas shifted between tasks. This fact seemed significant, but I was in no state to puzzle it out.

"Hello Judas," she said, eyeing my blue uniform with curiosity. "It's three hours to the next Commingling."

"I understand," I said. "I … simply want to enter the Shrine. To meditate."

She nodded, as if that were normal, and opened the second set of doors.

"I know the way," I said, in case she meant to follow.

Alone in the corridor, I began to lose my nerve. I could head toward the Shrine proper, or turn left, which was the way I suspected he'd gone. I'd never gone that way, and I didn't know if I'd be totally exposed. But I didn't want to lose him by delay. I forced myself to count to ten, then started down the unexplored hallway.

There were no side doors, and only a few dim lights. The path led straight until I could see where it stopped. This appeared to be a dead end. A blank wall stared at me. Relieved as I was not to have run into him, I was also confused. Had the Gray Man turned right instead? Stepping a little closer, I examined the dead end. I ran my fingers along the crease, and felt what I could not see in the dim light. This was a door. There didn't appear to be a reader, and anyway I was sure my glass wouldn't open it. Half-disappointed, half-relieved, I was on the point of leaving when the door slid aside.

Lit from the back, my quarry was a dark silhouette standing in the threshold. Though shadows obscured his features, I thought he was grinning.

"Hello Judas."

My teeth clenched together. But frightened as I was, there was also a kind of relief. Whatever happened to me now, even death, it would not be the same thing that happened every day. And I was tired of the stress of playing double.

"You … you were waiting for me."

He chuckled. "You could say I've been waiting for you for a long time. Waiting for the false disciple to show his true colors. But that blue is a nice color on you. For now."

"I only wanted to see—"

He waved me off.

"Please. I know what you wanted. And now you'll maybe get more than you bargained for. Come with me."

He turned and entered the small room behind the false wall. No sooner had I followed him in than it shut behind us. There was the sound of heavy bolts sliding into place. He led me to another door and waved his glass. It slid aside, and he beckoned for me to follow, whereupon the door closed. We were standing in what looked like a small closet, except that there was an inside panel beside the door, and a reader. He waved his glass, and pushed a button on the panel, and we began to descend.

He wasn't smiling anymore. I should have been frightened. Instead, my whole being fluttered with nervous anticipation. Even if they killed me, at least I'd have seen something new. If I learned more about where I was, and how I'd got there, that would be enough. Better than the yawning emptiness I felt; so I told myself. An easy thing to say, when your body's pumped full of adrenaline and fear.

The lift came to a stop, and the door slid aside to reveal a well-lit space. It teemed with people rushing to and fro. Many wore uniforms I recognized, but the Bellas outnumbered every other caste. As he led me through their midst, I drew a lot of attention, but he took me by the arm like a prisoner, and shook his head at them as if to say, "This will be handled." The way their faces turned away made me certain my fate was sealed. There was evidently little danger that I'd seen too much.

We came to a room with a large window facing the hallway, and a table inside. He sat me down and left me alone for a few minutes. From the inside, the window was black. I sat there, staring at my hands, expecting the worst. Finally, he returned, and settled in across from me.

"So," he said. "What do we do with you?"

I shrugged, and studied my fingertips.

"Protocol dictates you be wiped … or processed … but I'm hesitant. You've been very useful so far. I'd just have to find someone else. And I've been expecting this. The qualities that make you good at your work practically guaranteed you'd start sticking your nose where it didn't belong."

I felt a flash of anger. The fact was my curiosity seemed only natural. How can a person go on living without asking where he comes from, and why things are the way they are? I looked up at him, suddenly calm.

"If you're going to kill me, please let me see the outside first."

He tried to suppress a smile. It broke out anyway.

"It goes deep, doesn't it?" he said, half to me and half to himself. "You want to go outside, huh? Now that's an idea. Yes, that might be just the trick."

"What do you mean?"

He looked back at me, as if only just remembering I was still there.

"Come," he said.

He rose and bade me follow him back into the wide passage down which we'd come. Again, we passed through the midst of other workers until he led me far beyond the lift down which we'd come. After what might have been a mile walking in a straight line, we came to a set of heavily reinforced doors. He hesitated, then waved his key.

The doors came apart with a hiss, and a blast of very hot and pungent air hit me in the face.

"Step through quickly," he said.

I did, and the doors slammed shut behind us. He pointed at a rack of red suits on the wall. They were thick and bubbly, with large glass helmets built in.

"We'll have to suit up."

He grabbed one from its hook, and slowly took it apart. I had the sense he'd not done so in a while. He first helped me into a suit, double and triple-checking that each piece was locked in place. Satisfied, he took another down and secured himself within it with the same care. He tapped a button on his chest, and I heard his voice through the transparent helmet.

"Let's go outside."

We walked in near darkness to another thick door. He stood before it, shoulders rising and falling resolutely like one taking a plunge. He waved his glass, and the door began to creak as it rolled aside.

My immediate impression was of violence. Reds and browns coated the sky, and the swirling clouds, and the torn ground. Deep gashes and troughs rent the soil. The wind howled, and sand sprays swam the red air like puffs of dried blood. Someone had murdered this planet. Looking out on the vast space, I was overcome by a sense of panic. I felt I might fall out into it, and be swallowed up, and never stop falling. Then I did fall over, losing my balance and collapsing onto my knees. I began to feel sick and had to fight not to vomit inside my helmet.

"That's agoraphobia," said his voice crackling inside my speaker. "Breathe slow and deep, and try to fix your eyes on one point at a time."

I did as he said, and slowly worked my way back up to standing. I kept my eyes fixed ahead of me, seeing the rolling hills that wandered off for what must have been hundreds of miles. But there were also trees and shrubs. These were few and far between, clutching the planet for dear life, hunched as if they all suffered a common ailment. I looked back at the second level, the place I normally dwelt. A huge bracing arm grew out of its side and came down at an angle into the rocky ground. A few people wearing suits like ours walked down the arms toward the planet's surface.

"Labbies?" I said.

"Correct."

I was afraid that if I spoke too much, the nausea would win. "What are they doing?"

"Testing the ground and the plants. Every day. Waiting for the levels to dissipate."

"What do you mean?" I said.

"I mean—" he hesitated, "—well I brought you out here. I might as well. I mean that you people wouldn't take your medicine. We came here offering tranquility. Unity. But you fought us. You scorched your own world, and now it'll be some time before it's livable. If I let you go out without a suit, you'd succumb to the elements within hours."

My mind reeled. I couldn't remember any of that. And yet I saw living things, trees, bushes, and even grass, gnarled and sparsely distributed, clinging to life like vestiges of the past I couldn't recall. They were all so familiar; so alien.

"I remember trees," I said. "And there are trees. But I don't remember any struggle. Just a … a kind of deep discomfort. Why can I not remember? Why are there some who can?"

He didn't answer me at first. I had the sense that the Gray Man also was affected by the beauty and the horror of this world, the way the wind kicked up soil and swept it mournfully over hills once lush and green. Finally, he turned back toward the safety of the oasis, waving for me to follow.

When the doors closed behind us, we removed the heavy suits, and he led me back to the same room. Seated across from him, I repeated my question.

"Because, Judas," he said, "you didn't want to remember. The others did. Memory modification is still more an art than a science. When we came, bringing unity, there were some who saw the writing on the wall, and cooperated with destiny. There were others who clung to the old ways, to vestiges of your irrational past—chaos, breeding, fictions of transcendence, and all of that—and who fought us to the end. It's not our way to use force, but you forced us. We're saving all we can. When they let us, anyway."

I kept my silence, mulling over what he said. I hated taking his word for it.

"That's why I recruited you. One reason, anyway. You see, we wipe all those we can, but if someone has the will to hold on to who he was, he often does. This is a stubborn planet. Once it was well beaten, that recalcitrance took a new form. Some learned to feign compliance. They submitted to the wipe, but only with the plan of infiltrating the ranks of the infiltrators. One has to admire their tenacity, but their cause was always hopeless. Om knew. And there's no power in the universe greater than Om."

That name again. How it froze me to the marrow. But my desire was stronger than my fear.

"I've done what you asked. Can you give me back my memories?"

"No, and you wouldn't want me to."

I struck the table. "You don't know what I want!"

"I've read your file," he said, unimpressed by my show of temper. "I know who you were before. You did your part in our cause, but you didn't want to live with the memory of it. Trust me. Or trust yourself, rather. The you who decided to forget. Those others clung to the past, but you wanted to let it go. You must have had your reasons."

He had a point. If he was telling the truth, perhaps I'd be a fool to dig too deep.

"Why do I feel this … this guilt?"

He shrugged. "It's just a vestige. Something that was useful millions of years ago. Try not to dwell on it."

"Is Judas my real name? At least tell me that!"

He chuckled in that infuriating way he had. "It's *a* name, anyway. It's what they called you."

"Who?"

He didn't answer.

"Why did you bring me here if you're not going to either kill me or tell me what I want to know?"

He leaned toward me and laced his fingers together on the table.

"We all want things, Judas. Even me. And what do you really want? Is it knowledge? Escape? Pleasure? What is this 'something more' that stirs us all, even when we're fed and clothed?"

He was musing aloud to himself as much as posing the question to me. But what he said made me think of the coral. Of what I'd found.

"What's behind the door?" I whispered. "In the Shia sector."

"I think you know," he said.

"Why do you do it? And why the Commingling? It reminds me…"

"Om's wisdom," he said, cutting me off. "Don't try to understand.

Understanding isn't the point."

"I want to see how you make the coral."

"And then what? What will seeing gain you? I'll just have to wipe you again, or process you, or…"

But he sat back then, thoughtful. He stared at me, and the old sly smile crept across his wide face. With a kind of finality, he reached into his pocket, and retrieved his square of glass.

"Take yours out," he said.

I did so, slowly, sensing some odd tilt in his thoughts. His fingers danced over his glass. Biting his lip, he tapped his square to mine.

"Well. Now that's done. I've given you full privileges. Now we'll find out who you really are. Maybe we'll both get what we're after."

He stood abruptly, shoved the chair hard into the table, then he hurried us out of the room as if to prevent himself from regretting a fateful decision.

***

I entered the Shia sector. The many heads that turned my way reminded me that I still wore the stolen Jimmy uniform. I was no ghost today. A dozen of the brown-garbed ladies hurried over to me.

"Can we assist you?" they asked, in unison.

"No."

I walked forward quickly, pushing through them, making a straight line for the heavy doors. There was a pause. I heard feet scurrying after me.

"Uh … um … what are you doing?"

"Go back to work," I said. "This doesn't concern you."

I had a name, and now I held the keys to every door. It was remarkable how quickly the possession of these new powers acted upon me. Transformed me. Someone ran off, probably to get a supervisor. That made me smile. For once, I wasn't restrained by their rules. Now standing before the door, I pulled out my glass.

"You can't go in there, silly," said one of the ladies, trying, without success, to make her voice light.

I ignored her and waved it over the reader. I heard her sharp intake of breath as the doors opened. The scurrying of approaching feet told me that the supervisor had arrived.

"Stop!" said the man, in falsetto.

He put a restraining hand on my arm. I glowered down at him, my eyes boring into his soft, effeminate face.

"Take your hand off me. Or you'll regret it."

It was too much, I admit. Privileges or not, I would need to restrain this new sense of lordship. The Gray Man wore his office lightly. I should imitate that.

"I'm authorized," I said, more gently. "As you can see."

Pursing his lips, he withdrew his hand.

"This ... isn't standard."

"No," I said. "But it's not your concern."

He shrugged, and looked around at the nervous Shias.

"You can accompany me if you like," I said.

He laughed at that. "No. I cannot."

He slinked back, and turned his face from the open door, as if afraid to break protocol by looking too far into its hidden depths. I stepped through and waved my glass to shut the doors behind me.

I stood inside a very long, high-walled room. The place felt wrong. Nothing like this big, rectangular space existed anywhere else in the oasis. Columns of beds, ovular and transparent, stretched far to the right and left. They were fixed into a kind of belt that ran the length of the place. Inside each shell-like bed was a man or a woman, naked and asleep, their arms crossed over their chests. A similar line of bed-shells ran the opposite side of the room.

I passed through the line, into the center of the room. No sooner had I done so, than the column behind me moved. The belt in which it was fixed dragged it several spaces to the left, then stopped. Simultaneously, the column of beds in front of me did the same, but toward the right. Then I understood that what had appeared to be two separate columns were but two arms of one long belt that made an ellipse throughout the whole long rectangle. The belt conveyed the line in front of me toward a bulbous black machine far to my right. It was very large, and I could see from here that there was a gap inside large enough for a bed-shell to slide within. A thick transparent pipe snaked out of its back, and ran a dozen paces to where it curved, and pointed downward into a large metal cylinder. A dozen techs and Bellas milled about that machine. I started toward them to get a closer look.

They did a better job than the Shias of hiding their alarm at my presence. I walked right up to the machine, and watched the bed-shells pass through. Every few minutes, the belt dragged a new one into the gap. After undergoing some invisible process, each passed through, and its occupant continued to slumber as he or she made the cycle. The workers were gathered in conference, glancing my way. Finally, one Bella broke off, and approached me.

"Who gave you access?"

"The Gray Man," I said.

She seemed skeptical, but what could she do?

"Tell me what I'm seeing," I said.

She glanced at one of the techs, and they both shook their heads.

"You'd know if you were supposed to know," she said, then returned to where she'd been standing.

As each bed entered the gap, the machine whirred loudly. Perhaps this, and not the grinders, was the source of the low hum one always heard inside the corridors. I wanted to go over and duck my head down to get a better look, but I could feel the tension my presence was causing the others. Instead, I started to look more closely at the faces in those shells. I was good with faces and had gone about the place for months now. It was strange, then, that I didn't recognize any face as really distinct. Then the reason for it struck me with the force of certitude: these were the new people. The bred people. This is where they came from.

To test that theory, I walked down the columns, looking into each shell one-by-one. As so often happens, theory broke down in the face of new evidence.

All the populations of the oasis were mixes of bred and naturalized persons. Thus, there were three standard varieties of Shia, but there were also Shias who had, I assumed, been wiped and trained to this new life, former newcomers who'd graduated to the work. I saw several of the latter interspersed with those who were made to be Shias.

The breeding of the castes must have taken place off-site, or perhaps on some other floor. Maybe this room was a kind of final processing facility, the last stage before introduction. And yet there were more naturalized than bred workers inside the oasis proper, while here the bred sort outnumbered them. I wondered at the discrepancy, but I guessed it was a sign of things to come. The old people, the people of S-5, were slowly being replaced with those who had no past. People who gave no trouble.

I had just confirmed this to myself, when one more fact ruined my scheme. Inside some of the shells were men and women who were fully clothed, already vested for their caste. My heart began pounding in my chest. I didn't know why I was so frightened. But, as I increased my pace, and studied more forms and faces sleeping in the shells, I began to understand. These vested ones were the failures. The naturalized workers, who hadn't taken their medicine.

I recognized some of them now. Jimmy 821, my first conquest, looked up blankly at something only he could see. His eyes darted back and forth in his head, and lights and sensors blinked on the side of his shell. Black wires were inserted into his skull just above each ear. They were digging through his mind, trying to be certain they'd cleared out every vestige of his recalcitrant past. Evidently it was a long process, for I'd turned him in many weeks ago.

"We don't waste anything," said a voice beside me. "Everyone is useful to everyone else."

It was that same Bella who'd confronted me. I could sense her agitation. Privileges or not, I wasn't wanted here. I walked away, but she shadowed me.

"Is there something I can help you with?" she said.

"I'm just looking," I said.

"But what are you looking for?"

I ignored her. She huffed, a pretty, petulant sound, and stepped away from me. She pulled out her glass. I guessed she was contacting the Gray Man. Someone answered her call, and I saw her expression pass from concern to acceptance.

"Yes, sir," she said. "Oh, I see. Of course. Yes, sir, I understand."

"My apologies, sir," she said to me, without meeting my eyes.

She hurried back to her work. Finally alone, I continued to walk the length of the belt. I don't know if some part of me had already worked it out subconsciously, but when I saw her everything fell into place.

Inside one of the shells lay the woman from my first day. Like the Jimmy, she was dressed in her issued uniform, the white blouse and pants of a newcomer. Her eyes also stared at nothing, but she wore an anguished expression. I stayed by her shell as it inched closer and closer to the machine. When it finally arrived, I had to pass through the clutch of workers to get close enough to see.

The belt pulled her shell-bed alongside the machine. It came to a stop, and the wires retracted from the sides of her head. Her eyes fluttered, and she looked around. Her mouth moved. I could see she was trying to speak.

Several techs came over and looked down into the shell. They had their glass pads out, pens in hand, observing. Then the Bella with whom I'd been speaking came up, leaned over the shell, and placed her hand on its transparent covering.

"I hope you've had a pleasant sleep," she said.

The woman in the shell looked up at her like someone trying to see from very far away. Her lips quivered and smacked, making little popping noises, as if she'd never used them.

"How do you feel?" asked the Bella.

"I..." began the woman. "I'm afraid."

The Bella sighed. One of the techs shook his head, and marked something on his glass pad.

"We really tried with this one," said the Bella to me, confidentially and with a certain sadness.

"I want to go home!" cried the woman in the shell. "I want to go home! What have you done with my family?"

The Bella recoiled, as if the woman had struck her through the glass. "This *is* your *family*," she said, spitting the last word out. "The species. The world."

"Let me go!" cried the woman. "Please let me go back to my children. I remember them. You can't take them away from me! Let me go!"

"As you wish," said the Bella.

She nodded at the tech holding the data pad. He touched a button on the side of the machine, and I watched as it brought the woman, still crying for help, into the gap beneath it. The transparent cover of her shell retracted, exposing her to the machine's occult innards. There was a pause that might only have been a second, though it seemed much longer, and then five long, spidery arms shot down from the black machine and lifted her up into its dark insides.

She disappeared from view, and the obscene device began to whir and grind, not unlike those smaller devices that sat on the counters in the Labbies' sector. At least I don't think she was conscious for the process—perhaps the arms had injected her with something—for she never cried out again. I stepped away, and tried to understand what was happening. There was noise like water being siphoned and drained, and then a final pop.

Something entered the pipe that snaked out from the machine's back. It was a white material, foamy, but chalky. Perhaps sticky. It passed through the clear pipe, forced onward by pressure until the pipe turned down toward the large metal cylinder. *Clop, clop, clop.* The stuff dropped from the pipe bottom into the cylinder, until every last bit of it was gone.

I was shaking from my head to my feet. The poise and power I'd felt moments before—me, with my own name and my new rights—seemed to leak from my feet into the floor. Seeing my distress, the Bella came over, and placed a hand on my shoulder.

"It's alright," she said. "She was asleep before it happened. And now she can be one with us."

I looked at her, unable to form words. She shrugged.

"It's alright," she said, now frowning; confused. "I can assure you, sir, that nothing at all has been wasted. The machine is very efficient."

"Wasted?" I sputtered, incredulous.

"That's right. We're operating at ninety-nine percent efficiency now. You can expect a smooth transition."

I shook my head. "What are you talking about?"

The frown lines grew deeper, marring her perfectly proportioned face, but then her expression slowly softened, and she exchanged a knowing glance with the Labbies. They started laughing as if we were all sharing a joke. She turned back to me. Her shoulders fell, and her demeanor toward me was now coy.

"Oh, you can stop pretending now, sir. He's already told me."

I nodded, very slowly, considering that it was wiser under the circumstances to act as if I knew what she meant. In retrospect, I should have guessed it from the start.

***

Today is like every other day. The white walls and floors glisten in the artificial light, always clean, always the same, their monotony broken only by the comings and goings of the workers. When they see me, they nod, and pass by quickly, quieting their conversation lest it draw my interest. I am sitting here at my old table, sad, because now I am truly alone. The Gray Man has moved on, as was always his plan, and now I have only these memories to keep me company. He was never my friend. I know that. But he was someone to talk to. I wouldn't call Om "someone."

We met this morning, the Allmind and I, in the enclosure that sits atop this oasis. Its windows look out on this dreadful, dying world, and you can see the red storm clouds go tearing across the sky, dumping tainted rain on the pockmarked hills and the twisting, wounded weeds. Would that I could walk out there, without a suit, and touch the remaining plants with my fingers, and be torn apart by the wind, and be one with it. But I wouldn't confess such longings to Om. No doubt, they are only vestiges of that old desire for transcendence, the unhealthy illusion of escape from the here and now.

Yet speaking of forbidden things, I informed the Allmind this morning that no progress had yet been made in eliminating the genetic imprint of primeval superstitions, and so the ritual of the Commingling must be maintained in this oasis. I did not tell Om anything else. I hide things, even without reason, so that something of me is preserved until the moment comes when I can follow the Gray Man. The void inside me grows daily. I must get off this planet. Go somewhere. Anywhere higher, closer to that great Union with what truly Is—which I never find. But for now, I have my duties.

The Bella from the Shrine, that temple of Unity, enters my corridor. She doesn't see me yet, and she looks cautiously to the right and to the left, suppressing anxiety. Others wouldn't notice this, but I can see it in the way she carries herself; too stiff, a supercilious air, as if she disdained the whole world. It's what she's always done. Until now, this hostility has worked to throw attention off herself, and to set others on their heels. But it's an act. Beneath that shell of condescension, she's terrified that she's been made.

"Hello, there," I say.

I watch her freeze, then very deliberately relax.

"Hello, Supervisor," she says.

She stands there for a moment, uncertain, then strides towards my table.

"Have a seat," I say.

She sits. "You wanted to see me?"

I lean back, letting my gray jacket fall open in a casual way, giving off every impression of friendliness.

"Yes," I say. "You see there's a problem I'm hoping you can help me with."

"Of course," she says, too quickly.

I say nothing, letting her wonder. Giving her time to doubt her situation.

"I believe we have a regressive in the Shrine," I say. "You work there, so I thought you'd have unique insight into the matter."

Her face, porcelain and perfect, manages to go whiter, all except for the small birthmark on her cheek, the one she dampens with makeup because it reveals her naturalization. It's amazing to consider that someone born of flesh could be so perfect.

"I … I don't know. I mean, I don't think…"

"Don't think that could happen?" I say, finishing her sentence.

She nods. Then does it again, more fervently, because I don't say anything. Silence is a wonderful tool; a void which those under suspicion feel compelled to fill, as if the truth they held back might otherwise stand up and start announcing its presence.

"I'm there every day," she begins, "and I watch very carefully. I see everybody who comes and goes."

"Yes," I say.

"I pay close attention to what they say and do," she continues, "even among themselves."

I nod, inviting her to continue, waiting for her to step into my trap.

"I even review the Comminglings," she claims. "I study the vids to see if anyone's working against the process."

I smile. I wonder if my smile looks to her as the Gray Man's once did to me. "A rather perfect arrangement, isn't it?"

"What do you mean?"

"You encounter everyone of influence. You can observe them, catalog their behaviors and their quirks. You have access to data about where they come from, and where they're going."

Now her face is a sheet. We are at the point when the eyes give the mind away, for they flutter left and right, between the release of truth and the calculus of invention.

"I—"

"But you never participate," I continue. "Because of your unique role, you never have to taste what they taste. You can hide in plain sight."

"I—"

"Do you want to know what gave it away, Bella 142? It was your loyalty. You're too good at your job. Too faithful. Everyone around here needs change, even me. Something crawls inside us. We go around and around, and it gets to where nothing can help but a change of scenery. But not you."

The mask fell like scales from her eyes. I saw the relief and respected it. Lies, even in the service of a cause one deems worthy, weigh a person down.

But she takes one last stab at it.

"You can't prove anything."

I laugh. "Prove? Where do you think you are?"

I stand and walk over to the counter to grab a glass of water. I watch her eyes as I return. She knows what's coming.

"Share a meal?" I ask, plucking the coral from the tongs, breaking it, and dropping it into the water. She stares at it for a very long time. Just when I think she'll cave, the Bella clenches her jaw, and throws her heart into her mouth.

"Whatever you want, I won't give it to you. I won't tell you anything. *I'm* no traitor."

"You say it with such contempt. Do you remember me, I mean from before all this?"

I ask it with a lightness in my voice, as if that guilt-haloed gap in my memory didn't matter to me.

"I know what you did."

I shrug. "Everyone does what he has to do."

"And dogs return to their vomit," she says, shaking her head.

Several Shias pass by at that moment, then hurry on, not wanting any part of this.

"Even so, I've done nothing wrong," she says.

"Then take this coral with me."

"Go to hell!"

I shrug, and swish the white matter around in the glass, watching it fizz and dissolve, like all things do.

"Go ahead and wipe me," she says. "Or turn me into that. I'm not afraid to die."

I take a deep breath. "That's because you think it will be quick," I say. "But the more stubborn you are, the more work needs to be done. Sooner or later, we win."

She begins to cry. All that outer strength runs down her cheeks and chin and makes little puddles on the table.

"You're wrong," she mutters through her hands. "Someone will come! Someone will stop this!"

I let her cry. She's probably wanted to for years, and now the dams are breaking. I drink the coral down and place the glass gently on the table. I stand to go.

"When are they coming for me," she says.

"Soon."

I start to head back toward the bubble that looks out on S-5.

"I'll run," she says.

I sigh. "There's nowhere to run."

***

I stand inside the bubble, watching the wind whip red and black particles against it. The storm cuts the planet into ever more chaotic patterns, sapping the last impossible plants of their stubborn lives. I think that the patience of nature will outlast even the patience of Om. I hope it will, anyway.

She said that someone would come. I did not tell her that I hope she's right. Perhaps some avenger will rush in, captain of a deadly armada, flashing like lightning from east to west to bring a swift end to Om. Or maybe, the sky will fall on us. That would be enough. It would be good. But knowing what is good, and having the will to do it are two very different things.

I see myself in partial reflection in the enclosure's transparent walls. My suit looks grim and disheveled, and though my body stands safe behind that wall, the swirling whirlwind rushes through my image, as if I also stood inside that red and hopeless maw. With a sigh, I stand up straighter; make myself presentable again. If I'm ever to escape this place, I must first play my part. I am the Gray Man now.

THE AMOEBA

"Don't put that on yet," said Cass to Marco and Johnny.

The other boys frowned. They'd just hoisted a heavy branch over their heads and had been about to feed it overhand across the fort. Marco's little brother Lino looked up. He'd been dragging a big branch over the thick carpet of pine needles, with two chubby arms, doing his best to justify tagging along.

"You always change the plan," groaned Marco.

"I had a better idea," explained Cass. "Anyway, my yard, my fort."

Marco glared at him, then tossed his end of the log at the ground. They'd been building for nearly two hours, and Cass had altered the blueprint a dozen times.

"I'm gonna camp in here tonight," explained Cass, looking up at the sky.

The summer air had that spongy feeling that Cass had learned signaled sketchy weather on New World. "So it's gotta keep the rain out."

"By yourself?" said Johnny, raising an eyebrow.

Marco crunched his lip skeptically. Cass stared them both down to confirm he meant it. In his periphery, he also caught the uninvited guest leaning against his backyard fence. He went on pretending not to notice her.

"Yup, all night," he said. "And I need one more thing."

He darted inside. Mom was laying the table, and Dad was making a puzzle with Cass's little sister. He tromped downstairs to the basement, taking two steps at a time. In the back corner of a low-lit room adjoining the finished section sat a pallet of items that had been stacked haphazardly after their migration from Earth, and rarely touched since. He found the blue tarp he was looking for, and carefully worked it out from the stack. Cass shook it out at arms' length to avoid any fire-beetles. It was frayed on the ends, but he was pretty sure he could stretch it over the fort, tie it down, and then lay all the heavy branches across it. Maybe stick more clay in the gaps.

Cass rolled it up and climbed the stairs. So that his dad wouldn't see the tarp and tell him no, he held it on his right side passing through the living room. Mom came out of the kitchen as he slid open the porch door.

"Who are you playing with, Cass?" she asked.

He casually tossed the tarp through the gap and signaled the boys to wait.

"Johnny and Marco," said Cass. "Building a fort. Bye!"

He tried slipping through the door.

"And what about *her*?" said his mother, nodding.

Cass would have mimed ignorance, but his honest head looked out on its own toward the chain-link fence. He knew who'd been leaning there the whole time, watching them.

"Mom!" pleaded Cass.

"She's been there at least half an hour. Did you invite her to play?"

Cass looked up at the sky, stricken, a silent appeal to the anonymous powers of justice. "Mom, *please*!"

His mother laid down the steaming casserole dish. "It wouldn't hurt you to include her."

"We don't even know if it *is* a her!"

"Cass! That's cruel! Henry, please say something."

Henry Basil looked up first at his wife, and then, with profound sympathy, at his eleven-year-old son.

"Jen," he said, carefully, "I don't know if the boys feel comfortable. Anyway, won't it be time to call him in soon?"

Mrs. Basil glared back, unmoved, and evidently unmovable. After a few more seconds of agonized internal moralizing, Henry Basil decided that treachery had its uses after all. He turned to Cass.

"Look, why not include her in your game, Cass? Just this once."

Cass stared angrily at his feet. "Fine," he said.

Without waiting, he shot through the door gap, and slammed it behind him. He stomped toward the fort, scooping up the tarp on the way. Cass unfurled it in one sullen snap, and threw it out in the air over the fort, letting the tarp flutter down to cover the edges.

"*Now* you can put the branches across," he said.

The other boys watched him.

"What's wrong?" said Marco.

Cass spit on the ground. "We're being watched," he said.

The boys glanced over at the fence.

"So? Just ignore her," said Johnny.

"It," corrected Marco. "Ignore it, and it goes away."

Cass shook his head. "Mom said I have to ask her to play."

Johnny screwed up his face into an incredulous ball. Marco threw his head back and laughed. "Man, are you serious?"

Cass looked at him miserably. "Let's just get this done first," he muttered.

The fort was a framework of sticks, thin branches, and heavier logs; whatever they could find lying around in the woods. Following Cass's design, they'd first driven four forked branches into the pine-strewn ground, and then laid logs between the forks. This frame they'd lined with tall branches and sticks, driving their bottom ends into the soil, and filling in the gaps with clay from the creek that ran through the Basils' property. The end result looked pretty good, but Cass could see it was going to be top-heavy once they laid the remaining branches for the roof. If he'd had it to do over, he'd have made the branches for the frame and palisade walls thicker, and those for the roof slimmer and lighter.

The three older boys tied the tarp down, then resumed lifting the straight logs over their heads, and laying them one-by-one across. Too small to help, Lino made encouraging exclamations to which nobody paid any attention. As the big kids raised each log, he extended his short arms like a wizard.

After laying half the roof, Cass's arms were beginning to feel like jelly. The boys returned to the pile, preparing to hoist another beam.

"That's not going to work."

Arms above his head, Cass looked over at the speaker. The thing from the fence was now beside them. She was taller than any of them. Her hair was shorter than any boys', and she wore an unflattering jumpsuit like one of the bean brains back on Earth. She was no vegetable, of course, but something else was wrong with her. Even her voice had a quality not-quite-female; not quite anything. What marked her as a girl? It could have been the roundness of her hips, or her chest, which though flat, was flat in the wrong way.

"We don't need any advice," said Cass, after a brief pause.

He redoubled his efforts, trying to hurry the other boys along. Marco and Johnny averted their eyes from the stranger.

"I'm just saying it's not structurally stable," continued the visitor, in monotone. "Those big logs you're putting on top are all twice as thick as your support columns. One push and it'll all come down."

Cass glanced at her, frustrated. "If you want to help, come over here and help."

She paused, studying him like a bug under glass, and then continued, "And it looks like you've sealed the gaps with mud. That will make it even heavier."

She approached the fort, plucked out some of the gray sealant, and rubbed it between thumb and forefinger.

"Is this from your creek?"

Cass ignored her, walking his end of the log around to lay it in the last gap. She was in his path, but did not move, so that he was forced to stretch his whole body and lift the log over her while standing tip-toed.

"You do realize scooping clay from the stream bank speeds up erosion, right?" she continued. "The banks will fall in. Sort of like this clubhouse you've built."

Cass gritted his teeth. For his mother's sake, he was resolved to say nothing. But Marco had heard enough.

"Well, you've helped solve one scientific mystery today, *Amy*," Marco sneered. "You're obviously a girl. Friggin' know-it-all."

The girl's head swiveled suddenly towards Marco, rather like one of the praying mantises from the Capital Vivarium near Port Fair, where students went to view living specimens from Old Earth.

"I told you at school, I don't go by Amy. It's *Ahme*. 'Ah' as in 'Awesome.' 'Me' as in 'me.'"

"Shut up," he said. "You can't just make up a new name."

She stalked up to Marco and craned over him. Only a year older than the boys, she was much taller.

"I can make myself anything I want," she said. "But you can't even make a house of sticks."

With that she turned, surveyed the fort in a calculating way, and then shoved the wall with two hands. It wobbled for a moment, then leaned, before sagging definitively to one side. The boys looked on aghast at hours of hard work, now transformed into an irrecoverable mass of logs and mud. Marco's face twisted in rage. Cass looked from Marco, to Ahme, and back to the ruined fort in disbelief. Marco, the silver-tongued, sputtered for words.

"You … FREAK!" he screamed.

Ahme smiled, savoring his anger.

"Whatever you say, little boy."

Lino laid his chubby outstretched palms upon the fort, as if they held the magic to heal it. He began to cry.

"We're leaving," said Marco.

Johnny, who always did what Marco said, followed, shaking his own head in disbelief. Lino stumbled after them, drying his eyes. Cass looked at Ahme.

"Why'd you have to do that? You ruined all our work."

Ahme shook her head, correcting him. "Actually, I saved your life. If you'd have stayed in there, you might have been crushed."

"No, not unless someone came and *shoved the walls* while I was inside!"

She dismissed him with a gesture.

"Since you like creeks—"

"—I never said I liked creeks!"

"Since you like creeks," she continued, without altering her tone, "you should come to my house, and look at the pond."

Cass couldn't believe his ears. "You just ruined my house, and you want me to come to yours? Anyway, we're about to eat dinner."

Perfectly on cue, his mother's call reached him from the sliding back door.

"Get out of my yard," he said.

He made tracks away from her. His mother met him on the back porch. She held out a paper bag.

"Can I take it out after dinner," he asked, anxious to get inside.

"This isn't trash, Cass."

"What is it?"

She took a breath first. He sensed she was preparing herself for an argument.

"It's dinner," said his mother. "For you and Amy. I want you to go with her. Spend some time with her."

"What? No, I can't—"

"I want you to go," she continued. "And spend some time just being with that girl. I don't think she has any friends at all."

Unable to process the injustice of it, Cass again made his silent appeal to the sky gods. They were not at home today. He looked back at his mother, resigned.

"Why are you making me do this?" he said. "She's such a weirdo, Mom. She literally makes my skin crawl."

His mother took a deep breath. "Cassius, I know. But she needs a friend. Can't you see it? And if anyone on New World can help that girl, it's you."

He shook his head. "No, no. She doesn't even like me."

"That's not true, Cass. You know it isn't."

"What do you mean?" he said. "What are you talking about?"

Mrs. Basil glanced past him and lowered her voice further. "Cass … where do you know Amy from?"

"Ahhhhhhmeeee," he mocked.

"Ahme," she said, with a nod, waiting for him to answer.

"Just from school," he shrugged. "She's a grade ahead of us."

His mother looked at him, surprised. She took a half-step back, and suddenly seemed to doubt herself.

"You mean you don't…"

Cass shrugged; waited for her to continue. Mrs. Basil pressed her eyes shut. After a moment, she nodded, opened her eyes, and forced the warm bag into his arms.

"Go with her," she whispered. "Go to her house, and have a meal with her. Everyone can agree on food."

Reluctantly, Cass folded his arms around the bag. His mother left him standing there, and he turned around, hoping the girl had left. But she was still in his yard. Facing away from him, leaning forward and down like a bending willow, Ahme gazed into the burbling creek.

***

It was a fine house. Not so large as Cass's, but tall, and chrome, and built in the modern style, set on a rectangular grass plot with a fence about it, right in the middle of Port Fair. When they'd scaled the porch steps, the door recognized Ahme, and slid aside. Lights turned on or off as they passed from room to room. Cass's parents didn't believe in automation, but Ahme played her home like an organ; or it played her. They took a small lift to the second floor, and she led him to the dining room.

The wise table telescoped down to make their meal cozy. Cass set down the paper bag, and Ahme brought out plates and cutlery. He wondered where her parents were, and about whether the living house was something like a dog left alone all day, playing and sleeping at turns, or if its activity was just an extension of Ahme's own mind. They didn't have anything "smart" in the Basil home, but he'd heard that twitching was a skill in its own right, and it seemed to come naturally to Ahme.

"Sit," she commanded, when Cass stood there looking at the table.

He sat, and she took a length of bench opposite him. Cass felt as if he were on display.

"What did your mother make us?" she asked, filling the silence.

Without waiting for him to answer, he slid the bag over to her. There were two aluminum casserole dishes, one smaller than the other. The scent was intoxicating. Ahme seemed to recoil from it. With careful fingers, like she was unboxing a scorpion, she pried back the aluminum casing. She pulled off the cover, and a savory steam wafted up. Cass saw cheese, and noodles, and ground, browned sausage meat. Ahme shook her head, disappointed.

"I don't eat meat," she said.

Not only was Cass hungry, he'd been looking forward to the meal as an escape from talking to her. Now he was also irritated. His mother had made her a meal, after all.

"You don't?" he said. "Well … what the hell *do* you eat?"

"Lots of people don't eat meat," she said. "Don't act so surprised."

He shrugged and opened the other casserole dish. It was steamed broccoli, which he could at least tolerate.

"Ooh, that looks good," she said, grabbing it from him.

No "please" or "thank you"; but it occurred to Cass that he could have the main course all to himself. He cut out a square of casserole, navigated it to his plate, and paused in silence before eating.

"What's that?" she said.

"Casserole," said Cass.

"No, what were you doing just now? Blessing your food?"

He shrugged. He had been but was embarrassed to do it out loud. She made what he took to be a condescending little sound, then began shoveling broccoli into her mouth. They ate in silence for a moment, but he was not to be spared her strange conversation.

"I've read that on Earth, aboriginals in the Americas would sometimes bless their food before they killed it," said Ahme.

He shrugged.

"They didn't thank gods," she said. "They thanked the animal for the gift of its life."

"Huh," he said.

"I guess that's a sweet gesture," she continued, mouth full of broccoli. "But it doesn't change the fact that you're killing something."

Cass couldn't resist. "Well, *you're* killing broccoli."

To his surprise she nodded, and looked down at her meal with something like regret. Cass could have even sworn he saw a tear in the corner of her eye. She stared back at him, eyes wide, and glassy. He had the sudden, unnerving sense that he was all alone in a house with a madwoman.

"Cass," she said, her tone become softer, and more feminine, "did you ever think about me?"

With determination, Cass chewed his casserole, and pondered the best strategy for exiting the house immediately. He'd seen two horror movies over at Marco's, and was beginning to think he was in one.

"Can I come down now," said a disembodied voice; not Ahme's.

Cass dropped his fork on the table. Ahme studied him with a curious, sad expression. She sighed.

"Yes, you can come down."

After a moment, the lift door opened, and a woman stepped into the kitchen. She had shoulder-length black hair, and she wore a striped dress. Her nails were long and painted black, which was the same color as her lipstick. Though decidedly more feminine than Ahme, he saw an immediate resemblance. She was either her mother, or an older sister.

"Susan," said Ahme, "this is Cass."

The woman smiled at him.

"Yes, I remember."

Remember? Cass began planning his exit.

"I didn't want to invade your space," said the woman, apologetically.

"No, it's fine. Cass and I were just going upstairs."

"I—" he began, then didn't know how to continue.

Susan and Cass both looked at him, waiting.

"Why are we going upstairs?" he managed. "I should probably be getting home soon. It's getting late."

"You can stay here," offered Susan.

"No!" said Cass.

Ahme looked sad again. "But I … I just wanted to talk, Cass. I don't talk to many people, and it's been forever since you and I spent any time together."

Cass began to feel as if he were spinning in place. So far as he could recall, he'd never exchanged more than a dozen words with Amy-now-Ahme. And yet, as he looked at the girl and Susan, he had the odd sense that he'd seen them both before. He felt afraid and couldn't find a reason. But his curiosity was also piqued.

"Do you play checkers?" said Ahme.

"Huh?"

"Checkers? Do you know how to play it? I was thinking we could play and talk in my room."

He shrugged. Checkers seemed safe enough.

"Guess I could do one game," he said. "But then I need to get home."

He wasn't hungry anymore anyway.

"Great!" she said, sounding, for the very first time, like a girl.

Ahme took his hand, and led him toward the lift. As the doors closed, Cass caught a glimpse of the dark-haired Susan. For a moment, he was certain he knew her.

***

"King me," said Cass.

Ahme was forced to take one of her own pieces off the board.

"You're not very good at this," he said.

"Maybe I'm letting you win."

They were sitting on the floor of her room. Her bed was to his right. There was a small bookshelf to his left. The physical books made an odd contrast with her house, which was sterile, and mechanized, and so unlike his own. Each volume had something to do with the sciences, and he seemed to recall that Ahme was on the tech track at the Junior Academy. They didn't share any classes. Beside the shelf was a small aquarium that didn't seem to have any fish in it, only a green, scummy growth around the sides.

He looked back at her. She was studying the board; for once not looking at him. Despite himself, his eyes kept flitting toward the strange bulge of her chest. Something was wrong about it, but he didn't want to stare.

"You didn't ask me why I don't eat meat," she said, pushing a black piece forward.

"You're a vegetarian," he said, shrugging—and jumped her piece.

She smiled, and double-jumped him back. He hadn't seen that coming.

"If that's what you call it," she said. "But why?"

"I don't care why," he said, pushing a red checker forward to block her.

He was not at all interested in her reasons for anything. He found her repellent. But he also found her oddly familiar, and that bothered him. And he'd never been this close to a girl, in such a small room.

"If you're not curious about me," she said. "Then why do you keep looking at my chest?"

He froze. "I'm not … I didn't—"

"Yes, you did," she said, matter-of-factly. "And it's alright."

His head buzzing, Cass tried to focus on the board. So mortified he couldn't think, he made several foolish moves. Now he was losing.

"You always thought I was pretty," she said.

Embarrassed as he was, the comment was so obviously false that he found his voice at last.

"No! That has nothing to do with it. I just … I just wondered why they're so…"

"I tie them down," she said. "I don't like them."

"Oh," he muttered. "Fine."

She jumped another of his red pieces.

"They just get in the way," she continued. "And men stare at them. Their eyes always shoot over, like they can't control them."

He said nothing, wishing the embarrassing moment would come to an end so he could go home.

"I hate girls," she continued, "because they're soft, and needy. They can't even walk to the bathroom by themselves. I hate boys because they're stupid and gross. They'll do anything to anybody. But I have plan."

Cass too was making a plan—for escape. He pushed another piece forward, throwing the game now, so he could get up and leave. He sensed her staring at him, but could not meet her eyes.

"If you hate men," he finally said, "then why were you stalking me and my friends?"

She smiled cleverly, as if he were only asking a question she'd intended him to ask.

"I like the *principle* of the masculine," she explained. "It's fascinating. You and your friends, building a fort. Trying to command nature, instead of being subject to it. The masculine principle is active. It stands alone. But the feminine principle is strong in its own way. It receives, and brings forth. I'm going to find a way to combine the two. I'm going to be transcendent, Cass."

"What's transcendent?" he said, no longer even pretending to play checkers.

She smiled. "It means you're above everything. Nobody can pin you down. Put a label on you."

He shrugged again. "Why is that so important?"

She looked at him with disappointment and shook her head.

"Can't you understand? We fled the old world because we couldn't stop changing it for the worse. We couldn't change ourselves enough to avoid ruining it. We're leeches, Cass. We're parasites. But I'm not going to be a parasite. I'm going to change myself. Little by little, until I've become."

"Become what?" he said.

"Become," she continued, "and when I do, it'll be glorious."

He stared at her, for the first time looking her full in the face. There was a memory of a girl there, but she'd done much to erase it.

"Am I ugly to you?" she said.

He didn't know how to answer. As confidently as she presented herself, Cass felt that she might break with a word.

"Is Susan your mom?" he said, dodging. "Why do you call her Susan?"

"That's her name, isn't it?"

"Well … what does she think about all this? What's your dad think?"

Ahme laughed. "After what he did, he gets no say. But I'm glad he did it, in a way. It makes it easier to leave this prison behind."

"What prison?" he said. "You mean your house?"

She shook her head, incredulous, as if he were a simpleton.

"*This prison*," she said, cupping her hands over the pressed-down things that were her breasts. "This stupid ape-body. This parasitic, carnivorous husk that I was born into."

Cass looked away from her, his face hot with embarrassment.

"Do I make you uncomfortable?" she said. "It wasn't always that way. You don't remember though, do you?"

Before he could answer, she crawled over to the bookshelf, and pulled out a drawer from the bottom. Cass watched as she rifled through its contents, finally retrieving a small metal box. From it she took a notebook bound in a pink ribbon. It was tied firmly, and she yanked the ribbon so that it snapped. She rifled through the pages. In their center was a photograph. She took it out and showed it to him.

The girl in the picture could not have been older than six. She had glorious red-golden hair, and rosy cheeks. Her face was a cheerful warmth that washed over him with the power of a foundational memory; an old, familiar song; a phantom scent on the wind.

Cass had been only five when his family arrived on New World. He was three when they first stepped on the void ship, and he was now unsure if he even remembered Earth. The intervening time was mostly lived in the twilight of void separation, but for two days every week, he'd been awake in the nightland. Sometimes, in a dream, he remembered her. Sometimes, in waking life. They'd played together on those strange days when people were people, and not sleeping vegetables. They'd both grown up strangely, having aged two years in a succession of a hundred weekends that were bounded by irrecoverable twilight. When he'd remembered her in the time since, he'd never recalled her name. Now he knew.

Tears came to his eyes unbidden. He still cried of course, being a boy of eleven, and one whose mental growth—like all children on void ships—had been strangely foreshortened. He did not attempt to hide these tears. They were too real.

"It's you," he said, in a whisper.

"May I … hug you?" she said.

He nodded, and she did.

***

In the center of Ahme's backyard was an artificial pond. They stood staring down into it, silent, as if it were a crystal ball.

"This place is sacred to me," she said.

Night had fallen, but in the porch light, he saw a flicker of motion somewhere halfway to the bottom.

"What kind of fish do you keep here?" said Cass.

"I don't keep any fish," she said.

"But I saw—"

"I don't *keep* them," she explained. "They're just there. Birds land with fish eggs sticking to their feet. No matter what you do, you can never keep a place pure, and unspoilt. Something always gets in."

He shrugged. "But that's good, right? Life always finds a way."

"Life finds a way," she said, "to feed on other life. To take advantage of it. It's such a contradiction, Cass. It grows, and multiplies, only to eat itself in the end. That's the problem with this world."

He looked at her, and saw that she was sincere. Her eyes, always so flinty and outwardly assured, had tiny crystal beads in the corners. She lamented creation. She was mad.

"I think it's alright," he said. "I don't think it's bad that life spreads, and that things eat other things. That's the way things naturally are, so how can it be bad?"

Ahme left his side and walked around the pond. She crept close to the edge, leaning over it, as if she might plunge in. On the water's surface there floated a kind of barge of green growth. She crouched down, and with great gentleness, slid her hand beneath the undulating coating, and retrieved some in a cupped palm.

"Do you know what this is?" she asked, looking up at Cass.

"Like … amoebas?"

Ahme laughed. It was the first, pure laugh he'd seen from her since the twilight days. Some buried memory bit at his heart.

"It's a kind of green algae, native to this planet," she explained. "There's stuff just like it on Earth. And we've certainly brought our own here with us. But for once, that doesn't matter. Cass, this is what pure life looks like."

He frowned at it, wondering if he'd even want to touch the green sludge. "Just looks like slime to me," he said.

"That's your prejudice," pronounced Ahme. "Like most prejudice, it's just guilt talking. You eat animals and plants. In order for you to live, something else has to die. But this organism needs only water, and sunlight, and the stuff the world is made of. Sure, it'll eat the chemicals from things that have died, but it doesn't need to kill them. It doesn't need them at all. It doesn't need anybody."

"And it doesn't *do* anything," he added. "It's just floating slime."

"That's what makes it wonderful," retorted Ahme.

She held it up to her face, only inches from her still-feminine lips, and the strange, gaunt cheekbones and puffing jaw that were halfway boyish. Her eyes were wide with wonder, or horror, and now the diamond beads that had been gathering at their edges spilled out and rolled down her face.

"Don't you see?" she said. "It's simple, and transcendent. It stands alone, like a man. It receives, and brings forth, like a woman. This *slime* is the only living thing that is really pure."

Cass chuckled, nervously. "Why don't you marry it then?"

Ahme looked at him sadly. She sighed, and put her hand back into the pond, swishing it back and forth until the algae ran off. She stood.

"I've always remembered you, Cass. I remember the time you made me a flower out of paper, because there weren't any real flowers on the void ship. But, then, you couldn't have seen many on Earth either. Just pictures in feeds. There was something special about you. We were pure then. I thought … I thought maybe you would understand."

He looked away from her, feeling a strange mix of nostalgia, guilt, and something like love. She was still repellent. Looking at her made him uncomfortable. But now he knew what she had been to him once. A bright, beautiful light, now rendered odd, and inhuman.

"I don't understand," he said. "I'm … willing to be your friend, but I think you should stop dressing like a boy. Stop … stop thinking crazy things. Life is just life. You can't change the way things are made."

She walked around the pool, and right up to him. In her dumpy jumpsuit, designed to hide her natural curves, she still towered over Cass.

"Would you really be my friend?" she asked. "Would you want to be seen with me, with those friends of yours looking on?"

Unable to hold her gaze, Cass looked at his feet. He thought of Marco, and Johnny, and he knew the truth. Somehow, this moment mattered more than most others before it. It was a fulcrum point in his life, and in hers.

"No," he said.

His face was hot with shame. His mother, could she hear his terrible words, would have been appalled. But it couldn't be helped. For Ahme's sake, a strange price was being asked of him, but he simply would not pay it.

"It's okay," she said, and kissed him on the cheek. "You can go home now."

***

"Do you know what a soft touch is?" said Virtu Shaarawy.

She sat crossed-legged and several feet back from her desk on the thirty-fourth floor of the Chromley Building out of which Apex Security did business. Her legs were long, cocoa brown, and quite pretty, and the midday sun shone through the enormous window behind her desk, bathing them in adoring light. Captain Basil made a habit of not looking at them.

"I think so, ma'am," he said.

There were several hundred private security firms in New World. They proliferated on this planet, where the State was weak, because most institutions policed themselves. Yet Apex was one of only four with the coveted General Commission, the State-granted license to investigate public crimes. Not that they did much of that, but they *could.*

"Do you need an illustration?" said Virtu?

Captain Basil frowned, wondering if this was an insult, a sincere request, or—and perhaps he was imagining it—the type of work situation he'd much rather avoid.

"I'm guessing you don't want me to haul anyone out in cuffs," he ventured.

"That's putting it mildly," said Virtu. "We don't have any evidence of a crime. We certainly don't have a warrant. We can't afford for this to become a Lake Shilo-type incident."

Cassius nodded. Some years ago, following a rash of strange stabbings that had radiated outward from the Lake Shilo district in the city of Port Fair, there had been enough of a collective outcry that the Parliament of New World had hired Crystal Rock Security to investigate. Crystal Rock possessed the General Commission, but their methods had been deemed uncouth, and their conclusions unacceptable. It didn't help that the killings suddenly stopped at around one hundred victims, that the victims were dispersed and hard to connect to each other, or that Crystal Rock had employed mass arrests and a little old-fashioned waterboarding. Politics being politics, CRS had lost its General Commission, and thus set an example for the remaining large security firms about what *not* to do.

"Understood," said Captain Basil. "But then … why are we investigating?"

Director Shaarawy put her feet down, and rolled her chair forward, setting her elbows on the desk.

"Cass … can I call you Cass?" she said, lowering her voice, though there was no one else in the room.

"Sure," he said.

She smiled, indulgently. "This is called politics, Cass. Let me worry about the why. You worry about the how. More importantly, the *how not.*

Suffice it to say that someone important has asked us to look, and that … *parleying* with important people is my side of the business. Yours is more concrete."

He nodded again. "I get your drift, but who am I looking for? Some senator's kid?"

She shook her head. "Now that's just what I mean by 'soft touch.' Your approach can't be that specific. The company we're looking into is Unichrys. You familiar?"

"I've heard of it," he said. "They do body mods, or something like that."

"Something like that," she said. "But they offer more than enhancement clinics. Think religion. Or maybe cult. Here."

She opened a manila folder on her desk and tossed him a brochure. Captain Basil flipped through it. It was full of images of smiling people in various stages of physical transformation, but the image that most struck him was a pyramid graphic on which different levels or "perfections" were noted.

"Unichrys teaches a way of life," continued Shaarawy, "and the upper stages of that life seem to entail cutting off all family and historical ties. You won't find much about that in the brochure, but I have a whole folder on it."

"Let me guess," said Captain Basil, "the senator's daughter won't talk to daddy anymore."

The director nodded.

"And she's still a legal minor," added Basil.

"No."

He frowned. "Then, once again, why are we investigating?"

"Again, because of reasons," said Shaarawy. "Don't think of it as looking for a crime. Think of it as insurance. Senator Vellun is the chair of the sub-body that grants—and takes away—the General Commission. His personal family problems can become our personal family problems."

Cass nodded. "Understood. But even if I find her, I can't exactly bring her back."

Shaarawy smiled. "No, *you* can't do that. She's an adult woman—well, an adult *something*—and that would be kidnapping. There are, of course, other firms that can accommodate Vellun on that point, but that's not *our* business, in any sense of the word."

Cass's brow furrowed. He unconsciously chewed his lip and pushed the brochure back across the desk.

"You're nervous," she observed.

"This isn't the kind of work I usually do."

"No, but you're perfect for it. *Exactly* perfect, as it turns out."

He looked up at her, curious.

"This is where it gets interesting," Shaarawy continued. "You see, Senator Vellun asked that the agent we sent be a family man. A father, specifically. You're thirty-eight. Married, with four children. A real oddball, you have to admit."

"I'm not the only married field agent," he said.

"No, but you're the only one that Unichrys also seems to have its eye on."

Captain Basil sat up straight. "Huh?"

Shaarawy nodded. "You know that in this kind of visitation, if we're going to get them to even talk to us, we have to make a formal inquiry. As part of prelim, we told Unichrys that we were investigating a crime only tangentially related to one of their former patients, and that we'd like to send someone there to verify details. We gave them a list of possible field agents, and your name was on it. As expected, they refused."

"Well of course they did," said Cass. "Why play with fire?"

She nodded. "But then they *un-refused.* A week after the soft inquiry, I received a version of it back, with an approval and an invitation for a formal tour of Unichrys' main headquarters in Ostia. What they sent me looked like what I sent them, but only your name was left on the list."

Captain Basil became silent. Shaarawy studied him, her eyes narrowed.

"Based on my experience," she said, "our original inquiry went to the lawyers, who punted. But then someone else, someone higher up got wind of it, read it, and overruled them. So, I have to ask, Cass, do you know anyone at Unichrys?"

He shook his head. "I really don't think so."

But there was a doubt in his voice. He felt it. He wondered if Shaarawy heard it. Cass certainly had no contacts in that organization, whose goals and beliefs were so unlike his own. Yet he suspected things. From the moment his eyes had danced over the words on the brochure, a few old memories came back to him. Could it be? She pushed the folder across the desk.

"Her name is Trina," said the director. "Trina Vellun. Nineteen years old. You can decline, of course."

He laughed and favored her with a sardonic smile. If he wanted to advance at Apex, he could refuse nothing.

"I accept," he said.

***

Not content to modify only bodies, Unichrys' headquarters in Ostia had modified itself. From any angle, its outside appearance was highly debatable. Since Basil had approached from the east, it presented as something like a pyramid, going wide to narrow, before inverting the pattern, and going narrow to wide. What had at first seemed a mostly solid eastern face revealed itself to be a series of smaller, angled planes, like the bellows of a golden accordion. Near-random but aesthetically pleasing boxes and rectangles grew out like barnacles from odd places on the smaller planes, while to the southeast, over-the-shoulder, as it were, of the eastern side, another face yawned out, following a different pattern.

There were many openings at street level, which he took to be doors, and he entered one. Cass was no art critic, but even the front doors suggested to him a highly individualized and variegated experience of reality. They were not all the same size and shape, and they did not unify, but separated, any visitor off the street.

Upon entering, Captain Basil felt some relief. The architectural assault of the outside structure was not mirrored interiorly. All doors entered upon a vast, open space. Thousands of people in varying states of physical modification milled about, their many voices echoing off the complex surfaces above. Looking up, he saw that the distant ceiling was not one solid thing, but simply the under-surfaces of many individual rooms and corridors that seemed to float above the mighty lobby where he stood. He was looking for something like a reception desk, when he became conscious of a particular voice directed at him.

"What do you dream?"

He turned, and saw a man standing next to him. The speaker looked perfectly normal, at first. Though not in any uniform, a pink choker with the word "Unichrys" printed across it marked him as staff.

"All kinds of things," said Cass. "Right now, I'm dreaming of a tour."

"That can perhaps be arranged," said the man, in falsetto. "Do you have an appointment?"

In answer, Cass offered his pad. The man produced his own and touched it to Basil's. He frowned slightly at what appeared on his screen.

"Captain Cassius Basil, from Apex."

Cass nodded.

"Ooh, and I see you're here on *official* business."

There was sarcasm—or perhaps disappointment—in that word.

"Come with me," said the man.

Only after he turned to lead Cass across the lobby did Cass notice the face embedded in the back of his head. Above the man's neck, at the rounding of his skull, the hair was entirely gone. A set of blue eyes, a small pink nose, and full female lips perked out. The eyes sized him up lasciviously, and a red tongue rolled over the lips, before they suddenly puckered, and kissed at him through the air. Cass kept his expression even, and wondered whether the eyes could really see.

They crossed the huge lobby, walking perhaps a quarter mile, when his host came to a stop by a young woman who also bore the pink choker. They exchanged a few inaudible words, while the eyes behind the man looked eagerly sideways, as if disappointed to be left out of the conversation.

"Chira will give you the tour," said his host, turning.

Cass thanked him, and the man curtsied, and fluttered his fingers in a goodbye. Cass ignored him.

"Hello, Chira," said Cass.

"Hello, Captain Basil. What are your dreams?"

He smiled. "Mostly nonsense, I'm afraid. But I'd like to learn more about yours."

She smiled, devilishly. "Would you now? But I'm told you're here for a full tour. That should give us plenty of time to talk."

Cass smiled, and with real warmth this time. After all, she looked like what she was. Chira led him silently across the remaining stretch of lobby to a very standard-looking lift. She said nothing as they climbed. Though the levels had appeared uneven from below, this must have been an illusion, as the floors were clearly numbered on the display screen. They stopped at the forty-second floor.

"How many floors total?" he said.

"Depends on what you mean," she said, without explaining further.

She led him down a transparent, conical corridor. He could see others walking in their own hallways at acute angles to this one. It seemed a terrible waste of space for the sake of an aesthetic. The corridor came to an end and took a sharp left. After the turn, it became rectangular. The doors on either side seemed normal now—at least they were also rectangular—though each was only a doorway; a threshold without any hinged obstruction.

"These rooms are for discernment," she said, pointing out openings on the left.

"Discernment?"

"We help people understand what they want to be," she explained. "And what it will cost them."

He nodded. "I imagine some of these mods require a fair amount of coin."

She hesitated, then looked at him as if only just seeing him. "Yes, well, there is *that*, of course."

In the Discernment Rooms were many tables and couches spaced widely apart. At several of them, pink-chokered specialists sat across from prospective clients. The conversations all looked very intense. Chira led him further, and the corridor again banked left. Now there were several rooms on the right, like classrooms.

"We give workshops here," she said.

"On?"

"On Transcendence, naturally."

He nodded. "That's your religion, right?"

She smiled, curtly. "Religions purport to come from above. Transcendence emanates from within."

"Then how can it transcend? If it comes from inside, wouldn't you still just be stuck inside yourself?"

She stiffened for an instant, and Cass cursed himself for running his mouth. After all, he was supposed to be gathering information, not pissing off the management. Yet she seemed to recover her calm. Her body softened. She smiled.

"We did not make the veil. Nature—or *God*, if you prefer—made it. But we can pierce it. We can tear it, as our ancestors tore a void in space. Human beings were born to poke holes."

Cass nodded sagely and began to plan his next move. He'd hoped to speak to someone on the cusp of being changed so that he could find out what Unichrys said to make them go through with it. It was not a crime to fool people and take their money, but he imagined that the sort of people who went to Unichrys for that purpose might tend toward tight, cliquish groups. Perhaps some of these changelings would know what had become of Trina Vellun. For such people, a senator's daughter would be a real prize, a formal vindication of their radical choices.

But now that he was here, he doubted his plan. It would be hard to get away. Hard to speak to anyone one-on-one without being seen. He decided to go with his secondary plan. He needed a moment to think, and physical separation from his guide.

"Eh … I wondered if there was a restroom nearby," he said.

Chira studied him. "Back there," she said, with a nod. "On your left, going back the way we came, just after you turn the corner."

Near the Discernment Rooms, he thought. *Excellent.* He thanked her and began retracing his steps.

"I'll wait here for you," she said, as he rounded the corner.

The Discernment Rooms were on his right as he passed them, and the nearest restroom was just a few doors further on his left. It was, to his surprise, a men's bathroom, bearing the traditional icon. Chuckling at that, he went to the sink, and began washing his face. The water was good and cold, and the splash on his cheeks helped him think. It would do no good, he decided, walking around asking employees about Trina. At work, they'd be reticent to speak to him. Yet on the lapel of his suit jacket he bore a tiny surveillance camera. Up until now he'd kept it off just in case Unichrys scanned for such things. Now it would be enough to turn it on and walk around, letting it see as many faces as possible, faces that could be sent to his pad for identification. Even with their modifications, the software should be able to tag a good number of them.

Trina must have gone through the discernment process. Someone in those rooms would have seen her. In the time it took a person to use a restroom, he'd just walk through the Discernment Rooms, making sure to get footage of every employee. Later, when he'd discovered their names, he'd identify the soft ones, people with something to hide and a lot to lose. He could get to them outside of work.

He stepped into the corridor, checked for Chira, then quickly entered the first Discernment Room. He passed amid the tables and couches at an anonymous pace, turning left and right to let the camera collect the workers' faces. Most didn't even look up to wonder at his presence, and he was soon on to the second room. This was more densely occupied, and he had to be more obvious to make sure he got everyone. A few specialists had their backs to him, and he decided to return before Chira came looking for him. As he stepped into the corridor, she was waiting.

"Sight-seeing?"

He shrugged. "Just curious."

"About what? Are you looking for someone in particular?"

Cass was not a terribly good liar, but he owed her nothing. "If I was, I wouldn't look here. Modding isn't my thing. But I *am* supposed to get the lay of the land."

She cupped one hand in another near her waist, stiffly.

"This *crime* you're investigating, what is it?"

"I can't say."

"Who are you looking for? Does she have a name? He?"

"You know I can't say that either," replied Cass, with an apologetic shrug.

She hesitated, studying him through narrowed eyes.

"The tables are spaced like that for a reason," she said, nodding at the room he'd left. "People want to discuss their situation in relative privacy, but without feeling they're the only one. When you walked through there, you infringed on their privacy."

"I'm sorry," he said. "Won't happen again. I'm just worried that this tour will pass by some things that end up being important to my case."

To his surprise, the inklings of a smile grew at one corner of her mouth.

"Oh, I wouldn't worry about that, Captain Basil. This tour was made just for you."

With that she turned and walked down the hall. Cass followed, thinking all the time. For the next half-hour they passed more rooms, entered and exited the lifts twice, and generally wormed their way deeper into Unichrys' byzantine structure. Chira was a competent guide, narrating and naming most of what they passed, but Captain Basil found it hard to attend. His thoughts ran on his own, anticipated, presence there, and he couldn't shake the feeling that Chira was studying him, toying with him, and leading him by the nose. He seemed to catch, in the corner of her eye, the humor of the fox offering to ferry small creatures across a raging river. Finally, they came to a long, plain corridor that ended in a lift.

She entered with him but kept the doors from closing. Chira typed a code into the keypad below the lift's display screen, then stepped out. Before

Captain Basil could ask any questions, the lift doors shut again. He was alone. The lift whirred into action. He was going up.

***

When the lift finished its ascent, Cass looked out through the opening doors and was immediately confused. Expecting another hallway, he was greeted by an open sky. The lift had brought him to the building's roof and as he walked forward, he recognized the place as a sort of open-air temple. The temple's surfaces were all polished white marble, and a rectangular reflecting pool ran down its center. From the pool's far end, a wide marble stair climbed, terminating at a dais, which, elevated above the pool, seemed a fit place for a king. No throne, but rather a golden altar, jutted up from its center. On the altar, and seeming to roost, stood a large, many-colored bird. The bird looked alive, but even at this distance he could see that it was too big to be real. He could not locate its head, as if the bird were tucking it down beneath its plumage. A trapezoidal wall like an Egyptian pylon framed and overlooked the dais. Golden and emerald geometric patterns lightly etched the pylon's blue-black facade. White stone pillars trimmed in gold and green ran along both sides of the reflecting pool. It would have been a beautiful place, even in a hard rain, but on this stuffy afternoon, the milky New World sun fluttered in the center of the reflecting pool and made the whole place shine, even while a muggy heat in the air portended coming storms.

Standing at one end of the long pool, Cassius Basil squinted as the sky winds whipped across the roof, disturbing the waters, ruffling the Sun's reflected image, and whistling between the white pillars. Looking through them, Cass was surprised to see no ledge where the roof met the sky. He walked against the wind and passed beneath and between the line of marble columns toward the roof's edge. Carefully, he crept up and looked over, peering down tens of stories to the street below. Not even a guard rail stood between him and a drop through the strange architectural barnacles that grew from the side of Unichrys' building. Only the contrary winds offered any resistance to an accidental slip. Here was a place with no firm barrier between beauty and death.

The winds suddenly died, and he leaped backwards. Shaking his head, he began exploring the right side of the roof, making his way around the reflective pool in the general direction of the dais. Presently, he reached the pool's far end, and passed again beneath the line of white columns. He looked up at the large, life-like bird on the altar, and considered climbing up to it. But the water wrapped about the steps at the pool's end and washed up against the dais and the blue-black pylon that framed it. To get to the altar, he must descend into the pool, then climb out by the steps. He hesitated.

"Are you afraid of water?" said a voice.

Captain Basil looked at the altar. But the bird hadn't moved. Anyway, it seemed headless after all, and the voice had come from everywhere at once.

"Who's speaking?"

Cass's hand went instinctively to the metal bulge under his jacket.

"If you want Transcendence," said the voice, "you must be humbled."

He looked up again at the bird on the golden altar. Was it holding a different posture than before? Another gust of wind whistled over the rooftop, and now he understood why the bird had looked alive. Its feathers shimmered in the breeze. But the voice had not come from the bird; it had come from all around him, as if the wind or the sky was speaking.

"Maybe I like myself already," he said, directing his comments to the bird.

No answer. The wind died off for a moment, leaving a void feeling in its absence. Dark clouds in the east suggested rain. A storm was coming and already the sun was dimming. Cass wanted to investigate the strange, rainbow-colored bird, and now considered that if he stayed here much longer, he'd be drenched anyway. He checked that his pad was secure in the bladder in his jacket pocket, and then lowered himself into the reflecting pool.

The water came only to his waist. The wind picked up again, sending little half-moon radiations across the water. He waded swiftly toward the steps, climbed them, and reached the dais. The bird towered over him. Its feathers fluttered gently in the wind. Each was a solid color, but with no exact repetition. Each had its own, unique hue. The rainbow pelt was composed of thousands of tiny, individualized feathers. The bird opened its wings.

Cass cried out and leaped backwards, nearly falling into the pool. Open, the wings spanned ten feet. From the top portion of the bird's torso, a narrow, fleshy face peered out. Its eyes were diamonds set in gold rings; its nose, two long slits, and its mouth was that of a human woman, doubled in size.

"Good God!" cried Cass.

His hand went to his sidearm. The bird craned over him and sighed.

"Still a killer, Cassius Basil?" said the bird, from all places. "Don't be afraid. I do no harm."

Cass was shaking. It took all his willpower not to draw and empty a clip into the monstrous thing. Instead, he balled his right hand in his left, and stood before the bird as a suppliant before a god.

"What … are you?" he said.

The bird drew its wings around him, pulling him softly away from the edge, as if to embrace him.

"You know, Cass."

The large pink lips mouthed the words, but the voice came from elsewhere; from everywhere at once. Cass bit back vomit. Indeed, he knew.

"How?" he whispered.

The temple chuckled. "Do you want another lecture on nature, old friend?" said the voice in sweet, electric tones.

He shook his head. "Why have you done this to yourself, Ahme? It is Ahme, isn't it?"

The bird dipped its torso; a sort of nod. "That was one of my names. You may use it. There are many steps on the path to Transcendence, and each has its name. Each name was precious to me, for a time."

He waited for her to say more, but the Ahme-bird looked down on him with glittering eyes, its wings folded across his shoulders in a strange embrace. At length, the silence—and the embrace—became unbearable. He stepped backwards. She let him pass through her feathery appendages, then drew them slowly to her sides.

"You do not like this form?" said her disembodied voice.

"No," he said, incredulous. "How could you do this to yourself?"

"I have become," said the bird, matter-of-factly.

"But you're not *you*," he insisted. "I don't recognize you anymore. Your mother—Sarah?—she wouldn't recognize her own daughter."

Ahme clucked; a sardonic, avian laugh, or so it seemed.

"*Susan*. She birthed me, but now she lives alone, inside her electric home. But I have moved on, and up, flying ever higher into the possibilities of myself."

"I wish she'd stopped you," said Cass.

"Stopped me? On the contrary, she encouraged me. I cannot remember Susan ever telling me no. She envied me, Cass, because I was not afraid of becoming. She was always a slave to comfort. She lacks the will to slip the leash of taboo. To become."

"But *what* have you become, Ahme? This isn't your body. It's … it's a costume!"

She clucked again, and once more spread her wings. They were as radiant beneath as above.

"You disappoint me," she said. "When I learned that chance had again placed you in my path, it was almost enough to make me believe in Providence. Not God's, but my own. And now you're here, and as blind as ever. I am *not* artificial, Cass. I've merely gained the means to manifest what I truly am. You are the fraud. You, with your badge and your gun, and your little brood, trying so hard to be a real man. What is that, anyway? Have you ever seen one? All that you see here is me. My wings were fashioned from the bones of those silly ape legs that humans amble about on, doing mischief. My feathers were bred from my own keratin. At first, they were implanted, but now they grow from my own flesh. I am what I choose to be. I am."

He looked down and saw that her long legs were gone, and that her torso came to a single, large, three-taloned foot. Considered in herself, she was a picture of symmetry. Considered in light of his memories, she was a monster. Yet she was proud. *Her providence?* Whatever affection he might have felt for her was swallowed up in disgust.

"I didn't come here because you willed it," said Cass. "I came here to find Trina Vellun. And now that I see what you're trying to do to people, you can be damned sure I'll get her out of your cult."

Waves of motion went through her wings, and peals of laughter, high-pitched and musical, floated through the temple.

"Find her? But you already have. She led you to me."

Cass frowned. "Chira?"

"Indeed."

"But … she looks normal. You've only changed her face."

"*I* haven't done anything," said Ahme. "I do not dictate to others their paths to Transcendence. But I assure you, more than *that* has been transformed. It is, perhaps, a good thing that you did not try flirting with her. You'd have gotten more than you bargained for."

Cass shook his head, disgusted.

"You can try to persuade her," continued Ahme. "Tell her that daddy misses her and wants her to come home. I will not oppose it. But it would be a waste of time. She despises her father more than I did mine … when I still cared about such things."

Cass looked away from her. The dark clouds that had been far to the east now rolled westward. From this high point, he could see that they were emptying their contents on the world and would soon be upon the two of them.

"Better get out of the rain," he said. "Wouldn't want to drench your feathers. I've heard that makes flying difficult."

The great mouth smiled, wanly.

"I do not fly much," she said.

In her voice he heard the subtlest tinge of regret.

"At any rate," she continued, "I must change still more to make this form practical. And I don't mind the rain."

For a time, they stood staring at each other. Cass could think of nothing else to say. She was beyond his tastes, and beyond changing back to what she had been. Yet now he felt sure that, for all her bravado, Ahme had not yet "become". There was something more she longed for, of which her best designs and all the resources she could marshal had fallen short.

"Are you happy, Ahme?" he said.

Again, the avian laugh. "Eudaimonia is a *western* concept of completion. I do not subscribe to it. There are notions of fulfillment that incorporate the whole gamut of human experience, light and dark. I have no desire for some cheap bourgeois becoming. I am not a salesman, but a teacher. And a student, Cass. Always a student."

"Ahme," he repeated, "are you happy?"

The bird shuddered. Its glittering eyes bore holes in him. Ahme's outstretched wings slowly folded inward, until they covered her strange new face. Once more she was a statue. For a long time, he remained on the altar with her, unmoving. No further voice sounded from the temple roof. The indifferent rains finally came to pelt the white marble. There was nothing more to say.

Cass turned to leave. As he did, he saw upon the white steps a single green feather. Stooping, he picked it up, and rolled it by the shaft between his fingers. He smoothed the barbs straight and tucked the feather into his chest pocket. He made his way through the reflecting pool, and back towards the lift. Just before the doors closed, he saw the rain falling hard on the Ahme-bird and rolling down the altar like colored blood.

***

Cassius Basil stared into his glass of water, noticing the ice cubes. They were half-again as small as when dinner had begun, but you never saw them shrink. Time was like that.

"Everything okay, Daddy?"

He looked up suddenly. Martina Basil, Cass's youngest daughter, and the only one who still shared his last name, was essentially a woman. When had it happened? He wished there had been more time.

"Everything's fine," he said, straightening himself up.

When he did, his back creaked oddly, and he felt a rush of vertigo and a shortness of breath, as if he'd just exerted himself. *Geez, I'm not that old!* he thought. His wife Chelsea shot him a mocking smile. She always knew what he was thinking.

It was Monday morning, but Cass was semi-retired now, and didn't have anywhere he needed to be. Martina was off from secondary school for Thanksgiving break. They'd returned last night from another Basil wedding. This time it was his second youngest daughter, Chessy. The whole family—what was left of it—marinated in that after-trip inaction, the melancholy soup of jet lag and spent excitement.

"I think I'll go out," said Cass.

Cass threw a coat over his sweatshirt and stepped out into the brisk air. The gray sky and biting wind wasn't calculated to help his mood, but he walked hard against it, letting the heat in his body build until he felt active again, not mastered by externals, but himself the master. Half an hour later he returned, somewhat improved. The melancholy he'd been feeling had decayed into its second-cousin, nostalgia. He knew he shouldn't do it, but he did. Cass walked upstairs.

In his closet, inside a large wooden chest, Cass kept the things he couldn't throw away. He opened the chest and began rifling through. Inside he found dozens of old journals that he'd likely never read again, and printed photos of the girls' childhoods. Resisting, for a moment, the impulse to pull out an old photo, his eyes fell instead on a small metal box. He could not recall all that he'd put in there. He set in on the floor, flipped the latches, and began rifling through. Its contents were mostly things the girls had given him: hand-written birthday cards, "presents", and broken relics of one kind or another. He took them all out, then gasped when he saw what remained, pressed by pressure into one corner of the box. A single green feather.

He took it by the shaft, fearing it would break, or maybe disappear at his touch. Holding it up to the light, he saw that its color was still brilliant. Cass shuddered. He hadn't thought of Ahme in years. Now all he could think of was that she too had been somebody's daughter. He wondered if she was still alive.

It would have been better to put the feather back and forget. Instead, he packed everything but the feather away, and went to his office. It only took a moment on his console to learn that Unichrys was no more. It had gone belly up in the Big Crunch a decade earlier. Its strange headquarters, unusable for normal purposes, and tainted by a controversial past, had been torn down. He could learn nothing of the fate of its strange queen.

But he knew where she'd once lived. It wasn't far, as the bird flew. He set the feather down, set out clothes for the day, then marched purposively toward the shower. For once, Cass had somewhere to be.

***

The house looked vaguely unclean. Gray smears marred its chrome exterior. The yard was overgrown. Probably, the house had been abandoned. He went up and pressed the ringer anyway. When no one came, he felt relief. What would he have said anyway, if Ahme or her mother were home? Susan must have passed away by now, or else was spending her final days in a retirement home. But the dirty screen beside the door lit up, and a woman's face appeared there.

"Can I help you?" said the aged creature.

He named himself, and she did not know him. But when he asked for Ahme, her face betrayed her. She disappeared for a full minute. When the screen again lit up, her tone was sober.

"Come in," she said.

The door slid aside. He stepped into the entryway, which led to a small living room. It was lightly furnished, with two small couches and a bookshelf. A wide console screen was embedded in the wall. Old items lay stacked about the room, and the place had that vague, musty smell of old things or old people going to rot, their true scents living just below a veneer of perfume and cleaning solution. The old woman rose from the couch, and offered her hand warily. He could see from the depression in the sofa that she sat there often, perhaps all day. The place was silent but for a vague mechanical whirring in the floors above.

"I'm Cass Basil," he repeated. "Is Ahme around?"

She seemed afraid.

"Mr. Basil, I…" she began, "I believe my daughter has already paid her debts. I thought these things were behind us now. If there's something more, I'm afraid I'll have to refer you to our lawyers. But we don't have anything left. You can't get blood from stone."

The comment threw him. Then he realized that she didn't recognize his name.

"I'm not a creditor, or anything like that. I used to be a friend of Ahme's."

"Oh?" she said, like one coming up from a well.

"Do you remember me?"

He told her about the void ship, and his visit of years ago. Her face gave her away, going soft for a heartbeat, then setting into hard lines.

"I remember you now," she said. "I'm afraid I can't help."

"Is she here?" he pressed. "Do you know where I can find her?"

Susan looked just left of his eyes, like someone forming a lie. The vague buzzing he'd heard upon entering now grew louder. The lift doors opened, and something rolled out. A robotic vacuum cleaner, over-sized and antique-looking, zipped into the room, and began whirring along the walls, following its eternal, programmed course.

"I live alone," said Susan. "As you can see, I can't maintain the place anymore. The house and yard have gone to hell."

"They're not so bad," he lied.

She laughed, then looked sharply at him. "You won't find Ahme here."

"Does she ever come by?"

"I said she's not here!"

"Alright, alright," he said, putting his hands up, "but do you know where I can find her?"

She studied him, then slowly shook her head. The lie was obvious to them both, if not the reason behind it. He wondered if she knew about their conversation by the pond or the encounter at Unichrys and blamed him for not helping Ahme. Perhaps she blamed herself. The robot vacuum cleaner finished its preliminary cleaning of the edges, then began its course back and forth across the floor, deftly dodging the stacked items.

"I don't know what to tell you," Susan muttered. "It wouldn't be a happy reunion."

"You mean because she wouldn't want to see me?"

"I mean leave it alone."

He took a deep breath. There was little point arguing with an old woman. She knew where Ahme was, but she wasn't going to tell him. Still, he felt that if he left now, he would never have closure.

"Please," he said, "If you won't tell me where she is, at least give her a message for me."

The house lights flickered. Susan's eyes darted around, concerned, but she tried to disguise her reaction.

"Is that her?" he said. "Is she somewhere in the house?"

The old woman covered her eyes.

"Please, just go."

Cass looked up at the ceiling, as if he could see through the walls. He still remembered where her room had been. Ahme, he recalled, had been very good at twitching. She might be upstairs now, perhaps lying indisposed, but trying to let him know she was here. He thought of her avian form and wondered what age might have done to it.

"May I please go up to her?"

Susan backed away from him and sat down into her couch depression. The lights flickered again. Very softly, she tried to say something, but the whirring of the vacuum swallowed it up just before the thing rushed over and struck him in the shin.

"Ow!" he cried.

The large vacuum hovered menacingly near his feet.

"Alright, fine! I'll leave," he said to the house. "I just wanted to see you."

He started toward the door. As he reached it, the vacuum struck the back of his ankle. The pain was intense, and he turned around ready to kick it.

"I said I'm going," he almost shouted to Susan.

But the old woman did not seem to hear him. She stared at the vacuum cleaner. It perched a few inches from Cass's shins, ready to strike again. Keeping an eye on it, he reached behind him for the door. The thing rushed forward. This time he jumped out of the way, and it struck the door hard. Cass brought his boot down on the machine, then reared up to stamp on it again.

"Don't hurt her!" cried Susan.

He glanced at Susan, incredulous, then back at the large vacuum cleaner. It revved its motors, then shrank back from him and strafed left and right.

"What are you talking about?" he said.

Susan began to weep. "She's there. In there. Oh God!"

Cass felt the room shift under him. He found himself kneeling, going down to the level of the thing at his feet. It was only an over-sized vacuum cleaner. Susan, in the loneliness of old age, had made it into her prodigal daughter.

He took hold of the robot vacuum cleaner, looking for an off switch. The machine was a dull green color. He saw now that it was not round, but pear-shaped, with a smooth, flat top. The thing floated beneath his touch, no longer striking him, but seeming to encourage his exploration. It had about the depth of a guitar. When he touched its side, it immediately began rotating until his hand brushed up against a single, red switch. The switch was in the off state.

"Don't!" cried Susan. "You don't want to hear her!"

Cass ignored her and pressed "On."

The vacuum cleaner began to scream. It was not the whine of a machine, but of a woman, or perhaps of a bird; a long, high, desperate cawing that grew in volume until Cass's ears throbbed.

"Stop!" Susan yelled. "Stop it! Stop it!"

But the cry only grew more desperate and terrible. He grabbed for it, trying to shut off its voice, but the machine darted out of his grasp. Finally, he threw himself on top of it, pinned it to the ground with the weight of his body, and managed to hit the switch. He got back up to his knees and it rushed at his thighs. Cass grabbed it by its sides and lifted it from the ground. The machine was surprisingly heavy. He labored to his feet. Its wheels spun and whipped about the track on its underside. Holding them away from his body, he stared across at Susan.

"What have you done to her!"

Susan shook her head; wept into her hands.

"*I* didn't do it, Cass. She did. She just kept changing. Trying to become. And then it all fell apart, and there wasn't any money. And she, she made herself into … into—"

"—Then why didn't you stop her?" he sputtered. "Why didn't you ever tell her no!"

Susan pulled her feet up and wrapped her arms around her knees like a small girl. Cass glared at her. Then, like a man in a dream, he strode toward the backyard, clutching the vacuum cleaner like a tantrumming baby.

***

He'd set her down by the pond, wheels-up, so she couldn't roll away. Now he returned with a tool set from the house. One-by-one, he drew out the bolts that held her bottom cover in place. At first the wheels zipped about, trying to strike his fingers, but Cass spoke softly to Ahme, and told her what he planned to do. She stopped fighting him then. Her wheels spun in place. In anticipation.

He worked the green panel off and tossed it into the yard. Inside, beneath a transparent casing, lay Ahme. She was coiled up, a red and pink thing without bones. He watched her slosh about in yellow liquid. Cass turned the heavy machine over, and let gravity pull her out. Now the clear casing lay on the overgrown stone walkway that wrapped around the pond. Reversed, he could see that the fleshy, gelatinous form inside had eyes.

He found a flat screwdriver and worked it under a seam in the glass. Cass took his time. He didn't want to risk shattering the material. Finally, the top section came off in one piece. Ahme lay exposed to the brisk autumn air.

"Someone should have loved you," he said, gently working his fingers under the pink thing.

He cringed as it reacted to his touch, bunching up around his fingers, working its way up his wrist and forearm, then squeezing tightly around his elbow, like an octopus.

He sat down by the green pond. The pond had gone scummy, but the artificial pumps still moved its waters about. And, sometimes, he considered, there would be rain. A person could depend on rain. Cass cradled the heavy monstrosity against his belly. He wept, and it burbled and sucked against his arm, soaking the sleeve through.

"*I* should have loved you," he said.

The fleshy thing trembled and squeezed him till it hurt. The New World sun, which had been hiding behind the clouds all day, suddenly cleared them. There was no warmth in it, but a point of light came through and fell on them both.

"Light and water," he said, through tears. "It's all you ever wanted."

Cass came to a crouch and walked on his knees over to the pond, like a penitent. He could think of no way to pry the creature from his arm; not without harming her. He didn't understand how her formless form was put together. He lowered his arm into the pond, letting the dark green water come up to his shoulder so that it covered her too.

Ahme held onto him for as long as she could, or so it seemed to Cass. Finally, the temptation of water was too much for her. She released his arm and slipped away into the pond. Cass stood, and looked down into it, wondering if he'd killed her. But his fears were unfounded. He saw the waters moving, the green algae swirling about on the surface, as if dancing. As the light shined full upon the pond, Ahme swam up and broke the surface.

She floated, things like tentacles moving side-to-side in the pond's mossy covering, keeping her up. Her eyes were wide and flat, and they glittered up at him. She could not smile, for she had no distinct mouth. She was master of sun and water. Master, and victim. She was what she'd always wanted to be. Cassius fell to his knees and wept. Ahme had become.

THE WATCHERS OVER CRESCENT BAY

It was one of those middling days in young October when Solax still warmed the air, but fog lay over everything, chilling one's ears and neck, as if Nature sat bundled by a weak fire, sipping paradoxes. A ship built in Mercantus made its way along Bethany's southern shore. It was a large, double-masted yacht, one of those rich men's boats that could run entirely on steam if needed, and usually did—if a Mercantian baron were at the helm. The sails and rigging, though functional, were mainly there to suggest a certain ruggedness. Still, Custis Marks had plans for Bethany, and he intended to master natural sailing as well as any of its more rustic residents. He stood on the quarterdeck, taking instruction from a fellow whose expertise came with the boat. The latter appeared to regret this new role, no matter how lucrative. The instructor, whose ebony skin and wide, narrow eyes marked him out as Africhi, knew all about self-made men, and how it was a point of pride for such men to know everything, or else pay others to know it for them. He was therefore unsurprised to find the rich man finishing his sentences, anticipating his suggestions, and passing them off as commands to the deckhands, as if they had emerged from his own expertise.

Standing on the pulpit at the other end of the ship, Calvin Marks took in the spectacle. He could not see through the reefed mainmast, but he heard the instructor start and stop as Custis talked over him. In his imagination, Calvin saw Mr. Green flanking Custis, ever attentive and motionless, and perhaps with the barest hint of a smile at the corners of his eyes as he observed his master.

The yacht rolled steadily east. The Clover Islands disappeared behind Bethany's cliffs, and only the distant airships floating above the cities proved that the cities were still there. Calvin couldn't help but feel they were sailing into madness. Clearly, his father had some scheme in Bethany. Custis had already bought a villa on the shore and was now trying to adopt the habits of the locals. Calvin had no desire to live among such backward people, and he hoped he was wrong about his father's intentions.

Nothing was in his control. He leaned out over the sea and tried to recall the lines of old verse he'd found scrawled inside his mother's journal. Father kept Melania's memory locked away—in an iron safe of the most sophisticated make—but Calvin had, of course, defeated the safe, and studied his mother's long lost, and last thoughts. The boy had a way with mechanisms. He was like a mechanism himself.

"Out of the night that covers me," he quoted, "Black as the pit from pole to pole..."

How did it go from there? He'd brought the journal along. It was stashed below, in a waterproof skin, and he thought of going down to look. While there, he could visit the control room and study the mechanisms the made the modern engine work. His father knew of his abilities but seemed leery of letting his son "tinker around", as he termed it, and it was this lack of trust which, perhaps, bothered Calvin as much as Custis' hidden plans in Bethany.

But as the young man's gaze swept back over the main deck, taking in the grumbling deckhands who scrambled to execute Custis' sporadic commands, he realized that something else was amiss. It was something objective, beyond his own perpetual disquiet. He couldn't put his finger on it.

Presently, the southern shore cut inward in a deep arc, revealing a large bay. Misty from the morning, the inlet was defined by vast concave cliff walls that rose straight from the water. At their bottom, hardly visible in the fog, a line of dikes protected a little cave cut straight into the rocks at the water line. Evidently, it was a wharf, but for whom? Calvin's eyes climbed the great sea cliffs, and the white mist cleared enough for him to see the walls of a monastery. So, this bay was the fabled Crescent, and the monastery, Mt. Carmel. He'd heard of the place, but seeing it appear like that out of the ghostly fog gave him a chill. Over the walls, from somewhere within the protected structure, great white windmill arms turned endlessly in the sea breeze. Because of the enduring fog, they seemed to hover in the air like angels sent to judge the earth. Calvin recalled another bit of the verse:

"Beneath this place of wrath and tears, looms but the horror of the shade. And yet, the menace of the years, finds and shall find me unafraid."

As if on cue, deep, haunting bells rang out from the monkhouse, and moaned like phantoms off the sea-shorn cliff walls. It was a magnificent sight. It was a terrible waste of resources.

"Don' let 'er pash widdout making da sign!"

Calvin turned at the voice. A thin man with salt-browned skin looked up at him earnestly. Calvin recognized him. Custis had placed him in charge of hiring the crew, and this fellow, built from old shoe leather stretched over a frame, had been Calvin's first hire. But Calvin couldn't recall his name.

"What's that?" he asked.

The old man smiled and nodded at the monastery.

"Da' 'oly place, shir. Gotta pay yar respects."

He grinned and made the sign of the cross several times rapidly. The hurried movement looked more like a man securing a line on a block than the sort of piety of which monks would approve. Calvin smiled thinly.

"Well, I guess you've done it enough for both of us," he said.

He returned his gaze to the sea. The ship was moving at a good clip, and they would soon pass the Crescent. It was, he had to admit, a well-named location, but with such a moniker, wouldn't a mosque have suited it better? Not that there was any ultimate difference to him. There were men who made the world move, and there were men who made stories to explain its grinding machinations. That the latter divided themselves into many camps was perhaps inevitable.

Past the Crescent, the cliffs crept down until they hung only a hundred feet or so above the water. Bethany's southern coast began to round inward. Soon they'd be strafing its eastern shore. Having memorized the map, Calvin knew this side of Bethany was the longest, and also furthest away from civilization. Here, if anywhere, his father would try his luck at sailing the ship without the steam engines, and without advice from the instructor. There'd be fewer eyes to witness his initial failures, not that it ever took Custis long to master anything.

But as they rounded the island and bore north, Calvin saw that they were not quite alone. Two small skiffs, fast movers, circled the waters a quarter mile to their right. They must have been whalers, though Calvin didn't see the great green bodies breaking the Blue, nor the tell-tale spouting of the over-sized fish. The troubled feeling came back. He looked down at his hands on the pulpit rail, and pondered.

Two sounds caught his attention simultaneously. There was a scramble and thump somewhere above, while below him, someone loudly cleared his throat. Calvin looked up quickly and was surprised to see a large and very ugly bird on the mainsail's top yardarm.

"Excuse me, young master," said a familiar voice.

Calvin looked down, irritated. The salt-browned deckhand stood in the same place, eyes narrowed, and fixed on his.

"Ya ought not inore da' Powers, boy."

Calvin took a breath before responding.

"If there are Powers," he said, "then they can't *be* ignored, can they? Because they're powerful. And if they *can* be ignored, well then, they're not."

The deckhand frowned, puzzling it out.

"I been at sea longer'an you been livin'," he finally said. "A man ignores 'em, an' he meets 'em sooner."

Calvin laughed. "'No Kings. No Masters,'" he quoted. "That's the One Rule on Haven, isn't it? Well, no Powers, either. And *if* they've got it, let 'em show it. 'Put up, or shut up,' we say in the cities."

Calvin looked back up at the bird on the main yard. Never in his life had he seen a creature that ugly. It didn't look like a sea bird at all.

"Not everyting yields to money and plannin', boy," continued the old man. "Wind. Sea. Sharp shoals and dark movers under the Blue. When a man lives close to 'em, he knows what real powers be. Ye can't count on anyting but them. When ye feel the powers pressin' down, it's best to pray. An' I feels 'em all the time, boy. Been on the Blue dat long, have I."

"Thanks for the advice," sighed Calvin, eager to end the conversation.

He would have liked to inquire after the bird, but now wasn't the time. He'd clearly offended the old fellow. Calvin looked past him, toward the other deckhands. That was when he noticed an oddity. It was, he now realized, the very detail that had bothered him all morning. None of those deckhands looked familiar. He glanced back at the old sailor.

"What did you say your name was?"

"I? Didn't say, but it's Malachi."

Calvin nodded, remembering the sailor's pub where he'd hired him, and the others. He was terrible with names, but never faces. He descended from the forecastle and came to stand close to the old man.

"Who are those men?" he asked, his voice little more than a whisper.

Malachi glanced over his shoulder.

"Don't look," hissed Calvin. "Don't make it obvious."

Malachi turned back to him, sober. "Why, them's the men what was waiting at the dock for pickup this mornin'. I got there late meself, on account of I had to do me prayers. Got a missus in the house—begging your pardon—but she ain't my wife on account of she won't marry no seafaring man. 'Taint good Christian living, but I'm a fellow what hates a cold bed. So I always goes to see the priest 'fore I shove off."

He winked at Calvin. "I'm guessing they was larking, then?"

Calvin shook his head, confused. Malachi leaned in.

"I asked them boys what they was there for. Said they was the new crew, on account you fired the old 'uns and replaced 'em with more experience."

Calvin felt a chill. He'd made no such change. Then it occurred to him that this might very well be some interference from Custis. "*I trust your judgment implicitly*," he heard his father say. Indeed. Had Custis put a tail on him, and then vetoed his hires? The thought boiled his blood. On the other hand, he almost hoped it was true. If not, then the situation was rather serious. Here they were, a rich man and his son, out in an expensive new boat well past civilization. Past where the militia boats patrolled the seas. There was another loud clatter from above.

Calvin stared up at a second ugly bird. Evidently it had just alighted—collided with the yardarm, rather—and it dangled from the yard by one long claw, scrambling to right itself.

"Are those … vultures?" muttered Calvin.

"Aye," said Malachi. "Cliff vultures."

"Oh. I didn't think that type flew," said the boy.

Malachi took a deep breath, then seemed to speak from a place in his belly with no air in it. "Ye'd be almost right. But we're not far from those low hanging cliffs yonder, and they'll glide if they've a strong enough reason."

The old man swallowed hard, his Adam's apple seeming to claw against the mottled skin of his throat. Calvin looked aft and saw that three of the deckhands were watching Malachi and him. *There ought to be one more*, he thought.

"Please excuse me," he said.

He crossed the main deck as quickly as he dared; as casually as he could manage. A tall, swarthy fellow leaned against the main mast with his arms crossed, and a bit of chaw in his cheek. Two others, a stout bulldog with red hair and short, thick arms, and a dark-haired sailor who might have been the bulldog's fraternal twin, watched him pass. Calvin felt their eyes on his back. He continued toward the stern and pretended not to hear the splash of tobacco spit on the deck several paces behind him.

He ascended to the quarterdeck, hoping to get in a private word with Custis. His father was still embroiled in an argument with the Africhi sailing instructor. Custis was insisting on shutting the engine off, and unfurling the sails. The instructor didn't like the easterly winds whipping toward the cliffs.

"Dammit, man, I'll just move the boat out a mile," said Custis.

"Even so," said the instructor, shaking his head, "you'll find she's not so easy to control without the engine, long as that wind keeps driving, anyway. Wait a bit."

"I hired you to teach me to sail. So teach me."

"I will, sir," replied the instructor, "when the wind dies down."

Calvin stared at his father, hoping to get his attention. He knew that interrupting this "negotiation" would do nothing to improve Custis' temper. Custis made no movement to acknowledge him, so Calvin waved Mr. Green over to his side. The footman came wordlessly, and leaned in.

"Don't look now," whispered Calvin. "But something may be wrong with the crew. Make some pretense for meeting us in the officer's quarters. Are you armed?"

Mr. Green did not look up but rubbed his chin thoughtfully.

"Why yes, sir," he said, just loudly enough to be heard. "I believe I have the necessary ingredients. Would your father like some too?"

"Perhaps you could ask him for me," said Calvin, knowing that the two had certain signals and passwords of their own.

"Certainly," said Mr. Green.

Green walked over to his master and stood like a soldier at attention. Custis did not immediately acknowledge him but pointed his finger at the instructor.

"Go down and do it, or I'll do it myself, and you won't be paid a copper dime!"

The instructor scowled. "Tell the hands to do it. I won't be a party to your foolishness. And I'd take you to court to recover my fee. I don't care who you are back in Mercantus."

Custis laughed. "What sort of counsel do you retain in Mercantus? I could make you some good recommendations. I know all the good lawyers there. And all the arbiters. *All* of them."

The instructor shook his head, disgusted.

"Rich fool," he said, at length. "It's your ship. Your funeral. But if you sink her, I reckon I'll take that dinghy for my pay."

Custis laughed again. "You're welcome to it. Welcome to row off now if you'd like. Just go down and shut off the engines first."

"What sort of man buys a ship and doesn't know how to operate it himself?"

"A man who can afford to bring the instructor along, though, evidently, he hired the wrong one. Now do as you were told, or else take that dinghy and get out of my sight."

The instructor scowled, but walked away, defeated. He skulked toward the companionway that led down to the engine room. Custis glared after him.

"Sir," said Mr. Green.

Custis didn't respond.

"Sir—"

"What is it, Green!"

"I'm sure you must be hungry, considering the time and season."

Custis turned to him, then noticed Calvin.

"Time and season, you say?"

Green nodded.

"Is it so late already?" he muttered.

"Yes," said Green, looking at him meaningfully. "Let's retire to the quarters, you, Calvin, and me."

Custis' eyes flitted cautiously toward the deck, then back to Green.

"Very well, let's—"

He was interrupted by a shout from below. They heard the sounds of scuffling, and then a terrible, primal scream that couldn't be mistaken for anything but what it was. As the three of them stared, several more anguished noises floated up from the engine room. Calvin glanced quickly at the main deck. In the faces of those deckhands, he registered no surprise. Time seemed to stop. Presently, a dark hand appeared on the ladder. It was followed by its mate, stained scarlet. As the instructor climbed up onto the deck, his whole body seemed to stutter. He stumbled forward, dragging one foot at a time, face distorted in agony, arms bent and reaching futilely behind him.

"What is it man!" snarled Custis. "The engine's still on."

The sailing instructor flashed him a hateful look, fell forward, and landed at Custis' feet. A knife protruded from his back.

Mr. Green did not wait. Grabbing Custis with one arm and Calvin with the other, he dragged his masters toward the captain's quarters. It was well that he did, for though the fear of death was thick on Calvin, he could not make himself move. Instead, the boy stared out upon the false crew, and then past them, at the two skiffs he'd taken to be whalers. The deck crew surged forward. The skiffs now sped towards the yacht.

Green hauled them into the captain's quarters, slammed the door, and barred it. He went to a cabinet, removed rifles, and began methodically checking and loading them. Secure from immediate harm, Custis turned in fury.

"Pirates?" he said. "They think they can steal my ship!"

"They can, sir," said Mr. Green, calmly preparing the guns. "It's five to three."

Custis spat and turned on Calvin. "*You* hired these men."

"No, Dad," whispered Calvin. "Only one of them. I don't know where the others came from."

Custis shook his head.

"Dad," insisted Calvin. "The old sailor told me that the other men I hired didn't show up this morning. These men did instead. We've been had."

Despite this revelation, Custis seemed on the verge of making some biting comment, when Green intervened. The footman placed a rifle in each of their hands and spoke calmly to Calvin.

"You say the old one isn't one of them?"

Calvin nodded. Mr. Green considered.

"Then our odds are much better. If we can get him up here, we might make a stand."

Custis shook his head. "Fighting is too risky. These wretches are after money. Get one of them to come to the door, and I'll make a better offer. Then, when we're well enough away, I'll have them found and brought to justice."

Mr. Green looked at his master and smiled sadly. "I think not, sir. These men certainly wish to be paid, and handsomely, but not all pirates are of the same sort. These read their target, anticipated his plans, and waited patiently for the correct moment to strike. They won't be bought off, sir."

Custis looked for a moment as if he might protest, but finally shook his head. "Well, you would know. Very well. But let's think this through. They killed that old Africhi shark before he could shut the engine off."

Green nodded.

"If I can turn the ship around," continued Custis, "and drive her back toward the Clover while you two keep them pinned down, then we should be able to make it into safer waters. We'll send up a flare and let the militia take care of them."

"It's the only option," agreed Green.

"But what about the other ships?" asked Calvin.

Both men looked at him.

"Two small skiffs are also headed this way," he muttered.

Custis cursed and looked at Green. "Then we'd better move now."

As he was speaking, something struck the heavy door with tremendous force. Blow followed blow, and the gleaming edge of an ax-head made its brief appearance through the splintered wood. Mr. Green settled the rifle stock into his shoulder and glanced at the others.

"Ready?"

Calvin and his father nodded.

"Fire!"

They sent a volley through the door. There were muffled cries, and the sounds of scrambling bodies.

"Now!" said Green, "while they're on the back foot."

He ran to the door and threw back the bar. When Green pulled on the door, the corpse of a man fell in across the threshold. Green raised his rifle and fired again.

"They're on the run!" he shouted. "Pour out now!"

They scrambled forward, and immediately came under fire. Custis and Green dove to the ground, but Calvin slipped back into the cabin. He looked around, thinking. The pirates must have smuggled a store of guns onto the boat. That explained the missing deckhand. Perhaps the instructor had caught him below in the act of collecting the weapons. If they were to have any chance, they'd need a barrier. Calvin saw the heavy table in the captain's quarters. He dragged the dead pirate from the doorway, then went to the table, turned it over, and began sliding it toward the cabin door.

"Green," he shouted. "Cover me!"

Two shots rang out from the quarterdeck and were answered from below. Calvin began to work the table through the open door. Snatching up his rifle, he walked in a crouch beside the table, turning the corner, then edging the table out inch-by-inch until he'd positioned it across the front of the raised quarterdeck.

"Good work, boy!" shouted Green.

He fired another shot, then belly-crawled behind the barrier.

"We have to lay cover for your father," said Green, soberly. "They're keeping out of sight, but they'll pop out to shoot. With more on the way, we'll have to kill these men now if we can. Can you do it?"

Calvin nodded.

"Right then," said Green.

He swiveled up to his haunches, and was about to fire, when a bullet whizzed over his head. He ducked down a moment, then fired back.

"Keep it up boy!"

Calvin nodded, and imitated Green's method. Meanwhile, Custis was at the wheel, crouching behind it, turning the ship without standing so as not to make himself a target. Now he banked hard to starboard, away from the cliff walls, and into the wind. It was a taxing maneuver, better suited to smaller ships, and the yacht's engines whined with the effort. The boat lilted at a steep angle, and Calvin braced himself to avoid sliding. At least the mutineers would be in no better shape. Yet, as the boat banked, Calvin saw how close to overtaking them were the two pirate skiffs.

"Dammit. They don't even need to outshoot us," said Calvin.

"We could use that other man," muttered Green. "Do you see him?"

Calvin looked out for as long as he dared. Malachi was nowhere in sight. Perhaps the pirates had already dealt with him. He shook his head.

"Call him, then," said Green.

Calvin nodded, grateful that he'd learned the man's name.

"Malachi!" he began to shout. "Malachi! Up here, man! We need you!"

He peered back around the table. The hijackers, at least, had heard his cry. One emerged from the forward companionway, evidently looking for the old sailor. Green shot him in the head. The man dropped to the deck and blood poured from his skull, and began tracing erratic, semi-circular patterns, as the ship rocked to the chop of the sea. Calvin had never seen a man shot in the head. He hadn't known that the human skullcap, hit just right, could slide off like a hemisphere of onion. Green punched him in the shoulder.

"Come back, sir!" he said. "Call for that man!"

Calvin shook himself and cried out for Malachi. As the ship came out of the bank, righting itself, the table slid the other way across the quarterdeck, and Calvin and Green scrambled to stay behind it. There was a loud cry from midships, and Calvin thought the voice was Malachi's. Gathering his courage, he set his rifle over the table and prepared to lay cover. Malachi crawled out of the dinghy where he'd been hiding, and scuttled aft like a spider, looking up toward the quarterdeck with pleading eyes. The red-haired bulldog popped out of a companionway and trained his rifle on the old man's back. Calvin had a clear shot. He aimed, and meant to pull, but froze as if stricken by some ill-timed palsy. The villain's fiery red hair was the same color as Calvin's, and in a strange unreality, it was as if he were killing himself.

A shot ripped through the bulldog's thick throat, and Calvin knew that Green had intervened. The footman shook him sternly.

"You've got to fire when you've got a shot!" barked Green.

Calvin nodded, ashamed.

"Never mind," said Green. "They're upon us."

Calvin turned around. The two skiffs had reached the stern of the boat, and half a dozen grappling hooks already perched along the aft gunwales like the sinister metal cousins of the birds on the top yard. Malachi tramped up the quarterdeck ladder, then crawled behind the table with Calvin and Green.

"Hiya, shirs—"

"—Quiet!" said Green, passing him the third rifle. "We've killed two men, but there's two more on the deck, or below it. I'll cover this way, while you pick off the boarders. Don't be afraid. They'll be vulnerable as they come over."

Calvin stared at Green, then at the grappling hooks. Never before had the boy felt seasick, but the thought of killing men at close range—when he could see their faces—made him ill.

"It's your father's life or theirs," said Green. "Don't think about it. Do what needs to be done. I'll help as I can."

Calvin put his back to the table, and raised the rifle, waiting. He looked over at Malachi. The old man was grinning. Calvin's father stood gripping the wheel with his back to the stern of this ship. He glanced at Calvin once, asking with his eyes whether the boy would cover his unprotected flank. Calvin nodded and steeled himself.

As the ship cleared the southeastern corner of Bethany and rounded toward the Crescent, the first boarder came over the gunwale. Calvin fired. The shot somehow went wide, but a second shot from Malachi dropped the man.

"What'd I tell you 'bout da Powers, boy?" said Malachi, grinning. "Betcha wish ye'd minded them now!"

Another man scaled the ship's stern wall. Calvin aimed, and this time hit him center-mass. His man cried out and fell backward into dark waters. Calvin thought it strange that even murderers cried foul in their last moments, as if the whole world were a trick being played upon them.

"'Taint too late, boy," said Malachi. "Ye can shtill pray. Da Powers'll listen."

Three men, daggers in their teeth, came over at once, cleared the gunwale, and charged forward. Calvin shot the one who went straight for Custis. Malachi knee-capped a second, but the shortest of the three passed through. Malachi turned the gun on him, but not quickly enough to stop the man from snatching the knife from his teeth and flinging it. As his shot tore open the pirate's belly, the pirate's knife entered Malachi's body between chest and shoulder, plunging to its hilt, and pinning him to the table. At the same moment, the remaining deck hands struck from behind. One leapt over the table and grabbed Green around the throat, while the other popped up from the control room ladder.

Green's man choked him with one arm and pierced downward with a marlinspike. The footman somehow caught the wrist driving the blade and turned it away. He threw his head back into his attacker's, then flipped him over his back, driving the marlinspike into the man's throat just as his body slapped the deck. But while Green struggled, the man from the hold was already on Calvin. Though Calvin had managed to shoot him in the leg, the man struck him across the head with the butt of his rifle. Now he held him down, pressing the gun across Calvin's throat.

"Cal! Green, help him!"

Calvin heard his father's voice, but already his head was going fuzzy. There were savage cries around, and a flash of color as Custis fired a desperate flair into the sky.

"Pray, boy!" cried Malachi, pinned like a moth. "Pray 'an da Powers'll hear!"

Calvin closed his eyes. Presently, the pressure left his throat, and he knew that Green had come to rescue him after all. But it was hopeless. Swarms of men now came over the gunwale, and their whooping, triumphant laughter told him all was lost.

Green scooped him off the deck and cradled him in his lap. Calvin's head was still fuzzy from being choked, and his brain throbbed against his skull. Custis was grabbed and flung down beside them.

"Shoot 'em now?" said one of the boarders.

"No," said a new voice.

They looked up at a very tall man. He was neatly groomed, and, unlike his colleagues, dressed in the manner of a militia officer. The patch on his shoulder was a mockery of militia sigils, a grinning death's head with a human scalp in its teeth. He squatted down beside them, long cruel fingers hanging like talons over his knees.

"You put up a fight," he said. "I like that. Makes the job more interesting. What do you think: should I kill you all, or hold one for ransom?"

When no one answered, he sighed.

"Name's Zeb," he said. "You killed some of my men. I can't hold that against you. But the battle is done. Your fine new ship is now mine, and the militia are too far off to help. But I asked you a question. If you're going to be rude, it won't go so well for you."

Custis began to speak, ignoring Mr. Green, who emphatically shook his head.

"This is my ship," said Custis. "You've got no right to it."

Zeb smiled. "Oh, I disagree. Right of conquest."

"There's no such thing!"

"Says who?" laughed Zeb. "Suits in the cities? But they're over there, and you're here. On *my* ship. Under my thumb."

"What do you want, then?" spat Custis. "If you were going to kill us, you'd have done so already. Name your price. I can pay."

Zeb sat himself down on the blood-stained deck and began to laugh. Mr. Green slowly shook his head.

"Ain't that just like a stiff?" said Zeb, glancing up at his men.

They stood in a loose circle around the captives, leering down and laughing.

"All that money makes you feel powerful," continued Zeb, whose face had gone serious. "Makes you forget that you're only a man, and that you can't change one hair upon your head. But *I* can change it, sir. I can make it a muddy red."

He spat on the deck and called out to his men. "Bind 'em and get 'em on their feet! One of you go down, and shut the engine off, and drop an anchor. We don't want this beauty getting into the *wrong hands*."

There was another round of laughter, and the rough mob descended on them. Their hands were bound behind them with a thin cord that cut into flesh. The three of them were backed up against the bulkhead of the cabin. Calvin looked out and saw that they were again before the Crescent. The two pirate skiffs were lashed to the yacht. The ship's engines went quiet. The anchor spun free. The game was finished.

He risked a glance toward Malachi. The old man was still pinned by the shoulder against the table, and his wound bled profusely, forming a thick pool around him. Calvin supposed he was near dead by now, but the wily fellow, as if he knew he were being watched, opened and closed one eye, and mouthed a single word at Calvin. Calvin looked away, his gaze falling on the distant monastery. It floated above the gray cliffs, still shrouded in fog, staring down on him with impotent majesty.

Presently, he became aware that Zeb was also staring at him. The pirate smiled.

"How old are you, boy?"

"Don't answer him!" snapped Custis.

Zeb winked at a man, who promptly kicked Custis in the stomach. Calvin's father leaned over, wheezing. Zeb looked back at Calvin, eyebrow raised in a question.

"Fifteen," said Calvin.

Zeb smiled and looked at the sky ruefully. "Well, that was my age when I first went to sea. What's your name, son?"

Calvin looked uncertainly at Mr. Green. Zeb grinned and struck him hard across the face.

"I didn't ask the help, boy, I asked you! Your butler won't be cleaning up for you this time. He and Daddy are going to where the little fishies swim. But I like your face. Reminds me of myself, a long time ago."

Calvin closed his eyes, and his lips moved silently. Zeb leaned in.

"What's that, son? I can't hear you."

The boy looked up. "Please don't let my … please don't kill my father."

Zeb shrugged. "Well … that all depends."

"On what," said Calvin.

"On whether you want to join up. We need young recruits, and I don't particularly like killing boys."

Calvin nodded slowly. "I'll do it."

Zeb slapped him on the back. "That's a good boy."

He craned his long neck around, looking up at his men. "Get these two fellows comfortable."

He glanced at Malachi. "And we'll save grandfather for keelhauling. I can't abide a traitorous seaman!"

Zeb's men cheered approvingly. They dragged Custis and Mr. Green across the quarterdeck, lifted them painfully by their bound elbows, and sat them down on the stern gunwale. Calvin stared wide-eyed.

"But … you said if I joined up that—"

"—I wouldn't kill your father," said Zeb. "That's right. You're going to kill him."

He dragged Calvin to his feet and cut his bonds. Zeb extended an open palm toward the sky, and someone slapped a rifle down in it. His fingers closed like a trap on the long black barrel. He held it out to Calvin.

"Take it, boy."

Calvin shook his head.

"Take it, or we'll keelhaul the lot of you, then kill you anyway."

"I can't!" cried Calvin.

"You ever seen a man keel-hauled, boy? Trust me, this way's gentle."

Calvin found himself taking the rifle. He hadn't reached for it; not consciously. Now he glanced quickly around, and then at Mr. Green. In that brief look, he counted ten men on deck. Not one of them knew mercy. He looked at Green, at his father, and wondered if, after it was done, he would become like these vicious men. With shaking hands, he raised the rifle to his shoulder, and pointed it at the footman.

"I'm sorry, Green," he said.

The footman nodded. There was neither judgment nor fear in his eyes. Calvin put his finger on the trigger, then turned, aimed the rifle at Zeb, and pulled. The hammer clacked down, but there was no report.

Zeb's grin seemed to stretch from ear-to-ear.

"You didn't think I'd be so foolish, did you boy?"

Calvin went cold, all the blood rushing out of his face and hands, and fleeing to the bottom of his feet, as far as it could go from Zeb's devilish smile. In that moment, evil—a mere abstraction till then; a fairy-tale trope—leered down at him in living color. He looked away, unable to endure its terrible glance. Behind Zeb rose the expanse of the Crescent, shrouded in an eddy of white mist, like the obscure, arbitrary will of an indifferent god. High above the sea, the monks' windmills turned behind the clouds, aloof as angels. Yet Malachi's words echoed in Calvin's mind.

"You know what?" said Zeb. "I don't think we'll be hiring you after all."

"Go to hell," muttered Calvin.

"Maybe," said Zeb. "But later. A little la—"

Zeb's face lurched forward, and his body followed. He fell limply into Calvin's arms, knocking the rifle out of his hands, and then rolling sideways as Calvin leapt away. Only now, from the misty Crescent, did the gunshot's report sound in their ears, and whether it was followed by many more, or only echoed off those high cliff walls, none could say.

The whole company of pirates turned in unison, and those with rifles fired wildly into the mist. The Crescent ate their wild shots and returned its own. Another man fell to the deck clutching his throat.

"Doomed!" cried Malachi, pinned to the table. "Yer doomed! You oo'd shed blood in an 'oly place! The fiends are comin' fer ya! Already yer captain's speeding tor the depths!"

Calvin stood statue-still. The pirates looked around madly, cursing, and crossing themselves, their eyes drawn upwards toward the slow white arms of the giants over Crescent Bay.

"Well, dammit if I ain't seen enough!" said one.

He threw his weapon down and shook upraised palms at the misty bay in a plea for mercy, before running toward the stern wall, and clambering over toward the waiting skiffs. Another followed, and another, until only five men remained.

"C'mon, mates!" pleaded a ghoulish man with one eye and one leg. "Neither angels nor demons fire guns! Stand and fight—AAIEH!!"

He was struck in the chest and shoulder at the same time. As he crumpled to the deck, his last comrades threw down their weapons and fled. The abandoned man clambered up onto one foot, looked around madly, then stumbled to the gunwale and threw himself over. There was shouting below as the two skiffs detached themselves and raised their sails.

Green and Custis dropped to the deck, eager to be out of sight of the fleeing pirates. Calvin wandered over in a daze. He bent down and cut their bonds and helped his father to his feet. Malachi cackled behind them, but the three men looked silently into the bay.

"What the hell was that?" whispered Custis, finally breaking the silence.

Green frowned. "Not ghosts, I think. But monks don't shed blood. Even if they did, no one could make those shots from up on those cliffs."

He nodded up at the high monastery, which still seemed to float on a cloud. Then, out of the fog, came the white sails of another ship. It was slightly larger than the pirate skiffs, but not by much. A bearded man leaned against the pulpit rails holding a rifle. Beside him was another, an older fellow whose demeanor marked him immediately as a butler or footman. As the ship banked, and came up alongside their own, Calvin saw a young man at the helm. His wild black curls fluttered in the breeze. Beside the boy, and also armed, stood a woman whose dark hair and shapely face marked her out as his mother. All four rescuers were clad in black, like a deputation from the Grim Reaper. Then it struck Calvin that this was a family in mourning.

"Permission to come aboard!" cried a voice from below.

Custis looked at Green. The latter slowly nodded.

"Permission granted," answered Calvin's father.

A hooked ladder was fixed over the gunwale. The bearded man came first, followed by the butler, and finally the boy. The bearded man's face was kind but grave, like one who has suffered much, yet kept his hope. He offered his hand to Custis.

"Michael Tredder," he said.

"Custis Marks," said Calvin's father, taking the man's hand. "Thank you for saving our lives."

A round of introductions followed. Calvin was pleased to find that the young man was his own age. Indeed, this family was like a dark mirror of his, though Calvin's own mother had passed away while he was still a boy. Still, he found himself wishing that the woman on the boat had also come aboard. The brief glimpse he'd caught of her face reminded him of Melania, even if his mother's hair, according to a child's memory, had had tints of scarlet.

"Damned lucky you were there!" said Custis to Michael. "What were you doing in the bay?"

"Visiting friends," said Michael, after a pause.

As the two men talked, Calvin suddenly remembered the last member of their party. He looked over and saw Malachi still pinned to the table. There was so much blood beneath and around his aged body, as if someone had emptied a wine barrel onto a pile of old rags.

"God, Malachi! I'm sorry!"

The old brown sailor did not respond. His head slumped down toward his chest, and the left side of his body hung as well, dragging at the wound on his right side.

"Malachi," hissed Calvin, slapping him about the cheeks. "Dammit, man, wake up!"

So much blood was pooled around the table that Calvin was sure the man was doomed, but at last the old fellow stirred and lifted his head.

"Get this pin outta me shoulder?" he slurred.

Calvin nodded and grabbed the dagger's pommel. Try as he might, he could not pull it free. Malachi winced at his efforts, but the pain, at least, was keeping him awake.

"Can I help?"

It was the young man. Calvin nodded and moved aside. The dark-haired boy closed his hand around the pommel and drew it out swiftly. In almost the same motion, he caught the old man under the armpits and laid him out on the deck.

Malachi opened his eyes and smiled in gratitude. His head rolled to face Calvin's.

"Didja do it, boy?"

Calvin stared tight-lipped, and pretended not to understand. Malachi sighed.

"I ain't long fer this world, young master. Too much a' me's on the deck already, I figure. Give an old man comfort. Didja pray?"

Calvin did not answer.

"Jis before tings turned," pressed the old man. "I saw ye. Didja tell the Powers?"

Calvin opened his mouth to speak, then shut it. The dark-haired boy looked at him curiously. Calvin took Malachi's hand and squeezed it. He turned to the dark-haired boy.

"Let me have a moment alone with him," he said.

The young man nodded, and walked away. Calvin crouched close to Malachi and kept his voice low.

"Thank you for what you did," he said. "I'd say you scared the hell out of them."

Malachi laughed, then began to cough. "Aye. Sailors is a believing lot. Pirates most of all—on account a guilt. But did ya? Tell me, boy. I feels the long sleep comin' on. I don't feel no warmth coming from the other side. Help an old man's faith. Didn't ya pray?"

Calvin clenched his jaw.

"Didn't ya, boy? Say it for an old sinner's sake."

Calvin said nothing. Malachi's face twisted in agony.

"At least a bit of verse then? Somethin' what gives a dying man hope."

Calvin shook his head. "I can't. I don't know any…"

He stopped, considering. Almost, he began to speak, but thought better. Malachi squeezed his hand once, very hard, before his grip began to slacken. For the last time, he opened his eyes wide.

"Don't look … a miracle in the mouth … boy," muttered the brown old sailor. "Ya don't really think … it all depends on you?"

Calvin stared into his eyes and tried to answer. Presently, he became aware that, though the eyes still stared in question, the intention behind them was gone. The old rough hand went limp. Malachi breathed out and did not draw again. Calvin reached over and closed his eyes. For a time, he sat alone.

"A verse," he said at last. "Now that it won't trouble you, old man: It matters not how straight the gate. How charged with punishments the scroll."

He stood and walked away from the man. Now leaning on the starboard rail, he scrutinized the churning windmill arms, with an indifference to match theirs. He did not consider—could not; *would* not—what desperate words he'd flung their way only minutes prior. Already, he'd begun to forget, as if it had been a dream, for he, like them, was a thing of wheels and gears, and only what he understood was real for him. He would not surrender meaning to the mist.

"I am the master of my fate," he said to the white watchers. "I am the captain of my soul."

RILEY'S GAME

"So, why's he wearing a suit?"

Specialist Jenna Bradley leaned down until her faceplate touched Riley's. The man didn't look dead, but merely caught napping in the middle of his shift. His body was strapped in, and it leaned forward, balanced on the bend of an outstretched arm whose gloved fingers, splayed beside the keyboard, reminded her of a landing strut.

Bradley turned around and repeated the question for the two mission specialists. Rick Doski opened his hands in a shrug. Amen Gannet just frowned.

"Life support is good," offered the rookie, Gannet.

"He didn't seem to think so," said Bradley.

Aside from the rigidity that held him in that awkward posture, Preston Riley could have been some incorruptible saint. There was no bloating nor obvious decomposition, perhaps because the suit was designed to flash-freeze its wearer for proper burial. He didn't look frozen, but then Bradley had never seen that happen in real life. In her ten years working for Orecorp, "casualty" had always been a euphemism for "spaced". But there was *something* on his skin, and it sure as hell wasn't ice.

Bradley looked around warily, more concerned now about what she couldn't see than what she could. Riley's display screen went to sleep, and she woke it up. It seemed he'd spent his last moments tapping out the same message.

APPROACH. APPROACH. -APPROACH.

An odd thing to say, under any circumstances. Odder still that he'd kept typing it instead of just setting up one message to repeat. Bradley scrolled up though the log and found that the word was often misspelled.

APPROACH. APPROACH. DAPPROACH. -APPROACH.

And, further up:

DOAPPROACH. NPPROACH. OAPPROACH. APPROACH. -APPROACH.

Gannet walked around the other side of the prone Riley and began running more systems checks. He was the properly educated type—young, just out of Uni—and he oozed the charming expectation that everything fit into a system. And well he might; after all, the many lights blinking inside *Hector 4*'s small escape shuttle made it a tiny cosmos, a bubble of universe that had shrunk down to contain the four of them. But the shuttle's floor, ceiling, and bulwarks, were coated with a thin blue venation, barely visible except when viewed head on. The same material tainted the skin on Riley's face.

"It looks like we're going to be here a while," said Gannet. "Shuttle's got plenty of air. Let's rest the gear."

He meant take off their suits. Miner's suits were dexterous, but still too bulky for easy movement in close quarters.

"Leave 'em on," said Bradley.

Gannet, slightly miffed, slowly removed his fingers from his helmet clasps, and gently propelled himself toward another console. Bradley heard the beep of a DM inside her suit.

"Yeah?"

"What do you think?" said Doski.

"Don't know," she replied. "He was alive when he got here. Something in this shuttle killed him. Maybe he brought it with him from Den."

Doski nodded.

RESCUE PARTY, REPORT ON YOUR STATUS. FARFINDER, OVER, said Captain Meson on the general com.

Bradley hesitated, then bit her personal com. "Bradley here. Riley is gone. Life support seems good, but we're playing it safe. Suggest you stay put for now. Bradley, over."

She returned to the words on the screen and reviewed the facts in her mind. *Hector 4* had disappeared while investigating "Den", DNN-1336, that was; a small, forested moon of the lifeless DNN-1337. Habitable planetoids being at a premium in the explored universe, only a handful of higher-ups in Orecorp even knew of Den's existence. Naturally, *Hector*'s last tight beam before descent had been heavily encrypted, making interception from their competitors basically impossible. Riley's messages, also encrypted, had begun three days after that.

Now, a year later, *Farfinder* had arrived to find Riley's shuttle in a stable orbit. They'd got nothing when they pinged *Hector 4* itself, but the ship would have had to be functional to fire an escape shuttle while grounded. Had it self-destructed after that, or had it gone rogue, perhaps defecting to one of Orecorp's rivals? The latter seemed unlikely. According to their briefing, Orecorp hadn't even known Den was a living planet until *Hector 4* found it and told them so. The bonus for discovering living worlds was already enough to retire every soul on board, and it would have made no sense to spill the beans to Orecorp if treachery had been on the table. That left a desperate escape from the surface as the only plausible scenario.

APPROACH. DNPROHCH. -APPROACH. Jenna spun the pieces around in her mind like the colored hexagons on a Harley Sphere. Why hadn't Riley at least made a start toward Saxon Gate? Was he infected with something? The blue growth: that would be a reason to stay put, but then why the plain invitation instead of a stark warning? The general com squealed again.

FARFINDER TO RESCUE PARTY: WHAT'S THE SITUATION DOWN THERE? IS RILEY ALIVE OR DEAD? OVER.

With a sinking feeling, Bradley turned to look at the others. "Try hailing them again."

Doski did, repeating the same information about Riley and the life-support systems.

"Please confirm you read us, over," he added.

Nothing. After a very long wait, the com crackled.

FARFINDER TO RESCUE PARTY: IT SOUNDS LIKE YOU'RE IN SOME TROUBLE. WE'LL COME AND GET YOU. OVER.

Bradley bit her com on. "Negative, Farfinder! There may be a pathogen here."

Gannet looked at her with alarm, and quietly shook his head. He stared out the view port, then spoke to Bradley over his shoulder.

"In my opinion," said the schoolboy, "It's likely just some mold from Theonon that made it into the air recyclers. Anyway, he's coming for us."

She didn't bother to correct him. What was actual professional experience beside expensive book knowledge? *Farfinder* stowed its sails and pulsed toward their rescue shuttle.

RESCUE CREW, IF YOU READ US, GET BACK INTO THE RS-1 AND DETACH FROM HECTOR 4'S SHUTTLE. BRING RILEY, ALIVE OR OTHERWISE. OVER.

"Belay that," said Riley. "We're leaving him here."

"What?" said Gannet. "Disobey a direct—"

"—Do what I said," snapped Bradley.

Gannet shook his head despondently. Doski frowned at Bradley, but he shrugged, and patted Gannet on the shoulder before pushing himself toward the airlock. Meanwhile, the young specialist looked back and forth between Riley's body and the approaching ship.

"Leave him," she said, "or I leave you with him."

Gannet scowled, but he followed Doski into RS-1. Bradley took up the rear. She quietly regretted her generosity in suggesting Captain Meson send the junior engineer, rather than, say, Dr. Malcom. Unlike this green boy—probably the nephew of some Orecorp suit—Doc Mac would have grasped the danger they were in. He would have backed her, instead of dragging his feet. But Jenna soon scolded herself for caring. Were she ever to merit a command, she'd have to trust her own decisions without needing affirmation and agreement.

Back in the RS-1, Doski initiated the undocking sequence. *Farfinder* grew larger in the view port. Bradley sighed, anxious to be away from Riley's corpse and the stuff growing on the walls. Something nagged at her. Riley in orbit. The strange message. The com trouble. It formed a meaningful pattern, but she couldn't put a name to it. Then there was the little matter of her disobeying orders. Even if the captain agreed with her once he knew all the facts, he might still note her disobedience in the log. Notes like that could generate auto-inquests.

Jenna Bradley was no rebel, but she had secrets. Given the situation, she'd just have to risk discovery. They should all be quarantined, and Riley left to his eternal grave. That was the right call. Meson would *probably* see it her way. Doc Mac surely would, and he had the captain's ear. Once they were well away, she could explain it to them.

"Shuttle won't let go," said Doski.

Bradley slowly processed his words.

"What?"

"She's hearing what I say, boss, but it's like she's ignoring me."

The sullen Gannet, still smarting, looked up anxiously. The airlock doors stayed stubbornly open and stared at them like a dead eye. Through the portal, Riley could still be seen leaning forward in his chair, hard at the job of being dead. Bradley's stomach churned. As she watched *Farfinder* float toward them, the implications unspooled with mechanical finality. If they couldn't detach from Riley's shuttle, then they couldn't dock with *Farfinder*. They could only be towed. And, even if they survived going through the gates unshielded, the law strictly forbade bringing exotic contaminants back to the Theonon system. A breach like that, were it ever found out, would more than get her fired. It could bring the whole corporation down, and land them all in a prison colony. She looked at Rick, and the veteran's grave expression told her he'd been having similar thoughts.

RESCUE PARTY said the captain *WHY HAVEN'T YOU DETACHED FROM HECTOR 4'S SHUTTLE? OVER.*

Rick Doski shook his head. "Should I try again?"

"Might as well," muttered Bradley.

"*Farfinder*," said Doski, "this is RS-1. Do you copy? Over."

DOSKI, IT'S ABOUT DAMNED TIME! WHY'D YOU GUYS GO SILENT?

Bradley motioned to Doski, and he let her pick up the conversation.

"Captain Meson, this is Bradley. We *have* been responding, sir, but nothing's getting through. Something's sideways here. Also, we can't unclamp. Over."

There was a pause, and a series of choppy clicks, the radio equivalent of "ums" and "hmms".

IS RILEY ALIVE OR DEAD?

"Dead, sir. Possibly … possibly killed by an unknown pathogen. There's evidence of a lifeform on his person and in the shuttle. Begging your pardon, but we left him there."

She formulated her next words carefully. "Sir … if we can't dock with *Farfinder*, then you'll have to tow us. I don't know if we'll survive that. The thing is, even if we spacewalk to you, it's still a problem. Whatever killed Riley could be on us."

Gannet whirled around. "What are you trying to do?"

Doski swore at the junior engineer, and told him to stay out of it, but

Bradley caught her friend's sidelong glance. Rick had his own doubts about her read.

WE'RE NOT TOWING YOU, said Meson. *THAT'D KILL YOU SLOW. WE'LL GET YOU INSIDE, AND FIGURE THIS OUT.*

Gannet nodded triumphantly. Relief and terror danced like fire behind his eyes. This boy hadn't signed up to be a martyr.

"Thank you, Captain," said Bradley, soberly, "but how?"

INTABA SAYS BOTH SHUTTLES SHOULD FIT INSIDE THE HOLD. VALE WILL SCOOP YOU UP, AND WE'LL KEEP YOU IN THERE FOR THE VOYAGE BACK. WORST CASE SCENARIO, WE'LL DECONTAMINATE, AND HOPE FOR THE BEST, BUT THAT'S A HELL OF A LOT BETTER THAN IRRADIATION, OR LEAVING YOU HERE TO ROT FOR ANOTHER YEAR.

Bradley closed her eyes. They'd come straight from Theonon Prime on a rescue mission. She'd completely forgotten that the ore hold was empty. Plugged into *Farfinder*, quarantined in the hold, the life support systems on RS-1 might be sufficient to sustain them in the open space between jump gates. Bradley thought of Nina and fought back tears.

"Thank you, sir."

Shaking off her doubts, she followed Doski to the view port to watch the *Farfinder's* approach. At least she was confident that Vale Orissimo could pull off the tricky capture maneuver. The gunmetal-gray ship looked like a pudgy dog resting on four haunches. Those haunches were powerful thrusters, sufficient to get the mining lugger out of a planet's gravity but subtle enough to help her maneuver at sub-sail speeds. The dog crept forward, and the big ore hold opened to admit the conjoined shuttles. Because they were connected end-to-end, there'd be just a little wiggle room. Bradley had never seen a hold used this way but if Vale said she could do it, then she could. Soon *Farfinder* was on top of them. The ore hold, a black hexagon, looked too small to fit them. Bradley held her breath.

There couldn't have been more than a meter of clearance, but so smooth was Vale Orissimo's approach that the shuttle tapped the hold walls only twice before the bay doors closed and locked behind them. There was a jerk as the conjoined shuttles came under *Farfinder*'s artificial gravity. They struck the ground with a loud clang. It was a most pleasant racket.

***

Safe in *Farfinder*'s belly, Jenna Bradley stared straight ahead. She bit her tongue, a trick she had for holding back anxiety. This was too close. She'd been playing a dangerous game, and now she had serious doubts about the stakes. She made a good salary. There'd be a huge bonus for this job. She could quit, go to Agranor, and start a little farm. If they made it back.

When we make it back, Jenna promised herself, *I'm done. Probably.*

Rick noticed her, elbows on her knees and leaning against the bulwark. Bradley saw him coming over, so she did her best to look at ease. He slid down the wall and came to a rest beside her.

"You okay?"

"Of course," she scoffed. "Where's Gannet?"

"Messing around in Riley's shuttle," said Doski. "I think he's trying to prove it's perfectly safe in there."

She smiled. "Then tell him to take his helmet off."

Doski laughed. "I guess he's not *that* sure. Actually, I think he's just avoiding us."

Bradley nodded in quiet agreement.

"What really happened to Riley?" said Doski.

She shook her head. "I don't like it. There's something bad on Den."

Doski looked mildly skeptical, but he craned his head back, and stared politely at the ceiling. "Can't leave fast enough, right?"

Bradley nodded, but she couldn't summon any enthusiasm. Ever since finding Riley, a quiet fear had been growing in her mind. It was irrational, but she couldn't easily dismiss it. "God, what's taking them so long!" she snapped.

As if in answer, Captain Meson appeared on the dim display above the shuttle's console. Bradley and Doski came close so they could see him.

"Sorry for the wait. We encountered a slight problem."

"Problem?"

The word hit Bradley like stroid slag flying out of the black.

"It's nothing to worry about," assured Meson. "And we're not going to wait anymore. You three just strap in until we get moving."

"You were waiting on a tight beam from home," said Bradley. "And it didn't come."

Meson kept very still. The captain was not a tall man, but his broad shoulders and straight back lent him a confident, even imperial air. Adoni Intaba, the huge Sengari miner who'd befriended her on the voyage out, passed a few meters behind Meson's chair in the display. Even at that distance, he made the captain look small. Intaba's skin was so dark it glistened like flaked obsidian, and Jenna always had to force herself not to stare lest her attentions be misunderstood. Or worse, understood. The giant caught her gaze, and inclined his head ever-so-slightly, confirming her suspicions about the tight beam.

"It's not a problem," said Meson. "Where's Amen, by the way?"

Gannet walked up to join them.

"Great," said Meson. "One happy family. Strap in until I tell you it's safe to move around."

The screen went dark. Bradley and the others secured themselves for the coming gut-check. Vale would make a hard start with the engines at high burn before unfurling the stellar sails. If she hit Saxon Gate just right, *Farfinder* would skip through each of the subsequent gates like a well-thrown stone, and they'd adjust spin *in medio* to normalize apparent gees. Eventually, the crew wouldn't even feel the full assault on their bodies.

Bradley smiled a little. The hard burn meant the captain had taken her concerns to heart. She wouldn't need to worry about any inquest. Vale Orisimmo's silky voice came over the com:

BURN IN SIXTY, FIFTY-NINE, FIFTY-EIGHT…

Bradley checked her straps again, then made sure to pull her tongue far back from her clenched teeth. With the suit on, she wouldn't have the aid of a bite stick, nor of the drugs that rendered a hard burn more bearable. The anticipation of pain made her nervous, and suddenly she had to pee. She debated just going in the suit, but then worried she wouldn't finish before the gees hit her like a mallet.

THIRTY-SIX, THIRTY-FIVE, THIRTY-FOUR…

She checked to see if Gannet was properly secured. The boy-man's face showed every sign of stark terror. He'd probably never jumped inside a suit, and he might be worried about biting his tongue off. She quickly bit her com, and told him what to do. Gannet visibly relaxed; even smiled at her in thanks. She found herself forgiving him.

SEVENTEEN, SIXTEEN, FIFTEEN, FOURTEEN…

She really *did* have to pee, but now it was far too late. Jenna scowled, irritated that she'd have to add "bladder" to the long list of body parts to keep rigid or to relax while under heavy thrust. But at least she knew what she was doing. Even with her advice, Amen Gannet would likely shit himself, and probably break a bone. Would it be a wrist? A toe? She stifled a laugh and resisted the temptation to take bets with Doski.

TEN, NINE, EIGHT, SEVEN, SIX, FIVE…

Jenna closed her eyes, locked her molars together, and flattened her tongue against hard pallet.

TWO, ONE, BURN!

There was a colossal jerk, and the weight of the whole ship pressed down on her chest, crushing her breasts and stomach, and forcing air against her already-full bladder. Then, just as suddenly, the ship seemed to groan. Her chin snapped forward. The RS-1 struck loudly against the hold bulwarks, and only her suit's round faceplate stopped Bradley from breaking her neck.

Jenna's mouth opened in a gasp, and she lost control of her bladder after all.

Doski groaned. "What … the hell … was that?"

The shuttle floor began to shake. Bradley felt herself pushed forward against her straps, not violently, but with a steady, iron pressure. Captain Meson's voice came over the general com.

ALL HANDS ON DECK!

Gannet turned around to face her. "What's happening?" he slurred.

Bradley ignored him, and looked at Doski, her eyes asking him to verify what her senses had already made obvious.

"What's happening? What's happening!" screamed Gannet.

Doski shook his head in disbelief, then winced from the movement. He looked slowly around at the rescue shuttle's stark interior, as if recognizing for the first time how fragile it was. Gannet continued to shout his question louder and louder, as if sheer volume would force the universe to cough up answers. Doski reached out and put a hand on the younger man's shoulder.

"Burned failed, kid. We're being … pulled."

"Pulled?" sputtered the boy. "How? Where?"

Jenna Bradley shut off all her emotions lest they leave her crippled, useless in the coming struggle.

"Down," she muttered. "We're going down."

***

Under a milky white sky, countless blue-green fronds reached up from marshy soil, their tall tops swaying in the humid breeze, shuddering and twitching toward the low clouds like fingertips that beckoned noiselessly, "Come hither." Nothing moved in the thickly-grown understory, yet brambles and hedges and things like inverted roots covered the sucking ground. The soil, where it could support the mighty frond trees, was covered in a spongy film the color of bile. Elsewhere, it gave easily, as if Den were an endless swamp, a vast yellow-green stomach. Through the creamy cloud-cover, a boxy thing that could never have been born in this place came down to die in it. Dragging the enveloping clouds as it spun, the ship crashed through the frond tops, and spouted desperate blue flames. It struck the ground at an angle, and skipped through the hedges and root-things, crushing itself against the giant trees until it came to rest beneath a grove of them.

Farfinder's four burners belched smoke, but its entry heat had also boiled the moist ground. The smoke and steam curled together and climbed like a magician's rope toward the low-hanging sky. After a time, the noise of the ship's arrival died away, and *Farfinder* seemed but one more fixed item under the dark frond canopy. No birds had flown up crying to escape the ship's calamitous plunge, nor had any animal run howling in its wake. Only silence observed the fall. But the silence listened.

Does time pass without a mind to mark it? Is it then only motion? There was motion in the peristalstic squeeze of ichor through xylem and phloem. There was a constant pulsing among the tree roots and the vast fungal networks that joined them. Not far from the grove, bubbles formed and popped, beating out a strange tempo on slime-coated and bottomless pools. Even the clouds changed shape at intervals too long to be observed. But from the grove where *Farfinder* had ground to a halt, these and other anonymous turnings were once more given quality by minds that could mark their passage.

The ship lay on its back like a dead dog. Its thrusters still smoked, but the wet ground had finally overcome the heat from its entry. Its metal skin was growing cool. From *Farfinder*'s belly there came a frantic beating. The skin of its chest was torn back, and white figures spilled out in a strange birth. They clambered down, dropped carefully to the spongy ground, then climbed onto the upturned bridge. With torches and prying tools, they breached the ship's smashed hatch, and soon began pulling others from its interior. It was hard, hot work, for the bodies of the dead outnumbered the living, and few of the crew had entered this world in one piece.

One by one, they pulled the survivors out. Those who remained looked with horror on an indifferent forest, and wondered if living had really been the better fate. They inhaled foreign air into unprotected lungs. They saw the wreck of *Farfinder* and knew in their hearts that escape was near hopeless.

The survivors raised a pavilion. The bright orange tent was stretched over gray metal poles, which had to be thrust very deep to stay put in the soft ground. The tent's loud orange color, which had meant rescue back home, stuck out like blasphemy in this silent world. Already the thick white mist was dulling its brilliance to a muddy ochre. The survivors spoke in hurried whispers, unsure what creatures might be watching from under the tall trees. Meanwhile, the dead lay still.

Bradley and Doski crouched with Doc Mac beside Captain Meson. The captain was dazed, but alive. His left leg had a hairline fracture, but Malcolm had already put it in a dynacast splint. Like him, the captain's life was spared by the ship's own architecture. The bridge was centered up and away from the sides. Much of the crew—support technicians, along with *Farfinder*'s skeleton mining team who were there only because Orecorp thought they might want to do a little rock collecting on the way home—had been secured near the outer bulwarks, above the thrusters. Those sections had struck the frond trees first and dragged the forest as the ship skipped through it. Numerous tall plants and vines had wrapped themselves around the ship's arms. The engines were buckled-in, and their only escape shuttle was somewhere in that mess, mashed to powder. With such dense forest to greet them, even the hardiest of the miners had died on impact.

Bradley thought then of Adoni Intaba. She hadn't seen anyone pull him out. She rose, without much hope, leaving Doc Mac to attend to the captain.

To her surprise, she found him quickly. The ebony giant lay sprawled upon the mossy ground, a felled tree of a man. Several ugly, root-like plants had broken under his body, and their insides oozed out so that he appeared to be lying in a pool of black blood. She wondered why Intaba was here, and not trapped in the debris. Being a miner, he'd have been housed in the arms of the ship. It was a wonder that his corpse had even remained in one piece. The man was likely too big for anyone to have carried him out this far, so she could only assume he'd been flung through the breached arms when the ship ground to a stop.

Adoni's face, pleasantly chiseled, remained peaceful even now. She hadn't forgotten that it was his idea to use the ship's hold to capture the two shuttles. He'd saved their lives—though to what end she hardly knew. She'd shipped with him only two or three times, but had lately come to admire him. Partly it was the knowledge that they were both among the best in their respective classes, handpicked for this rescue mission. That made him familiar, almost a peer. Not long ago, after a nightcap, she'd even caught herself speculating on what sort of father-figure a man like Adoni would make for Nina. She hadn't known if he was single, let alone attracted to her, but she could assume most of the crew were unmarried. Nowadays, Orecorp employed only the childless. No more orphaned miners' kids to go after them in court. Not on the record, anyway.

She suddenly cursed her own selfishness. What kind of person was she to think about what the man could have been—for her—when he was lying there dead? But it wasn't just these broken castles in the air that made Jenna bitter. Intaba had seemed invincible, and Den had already managed to kill him. What were the odds, then, for the rest of them?

"Dammit," she said.

At least Doski and Meson, Vale and Dr. Malcolm, had made it out alive. She could count on them. Probability be damned, she had no choice but to believe they could escape this death-trap. Someone was waiting for her back home.

"Adoni," she said, shaking her head, "we really could have used you."

The black statue at her feet opened one eye, and then another.

"Is that a fact, ma'am?"

His voice was hoarse, but his spreading grin brought Bradley to her knees. She hugged him, hard. Adoni grunted and brought up one hulking forearm to pat her on the back.

"That hurts ma'am."

"Oh," she said, letting go. "I'm sorry. Anything … broken?"

He closed his eyes and hummed like a ship running diagnostics on itself. "Um … don't think so. My ribs are bruised. That could be from the straps."

Jenna looked over at the smashed-in sides of the ship, then back down at Adoni.

"How the *hell* did you get out?"

"Just climbed out, ma'am," he said. "After you made the hole. Figure I'm too big for you people to lift anyway. Meson had me up on the bridge, remember? I was secured in the back, near the crew quarters."

She laughed. A tear beaded up in the corner of her eye, and by instinct she tried to wipe it away. The suit blocked her.

"You gonna keep that on?" asked Adoni, reaching up to tap her faceplate.

"For now," she said. "I still think something here contaminated Riley. I don't plan on catching it."

She winced after she said it. Assuming she was right, Intaba and the others were already exposed. He gently touched the arm of her suit. "It probably got us all, then."

She looked down and saw the large rip below her elbow.

"Shit."

But if the suit was breached, then she'd already been breathing filtered air from Den for some time, rather than her own supply. She'd been too busy setting up camp to notice the rip, or the change in air quality. But in that case, there was no point putting up with the ungainly suit.

"How is it?" she said, nodding skeptically at the milky sky.

"Mmm … musty," he said, "But not too bad. When it isn't hot here, it rains hard."

"How do you know?"

He frowned at her. "Taste the air, ma'am."

She stood, nodded once to herself, and began removing the suit. As she did, she remembered her loss of control during the aborted burn.

"I've got to…" she glanced down, bashfully.

He smiled, understanding. "Come back and say hi when you're ready, ma'am."

Jenna said she would. She began marching toward *Farfinder*. Climbing inside, walking on the ceiling that was now floor, she quickly made her way to the crew quarters, where she found a locker with clean jumpsuits, and a detachable shower head that still worked. To her surprise, the stall was already wet, and she wondered who had had the time to come in and use it. Jenna lifted the laundry chute cover, saw "Orissimo" on the name label, and shook her head.

"Typical."

But there was no time for personal dislikes. Jenna thanked God that *Farfinder*'s command center still had power. She wasn't overly concerned about using up the ship's water reserves. Den clearly wasn't short on water, which they could siphon up and purify. The question of food was more vexing. Were any of the plants edible? Were there animals here? She'd seen no sign of them so far; not even insects. But there ought to be enough dry stuff to keep them while they figured it out. And, of course, fewer mouths would need feeding.

As she showered in the upside-down stall, Jenna considered the awesome duty of burying the dead. But no, that would be unthinkable. There were too many. Cremation was the only practical option, if they could get a fire hot enough to do it. There were fires still burning in the nearby woods, so perhaps they ought to act quickly. God only knew what scavengers might be hiding out there, waiting to dig up their comrades as soon as they put them into the alien ground. With these unpleasant thoughts in mind, she re-entered the bridge, as clean and fresh as was possible for a castaway. Rick Doski had joined her there, and now stood on a supply crate so that he could reach the inverted console.

"Any idea what brought us down?" she said.

"An idea, yeah," he said. "But it makes no sense."

"Well?"

He shook his head. "Computer says something on Den pulled us down."

She frowned. "Yeah, that's obvious. But if this place harbored advanced life … I mean sophisticated enough to build a gravity gate…"

Rick shrugged. He exited the diagnostic screen and began scanning the surrounding area. A structure appeared on the sweeper. Bradley squinted.

"What is that?"

Rick shrugged again. "Don't look like much, does it? Maybe a small mountain. Indications are that's where it came from. Hold on."

He kept sweeping the area, widening the arc until it was at the limits of *Farfinder*'s sensors. In a few seconds, to both of their surprise, something talked back. Doski whistled low.

"Don't know about the mountain-thing, but that's Hector. And she's still got power."

He tapped in a few more commands, and *Hector 4*'s location relative to *Farfinder* came up on the display. Without satellite data, the ship could only use radar, ladar, and whatever it had auto-scanned from orbit before its fall. The image of Den thus rendered was only partial and frayed at the edges like a treasure map.

"There be dragons," whispered Bradley, mostly to herself. "But hey, why is Hector talking now, when it wasn't before?"

"I have no idea."

Bradley chewed her lip. The situation felt eerily familiar. The wheels in her mind were turning, and she didn't like where they wanted to settle.

"Maybe somebody didn't want us to find it before," she said. "But now that we're here, it doesn't matter."

"You think it's … some kind of intelligence? Targeting us?" said Doski. "But there's no evidence of cities, or development of any kind. I mean other than the … the thing. I'm inclined to think it's something natural that we just haven't seen before."

Bradley considered a long time before answering.

"Maybe, like you said, intelligence of *some kind.* Do me a favor and look up the communication logs between Farfinder and us when we were in Riley's shuttle."

"Why Riley's shuttle?"

"Just indulge me, please."

He nodded and went to work. Rick had to pull his arms down and shake them out a few times, and she realized that reaching up to operate the console was pulling all the blood into his chest. Finally, he found what he was seeking. He let his arms rest again while he read the screen, then turned to Bradley with an incredulous frown.

"The log shows a record of all of our calls back and forth," he said, "even though Farfinder couldn't hear us when we were there. But the way the system works, if those calls went through, they should have heard us. Makes no sense."

She shook her head, disagreeing. "It makes sense, if somebody on Den interfered with those transmissions."

Doski didn't say anything to that, but he exited the screen, and went back to the scanner. She saw that he was re-processing the scanner data to try to generate a better map. He tapped the screen, and the partial map expanded in scope, though not greatly in detail. Something else appeared as an undescribed point with fuzzy edges. The map now highlighted three locations: their own, *Hector 4*'s, and this point some distance to the southwest.

"And that is?"

"Don't know," said Doski. "That's the mountain-thing I was talking about. Let's call it the Anomaly. Whatever pulled us down came from there. It's roughly hill-shaped, but it's not mountain-sized or we could see it from where we're parked."

Jenna laughed grimly at "parked", then raked her fingers through her damp hair. "A small planetoid like this can't generate enough gravity to pull us from orbit. And any technology that could, would leave its imprint on the surface. I mean, even if the … inhabitants … even if they live underground, where are the vents? The power plants? The infrastructure?"

Doski nodded but repeated himself. "Computer says we were grabbed from orbit, and dragged all the way here. But Hector's shuttle was in orbit too, and it stayed there for over a year."

"So, we *were* targeted!" said Bradley. "And Riley's shuttle was the bait!"

She wanted to sit down to think, remembered the crew chairs were all fixed to the roof, and began pacing in frustration.

"What about Hector's crew?" she said.

Doski nodded obligingly. "I mean, I can *check*. Hector's talking, so I should be able to port in remotely."

He went back to work. She watched as he accessed *Hector 4*'s systems and began to run diagnostics on them. He shook his head but kept digging around without speaking. After a few minutes passed, she became impatient.

"Hey, Rick, I'm still here."

"Sorry," he said. "I get hypnotized. So, as I suspected, nobody's alive, at least not on board, and the engines are damaged beyond repair. That's the bad news."

"What the hell is the good news?"

Doski favored her with a grim smile. "Stroid slaggers. Remote mining charges. Ship's still got two missiles in the bay, and they look intact."

"Okay," she said. "So if we can recover those, we might be able to use them against Den."

"Den?" said Rick.

"I mean whoever or whatever on Den captured Farfinder and Hector," she quickly amended.

Rick hopped down from his crate and sat on it. "Speaking of that, we don't really know that it *is* somebody. Could just as well be an unknown phenomenon, like I said … like, I don't know, a gravitational … geyser. Something weird, that flares up from time to time. I mean, the place is covered in greenery, and we haven't even seen herbivores, let alone intelligence. I think it's better to deal in what we know. There's something about a lot of tall, leaning trees that makes you feel a little paranoid. Let's just stick with facts."

"Oh, yeah," she said. "It's just the trees making me paranoid."

She came over and sat on the crate. It was so small that they had to face in different directions, like points on a compass.

"The facts are that something plucked a Venture-class mining lugger from orbit, but let its shuttle escape to lure us in too," said Bradley. "Whatever it was interfered with all the communications that could have helped us, but still let through an invitation across space. And now, if we call for help, we'll become the new Riley. A worm on a hook."

"Maybe," said Doski. "But we've got what Riley didn't have."

"Which is?"

Rick gave her a surprised, chiding look, and stamped a few times on the ground, or, rather, the ceiling.

"We've got a fifth burner. Farfinder's a third-generation Venture."

Jenna stared at him. She'd been sailing so long on the old series, she'd hardly given it a thought when Orecorp sent them out on this newer, faster rig. But it wasn't just faster. Its bridge was also a detachable skiff, with its own thruster. They could just right the thing and make a run for it. But if they tried it now, wouldn't Den just pull them back down?

"So, if we can destroy this ... anomaly, we can blast our way out of here!"

Doski laughed. "Yeah. I mean, I hope 'yeah'. Plus, we know whatever did it ain't always running. Otherwise, Riley's shuttle wouldn't have stayed up there."

Jenna leapt to her feet. Now there was real hope. But even as she rejoiced, that quiet doubt stirred inside her, and she wondered, as she had on RS-1, if it could possibly be that easy.

***

Night came quickly, then came again. Den made one rotation every six hours. DNN-1337, Den's lifeless mother planet, orbited an orange dwarf star. Barren though she was, this mother seemed to have all the madness and all the tenderness of a human mother. At times, her bulk blotted out the sun, drenching her child in an indefinite night, but at other times she also amplified the sun's yellow-orange rays off her slaty surface, extending Den's daylight past its natural three hours. In her shadow, Den starved; Den thrived.

Not until fourth light did they locate a burning site, a rocky hill that rose out of a swamp about a kilometer from camp. It was littered with dead branches, which was lucky, because they'd had a hell of a time trying to find any deadwood under the frond trees. Now they stood at a distance and watched the great cairn consume itself upon the hill. In the center of the cairn, by now crumbling to ashes, were a dozen men and six women wrapped in black sheathes. Of the dead, only Riley remained, in the hold, left unspoiled in his suit for further examination.

It seemed to Bradley that Preston Riley was one lucky bastard. Burning was no way for a miner to pass on. The destruction of disintegration was too impersonal, too much like getting spaced off a stroid. And at least then you were dying in your boots. Yet far better this than to let Den have their bodies. There was something in its spongy soil, its drooping, inquisitive branches, the erect rootlets that twitched even when there wasn't much breeze, that made the very ground seem hungry. She didn't give voice to these feelings, but she wondered if the others felt them too.

"When's next nightfall?" said the captain.

Meson stood leaning on a crutch, keeping his broken leg straight to let the dynacast do its work faster. When no one answered him, he looked sharply at Rick. Doski cleared his throat and fumbled for his data pad.

"Should be ... *should be* half an hour," he said, "but based on our location, and the turn of Den's planet, we might have lingering glow for another hour. Might. To be honest, sir, I'm still trying to get a handle on this cycle. There are irregularities, and we don't have satellite support, so—
"

Meson raised his hand to silence him. "Then we'll have to plan without it. But we'll only be going after Hector in the day cycles."

He glanced around at the others. Everyone liked Doski's plan of trying to get *Hector 4*'s intact mining charges in the hopes of destroying, or at least disrupting, whatever had pulled them down. But the Devil was in the details.

"The light's the main problem," Meson continued. "We don't have much of it in any given six-hour period, and that ship is at least eight hours hard march from here. That's assuming we don't hit an enormous swamp, or fall into a hidden cave, or get poisoned by something."

"Or eaten," offered, Vale Orisimmo.

She was smiling when she said it. Nobody laughed.

"Lieutenant," said Meson. "that's neither helpful, nor accurate. The planet doesn't appear to have any native fauna."

"Appearances can be deceiving," said the pilot, shifting her weight heavily to the other hip.

Meson frowned. Everyone knew that Vale took liberties. Sometimes, after a dangerous run, she even hit the bottle while she was still on duty. Vale did these things because she thought she could. She was that good. But they weren't hopping gates now, jump-slagging pirates, or corralling copper-rich stroids for big, big money.

"Indeed," said Meson. "For example, you *appear* to have forgotten your station. Or maybe you've been drinking something other than water. I suggest you stop talking for a bit, so I don't get the wrong impression."

She laughed, but bit her lip and turned away. That laugh bothered Bradley. "You still wanna play 'in charge', Old Man?" it seemed to say. Vale Orisimmo was temperamental, even petulant, but they'd want her fully functional to get out of this place.

"We don't know the topology," he continued. "Our map is only partial, but Hector's wreck lies about four clicks southeast of camp. The Anomaly, or gravity surge, or whatever, is about six clicks to the southwest. It'd be nice to know what the hell's there, but we'd better not get too close until we're holding the means to destroy it. That's why I've decided that we'll all make the trek to Hector together. First—"

"—I think we should split up," said Vale. "Captain," she added, seemingly as an afterthought. "You take one half. Bradley takes the other to recon the Anomaly. Save ourselves a lot of time that way."

"Vale," said the captain. "Shut up."

Malcolm, Doski, and Intaba observed the stand-off with quiet concern. Amen Gannet also looked uncomfortable, but not, it seemed to Bradley, for the same reasons. While the veterans wondered if Vale would keep escalating, the junior engineer stared wide-eyed into the surrounding alien jungle, almost pleading for the captain to change his mind. Meson flicked his gaze briefly in Gannet's direction and continued.

"I've done a fair bit of jungle hiking in my time. This terrain looks as bad as anything I've seen. That's why I'm estimating eight hours. I know that *some of you* will want to shorten our stay as much as possible. So do I. The problem is, we already have reason to believe that the Anomaly can stop us from leaving. It caught Riley. It pulled us down, and presumably Hector too. So, we need to do this right."

He tapped his wrist gauntlet, then pointed to the southeast. "We can follow Hector's beacon. We shouldn't have trouble locating it, but based on what I've seen of the terrain, I don't expect to make more than half a click per hour in daylight. There's a lot of weird terrain, and poor visibility. We're gonna take our time, and get back in one piece. With the short days, we'll have to camp once, maybe twice on the way there. Same thing on the way back. A lot can go wrong when you don't know what's in front of you. If one person gets in trouble, the whole group stands a better chance of getting him out. So that's what we're going to do."

Vale shook her head in silent protest. Bradley had her own doubts about the plan, but remained silent, knowing the captain expected her support. She glanced around to hide her unease. Doc Mac looked pensive, but Amen Gannet was white in the face. Meson studied the young man, then turned to the medic.

"Malcom," said Meson, "out with it."

"Captain," he began, "as your doctor, I have some concerns. I'd prefer to raise them in private."

"No," said Meson. "In the open. What is it?"

"Your leg, sir."

"To hell with the leg, Mac! It's in a dynacast, isn't it?"

"That's to let you walk on it if you *must.* As your doctor, I suggest staying behind with the ship. We'll need to repair the hatch anyway."

"I'm going," said the captain. "But you're right. Someone should stay behind. Since you'll insist on coming with me to fret over my leg, it's got to be … Gannet."

Gannet looked up at his captain like a prisoner just spared the gallows. So obvious was the young man's relief that it was a full two seconds before he remembered to affect disappointment.

"Are … are you sure I can't come along, sir?"

"Sorry to do this to you kid," said Meson, "but I need you to fix that hatch, and keep those life support systems running. We don't know what we're up against, or what kind of time window we'll have to blast out of here after we get the missiles."

Amen nodded vigorously, but not *too* vigorously. The captain looked away, pretending not to notice.

"Very well then. We'll prep with the daylight we have left. Then catch some sleep, all of you. We leave with the first new light."

Everyone began to shuffle away toward the ship. Everyone, that was, except Vale Orisimmo. She stayed behind under the canopy and waited until the captain had hobbled ten or twelve steps.

"Robert," she said.

Captain Meson stopped in his tracks. Planting his good leg in the soft ground, he pivoted towards her very slowly. Bradley noticed that the vein on his neck had swelled in size.

"Orisimmo, *what* is it?"

"Just a simple question, sir. I hope I don't seem disrespectf—"

"—Just spit it out!"

She nodded. "Okay, fine. Don't you find it odd that this anomaly dragged us from orbit only to plant us within a few clicks of Hector? Or that we couldn't hear Hector before, and now we can? That's a lot of coincidence. Are you sure you're not walking us into a trap, sir?"

Captain Meson broadened his shoulders. Slowly, he unclenched his hands, and Bradley saw in an instant just *why* he was captain, for the man not only heard the defiance in her tone but controlled himself enough to consider the merit in her words. He cleared his throat and spoke so that all could hear him.

"Lieutenant, if this *is* a trap, then we have no choice but to spring it."

He turned away from her, and began marching toward *Farfinder* with the same hobbling gait.

***

"Do you hear that?" said Bradley.

She came to a stop at the crest of what turned out to be just another bramble-choked ridge, one of perhaps thirty they'd had to scale and descend since first light. Indeed, the forest floor seemed to be nothing but tangled ridges, set one-after-another in an endless line. They were not high. In shape, the ridges were like long sand dunes, but instead of merely giving, as sand would, the spongy turf constantly sucked at one's feet, or else enmeshed them in the thick brush that somehow managed to grow out of the sucking soil. Indeed, the forest floor was so notional, so gummy, that the growth of any flora, let alone this busy shrub layer and the long thin trees that ribboned up everywhere, seemed a horticultural miracle. Meanwhile the upside-down root-things would sometimes twitch, making Bradley wonder if they also shifted below the soil, swimming to keep pace with the fickle ground.

Rick stopped beside Bradley and allowed himself a few deep breaths. "What? I don't hear anything."

She nodded. "That's exactly what I mean."

Meson and Doc Mac were struggling up the next green ridge. The captain looked back to make sure the others were following. Vale and Intaba were at least one crest behind Bradley. For her earlier outbursts, the captain had made Vale carry the extra water containers. Under their weight, she'd fallen into one of the swamps they'd crossed, and was now thoroughly wet and miserable. Intaba, pretending to be tired, had dropped back after this to take one of the water packs onto his own shoulders. The cursed forest ridges, sucking at their heels, and forcing them to mind their ankles on the down-climbs, also made it doubly important to keep each other in view. Yet this terrain was far better than the swamps they'd had to ford before reaching this "solid ground." Their expedition was making awful time, and they had only an hour or so till the next nightfall. Glancing behind him again, Meson frowned to see Bradley and Doski stalled, but he soon straightened his leg, and leaned against a black tree to wait for them.

"You gotta be more specific, Jenna," said Doski.

"There's nothing in the trees," whispered Bradley. "No sounds of scurrying. Nothing flapping or clicking away. Not even an insect to scatter at our approach."

"Maybe animals haven't evolved here," shrugged Doski. "Or maybe they've just got worms and bacteria and stuff like that."

She shook her head. "Yeah, but I don't believe that. There are so many available niches here. Nature abhors a vacuum. And anyway, I *feel* something. Don't you?"

He shrugged, but then looked around into the tangled darkness. Almost casually, he slipped his jamstick from its holster, and expanded it. The stick was a common miner's tool. It looked like a cross between a short spear and a bad prosthetic. The business end concealed a diamond-sharp vibrating blade that could also be expanded or retracted. Four delicate "fingers" grew from the circular housing that held the blade. These were strong enough to let a miner rip a chunk of rock from an asteroid; good for excavating hidden ores, but also quite useful for grabbing hold should one suddenly get knocked off his feet while careening through space. Doski spun the jamstick in his hand and set the blade vibrating. Each expedition member carried one, but Rick had come up through the ranks. He knew how to use his.

"Hope you're wrong," he said. "Captain gave Gannet the only gun."

She sighed. "Of course he did."

Rick smiled. "Oh, c'mon. Give the kid a break. We'll be okay with these." He spun the jamstick again, and its blade made the air ripple like water. "You're not starting to agree with Orisimmo, are you?"

She laughed. "Even when Vale and I agree, we disagree."

Doski chuckled, but nearly tagged Bradley with the blade. He grimaced and slipped it quietly back into its holster. At that moment, Vale Orisimmo crested their ridge, followed closely by the cheerful giant. Vale was breathing hard, her face a shade of red nowhere else to be seen in these woods. She squinted at them both.

"Something funny?"

Vale caught her breath and leaned rudely against Intaba. The big man did not seem to notice the added weight. Jenna felt a flash of emotion. It wasn't envy. She could never envy Vale. Perhaps she just felt sorry for Intaba having to put up with Orisimmo's bitching. All that mattered to her was getting back to Nina, getting that finder's bonus, and—maybe—getting the hell out of Orecorp.

From the next ridge, the captain waved them forward impatiently, much to the apparent dismay of Doc Mac, who looked ready to drop. It was not lost on any of them that the captain, on a bad leg, was outpacing his crew.

"Still think this is such a great plan?" crowed Vale, under her breath.

Though the comment was directed at a fluttering root-bush, Bradley knew it was meant for her.

"I follow orders," she said, trying not to put too fine a point on it.

"Yes," said Vale. "You do."

Vale hitched up her pack, and re-tightened the shoulder straps, which the heavy water cannister kept trying to loosen. It was a noisy process, and rather pitiful to watch. She was a wiry woman, tough for her size, but that was not very great. Doski suddenly held up a hand.

"Quiet a moment."

The four of them stopped dead. Bradley again felt the touch of some indefinable fear. It wasn't of the forest, as such, but of something else, something *other*; faceless. Doski crouched low. He tapped her ankle.

"Jenna," he whispered. "Move."

She'd been standing in the only clear patch on the ridge. Now she stepped aside, and watched Rick put his ear to the ground. He remained there a full minute before coming to his feet.

"What is it?" she said. "Something … living … down there?"

He shook his head. "It's funny, because now I realize I've been hearing it all along. I just didn't realize that I heard it."

Into her mind crept half-formed images of large, black, burrowing things, or worse, of minds and hearts uncanny, things wholly other, for whom light was but a passing illusion, and darkness the only solid, constant thing.

"It's water," said Doski, nodding as if to reassure himself. "Yes. Miles of it. Floods of it. Rushing just below our feet. It's everywhere."

He looked around at the oddly shaped forest floor with a new mix of wonder and unease. Vale kicked hard at the spongy moss where Doski had just been pressing his ear. It gave, becoming concave, then slowly reformed.

"Wonderful!" she scoffed, hiking up her pack once more.

She marched down the next slope ahead of them, while the heavy water containers clattered arrhythmically against her frame.

***

An hour later it was time to make camp. They found a stretch of level ground in the defile between two green ridges. It was like a valley in miniature, and the elevated ground east and west of them gave a sense of security. They'd hardly erected their three pop-up shelters, not bothering to stake them into the soft ground, when the ochre light failed entirely. The captain ordered them into their shelters, and Jenna and Vale retired for the night without saying more than a few words to each other.

Lying awake in her sleeping sack, Jenna listened for the comforting sounds of night, but none came. Vale fell asleep almost immediately. The pilot's snoring made a poor substitute for the night's missing rhythms. Between Vale's racket, and their combined, unwashed odor from the hard trek, Jenna wondered if she'd ever fall asleep. Then she thought of Nina, and sleep became impossible.

If she never returned, Nina would be worse than spaced. Alone in their apartment on Settlement C, her identity disguised lest Orecorp connect the girl to First Officer Bradley, she wouldn't even be informed if her mother disappeared. If she were lucky, she'd find out about it from news feeds. But no, this had been a secret mission. And even if Nina did learn the truth, she'd get no survivor's pension. When Amos, a plague orphan like Jenna, had died in the second wave, it had fallen on her to provide for the girl alone. She'd changed her name, concealed her daughter's existence, and tested into officer apprenticeship in Orecorp. She'd not even listed Nina on her insurance as a distant relative or favorite niece, because the company was wise to such tactics.

How long would the girl wait for her? At twelve years old, she'd have some resourcefulness, but Jenna had never been gone this long. If she left now, Nina would be halfway to fourteen when Jenna returned. There was, thought Bradley, food in the house, and credits the girl could spend, what remained of the dwindling insurance payoff from Amos. But when these ran out? At what point would the girl give her mother up for lost?

There were bad men in Settlement C. Some lived in their own tower. She'd seen their eyes following Nina as the pretty girl walked swiftly beside her mother. The Towers were a place to live only if a person had no future, or was scraping by for a better one. Who would protect Nina from the mangled men, those pock-marked creatures without hope?

It was with such thoughts as these that Jenna tormented herself until her eyes finally closed. Worries passed into troubled dreams, and these to a deep, thoughtless blackness without imagery. She didn't know she'd slept until she was suddenly roused by the captain's voice outside her tent.

"Wake up you two. Sun's out."

She looked at the time. Only three hours had passed since they'd entered the tent. Bradley forced herself to a sitting position, and saw that Vale was gone. She must have risen before reveille, perhaps to spite the captain. Bradley quickly dressed herself, rolled and stowed her gear, and crawled out into the morning sun.

The brightness was a kind of blasphemy. Every sinew and organ cried out that it was still night, but the oblivious day defied her. It occurred to Bradley that this planetoid was of little value for human settlement, unless Orecorp was planning to sell it to the Commonwealth as a high-security prison for the worst felons. Anybody living here would eventually go mad.

She threw Vale's gear onto the loamy ground and set to work disassembling the pop-up. The memory frame had to be folded just-so to get it back in the bag, which was difficult to pull off without help, at least when you were still half-asleep. She struggled for a few minutes, then lost her patience.

"Vale! Get over here!"

"I wouldn't yell," said Adoni Intaba.

He glanced around into the woods, then took hold of the far end of the frame and began folding it.

"Thanks," said Bradley, pressing down on her side.

She didn't bother asking him "Why?" He must have felt it too. If this jungle were truly without animal life, then it made up for it by seeming more aware than any forest had any business seeming.

The shelter's memory frame had to be untwisted several times, but they finally succeeded in collapsing it, and sliding it back into its tiny bag.

"Sorry, Adoni," she said. "You shouldn't have to do this. She just expects everyone to pick up her slack. Please don't let her use you today. Make *her* carry the damn water."

Intaba looked up, troubled. She wondered if she'd offended him, but the other men approached, wearing the same grave expression. Then it hit her.

"Where is Vale?" said Bradley.

Captain Meson sighed. "She wasn't in your tent? Just now?"

"No," said Bradley. "Her side was empty. All her gear is right there on the ground. Where I threw it."

The captain shook his head. "Not all of it, I'm afraid."

He bent down and lifted the backup water cannisters. He turned them over, shaking them to emphasize that they were now empty.

"Perfect," said Bradley.

She looked past them into the faceless jungle into which Vale had, evidently, fled.

"What are we going to do?" she said. "What if she gets lost or injured on the way back to the ship?"

Meson's face was hard. "Do? Nothing. When we return with the mining charges, if she's still in one piece, then I'll have something to do. I promise you that. Until then, she's on her own."

The others looked away. Bradley bit her lip, wondering what the captain *could* do. Clearly, Vale was betting on her own indispensability. Would Meson put her under lock and key, and risk making the escape flight himself? Would he make Bradley do it? He might. It was one thing to tolerate Vale mouthing off; quite another to permit open disobedience. Meson might very well judge that the risk to life was relatively better than the risk to his command, letting Vale walk all over him like that. Rick suddenly chuckled and shook his head with a low whistle.

"Hell," he said. "At least little Gannet will have some company."

He stopped laughing when he saw Meson's expression.

"Some company," spat the captain, hoisting his pack. "Let's go."

***

When Amen Gannet found that he could neither keep awake, nor remain alone outside under the orange pavilion, he resigned himself to the ship's bridge. The place was still upside down, and, despite the repairs he'd made to the hatch and air scrubbers, it still smelled vaguely of death, and cleaning solution. The air scrubbers were working fine, but the ghosts of the dead crew lingered to haunt him, not unlike those bloodstains, charred into the bulwarks, that he'd been unable to remove. At first, sleeping on the bridge had been unthinkable, but the naked night made it bearable by contrast. He couldn't name what he feared. It was just that silence, that starless sky, and the thought of closing his eyes on a world that might be watching him.

He spread his sleep sack on the flattest portion of the command module's ceiling. It was just curved enough to make him feel the bend in his spine. While the ground under the canopy had been softer, every time he'd closed his eyes a part of him had worried that the planetoid was only waiting for him to sleep so that it could swallow him whole. Better an aching back, than that. He glanced up at the locked hatch, and once more he reached out to tap the bolt rifle to his right. He sighed, and drifted off.

When he woke the first time, it was with the cold suspicion that he wasn't alone. But the sun was out again. Light seeped up from the corners of the transparent metal view port, which faced the ground, and that gave him comfort. He reached for his volume of *Foster's Scrivenings*, a small chapbook bound in real paper, which he very much treasured. A graduation gift from his father, it consisted of excerpts from before the great flight from Earth. He liked to open the volume at random, letting his eyes fall upon cryptic passages that had once held great meaning for the Ancestors. Without context, it wasn't always clear to Gannet why some had been considered valuable. Still, he found that reading slowly, "chewing the ink", Dad called it, usually left him with a general impression of burgeoning wisdom. Or else it left him utterly confused. He ran his thumb along the book's edge until it dipped in, and then he opened it and read aloud:

"And the Lord God said, Behold, the man is become as one of us, to know good and evil: and now, lest he put forth his hand, and take also of the tree of life, and eat, and live forever: Therefore, the Lord God sent him forth from the garden of Eden, to till the ground from whence he was taken. So he drove out the man; and he placed at the east of the garden of Eden Cherubim, and a flaming sword which turned every way, to keep the way of the tree of life."

Gannet frowned. Why wouldn't God want mankind to have knowledge? What exactly did the phrase mean, "to know good and evil"? He floated several possibilities, then became tired again. Whether or not it made sense, the book had done its real job. Amen closed his eyes and drifted off once more.

Amen woke a second time. Now it was pitch dark. His face was cold, and there was a thin layer of frozen perspiration where the skin of his neck met the warmth of the sleep sack. He'd forgotten to adjust the module's temperature, but nothing short of impending death, or a powerful need to hit the head, could have induced him now to leave his sack. Even behind steel, he didn't feel entirely safe from the cold dark outside. That he'd so far seen nothing out there with the power to move itself was hardly comforting. Not having seen a thing was vastly different than *seeing that there was nothing*, and that distinction—mere logic-chopping in the day—became very sharp for him under the cloak of darkness.

Amen loosened his sleep sack just enough to slip his head further into it. Bad breath be damned, he was not going to have his face freeze! It didn't hurt that being in the sack was like hiding under covers. So cocooned, he drifted off for an hour or so before the noises woke him.

Surely, it had been the patter of rain. He slipped his head out of the sack and listened. Rain was rain, wherever you were. Nothing to be afraid of. There was another sound, but that was probably a branch in the wind knocking against the upturned hold from which he and Doski and Bradley had escaped. The ship was leaning against several tall trees, and the breeze was making their limbs scrape the portion of the ship that overhung the command module. That was all.

Thunk.

A clear, clean sound. Amen Gannet sat up.

Schiff. Schiff. Thunk.

Amen Gannet stopped breathing. His knuckles found their way into his mouth. He bit without feeling. There was silence.

Pft ... Pft ... Pft. A pause. *Pft-Pft-Pft!*

Amen grabbed the bolt gun. He extricated himself from his sleeping sack in a kind of frantic, wiggling leap. Never had he been more sober; never so alert. His focus surprised him. Fear, he knew, scrambled reason, but this kind of pure terror sharpened it to a fine point. He felt every vibration above. His body, utterly wired, prepared itself for he knew not what. Rifle clutched in ready, Gannet strafed into the bridge's center, and tried not to make a sound.

Something was climbing around the outside of the ship. It was not rain. It was not a branch. It wasn't something dead, tossed and turned by the wind. It was very, very alive. He could feel that through the metal. And now it was moving down the outer hull.

Gannet tried to gather something from its weight and motion. Whatever it was walked a little, slid a little, and stopped from time to time, as if to listen. As if it knew he might also be listening. It had legs because he heard and felt their tread. It was there, above him. It was waiting.

Amen decided to come out shooting, but just before his muscles responded to the order, the living thing slipped down to the grass beside the command module. It tried the hatch—at first tentatively, then with force—but found it locked.

He heard it shuffle around on the spongy ground and move to the other side of the module. Gannet backed toward that side. He listened to the muted footfalls just beyond the thick hull. No longer sure he could even hear them, he put his ear to the wall. His heart was beating so hard, he began to wonder if he'd be able to hear anything but the noise of his own body. Worse, he began to imagine some huge, eyeless creature, too big or too awkward to open the hatch, its feelers vainly flailing on the cold metal, yet still tasting the *thump*, *thump*, *thumping* of his terror.

BANG!

Something slammed the hull. Gannet screamed, leveled the bolt gun, and fired. Immediately, he screamed again, for the bolt that struck the inner hull bounced off the super-folded steel and came back to furrow a path across his cheek. He put his hand to the wound, and it came away red. The sight of his own blood, this first taste of the worst possibilities, seemed to break a dam inside Amen's mind. In one heartbeat, he exchanged his boyish terror for a cold, killing resolve. He would burst from his enclosure and kill the loathsome thing. He was on the point of doing it when flashing colors broke in through his fugue state.

His data pad lay beside his pack, flashing a green alert. Someone had sent him a message. Meson, or Bradley, or Doski. *God in heaven, he was not alone!* Clutching the rifle, he darted over and swept up the pad. The message was indeed from Meson. He stabbed it with a trembling finger, and read:

Vale abandoned mission. Assume she's coming back your way and could arrive anytime. Try not to shoot her.

Amen sank to the floor. Vale was here! It was Vale outside, trying to get in. Probably she was in one of her sulks. No wonder she hadn't called out to him. Of course she'd have avoided seeking the rookie's help. She'd probably tried to sleep in the breached hold above, but that had been too cold. Then she'd come down here, wanting to get inside for warmth, reluctant to admit that she wasn't equipped to hack it alone. And now, of course, she'd be afraid of getting shot. It all made sense.

Now that he understood, the cold terror that had before made him strong suddenly left him, replaced by a warmer fear of what might have happened had he managed to shoot her through the hull. *Shoot the pilot!* Then they'd really call him a rookie. He'd have to go out to her and explain. She'd treat him with contempt, but what of it? He couldn't have her lying out there all night under the pavilion, cold and raging at him.

Gannet went to the hatch—he could at least take pride in the work he'd done to repair the thing—and opened it up. He stepped through, gun first, then hesitated, wondering if he should really be carrying the gun when he found her. She might think he was a lunatic, or worse, a frightened little boy playing sailor for a while, putting a notch on his resume so that a later, corporate Amen could claim he'd come up through the ranks. Never mind that he'd fixed the damned hatch and repaired the air scrubbers! She'd just laugh at him with that trademarked condescension that Vale wielded like a knife.

The decision was made considerably easier when he finally spotted her, standing under the pavilion. He put the safety on and set the rifle down against the hull.

Vale was twenty meters or more away, clothed in shadow near the far end of the outdoor shelter. She was staring back into the woods. He imagined she regretted her decision, or else was trying to convince herself that leaving the expedition had been entirely justified. He could not guess at the reasons, but people like Vale Orisimmo never admitted when they were wrong. Gannet's father was like that: proud to the end. And Amen was far from understanding the nuances of shipboard politics, especially among old hands, with many years of shared loves and hates. Amen Gannet was here—he had no illusions about the matter—because of a very different sort of politics, the kind that happened in corporate boardrooms and among well-connected families. He was not one of them. He'd not really earned his spot on this rescue mission. For all the crew knew, hell, for all *he* knew, he was little more than a spy. The others probably saw him that way. He so wanted to earn their respect.

As he drew closer, Amen was surprised at the play of shadows on Vale Orisimmo's body. He'd always thought she was a pretty woman, shapely, if in a Tomboyish way, though he'd never dared to stare at her. Now that he was approaching her, he was surprised by how flat and angular she was. From behind, she really didn't look like a woman at all. Only when he was nearly beside her, too close for the shadows to conceal her form, did the figure he'd taken to be Vale Orisimmo turn, and meet him face-to-face.

Preston Riley grabbed Amen with vice-like fingers, and smiled a big, dead smile. Amen Gannet screamed, and kept on screaming, until he lost his mind.

***

Bradley stared at the barrier, dumbstruck.

"We could try to go around," said Doski.

Captain Meson flipped open the mud-flecked cover of his gauntlet. The device gave him remote access to *Farfinder*'s brain, and so also to the map the brain had generated for Doski. The others crowded around to look at the small display. *Hector 4* was represented as a blinking orange dot on one side of some blob-like textures, but these textures gave no real indication of either the nature or the extent of the obstruction. Meson had led then confidently thus far, but clearly hadn't expected this obstacle.

A wall of long brownish tubes in dense clusters stretched thirty meters above them and as far as they could see to the left and right. It grew around and among the tall frond trees, forming a thick network, one that seemed to go back into space for quite some distance.

They'd all thought it was good fortune when the last ridge had sloped downward, becoming a relatively level plane. The plane had led them to this wall of godforsaken vegetation. Bradley wondered how the trees could tolerate such a thick infiltration without being choked. Meson looked down at his screen for a long time, considering.

"If we go around," he said, "assuming we *can* go around, the detour might take us far out of our path. Who knows what else we'll run into? This is ugly, but it's a straight shot."

"Straight shot?" said Doc Mac. "Straight into a thicket, you mean! Captain, we have no idea what this stuff is, or what kind of toxins or—"

"—A straight shot," repeated the captain. "Take out your sticks. We'll all stay together and cut our way through. Let's have two at the front to blaze the trail, and the others can cycle in when the first group gets tired. The growth looks stable; very dense and matted. I'm thinking we can tunnel right to the other side."

Doctor Malcolm made no move to comply. He pulled out his canteen, which was filled with water he'd siphoned up and purified from under Den's soil when they'd descended to the level plane. He took deep draughts, gulping it down noisily, and the hand that held the canteen shook like a drunkard's.

"Get behind us, Mac, if you're not going to help," shouted Meson.

The doctor took the canteen from his lips, and said in a small voice, "I'm afraid, Robert. I have … I have a terrible feeling about this place."

"Right now, I don't care," snapped Meson.

The captain took him by the scruff of his jacket and drove him gently toward the back of the group. Bradley couldn't blame the doctor. He hadn't been trained for this; not that she had either. The thought of being contained within that pandemonium made her uneasy too. She bit her tongue, pulled out her torch, and pushed the fear to a place in her soul where there was no air to feed it. Adoni stepped forward, the blade on his stick already bared and making the air around it fuzzy.

"I go first," he said.

"*We* go," said the captain.

Intaba nodded. The two men began to cut a doorway through the tangled wall, Intaba working the top half, and Meson working from chest-height down. They were cautious at the beginning, both trying to get a feel for how the tangle-vine broke under the blades' hypersonic movements. When they saw that it gave easily but kept its form, they increased their pace. Soon they were in a rhythm, Adoni cutting on the left side and Captain Meson on the right. As they worked inward, Bradley and Doski followed at a safe distance from the blades. Doc Mac shuffled along in the rear, hugging his elbows, and looking down shamefacedly. He was only a doctor, after all, and Bradley pitied him.

As they moved deeper, the hedge of vines swallowed most of the daylight. Doski and Bradley flipped on their torches, and the darkness receded. Whether it was more bearable was a different matter. Flooded in white light, the tangle-vine became more sinister, an endless brown tubing of irregular girth coiled up and around itself, like an ugly hedge maze with no exit guaranteed. From the thicker tubes sprouted thousands of finger-width vines. Some of these were covered in thorns, while others were fused together into little nooses.

Bradley tried to make sense of the stuff. Overall, it reminded her of fungus. Its growth pattern was approximately modular, and the vines also wept a clear, vaguely pungent fluid. But if it was fungus, what did it eat?

She knew that fungal mycelia grew by excreting digestive juices and lapping up the resultant soup. That was a good way for nature to dispose of fallen trees, or to infiltrate living ones, yet this damp matrix reached far above the ground, and suspended itself between the tree trunks, as if it were only using the trees for scaffolding. The trees looked healthy enough, so what was the fungus actually doing?

She turned her torch up until the brightness was almost blinding, and squinted into the dark gaps between the tangle-vines. The captain was breathing hard. His strokes had begun to slow. He stopped, and put his hands on his thighs. Observing this, Adoni decided to rest as well, out of mere deference, it seemed, for the big man hadn't yet broken a sweat.

"Can you turn that down?" said Meson, holding a hand up to block the torch light. "It's hot enough in here."

"Sorry," she said.

But Bradley did not turn the torch down; only directed it away from him. Now pressing her face up against the damp wall, being careful to avoid the thorn-bearing vines, she pushed the torch in as far as it would go and squinted into the gaps. Her lips parted in silent surprise.

"What," gasped the captain, "are you looking for?"

She handed him the torch and popped out the blade on her jamstick.

"Our turn," she said. "Rick?"

Doski nodded and took his place beside her at the front. They began to cut into the tangle-vine, deepening it by about a body-length every minute. Gradually, Jenna edged the corridor to the left. She hoped the captain would be too winded to notice this detour until she'd had a chance to verify what she'd seen.

"Bradley," said Meson, "you're not going straight anymore."

"I know, I know," she sighed. "Just hold on."

She began to cut more steeply to the left. Now she was taking off long vertical sheaves, impatient to prove her hunch. Suddenly, the blade on her jamstick made a screeching sound. When she yanked it back, it was smoking.

"What did you find?" said Meson.

"Shine the torch in there," said Bradley.

The captain did and frowned. Planting his casted leg wide, he used both arms to pull back the thick brown filaments. A thorny vine snapped down, and one of its spines lodged itself in his palm. He tore it out, cursing, and tried again. Intaba helped by using his long arms to spread the tangle-vine, while Doski stood behind them lighting the way.

"My God," whispered Meson.

"But that can't be Hector," said Doski.

"No," said the captain. "That's not one of ours."

One smooth corner of a very large, metallic structure showed through the tangled growth. A ship lay on its side, and the topmost arch of its sloping hull stretched as high as the lower canopy. The vessel was not merely exotic; it was plainly alien. It stood encased in a thick mass of the damp tubes and filaments. In the torchlight they could see how the filaments oozed upon it, and how the hull's inky metal had been lacerated in many places. The "fungus" hadn't been feeding on trees at all, but on the craft. God only knew how long ago it had crashed here, but from the looks of it, the job was more than halfway done. Yet despite the ship's advanced state of disassembly, red light from within still burned, and a low hum proved that the craft was in some sense functional. It was impossible to look at the weeping vines and the living ship without thinking of parasites who kept their hosts alive until the bitter end.

Captain Meson stared gravely for a time, then slowly let the tangle-vine fall back into place. He stepped away into the gap, pondering, and rubbing the spot where the thorn had pricked his hand.

"Guess we're not the only fish to get reeled in," offered Doski. "I wonder who they were? What star they came from. How'd they end up on Den, of all places?"

The captain shook his head. He continued to rub the fat of his right palm. "Let's press on. If this stuff is massed because it's eating that ship, we must be close to the other side of it."

Meson checked his gauntlet and began angling the corridor away from the alien ship. After about an hour, they broke through to fading daylight. The captain led them a dozen paces from the tangle-vine wall, and abruptly fell forward. Intaba caught him easily and laid him down on the mossy forest floor.

"Sir? What's wrong?" said Bradley.

"Damn," slurred the captain.

His breathing was heavy, with long pauses between each breath.

"Mac, get over here!" she said. Then, more quietly. "You're overworking the leg, Cap. You just need rest."

He shook his head. "No. It's my hand."

Bradley looked at the captain's hand, and stifled alarm. The hand had doubled in size, and a deep purple bruise spread from the palm downwards, extending into the captain's forearm. When she touched it lightly, he winced.

"Let me take this off," she said, undoing Meson's gauntlet, and reluctantly securing it on her own arm. "Malcolm, come on!"

She looked up angrily, only to see Rick's serious expression.

"Jenna," said Doski, shaking his head. "Mac didn't come through."

Bradley rose and stared back into the tangled hedge. When had they lost him? When had they last seen him?

"We've got to go back!" she said. "Maybe he got turned around when we stopped at the ship, and then he headed back to the other side."

She marched forward and ran into Adoni Intaba's extended arm.

"No, ma'am," said Intaba. "Look!"

As Bradley watched, the rough corridor grew smaller. Now it was a depression, and now only a suggestion. The hedge wall had closed behind them.

"Dammit, he was right behind us!" she snapped.

"But the captain needs you now," said Intaba.

With a sick feeling, Bradley nodded, and tore her eyes from the hedge wall. She tried not to think about what might have become of Malcolm.

"Captain," she said, kneeling beside him.

Meson's eyelids fluttered, but he didn't respond. His breathing was heavy, his breaths far apart. The man was in deep sleep. Bradley studied him for a while, considering. *Farfinder*'s medical kiosk was still functional. All they had here was a field kit, but the light was waning. Doski crouched beside her and spoke low.

"This looks bad. We've got to get him back to the ship."

Bradley considered the matter. If they retraced their steps exactly, and marched hard through the night, they could make it to *Farfinder* in about five hours. Maybe five and a half. But *no,* they'd have to carry Meson, and hack another path through the hedge, or else go around it, and rediscover their trail. And now they had reason to fear that *Hector 4*'s mining charges wouldn't wait for them. Had that stuff eating the alien ship already gone to work on *Hector*? Jenna had seen the tangle-vine close the hole they'd made in real time. It could work fast; diabolically fast. True, there was no way to tell how long ago that alien ship had crashed here, or how long the growth took to get started, but if they couldn't recover *Hector*'s mining charges, they'd be without weapons against whatever strange technology had pulled them down. Hell, that stuff might be eating *Farfinder* right now!

"The light is fading," said Bradley. "Make camp."

"Jenna!" shouted Doski.

She shook her head resolutely. "We need those missiles. We'll do what we can for him with the medkit, then let him sleep."

"You're taking a serious risk with the captain's life."

"And it's mine to take," she said.

"Jenna, listen to me for a second—"

"—Specialist Doski," said Bradley, fixing him with a hard stare. "I am First Officer. For the time being, I'm acting captain. We'll give Captain Meson the best care we can, but we're going to continue with this mission. That's what's going to happen."

"What if he slips into a coma? We have no idea what he's infected with."

"In that case, you'll stay here with him, and Adoni and I will push through to *Hector 4*. We've got to get those charges. It's what the captain would want."

It hurt her to speak to Rick in this way, but she buried her feelings under ice. Rick closed his eyes and sighed deeply.

"I do not agree with this decision," he said. "I do it under protest."

"Duly noted," she spat. "Now pop your tent and get inside with the captain. Night is almost here."

***

The night was dirty. Den's sun seeped over the edges of her mother planet, casting her moon in illuminated muddiness that did not so much temper her darkness as further corrupt it. Vale did not seem to need that light, even if it had been able to reach her beneath the trees. She shuffled forward, making a straight path for the Voice that called her, never varying from her course except to walk around a tree or boulder in her path. She'd crossed the swamps this way, even walking along their sticky bottoms, letting the dark water cover her head.

Her jumpsuit, now soaked through and clinging, chilled the life inside of her. She tore it off, easily, as if she were a gift, and her clothing only wrapping paper. The Vale whom she had been before now sat inside of her like a homunculus, observing these changes with passive interest. Her naked skin, still clammy and cold, began to sprout a thin green covering that better suited her new home. *This is only the first change*, said the Voice to the Vale inside of Vale.

She came to a place where the gaps between the frond trees were thick with thorns and trembling rootlets. She walked straight through the brambles, and they didn't hurt her the way they ought to. The new green covering made her slick, like a walking slime, and she seemed to slide between everything. Finally, she escaped the underbrush, and entered a small clearing. There were others.

She noticed two creatures. One walked upright, and the other crawled behind the first, pulled along by a bit of rope. The upright man was only vaguely familiar, but the other, the one being led like a dog, had a name she ought to remember.

The Voice asked her about it, but Vale could not recall. The Voice asked again, more insistently. What was the crawling thing's position? What power had it wielded? It squeezed her to get an answer.

"None," gasped Vale, speaking with her own mouth. "A boy. He poses no threat!"

The Voice relented, and Vale slipped back inside herself, where it was safe. Her body kept shuffling toward the strangers. When she reached them, she saw that the crawling man was not being led by a rope as she had thought. Rather, a vine grew from his forehead, and into one of the walking man's fingers.

Where are others?

She didn't know if it was the Voice speaking, or the man. She supposed it didn't matter. It was all the same Voice. Her own mouth moved, but this time she was only observing it.

Alone, said the Voice in her voice.

The man grinned. *Not much longer.*

Then the walking man's fingers grew out and joined with hers. As Vale watched from within herself, the three bodies fused together, their minds and matter mingling until it was hard to say where one ended, and another began. The Vale inside of Vale tried to pull away. She remembered, vaguely, being a separate thing. She forced her mouth to move.

"Let … let me go!"

The familiar man turned toward her. Where had she seen his image? It didn't matter now.

Go where?

"To … to … freedom," she managed.

For what? For whom?

"I don't know," she said, to her own great surprise.

Knowledge, said the Voice. *I give. Sleep now.*

Vale went to sleep for a while. When she awoke, there was less of her. The three figures, of which she was now but one extremity, crept like insect pilgrims toward a great, strange mass. Vale and the young technician were crawling through red grass, their bodies joined to that of the familiar man by a sort of green scaffolding. Vale suddenly remembered the man's name, but she didn't care that she'd remembered. She didn't care.

***

The morning was already oppressively humid, but Bradley had broken out the camp stove to brew coffee. It was reckless, maybe. Their water supplies were running low. She remembered that Doc Mac had purified some extra water from under the soil to replace what Vale had dumped, but it was only a liter, and he'd been carrying it on him when he disappeared. They'd just have to siphon more before returning.

She sat on a stone, numbed by fatigue, half-vegetable. Adoni sipped his coffee beside her. The lids of his eyes were wrinkled, and partly closed. A rustling came from within Rick's shelter. She hadn't woken them immediately, wanting to let the captain sleep longer, and keeping at bay the possibility that he never would wake up. Doski cursed loudly, then went silent. She heard him struggling with the tent zipper. Bradley and Adoni shared a worried look.

After a few moments, he came to stand by them, then hovered without speaking.

"Well," said Bradley, staring into her coffee, "how is he?"

When Doski didn't reply, she looked up at him. His eyes were a nest of dark circles under milky glass. Hollow.

"Jenna," said Rick, shaking his head, "the captain's gone."

Bradley tried to arrest the despair that washed over her like a flood. After all, she'd already been half-expecting the news, and it wouldn't do now to let on that she was terrified. She felt the weight of command as a crushing, physical force. And there was Nina, all alone in the Towers; someone else she could fail. Intaba's large hand closed gently around her shoulder, and some of his strength seemed to enter her soul.

"I take responsibility," she said, standing to face Doski. "It was my decision to keep going."

She didn't know if there'd really been an accusation in Rick's tone, but she'd felt it anyway.

"Now I'm going to make another call that you might not like," she continued. "We don't have time to bury the captain, or burn him. We need those missiles. Once we've got them, we'll figure out what to do with the captain's body."

Rick shook his head, perplexed, but she pressed on, not caring to hear his opinions.

"Wrap him up. Try to seal him inside his sleep sack, and then we'll zip him into the pop-up. That might slow the decay a little while we find Hector."

"No," said Doski. "The captain isn't here."

Bradley stepped back. Somebody, it seemed, had just kicked her in the stomach.

"How?" she stammered. "You were in the same tent together!"

Doski waved his hands. "I don't know, okay? And it's weirder than you think. After what happened with Vale and Malcolm, I got … superstitious. I planted myself between him and the door. I tied twine through the clamps so you'd have to actually cut through it to open the shelter. The twine was still there this morning. Meson wasn't."

A shiver went down her spine.

"He cut his way out, Jenna. Right along the seam with the blade from his jam stick, and he crawled out while I was sleeping. The stick and blade are still there. He didn't even bring a weapon with him."

Adoni strode over to the far side of Doski's shelter. He crouched, felt around the seam, and then pushed into the material, revealing a hole just large enough to let a grown man wiggle through. The giant stood up with Meson's detached blade and began turning it over in his hands.

"Did he take any other gear?" asked Adoni.

Doski shook his head. "Far as I know, he walked out in what he was wearing. Boot tracks go off that way, right into the woods."

Doski indicated the general direction from which they'd come. "So, what now?"

"Give me a moment," said Bradley.

She began to pace. One-by-one, their little company was disappearing. Perhaps, like Riley, the others had been infected by something on Den. The captain had pricked his palm on a thorn. Vale, she now recalled, had fallen into the swamp, face-first. She couldn't think of any injury to Doc Mac. But…

"*Shit*," she said. "What did Malcolm say was in the water he siphoned?"

"What? Um, a metal of some kind, but in microscopic amounts. Anyway, he boiled the hell out of it, so—"

"—Maybe not enough," said Bradley.

Intaba tilted his head. "What has this to do with the captain?"

"It's just a hunch," said Bradley. "But they've all had especially close contact with Den. There are organisms that drive their hosts to act strangely. Nina—this … friend of mine—used to be obsessed with that kind of thing. Fungi that take over ants' minds, or parasites that use cattle to help them reproduce. Maybe Meson was infected by something like that. Under its influence."

"Hell," said Doski. "*I've* been in close contact with this place. Got cuts and scrapes all over."

"Me too," said Bradley. "But that's just the thing. There's a logic to it. The disappearances. It feels like we're being hunted, except not by an animal. It's Den. I think she's hunting us."

"She," repeated Intaba, utterly without inflection.

Bradley pressed on, becoming more convinced. "First, she lures us down from orbit, and crashes our ship. She gives us one option for escape and maneuvers us out here toward Hector. She takes our water, and then our medic. Then the captain. Probably, she can take any one of us, at any time."

Doski glanced at Intaba with obvious concern.

"Bradley," he said, speaking softly, "You *are* the acting captain, but we're all running on very little sleep here."

Her eyes were wide; bloodshot and unblinking. "Listen to me!"

It was hard to keep from shrieking. Why couldn't they see it?

"The order of their disappearances can't be an accident! Den knew Vale didn't want to come. She said it out loud! The captain was our leader, and he was injured in the crash. So she took Vale first, and then she waited to take the captain until she had Doc Mac, otherwise we might have been able to help Meson."

"Come on, Jenna!" said Doski. "The only thing Den's infected you with is sleep deprivation! This is paranoid!"

He took a step toward her. Bradley backed away from him, and toward Intaba. She glanced at the big miner, hoping for support, but he kept his thoughts concealed behind a troubled brow. Doski laughed nervously, shaking his head.

"Look, think about it," he said, "if Den were somehow … conscious, purposeful … wouldn't it kill Adoni first? I mean the guy's stronger than all of us put together, and he got plenty cut up when we crashed!"

Bradley stopped, suddenly struck by the implications of Rick's words.

"It's because … she *isn't* trying to kill us," said Bradley.

"Oh?" muttered Doski, "and why is that?"

She stared at him, stunned. "Den doesn't kill her victims. It isn't our nutrients she wants. Don't you see?"

Rick brought his hand to his brow, a gesture of long-suffering. "Jenna—"

"Remember Riley? Did he look dead to you?"

"Come on!"

"And the alien ship. Den was consuming it, while all the time keeping it functional. But we're not *things.* We're people. Animals with minds! Maybe there aren't any lower animals here, because Den *is* the animal, a single, green, hungry mind, feeding on machines and minds that stray into her path! She doesn't have to *think.* She doesn't even have to be alive. A ship's brain isn't alive. A virus isn't alive, but it wants to be."

"That's insane!" spat Doski. "Look, I'm sorry to do this, but I'm taking command. You're not in the right state to give us any chance of getting off this rock!"

He stepped toward her again. She flinched, and Doski hesitated.

"Jenna," he said, more softly, "I'm just … taking command, okay? It's not personal, you know that. Intaba—"

Adoni moved closer to Bradley. She wheeled around on him, fearing betrayal, but the miner made no move to restrain her. Instead, he again placed a hand on her shoulder, dwarfing it within his huge palm.

"No, I don't think so, Rick," said Adoni. "She is captain, until the captain returns."

Doski assessed the situation, sizing up the big man before shaking his head with a look of futility. "Fine. Fine. But we're wasting time. There's no point going down this rabbit hole of Bradley's."

Adoni inclined his head thoughtfully. "I *do* see a point. Let us check-in again on Gannet. If Bradley is correct, then perhaps the young man will have seen something to confirm it. But, if all is well with Amen, we shall then have some reason to doubt Bradley's view."

Rick shrugged. "That's a damn good idea, actually."

He hit the com on his data pad, and hailed Gannet. Intaba and Bradley looked on, listening to the static. After a minute, he tried again. Silence.

"Not answering," shrugged Doski. "But that doesn't mean much. If I were him, I'd still be asleep."

"Locate him," said Adoni. "We're not so far. You can access Farfinder's scanner from here, no?"

Rick conceded this with a wobble of his head.

"May I?" he said, indicating her wrist. "I can probably port in from my pad, but the captain's gauntlet has direct access to the ship's scanners."

Bradley looked at him skeptically.

"I'm not gonna take it, okay?" he said. "You're the boss."

She took a deep breath, and offered him her wrist, silently conceding that she didn't really know how to use the thing anyway. He craned over her arm and began tapping away. They watched his expression pass from irritation to confusion.

"Shit, he's ... not even there."

Adoni sighed. Bradley felt his grip on her shoulder change. She realized that the strong man was actually worried. "Now let us see what has become of Hector 4," he said.

Bradley frowned at him, confused. Adoni's huge Adam's apple made a circuit up and down his throat.

"Please," he said.

"Why?" said Bradley and Doski at the same time.

"Because," said Adoni. "I also have a hunch."

With Doski offering guidance, Bradley tapped the screen. She fumbled with the interface, her fingers shaking as if they did not wish to make any more discoveries. Finally, she opened the map module, and located their own position. She scrolled to the southeast, looking for *Hector 4*. Not finding it immediately, she navigated to a wider view. Still, it was nowhere in sight.

"Search by tag," said Doski, softly.

She shook her head, uncomprehending.

"The captain would have tagged it," he said.

Doski tapped the screen and pulled down a sidebar. It listed their current location, and those of the ships, along with several topological features that the captain had evidently labeled during their journey. The last option was "View Array". Doski touched it, and the map pulled back. They saw themselves as a tiny blinking dot. To the northwest lay *Farfinder*, highlighted in yellow. Far south and slightly west of that, the Anomaly's estimated location, tagged in blue. Now halfway between the two, a third item appeared where it ought not be. It was *Hector 4*. The ship had moved.

"Impossible," Doski whispered.

Bradley leaned against Intaba, feeling lightheaded. "I thought … I thought it wasn't functional."

"She's not," said Doski. "Engines are smashed. Just the onboard, basic systems were running when I ported in from Farfinder. I don't understand."

"I do not think it moved itself," said Intaba, his voice cold. "It does not need to, remember?"

Doski looked at him. "You're saying … that the Anomaly moved Hector *towards* itself?"

"Or the forest moved it," replied Adoni. "Or, like the ship we found, it's being kept partly alive for some purpose we cannot guess."

"But then why wouldn't it have just dragged Hector right to it when it crashed? That ship's been here over a year. Why not snap up Farfinder too, for that matter? It doesn't make sense to bring us all the way out here only to have us turn around and go back?"

The big man shrugged. "Perhaps to separate us. Perhaps Den's mind is like that of a spider, or like the programs that manage the flyways and auto shuttles. Maybe she is clever, in a way, but not so strong when matched against true minds. I once saw a group of children disable an auto shuttle by setting a cone upon its hood. Do you know the tale of the lioness and the wildebeest? Individually, we are prey, but in numbers, we might resist her."

Bradley groaned. "Riley *was* fighting back! Remember his message.

Letters in all the wrong places. I understand now what he was trying to say: Do not approach! Do not approach! He kept trying to warn us, but Den wouldn't let him get the words out straight."

Doski looked at her in astonishment, then slowly turned to face the trees that, even in the morning light, seemed to encircle them like a pack of hungry dogs.

"If you're right," he said, "then it's only a matter of time before it gets to us. As soon as someone stumbles behind ... maybe the next time we go to sleep."

He pronounced the last word with terrible emphasis, for sleep was the one thing they all craved.

"Then we won't," said Bradley. "We'll tie ourselves together, and go after Hector, whether it's light or dark."

Doski nodded, but glanced towards the shelters and gear that would now have to be collected and hauled on their backs. His mournful expression spoke louder than words ever could.

"I can carry more," offered Intaba.

"No, Adoni," replied Bradley, sharply. "Food. Tech. Whatever water we have left. We'll put them all in one pack and take turns carrying it. Leave the rest to Den, or she'll get it anyway."

As she finished speaking, the whole sky seemed to groan. The morning light shifted from muddy orange to brown and finally to gray, in rapid succession.

CRIIIKIKAKATOW!

The clap of thunder broke so loudly over Den that for a moment it seemed that the whole moon had exploded. Even Adoni flinched, crouching down on his tall legs, his hands shooting up to cover his ears. There was a short pause, and then a sound like an aluminum sheet being torn from east to west. Rain followed—heavy, angry—as if the rain didn't know whether to drown them or pummel them to dust.

***

It is a place on Den like no other. She is there. She defines it as a place. All the rest grows out of her, or into her, or slowly becomes her. Only a thin red grass shows its face beside her bulk, but she has coaxed, and cajoled, and finally twisted the encircling trees to thread their canopies together, to hide her from things that probe the sky, things she craves but cannot understand, which might spy her true form at an awkward moment.

Presently, she appears as a great udder bulging up from the soil, mossed, membraned, and veined-over with many green and black tracks, like the capillaries under leaves, or the fruiting bodies of vast subterranean molds. She's never the same from day to day, her appearance being purely notional, ever-subordinate to the function she strives to execute: to feed; perhaps to know. To swell, but never to reproduce, for she would not permit an equal, a second that might lay claim to that same lush world. Whatever she touches she captures, and whatever she captures becomes her. She has threaded herself throughout Den, and all that comes to Den becomes her. She is the fallen star of living things, a self-referential green hole, a consumption consuming itself, a tree that has grown eyes to see, mouths to eat, and a hollow Voice that lives to speak against all limits and definitions.

Others have come to her. Many, many. Fools who fell from the stars. She has drained them dry, broken them down and reassembled them, gaining always in function but never in wisdom. This thing, this cursed, blessed thing floating just beyond her horizons in minds she can dissect but never penetrate. Never become. But tomorrow; there is always tomorrow. She has strung them about her like pearls and made them into the Process that is the Consumption that is the Remaking that is Den. Flesh and wire. Metal and bone. Blood and sap. All of it is She.

***

The rain fell in sheets. They were soaked to the bone, but the torrent seemed to increase whenever they slowed. Lightning struck less than a kilometer behind them, as if to contain them, to drive them ever forward. The three pushed on for *Hector 4*, following the gauntlet on Bradley's wrist. Meson's gauntlet was more than a convenience; it was a mark of state, granting him command over his whole ship. With it, he'd had power to enforce his orders, to belay any mutiny, to blow the ship up, if he'd wanted to. Bradley couldn't use it in all those ways, not without possessing Meson's unique biomarkers, but the captain's technological bracelet still functioned as a symbol of the weight she now carried. It was all dead weight.

For perhaps the twentieth time there came a deafening crack and a blinding flash. Close. Too close this time. Jenna groaned, and, despite her best efforts at dignity, slipped and fell forward. When she hit the ground, her knees slid on the river of mud that poured down from a distant rise, and she landed in the muck face first.

She lay there for a moment, exhausted. Adoni crouched down beside her, saying something she could hardly make out over the pounding storm.

"…must keep … no time to…"

His strong hands grabbed her by the scruff of her jumpsuit and set her on her feet. Though still connected to the others by a rope, Rick Doski was trudging forward with his head down. The rope went taut. Jenna shook off her discomfort. She could not be the weak link in the chain. She checked her gauntlet again and felt a sort of tainted relief.

Hector 4 was close. Despite Den's best efforts, they'd gained upon the ship. Even since the storm had begun, the ship had moved steadily toward the Anomaly, and yet their little company had moved faster. But their good pace was also unsettling. She felt the moon could have killed them if it had wanted to. Instead, Den was moving the ship just ahead of them, like a carrot on a stick. She was certain that what Den really intended could only be something worse than killing them. But what did they have that she wanted?

Their pursuit of *Hector* led them back through different terrain than they'd originally traversed. The crests were farther apart, but more thickly matted with the strange root-shrubs. In the heavy downpour, these anti-roots twitched and stretched like children catching raindrops on their tongues. If she stopped and listened, Bradley could even hear a distinct gulping sound. Den was nursing her multitudinous babies, gorging them from above and below. It made Bradley want to vomit.

BEEP. BEEP. BEEP.

The three of them stopped and looked at Bradley.

"Proximity alert," she said. "We're within fifty meters."

Doski stared in the direction indicated. He shivered and rubbed his arms. "I don't see anything. Just the rain, and these damn suckers."

Intaba pointed. "I do. Look there, between two tall trees."

Bradley squinted, but through the sheets of rain she could see very little. The terrain climbed in a roughly uniform way, a giant version of the ridges they'd passed over on the journey out. There was indeed a dark mass between two frond trees, but it didn't look anything like a ship.

"Let's get closer," she said.

Releasing the blades on their jamsticks, they took off jogging toward the dark mass. The gauntlet's insistent beeping left no doubt that Intaba was right, and that the black-green tumor under the trees was somehow *Hector 4*. Within a minute they'd overtaken it. They stopped at its feet and stared up in awe.

"Good God," said Rick. "What are we even looking at?"

The mass was dark green, and roughly ovular. It was so big around—perhaps twenty meters at its widest extent—that they would have noticed it earlier if not for the tremendous rain. Formed of thick vines and other clotted plant matter from which only small metal corners protruded, it swelled and contracted. Its form suggested, but did not really look like, the fungal wall they'd passed through earlier. Tightly braided vines gave it the appearance of a large and partly squashed ball of wet yarn. It ought to have rolled backwards, down the slope. Instead, as they watched, the mass scooted up a few meters.

"What's moving it?" whispered Bradley.

Doski crept toward the thing, holding out his jamstick like a spear. He bent down to get a closer view, then suddenly leapt away.

"Son of a bitch! Look at this!"

The others approached, but slowly. Doski reached out to jab his stick at the lower surface of the green mass. From the tiny spaces between the vines, thin gray tubes flicked in and out, some seeming to taste the rain, others boring into the wet ground. They might have been insect legs, though they were irregularly sized and spaced. Bradley shivered from the cold.

"Those are the root shrubs we've been seeing, but they're ... embedded into the structure."

"Yeah, and they're working together," said Doski.

As they watched, root-arms pierced through the front of the spheroid and dug down into the hill, while those near the bottom slowly released. One group of root arms handed off the task to the other, and the mass climbed up a few meters.

"Hector's inside all that," he said, looking dubiously at the green horror. "Or part of Hector, anyway. What do we do?"

Bradley cocked her head, considering. They could cut into it, but she wasn't sure how the mass would react.

"Let's wait until it reaches level ground," she said. "I don't want it rolling back down into all that mud. Once it's on the flat, we'll saw out a big enough hole to see what we're dealing with."

They had to wait another five minutes before it reached the crest of the hill. That was enough time for Bradley to wonder how the bulbous thing had been able to navigate the forest, and how it planned to get through the taller stands in front of it.

Planned. The word stuck in her mind like a thorn. The rain that had driven them there was already starting to taper off. The lightning, she observed, hadn't struck again since that last blast disoriented her. The trees here, though tall, were widely enough spaced that the wet spheroid could probably weave through them. It had found the path of least resistance, a path that led inexorably toward the Anomaly.

"It's level," she said. "Let's get started."

Standing as far away as the length of their jamsticks permitted, they began cutting a wedge-shaped hole out of the vine wall. As they did, the root arms shot out spasmodically, flailing like living wires. Bradley tasted bile in her mouth, but she swallowed it back down. If the thing was in pain, at least it seemed to lack any defense.

"Careful," said Bradley. "We don't want to cut into Hector."

The matted green stuff shriveled up under their blades, and a wedge of green carpet soon dropped off the spheroid with a muddy splash. Underneath lay a section of hull with no markings, and what appeared to be a single tooth of one of the brackets that joined the primary thrusters to the side-arms on Venture class mining luggers.

"Cut it wider," said Bradley.

They did, revealing the bracket.

"We need to get into the bridge," said Doski. "That'd be…"

He pointed up, tracing the air with his finger.

"About there … shit!"

Hector 4 shot forward again, the roots clawing frantically now, like a claustrophobic caterpillar having second thoughts about its cocoon.

Doski swore. "The whole thing's a single organism."

The rain tapered off to a drizzle. The many-legged tumor repositioned itself on its bottom axis. It was not lost on any of them that the thing was orienting its bulk so that it could pass between the next stand of trees.

"Now!" said Bradley. "Run alongside it."

Its pace was steady, but slow, and they had no difficulty getting hold of it. That was a horrible feeling, like riding an intestine. They went to work, and soon opened another gap in the matting. They exposed the starboard hatch, then cut the hole wider so that the hatch could slide out when opened.

"Moment of truth," said Doski.

He lifted a hinged flap to expose the handle that manually opened the hatch. He pulled and twisted left. With a loud pop, the hatch lifted, and slid out. A stench hit them from the interior, but it quickly dissipated. The hazard lamps were on inside, and many small indicator lights blinked maniacally, as if *Hector* were locked in a state of panic. But wounded as she was, the ship seemed relatively well-preserved on the inside.

Rick clambered in, then stopped at the threshold.

"Damn," he said.

Inside the bridge, a familiar blue venation decorated the walls and surfaces. Intaba and Bradley held back, peering in dubiously.

"You sure you want to go inside?" said Bradley. "That looks like the same stuff in Riley's shuttle."

"Isn't that why we're here?" said Doski. "I have to get control of those charges."

Doski entered, strapped himself into the tech's chair, and immediately went to work accessing *Hector 4*'s computer. As he typed, he talked to himself, becoming excited as each little system woke up. The panicked lights stopped flickering, as if *Hector*'s meta-brain were relieved to once more fall under the command of its rightful masters.

"Alright!" exclaimed Doski. "Two missiles still in good working order."

Bradley and Intaba finally pulled themselves up into the bridge and came to look over his shoulder. As they did, the ship lurched, sending Bradley into the back of Doski's chair, and dropping Intaba into a bulwark.

"It's still going strong," said Bradley. "Even with the huge holes we cut."

"But, that's what we want, right?" said Doski. "Otherwise, we'd have to hand-carry these things all the way to … to wherever the hell it's going. Assuming it's going where we think it's going. How far away are we from the Anomaly, anyway?"

Bradley braced herself against Doski's chair and checked. "About two-and-a-half clicks. What's your plan for setting them off? The missile bay's completely blocked by that green stuff. We can cut it out, but there's no guarantee they'll still launch."

"I've been thinking about that," said Doski. "We're in the middle of a damn forest anyway, and these charges are designed to be launched in space. But I can still make 'em go 'boom', one way or another. Plan A would be cutting down to them from inside the bridge and removing them manually. That way we can stick them wherever we want. Plan B is to set them off inside Hector. I just have to override the safeguards. Normally, only a captain can do that, but I'm sure I can write a script that will get me in through the back door. Just need a little time."

"But won't Plan B kill us too?" said Bradley.

Doski shook his head. "Only if we're standing nearby when they detonate."

"Then what?"

Doski took a deep breath. "Even inside a missile tube, these mining charges aren't weapons. They're designed to be carefully placed, and they've got to be specifically triggered, or they won't go off. You can do that in one of two ways: either you fire the charges from the bay and get a precise hit—in which case you remotely detonate once your ship is in the clear—or your mining team walks them down to a stroid, sets them in place, and pulls the regulator. The regulator's like the hammer on a gun, only it takes a few minutes to strike. Either way you have enough time to get out of the blast radius … assuming your ship is nearby."

Hector picked up speed. This time Bradley caught herself before sliding.

"What's a regulator? I've never heard of anyone arming a missile by hand" she said, frowning.

"That's because it's almost never done anymore," said Doski, speaking quickly, and with some irritation at the need to explain himself. "A century ago, manual detonation was more common because it's more precise. But there were a few cases where the handle snapped right back after they pulled it. Or maybe somebody just knocked into it. We don't really know because the SOBS blew up before they could tell their story. Lawsuits followed. You know the drill."

He trailed off for a moment, lost in his typing, before he continued.

"That's why it's always remote now. All I gotta do is get inside the source code, and slave the charges to my data pad instead of to Hector. If I can do that quickly, which is a big 'if', I'll get under the floor and try to bring them up through the bridge. That could take a while. You two need to get to Farfinder and free the bridge module. Then put it in skiff mode and land it somewhere near the Anomaly. We place the charges, take off, and blow it to hell. Then blast our way out of the atmosphere, hopefully."

Bradley looked around the network of blue veins that had grown over everything.

"How much time do you need? This place is crawling with—"

"—I'll be fine."

"You can't know that. Riley—"

The ship stalled, then suddenly shot forward. Probably the walking tumor had just squeezed itself between a few trees.

"Hell," said Doski, "I don't even know if I can slave the charges, but at least I have to try. We'll need Farfinder's skiff either way, and you're the only one left who's had any flight training. Anyway, I'm the only one here who can do this kind of stuff."

Bradley shook her head. "Meson didn't want us to split up."

Hector seemed to be picking up speed again.

"Meson's dead," spat Doski.

"Maybe he's not."

"Dammit, Jenna, you know what I mean! If he ain't where we're going, we can't wait. You shouldn't go after Farfinder alone."

Bradley hated it, but he was right. There was nothing more she could do here, and without the skiff, nobody was going home.

"Alright," she said. "We'll meet you at the Anomaly, but, please, just get out of this thing as soon as you've done what you need to do! I don't trust it."

Doski saluted. "Yes ma'am."

"And if we need to communicate?" said Bradley.

Doski tapped the rectangular bulge of data pad under his poncho. "Get going. And don't crash the skiff. You're not Vale, you know?"

That's for damn sure, she thought.

Bradley nodded at Intaba. A thin green film had already grown over the hatch door, and the miner sliced it away with his jamstick. Outside, it was only drizzling.

"Stay alive, Rick," said Intaba.

Doski nodded but did not answer.

***

Bradley kept up a steady jog for as long as she could manage. The soil of Den cloyed at her boots. She looked back and saw that the big man was once again lagging behind. Grudgingly, she stopped to wait. Her boots sank into the soil. Intaba lumbered up beside her. He crouched down, balancing his jamstick across his thighs, and drew long, heavy breaths.

She waited for as long as she dared. Adoni might be strong, able to swing a blade all day or dig into an asteroid, but his body was clearly unused to sustained running. And it was worse for him than for her because Den's marshy surface sucked harder on his heavy footfalls.

"How much longer, Captain Bradley," he said.

"About a kilometer, I think. And it's just Bradley. You can sit down for a moment if you need to."

He shook his head. "I do not trust this ground. It is … like a thing feeding."

She nodded. Strange noises had started sometime after the rains stopped. These were reminiscent of the little gurgles from the root arms, only deeper and more sustained, more like the croaking of many bullfrogs. Though the soil was still muddy, she was surprised at how quickly the rushing groundwater had begun to dissipate, almost as if Den were lapping it up. Folds and fissures appeared in the ground, and water seeped in, but most of it rolled downhill ahead of them. They'd been descending in the dark for a good half-hour but had yet to reach the bottom of this long defile, where the bulk of the rainwater presumably collected. They'd yet to see a real river on Den, and she hoped they wouldn't have to cross one.

Intaba forced himself to stand. His boots had sunk almost to the laces, and he struggled mightily to extract them. Once free, he jogged in place to keep himself from sinking. Bradley freed her own boots and began running again at a smart pace.

Her torch hung around her neck by a lanyard. Its jostling made the tall frond trees seem to dance. A cool night breeze ruffled her hair, and buffeted her face with the same thick mist that obscured their view of what lay ahead. Presently, the terrain dipped sharply, almost vertically, and she stifled alarm. Intaba was still barreling down behind her, so she began running blind lest he lose his footing and crash into her back. The source of the croak-gurgling was now very near. It stood between them and *Farfinder*.

Mercifully, the terrain began to level out. She wanted to rush forward, letting the downward momentum give her wings toward the finish line, but some instinct warned her to stop.

"Adoni!" she called out, over her shoulder. "Wait."

He tumbled down beside her, sucking wind.

"What … do you see?" he said.

"Nothing yet."

Many croaks sounded in near-tandem. She raised her torch and gripped her jamstick. In the mist before her dozens of black spots stretched out upon a level plain. At first, she couldn't make sense of the vision, but, presently, the croaking started again. The black spots resolved into distinct shapes.

"Like mouths," said Intaba, beside her. "Opening to feed."

Bradley shuddered. "What the hell on?" she said.

"The rain, I think," said Intaba. "And, perhaps..."

He turned and walked back into the darkness behind them. She watched him scale the steep decline they'd just run down. It was rather thickly grown with root-shrubs and stunted, sideways frond trees, and she realized how easily they might have broken their necks running down it.

"What are you looking for?" she called.

He bent down with his jamstick and sawed at something on the hillside. Adoni put his boot on the bole of a frond tree, and strained. Three hard heaves, a loud crack, and the thing he was pulling at snapped free. He nearly fell backwards, but kept his footing, and ran to her. He leaned on his jamstick, catching his breath. His other arm was wrapped around a thick section of tree root. She waited.

"A solution," he said. "To something that has vexed me."

Bradley tilted her head inquiringly.

"A forest," he explained, "ought not be so clean. We have seen many trees, but few fallen ones. Remember how difficult it was to find branches for the cairn? Except in that raised, rocky place. And now see how quickly the rain disappears."

She nodded.

"Alright," she said. "I think I see what you're getting at."

Intaba strode forward, dragging the large root along the ground. He crept carefully toward the nearest of the black mouths. When he was within a meter of it, the hole made an awful croak, and doubled in size. Intaba leapt backward, just out of its radius. Now the mouth opened and closed, whooping, sucking, and gurgling all the time. Dark waters within bubbled up, then pulled down. Carefully, Intaba lifted the long root and moved it horizontally toward the hole. The black hole quivered beneath it. Bradley did not understand how soil and loam could open and close this way. Like lips. Intaba put the root in the hole's center, and the "lips" slapped shut.

The big man stumbled back in a crab walk toward Bradley. As they watched, the green and brown edges began working the root inward. There was something horribly autonomic in the motion, like a robot herbivore munching grass. After the frightening initial speed with which it had closed, there was nothing particularly hasty or deliberate about the way this mouth engulfed the root. It consumed indifferently, yet absolutely.

Bradley's own mouth fell open. "So … let's get the fuck out of here."

Intaba chuckled. "Don't we have to pass through, ma'am?"

She looked at him. "Can we, you think?"

In answer, he gently lifted the torch from where it hung at her chest and shone it into the mist ahead. He swept it left and right. The plane continued as far as the light extended. There was no hiking around it, not in any timely manner. This gorge was a kind of collecting site, a natural garbage disposal. Whatever made its way into those mouths was quickly snapped up—and perhaps re-used. Intaba raised the torch, aiming it far and straight ahead. Bradley saw that the ground rose steeply on the other side. Past the plane, rocks and boulders climbed up toward more forest. If they could make it, the rocky terrain would be easier to scale than this wet, sucking loam, and the ship couldn't be far beyond.

"We run fast," said Intaba, "and do not step too near any of the holes."

He looked at her. "I am taller. My eyes, I think, are sharper than yours. Perhaps you will let me lead through this section?"

She nodded, in no mood to argue. Intaba brought the torch beam back to the ground and took a deep breath. She saw him close his eyes; move his lips. The strong man was praying. It touched her, and frightened her, at the same time.

"Let's go," he said.

He dashed away. Bradley was soon running as hard as she could. Long distance running might not be his strength, but here Intaba moved like a lion, tearing left and right, but always driving forward. He did not wait for her, trusting her to keep up with his tremendous gallop. Bradley tried to set her feet only where he did, but the many mouths gaped to cover the spaces where Adoni's boots struck down. She was forced to leap between new, smaller gaps, the scant ground left over when the mouths croaked and swelled, and so she deviated from his course many times.

As she ran, she tried to force her eyes away from the safety of the other side. The distant boulders grew larger, and she knew the two of them must be nearing the end of the plane, yet whenever she dared a glance, she'd invariably lose track of her footing and step too close to danger. But fear kept her running hard. After a time, Bradley once more chanced a look at the approaching wall of rocks. She gasped and stopped in her tracks.

"Come on!" yelled Intaba, glancing behind him.

He was afraid—she could hear it in his voice—and his pace had begun to slow. Had he grown tired, or had he seen it too? Deep croaks and wet snaps grew to a crescendo, warning her to push on. The mouths seemed to have gone into a frenzy, sensing their prey would soon escape. Intaba looked back again, stopped too quickly, then stumbled from the momentum. She collided with his back, then tripped over his huge body. He was on all fours, sucking wind.

"Get up!" she said, scrambling to her feet.

Three spreading inkblots converged upon them. She tugged at the miner's arm.

"We're almost there! Please, Adoni, I need you!"

He struggled to his feet, then to her surprise, swept her up like a child, and rushed forward. She looked over his shoulder to see the mouths come together, forming one great, angry hole. He clutched her to himself, moving in great, loping bounds. Only five meters or so stood between them and the safety of the rocks, yet Intaba suddenly skidded to a halt. The ground before the rocks fell away, parting to form a fissure too wide for even him to leap over. He hesitated only a moment. With a loud cry, Intaba hurled his jamstick into the opening. No sooner had the stick broken its plane, then the great darkness snapped shut upon it. The miner rushed forward across the earthen lips that now sucked greedily at his weapon, and he crossed the last two meters onto the rocks. Exhausted, clutching her to himself, he began to crawl up the rocky hill on three limbs. As he made for a boulder that jutted out from the smaller stone, he still tried to press her close to his chest, though his strength was beginning to fail, and her feet dragged along the rocks, slowing him down. He managed to scale the boulder, dragging her up behind him, before he collapsed on his side, utterly exhausted.

Bradley rolled out from underneath him. Tired as she was, she remembered what she had seen.

"Get up! Get up! We're not alo—"

The blow came swiftly, and Bradley fell from the boulder, and landed on her shins on the rocks below. She cried out in pain, then gazed up in horror to see Captain Meson craning down like a gargoyle. His face was gray; his eyes, once blue, were the color of soil.

He cocked his head, curious if she would run. But there was nowhere to go. Intaba stirred and reached up languidly. With no change in expression, Meson kicked him hard in the face. Intaba tried to prop himself up on one elbow. Meson looked down at him, fascinated, then laid a hand over the miner's head.

Still, said a voice that came from the captain.

Intaba continued to struggle, then went limp. He pitched to the side, and now leaned over the boulder's edge, staring without blinking at Bradley. Meson leapt down and landed like a spider beside her. The dynacast was gone from his leg. His whole body seemed to bristle with energy.

Here to me, he said.

But the voice was only in her head. She didn't think that his mouth had even moved, at least not in time with the words it had spoken.

"Leave us alone!" she screamed. "We just want to go home!"

This home, said the voice.

He sprang, and grabbed her by the hair, yanking her from her feet. Bradley screamed as he dragged her down the rocks, toward the sucking plane.

You do not, said the voice, Y*ou will. We will. I will. Understand.*

"Let go of me, please!"

Meson moved inexorably toward the plane. She twisted around on her knees and saw a great mouth open. Meson raised a hand toward it.

Stay.

He stepped down into the mouth and began a careful descent as on unseen footholds. The lips trembled at the restraint he'd imposed upon them. In that instant, Bradley's fingers brushed a sharp rock. She raised it high and brought it down on the hand that held her hair. Meson flinched, and let go. She turned to run, but he caught her by the ankle.

She clawed at the rocks, but the captain seemed not to notice. His grip was a vice. A strange numbness crept up her foot. He slipped further into the mouth, disappearing in darkness.

Feed, said the voice.

The lips shut hard on Bradley's foot. Sharp things pierced her around the ankle, and she felt cold threads weaving themselves between her sinews. The mouth gulped once and sucked her in further. Yet, even as it fed, the pain of its bite dissipated. A cool, pleasant numbness ran up through her ankle, into her smarting shins and knees, and up her belly. Something not unlike peace swept over her, and the desire to escape fled.

"It won't kill me," she found herself saying.

It won't kill you, the voice mimed.

"It didn't kill Meson. It didn't kill Meson," she said, slipping down.

Meson is precious. Meson is me. Sleep, child.

Her eyes closed.

"Child?" she muttered.

The mouth had swallowed her right leg only centimeters from the knee. Her mind was a dark room, the door and windows shut tight, registering no light, no taste, no smell. Yet thought remained. She forced her hand to find the jamstick in its holster, and with a feeble moan, stabbed downward. The mouth opened briefly before snapping closed around her waist. Bradley was lifted from the ground. Still without feeling, she sawed around her body, twisting her torso as she cut, until the lips that held her slowly relinquished, and curled back upon themselves. She dropped, landing on the rocks. Numb from the waist down, she clawed back up onto the shore.

But she could go no further. The toxin that had made her calm, now threatened to lull her to sleep. Meson clambered back out of the wounded mouth. He'd not quite cleared its twitching lips when Bradley turned and swung the jamstick toward him like a sword. The blow was wild, but the vibrating blade made up the difference. She'd cut him in two from chest to thigh.

His left half flopped down like a sandbag. The one arm still attached to his torso reached for her, the fingers spasmodically closing and opening. A black fluid ran from his lips. For an instant, she saw the old Meson behind those eyes, terrified, and perhaps grateful, but the dark mouth opened wide and swallowed him whole. Bradley put her head down and cried.

***

Jenna was in her apartment in the Towers. She was making dinner, and she could see Nina through the kitchen cutaway wall. The twelve-year old puffed a hanging strand of brown hair out of her face. She was now doing math that Jenna herself had barely made it through, and she was learning it at home, without the benefit of a teacher. Nina slammed her data pad on the table in frustration.

"Nina! Come on!" said Jenna. "Those are expensive."

Nina ignored her and did it again. Jenna put the soup on simmer and strode into the living room.

"I'm serious!"

Nina stood, and without looking at her mother, walked toward the apartment door.

"How am I supposed to do this without help!" cried the girl.

She threw the data pad so hard that it cracked against the door, and then she kicked it again for good measure. As Jenna watched, appalled, Nina undid the four locks, flung the door open, and entered the corridor.

The corridor was lined with men, some hunched over like plague victims, others tall and spindly, their fingers like hairs and roots. Nina walked off, and all the men turned to follow her. She didn't seem to notice them.

"Stop!" cried Jenna, running into the hall.

Nina walked faster. Doors opened all along the corridor, and more strange men poured out. Soon her daughter was surrounded by an army, some walking, some clicking noisily along the ground on insect legs, others crawling along the ceiling. Jenna began to run. Her feet moved, but she did not advance. The party of admirers trailed Nina all the way down the corridor, but Jenna still went nowhere. Her daughter disappeared around a corner, and the mutant hoard pursued, cackling with delight.

Jenna sat up screaming and hit her head. She recognized the inside of the tube in the bridge's medical kiosk. Memory rushed back, and she tried to move her legs and toes. The numbness from before was gone. She opened the med tube and sat up.

Intaba sat across from her. His face flushed with relief when he saw her.

"You're not harmed?" he said.

She kicked her feet like a swimmer, and suddenly realized that she was naked under the sheet. Since it was against procedure to place any foreign material inside the medical tube, where it might contaminate the patient or confuse the nanos, Intaba must have waited to cover her until they'd finished their work. Even as she fought panic over all that had happened, Jenna was touched by this gesture to preserve her privacy.

"I'm well," she said. "You … you saved my life."

He shook his head. "You saved yourself. I could not help. I wanted to. I couldn't move, ma'am."

"No, Adoni! I'd never have made it across without you."

He looked dubious, and a little ashamed.

"And no more of this 'ma'am'," she continued. "From now on, it's Jenna."

Intaba frowned, then slowly nodded.

"May I have my clothes?" she said.

He rose immediately, and she saw that he was already holding a fresh uniform that he'd been waiting to give to her. With his gaze carefully averted, he held it out in her direction.

"Just a moment," she said.

She dressed herself quickly, then climbed out of the tube. After two steps, she stumbled. Intaba caught her and set her back on her feet.

"You just need to get your blood flowing," he said.

He began to move away from her, but she held him fast.

"Wait a second," she said. "We're upright!"

He nodded. "I was able to detach the bridge from Farfinder's body and winch it over."

"By yourself?"

He shrugged. "You have seen the monuments made by my people, the Sengari?"

"Just images," she said. "I've never been."

"Well, we work with stones much heavier than this hollow shell. There are many trees about. Our wise men say that with the right lever, a man might even move a planet."

She smiled. "Didn't one of the Ancestors say that? Anyway, if you can flip the command module, maybe you can help me to the command console."

She didn't know if she'd need the help, but it was peaceful, holding onto him. She clutched his waist, feeling the solidity of his body under her arm and hand. Intaba walked very slowly, while she leaned into him. It was strange that someone so powerful could be so gentle. Then her peace was broken by the memory of the dream. She remembered crying out for Nina just prior to waking. She glanced up at Intaba.

"Did I … did I say anything while I was sleeping?"

He shook his head. "It was a nightmare, wasn't it ma'am?" said Intaba. "Jenna," he corrected. "What about?"

She almost told him, then thought better of it.

"Maybe some other time."

"May I make a guess?" he said, taking another step.

She hesitated. "Well … alright."

He stopped, and looked down at her, a twinkle in his eye. "I think you were dreaming of your child."

Jenna froze. "I don't … I wasn't … Did I say a name out loud?"

He shook his head. "I watched you fight," he said. "When Meson touched me, I felt a pleasant sting, an invitation to surrender. And it overcame me. But I saw you from the rock. You also felt this sting, I think, but you found strength that was not for yourself. We have a saying among the Sengari warriors. You will, perhaps, be offended by it. We say, 'A man exults in pain, but only for the sake of honor. A woman despises pain but suffers ten deaths for the sake of her child.'"

"But there was no pain," she said, looking away, wondering if there was still a chance to keep her secret.

"Not in the body, Jenna. In the heart ... if you had succumbed."

She looked into his eyes. They were deep, and very dark.

"I have a daughter," she whispered, glancing around as if the bridge were listening. "I have to get back."

He nodded, and, trembling a little, pulled her in close.

"I ... I have nothing like that," he stammered. "I always expect to die, and so I do not fear death. But now I understand that it is easier to die for oneself than to risk living for another. Death is an escape from the pain of rushing through space all alone. If I die here, Jenna, it will not be for my honor. It will be for you and for your daughter."

She leaned in and laid her head against his broad chest. They stay like that for a long moment, floating in blessed silence, as if the darkness of space had somehow broken through, and wrapped its mantle about them, and had become meaningful. A warmth danced over her soul, a gentle fire of which the two of them were both the kindling and the flame. The fire was somehow before them, behind them, beyond them, their origin and their end, a little fragment of the first flames of creation, now born anew for the millionth and for the first time. She did not understand it, but she knew its name.

"Thanks for the offer," she said, finally pulling back. "But I'm not leaving this planet without you."

***

It hadn't taken Rick long to slave the mining charges to his data pad. A surprise, because he'd secretly thought that hacking *Hector* would be the difficult part. But the difficulty came afterwards, with the missiles themselves.

The ship was like a greenhouse. It had been such a relief to get out of the pouring rain, to finally be warm, that he hadn't figured on such a prolonged, smothering heat.

He was sweating like a pig, and the moisture of his body mixed with the rain that still soaked his jumpsuit. *Hector*'s bridge was foggy, and all its surfaces were slick. There was an unpleasant musty odor; the same that had hit them when they'd first opened the hatch, but now it was concentrated around him. By the time he got the first floor panel off, he felt nauseous; even a little sleepy. Whatever their nature, the little blue veins that covered everything seemed to put off a lot of heat. Finally, he couldn't take it anymore. He stripped off his jumpsuit and flung it across the room.

Now practically naked, he lowered himself into *Hector*'s innards. The blue growth was down here too, and that gave him the creeps. He balanced each foot on the covered portions of two skeletal pipes. The pipes were hot, but not quite enough to burn him. The real issue was balance. His feet were sweating, and that made it hard to stand. Rick curled his toes around the pipes and hoped for the best.

Below him, in the space between the pipes, sat a small round cover, which granted access to the missile bay. He squeezed inward, and carefully repositioned his legs so that his shins were flush with the pipes, then wrapped his ankles around them to anchor himself in place. The heat of that cavity and the metal on his shins, each barely tolerable in themselves, combined to make him miserable. He reached through, arms dangling, and began working the round cover off. His own body blocked the dim light from above so that he was essentially working blind.

It took him numerous wrenching twists to loosen it, and it was hard to apply pressure while also keeping his balance. *Hector* jerked forward, and Doski slipped off the pipe and slammed his kneecap into the cover's handle. The pain went right down to the bone, and he screamed. He pulled the leg up, secured himself, and kept twisting. Eventually the cover loosened, and finally popped open. Doski turned sideways and slid down into the missile bay.

The lights came on in there, and he thanked whatever power sustained the universe for that little favor. He realized that his knee was bleeding pretty badly. The cut wasn't all the way to the bone, and he couldn't worry about it now anyway, but the blood was already running down his naked shins and making little streams along the veins and tendons in his feet. He looked up through the narrow hatch and began to doubt his original plan. Getting even one missile out of the bay and through that squeeze without someone to hand it off to seemed close to impossible. And yet, it *might* end up being necessary. He'd thought so, back when he was thinking clearly. He muttered an obscenity and went back to the grind.

It took him an hour to get the first missile out, with *Hector* shifting underneath him constantly, and threatening his precarious balance. An hour was enough time to start wondering what would happen when he reached the Anomaly. His imagination spat out contradictory images of the thing, but only in the brief moments when he let himself rest. Soon he was going back down for the other missile. Mercifully, the second attempt went a little faster. Now he knew the places where he could wedge the heavy thing on the way up so that he didn't have to carry it while he climbed. Feeling triumphant, he dragged both missiles across the bridge floor, set them by the hatch, and allowed himself a real break. He cleaned and wrapped his knee, then closed his eyes, feeling very serene until he remembered that he'd have to put his soaked jumpsuit back on.

As he sat there gathering his strength, a single blue filament touched his bare foot. He did not feel it as it followed the thin trail of dried blood. Numbing as it touched, it inched up his shin, slipped under the bandage, and entered the wound on his knee.

Rick did not know that he stood up only minutes later and walked over to the console with his data pad. When he found that he was typing, he did not know why. The strange life growing inside him did not *know* either. It—she—did not comprehend, though she excelled at rearranging and reshuffling what others had made. She could not create, only re-purpose. And she could break, especially complex and intentional things, like the program Rick had so carefully written. That was the weakness of carefully formed things; pull enough threads, and they came undone. That was the strength of her formlessness; her structure was only the shadow of her whims. At her whim, Rick did something, even watched himself do it, but couldn't summon the will to do otherwise. When it was done, at her invitation, he let go of the troubling memory. A few moments later, he found himself on the bridge floor, waking up from a dream. The ship had stopped moving.

Doski got to his feet, alarmed that he had fallen asleep, and quickly dressed himself. He cut away the new growth blocking the hatchway and saw that he was not far from the ground. After searching around frantically for his data pad—why was it sitting on the console when he'd left it on the floor?—he crouched down, wrapped an arm around each missile, and managed to stand. His knee quaked, but he jumped from the hatch, landed painfully, and ran for the nearest leafy cover. Only when he was sure he was out of sight did he finally dare to come back and have a glance at the thing he meant to destroy.

He saw it, and he feared.

***

The skiff wobbled as it flew, and Adoni Intaba did not say, "Are you sure you can fly it?", though the question had crossed his mind. They skated up and down over the treetops, and it appeared that at any moment they'd clip the canopy, a good portion of which lay concealed in Den's cloying mist.

Night was coming too, making a collision even more probable, but the Anomaly wasn't far. They could already see it through the view port, or at least its fingerprint. Something had bent the tall trees, making an enormous dome out of their highest branches. No tree would willingly grow in that way, against its own ends and purposes. But finding was one thing, and landing another. The forest was too thick there, and the nearest clearing was perhaps a thousand paces from the dome. *At least,* he thought, *escaping Den's gravity will be easier for Jenna than flying or landing … if we don't die first.* He hoped so, anyway. Jenna glanced back at him.

"Thanks for the vote of confidence!" she said.

"Ma'am?"

"Again, it's Jenna. And you don't have to hold onto your chair so hard that the veins in your face bulge out. I've done this before."

He chuckled and tried to relax.

"In simulation," she admitted, shrugging her shoulders. "And it wasn't the same craft. But the controls are the same, basically."

He nodded again. "No need to explain. I am … sure you will do it."

She smiled at the encouraging lie. Meson's gauntlet beeped, and she glanced down at it.

"Looks like Doski, but I can't really open it and look. I'm a *little* preoccupied."

Adoni smiled, relieved that she was not going to make the attempt. The big man surveyed his body, trying to reconstruct how he'd managed, through various loosenings and reroutings, to secure his enormous frame into the straps. He carefully freed himself, and even more carefully took a few steps to where Jenna piloted the bridge skiff. Bracing himself, he reached over and gently tapped her wrist. She turned the gauntlet toward him.

Intaba read Doski's message, frowned, and read it again.

"Adoni?" She glanced at him curiously. "We're almost there? What does he say?"

Adoni nodded. "Sorry. He says … something very strange. Hector is going into the Anomaly."

"*Into* it? What does that mean?"

Intaba shook his head.

"I'm going to make my approach," said Jenna. "You should probably strap in."

Intaba quickly returned to his seat and resumed his struggle with the straps. Jenna pulled the yoke left, and the ship banked steeply to port. He had to pinch his thighs against the seat to hold himself in place, while he struggled to force the straps around his torso. He finally got them and heard a satisfying click. She leveled the skiff out, a much smoother movement this time. He put his head back, and closed his eyes, deciding it was better not to watch. Jenna's gauntlet beeped again. He groaned.

"Let me get this thing on the ground first," said Jenna.

He sighed. "It could be important. I'd better look."

"No," she said, "I've got it!"

She let go of the yoke entirely, and flipped open the gauntlet's cover, and started reading. The skiff shuddered, then dipped hard toward the canopy. Jenna cursed and pulled up on the yoke stick. The sudden motion flung Intaba's head back painfully.

"Please do not do that again," he said.

"No, it's … we have to land now!" cried Jenna.

Intaba rubbed his neck. "I think you should take your time—"

"Can't," she said, pushing the throttle forward. "The Anomaly. Rick says it's opening its mouth."

***

Abomination. That was the only way to describe what he was seeing. After he'd set the missile charges down in the driest place he could find, Doski had finally ventured out to look at the strange cause of all their problems. He didn't know what he'd been expecting. Not this. Perhaps a machine, or at least something large and metal. Fueled by nothing but its effects, the heart of Den had taken many shapes in his imagination while he'd labored inside *Hector 4*, crawling toward it.

When he'd thought of how it had interfered with Riley's shuttle, he'd pictured the Anomaly as a great black satellite dish. Then he imagined it as a metal mushroom, the fruiting body of some vast subterranean cyber-fungus. But the true artifact was more obscure, and, in that sense, more unsettling, than any of those vague images.

It swelled like a pustule in the center of a clearing thick with scarlet weeds. He supposed it could be called a mound, though "pyramid" better captured its flavor. It lacked any proper form, for it was constantly moving, swelling up, squeezing in, and foaming out—adding little layers to itself. The field of red grass might have been a carpet laid for a god-king, or centuries of blood, pooled and still pooling at the base of a living temple. The Anomaly had, so far as he observed, no fixed, definite anatomy, but in it were embedded all manner of taxonomies, both organic and mechanical. He saw what looked like the skeletal frames of space-faring craft, and the pulsing lights of some exotic make, along with tubes and pipes, clearly artificial, but re-purposed, and running side-by-side with black vines that ported into them and completed them. There were engine-things that spun, and wet grooves in the shape of circuits, or fingerprints, or logic gates. There were holes that opened and closed, possibly to help the Anomaly breathe, or to vent its heat. One long section running vertically reminded him of a human lung, if only it were giant-sized, and stripped of flesh. Folds near its peak—the only part of the structure with any regularity—resembled gray matter. Perhaps it was not a "mound" at all, but a brain, naked, and without the pretentious addition of a face.

He watched as the ship that had once been *Hector 4* dragged itself toward the Anomaly on those horrible legs. It stopped before the mound. For a moment, he thought the green tumor was stooping to make some form of alien obeisance. The tumor's foremost portion unraveled from the ship it contained, then reached out toward the mound. The mound was many times the size of *Hector 4*, even in its green wrapping. A section near the bottom of the mound split apart, then folded back against the Anomaly making a rude orifice. *Hector 4*'s organic straight jacket would now formally be accepted into the body of this greater organism. The ship plunged into the hole, and its many little legs drove hard, and forced it inwards.

"That … is …. gross," muttered Doski, punctuating the observation with a few well-placed obscenities.

There was nothing really purposive, or natural, or even mechanical about the process of entry. The *ad hoc* orifice in the Anomaly's side was not *made for* the Hector-thing; that was merely its present use. Doski felt disgusted. Or he had, only moments before. On some abstract level he still was, but the part of him that ought to *feel* this way was becoming curiously passive, his outrage slowly submerging itself deep inside of him, watching it all happen through a semi-opaque film. He was more distant now than afraid. What had been repugnant was now a grim inevitability. The instinct to wretch, to recoil—to run away, before the thing ate him too—went dormant.

He decided that he should let the others know, more out of duty than any real sense of urgency. Doski took out his data pad and sent a quick message to Bradley. He hoped, in an almost academic way, that they were coming to get him. And probably they would want to be informed that the Anomaly absorbed things and made them parts of itself.

He yawned. Was he sleepy? When he looked up from his data pad, he saw that *Hector*'s tumor had jammed itself nearly all the way into the great mound. The mound shuddered. Its skin made efforts to close, but *Hector 4* continued to tear the hole deeper and wider. Doski thought of a baby being born, but in reverse. The violence of the process had left a gaping tunnel, and both the ship and the Anomaly oozed black blood. Perhaps he ought to go into the tunnel and investigate. He couldn't imagine *why* he'd want to do something like that but…

Activity at the mound's peak drew his attention. The ring of folds that had reminded him before of brain tissue suddenly thinned, becoming rope-like. The peak expanded. There was a deep, semi-rapid, whooping sound—*gluppa, gluppa, gluppa, gluppa*— like a cat about to vomit. And something came up from its innards, while the folds squeezed wider and thinner. It wasn't something Den had made, but another thing that she'd captured and absorbed, perhaps long ago. She must already have been a killer before it came to her, but the fateful capture of this one item had made her terrible. He recognized the sort of thing it was, if not the exact make. A tractor gate. A gravity ring. Not from the Commonwealth. Probably not even human. But there were only so many ways to manipulate gravity waves, and thus only so many forms such a device could take. The disgorged object bubbled out of the mound peak, then rotated on a noodle of brain-flesh, like an eye scanning the dense forest. The air above it went fuzzy, and leaves and branches and all the matter in its path bent down and tore free, flying at the mound in a messy vortex. Rick understood what was happening. What had happened before. What would soon happen again. Shuddering, mind foggy as it pushed back against some other will, he began a message.

IT'S OPENING ITS MOUTH. DO NOT APPROACH!

He forced his fingers to type those final words, knowing Bradley would understand.

What are you saying?

His hand fell away from the data pad. Den had caught on. She made him tired again. Again, the tunnel beckoned. He knew entering it would seal his fate. Somehow, he didn't care. It was more frightening outside, in the woods, under the dark trees. He understood, even then, that he had a choice. Den could bring a mechanical horse to water, even make it drink, but some strange power limited her dealings with rational minds. She threatened. She cajoled. Mostly, she dulled, blurring lines of self and will until acquiescence seemed natural, or at least inevitable. Rick Doski was a builder. She'd keep him around for quite some time, until he faded. Wouldn't that be nice?

"I don't want to go," he said, weakly.

Yes, you do, said the voice.

"I have others," he protested. "I don't need you."

As if in answer, others came. Five silhouettes appeared inside the tunnel made by *Hector*. It was dark, and he couldn't see their faces, but their shapes moved toward him with clockwork grace. They stepped into the failing light of another short day. He recognized Amen Gannet, no longer afraid. No longer anything. And there was Vale Orisimmo, jaws fixed in that same sardonic smile, now made permanent. The top half of Captain Meson skittered out on long root legs, and Doc Mac rested one avuncular arm on the captain's shoulder, as if he'd just completed a successful surgery. Oddly, these familiar faces did not frighten Rick. In some way, he'd expected them. Only when Preston Riley stepped out from the throng did real terror awaken in Rick's heart. It was a face he'd never seen alive, but which must have watched him, and known him, biding its time.

Come, said the voice, in Riley's lips; in Rick's mind.

"Why should I?"

Rick's anesthetized intellect counseled him to run. Now, or not at all. Otherwise, he must eventually give in. He wasn't strong enough to keep saying "No". Not for himself. But Jenna and Intaba needed him.

"You have nothing that I want."

In me, you will understand. In me, you will do and do and do and do. And like.

"I'll bet you don't understand anything," he said, "That's why you need—"

Hush, said the voice. *Come here.*

And he was tired, too tired to refuse. But if he could not resist, he could still deceive.

"I will come," said Rick.

He bent down, into the brush, and sent a final message. It was very difficult to make his fingers work, but soon his struggle would be over. He walked a few paces and gathered up a missile under each arm.

What do you carry?

Rick sighed. Somewhere he'd heard that the Devil lied by telling half the truth. Perhaps he could beat her at her own game.

Weapons, he said, in the common voice. *For our defense.*

Rick kept the other half of the truth locked away in a cellar in his soul. The others came out to meet him. Riley extended a hand, as if to help carry the missiles. Instead, his fingers grew out like needles and pierced Rick's sternum. Blue vines burst from Doski's pores, and crept along his skin, going dark green as they hit the air. He smiled. He had joined the black parade, but on his own terms. The whole company turned in unison and marched toward Den's gaping mouth.

***

Something passed through the green dome over the Anomaly. Bradley saw it in the distance as a distortion of light. It became a concavity pulling down the sky. The dome of trees began to disappear. All the matter in its path rushed inward; not only the trees, but Den's thick clouds, presently painted red and orange by the setting sun. The gap widened, and for a moment she caught sight of that strange protuberance beneath the canopy.

"It's looking for us!" shouted Intaba.

"I know," she said. "I'm trying!"

But there was no easy place to put the bird down. The small clearing ahead had been her only viable option, but Bradley was years out of practice, and didn't think she could make a true vertical landing. She'd planned to circle the landing zone, making smaller and smaller loops until she could get right above the zone, and drop down on the repulsors. It was what they called a "chip landing" in basic training—as in, "chip your tooth."

The implosion field widened rapidly, and she could now see the gravity cone clearly, for the things that swirled inside it gave it form. The cone swept about like a searchlight, and its motion tore at the atmosphere around the skiff. The ship flipped over, and she struggled to regain control.

She righted it just in time and had to pull up hard to avoid slamming into the trees. Then she had an idea.

"Okay, I'm just going for it."

She dove back into the trees, then banked to port, threading the narrow spaces between the frond giants.

BANG!

The skiff's belly clipped a trunk. It shuddered, but she held it in the same orientation. She was so close! All at once, the trees opened up, and she saw the small clearing covered in tall yellow grass.

"Hold on to something!" she yelled.

Bradley righted the skiff above the clearing and dragged the yoke hard left. She held it there and punched the boosters for mere milliseconds to send the skiff into a gut-wrenching spin. Now disoriented, she killed the engines, and quickly pulled the repulsor handle. The skiff dropped, still spinning in place, and its belly crashed down on a field of roiling energy. When she could hold it no longer, Bradley released the handle, and wrapped her arms around her head. The repulsors stopped firing, and the skiff slammed onto Den's surface.

Silence. Bradley felt the world turning long after the ship's motion had ceased. She was surprised that her teeth hurt more than her neck or back.

"Jenna!" shouted Intaba. "Are you alright?"

Bradley explored her mouth with the tip of her tongue and laughed.

"Captain?" said Intaba, looking baffled.

"I actually did it," she muttered. "Chipped a tooth, I mean."

Intaba freed himself from the straps, then began to do the same for her, working carefully, as if she might break. But Jenna was far from breaking. On the contrary, she felt strangely, furiously alive. She looked up at him, and grinned, taking care to display the broken incisor.

"Still pretty?" she asked.

He shook his head. "Yes, ma'am. Pretty crazy."

Bradley laughed again. "Adoni, did you just make a joke?"

The big man took a jamstick from its rack, waved it in her direction like an accusing finger, then hit the button to expand it. He opened the blade and set it whirring, and, satisfied that the stick hadn't been damaged in the crash landing, closed it down.

"The Sengari celebrate when battle is over," he said, slipping the stick into his empty holster. "Not before."

He stood before her, a black tower of destruction, but with smooth, hard edges. She nodded, chastened by his comment, yet unable, with him standing there, to keep her mind entirely off the celebration.

***

They tracked Doski by the signal from his data pad. They found it resting by itself in the raised bed of a bramble bush. Not until the landing had they seen his final message, and reading it threw cold water on the brief, manic levity that came from facing death.

Execute sequence. I'm already dead.

The horrible thing before them—animal, mechanical, whatever it was—raged at the sky above. Openings around its base, mouths or sphincters, who could tell, sucked air and expelled matter at intervals. The things that the Anomaly devoured rushed out of it in torrents of black waste, and the waste pooled around its base. There was one opening larger than the others. Nothing came out of it, but Bradley felt certain that this was where Doski had entered.

Intaba lifted Doski's data pad from the thorns and touched the screen.

"It's locked," he said.

Bradley continued staring at the obscenity in the clearing. She felt certain that it stared back at her. In confirmation, the gravity gate went silent.

Come to me.

"Jenna." Intaba shook her. "You need to override Doski's lock."

She looked up at him, distant, then slowly understood. Bradley tapped her gauntlet against Doski's data pad, and the screen came to life. A window had been left open in which a small green button was labeled "Activate."

Intaba shrugged. "Well, that's that. The charges must be inside. Let's get back to the skiff and set them off."

But he made no move to go, instead staring into the forest, a look of disgust and guilt on his face.

"He died to make this happen," said Bradley. "We have to see if it's not too late to save him."

Intaba dragged a big hand down the flat of his face.

"How, Jenna? How?"

"We go in," she said. "As he must have done."

"And how do you know he'll come with us?" countered Intaba. "Remember Meson. He could be … like that."

Bradley stared at the Anomaly. Suddenly her brain was filled with mud. She shook herself, snapping out of the fog.

"We have to go in," she said, and started walking.

***

The tunnel was just wide enough to admit a human body, and it was tall enough that Adoni could walk without crouching. It was almost as if they were expected. The corridor walls were ribbed above and below. They swelled and waned as if the whole structure were breathing. Jenna tried not to notice thick, tubular things that moved just behind the walls. The close air had a musty scent, like a wet dog, or an unwashed body. The air tasted strangely metallic. It was, she thought, the smell of raw stuff, matter mixed together, and blended; caught in a state between life and mechanism. There was a subtle hum, hardly audible, that might have been the rumbling of a distant engine or the warning growl of a predator.

Presently, the passage narrowed, and the roof came down. Bradley looked behind and saw Adoni crouching.

"I don't like this," he said. "We're being hemmed in."

Adoni opened his jamstick, set the blade humming, and brandished it menacingly at the walls. Perhaps it was only her imagination, but the corridor seemed to retreat a hair's breadth.

"There," said Bradley, shining her torch. "Just ahead."

The passage terminated at a larger chamber. Bradley went down on her haunches and hesitated near the threshold.

"You'll have to crawl," she said. "But it opens up on the other side."

Adoni's low grunt made his displeasure clear. Bradley waited, gathering her courage. *Either go now, or run now*, she thought. She scrambled through.

The chamber was a near-perfect sphere, or hemisphere, rather, for the bottom was flat. In the floor's center lay the charges from *Hector*, still in their missile tubes. Jenna wanted to shout for joy, but she was suddenly wary. Had Doski carried the charges in here, or had the Anomaly somehow extracted them from the ship? What if Den understood what the charges were, and how to dismantle them? Already black and green vines, wire thin, had begun to wrap themselves around the missiles, looking for openings. They'd have to set them off soon.

She raised her torch to scan the walls, and promptly let loose a scream.

Vale's face looked out from the wall, where it was embedded. Her eyes were closed, but her fingers pierced the wall's surface, stretching it, sheet-like, over themselves. Bradley stumbled back, catching her heel on something that jutted out of the ground. She recovered her footing and shined her light on a root-like protuberance. It was an elbow, flexed at the wrong angle, the hand and shoulder buried beneath the floor.

"Adoni!" she screamed.

Intaba forced his bulk into the room and ran to her. He looked down at the tortured limb.

"Gannet, I think," he said. "Let us go."

"Okay," she said. "Okay. Just let me…"

Bracing herself, she explored every square meter of the chamber. Doc Mac was there, his naked back and feet bent outwards, his face stuck in the wall. Beside him, an agonized mouth stuck open belonged to Meson. She shined the torch at the chamber's ceiling and found the last member of Meson's crew.

Doski's arms were stretched out to either side; his feet tied together with some black, spongy material. The same bonds encircled his torso, neck, and wrists. His skin, beneath the blue venation, had turned dark green, and seemed to be sprouting moss. Rick's eyes were open and filled with tears.

"God!" said Bradley. "Can we help him?"

Intaba gripped her hard around the wrist and shook his head.

"I don't think so. Look at the others."

Rick's jaw moved, sawing from side-to-side.

"Jenna," Intaba hissed. "We must leave this place."

He glanced at the missiles. "And set them off, if that's still possible."

"Wait," she said, "he's trying to speak!"

Rick Doski closed his eyes and clenched his teeth together. He appeared to be summoning all his strength.

"Plll … puh … pull!" he said.

"He wants us to pull him out!" she said. "Can you reach?"

Intaba obediently stretched toward the ceiling. One of his fingers grazed Doski's boot.

"I could jump," he muttered. "And get my hands around him."

"No," she said, "You'll get that stuff all over you. Lift me instead. I'll see if I can cut him loose."

She took the jamstick from his hand and stood board-straight. Intaba clutched her just below the knees and lifted. Now her face floated only inches from Doski's.

"I'm going to try to cut you out," she said.

His eyes moved back and forth rapidly, trying desperately to tell her something. She had no time to decipher it and began to slice away at his bonds. The material gave easily. The blade only had to graze it before it snapped and slithered back into the wall.

Bradley soon succeeded in freeing his hands and feet. She went to work on the vines around his throat, shutting off the blade to avoid killing him by accident. Finally, she had only the stuff around his waist to deal with.

"Get ready to move me," she said. "He'll fall."

She sliced through quickly, and Intaba swung her to the side.

But Doski did not fall. He hung there, though his arms and legs drooped downward.

"Let me see what's holding him," she said.

Intaba moved her back into position. She pressed her head to the ceiling to peer behind Rick's back. The flesh of his waist, neck, and torso grew up from his body, becoming one with ceiling itself.

"Shit. I'm just going to pull him. The worst it could do is kill him!"

She grabbed his arms at the shoulders and wrenched. Doski inched toward her, and she felt the flesh tearing, as if he were a rodent in a sticky trap.

"Jenna, stop!" thundered Intaba from below.

"I can get him! He's coming loose! We can put him in the medbay."

"No!" shouted Intaba. "Look at the door!"

She looked. Not only was the passageway shrinking, but the chamber itself was crowding inward.

"Just a few more seconds," she said.

She pulled at his waist, only to watch the tendrils she'd cut before grow back and suck him into the ceiling.

"Enough," said Intaba.

He let go of her legs and caught her before she hit the ground.

"We are leaving. Now!"

He plunged into the passageway, dragging her by the wrist. Bradley did not fight him, but she wept for Rick.

Where are you going?

The voice was joined by others; some familiar, and some strange. Now it sounded in the chamber behind her, coaxing her to return, asking her about Rick's gift, taunting her that it would find out anyway. *Damn right, you'll find out!* she thought. They squeezed through the closing corridor and crawled out onto red grass. Intaba yanked her to her feet and took off running for the shuttle. She came along without resistance.

It wasn't right, leaving him, she thought, not knowing if it was her own voice, or that of another.

But she had little strength to fight, and what she had was for another. At least they could blow the damned thing up and put Rick out of his misery. That gave her strength, and she ran all the harder.

They reached the clearing and found the skiff where they'd left it. When they were secured in their seats, she drew out Doski's data pad, unlocked it, and tossed it to Intaba.

"Wait until I tell you," she said.

Bradley started the repulsors, and the skiff floated up from the yellow grass. She hit the engine, and the thruster roared to life. The skiff rose slowly to a height of about seventy meters, far enough away to be outside the blast radius, close enough to see it go off. Intaba's finger hovered above the activation window.

"Okay, get ready," she said, "in three ... two... one ... kill it!"

Intaba touched the button. They waited. Nothing happened.

"Oh no!" said Bradley.

Intaba touched it again. She turned the skiff toward the Anomaly, now partially visible through the trees.

"What's wrong?" shouted Bradley. "Are we not close enough to set them off?"

"Perhaps the missiles are damaged," said Intaba, softly. "Or perhaps..."

"What?"

Intaba closed his eyes and sighed deeply. "Yes, he said. I think I know. Set the skiff down again, but over there, at the far edge of the clearing."

"Why—"

"—Please," he said. "No time to explain."

She let the ship descend, and floated over slowly, dropping a few meters every second. Soon they were hovering on the repulsors.

"Jenna," said Intaba, "set the skiff down."

"What are you going to do?" she said, turning around to face him.

She noticed that his straps were already off. When he didn't answer, she finished landing the skiff, this time managing to do so without much violence.

"Jenna," he said, "I want you to know two things. First, I have never harmed a woman. Also, I believe, ma'am, that I love you."

He sprang forward and placed his massive forearm across her throat. Jenna struggled to breathe but could get no air to pass through her windpipe. She slapped and tore at his flesh with her nails. In less than a minute, her eyes closed, and her head drooped forward.

Intaba released her. He leaned in close, and sighed heavily when he heard her drawing breath.

"I'm very sorry about it," he said. "But you'd never have let me go."

Intaba opened the hatch and took off running toward the Anomaly.

***

It wasn't hard to find the opening through which they'd escaped. Whatever sort of being the Anomaly was, it seemed to spread its focus in many places at once, and the energies given to one task left less to others. The hole was now child-sized, and still shrinking. Intaba set his blade humming, and went about the work he knew best. Mining was all the meaning in his life. Let it then be the means of his death. That would be a good death for a man of the Sengari.

He cut in broad circles, tearing out materials as he went. As he mined, things that moved under the muck crawled over his hands and forearms. He never saw them, only felt their rough slide, and the little nips and bites that seemed to taste him, learning what he was.

Come in! Come in! said the voice.

"Shut up," said Adoni.

It took him ten minutes, for the passageway had sealed itself near the chamber. Finally, he burst through and found the cramped place where the missiles lay. It was small now. He had to crawl. Adoni activated his torch and set it on the floor. The missiles were entirely coated in green fibers, which he proceeded to cut away with the greatest of care lest he damage the firing mechanism.

Rick had planned to destroy the Anomaly by setting it off from a distance. Adoni knew that the man was an expert at his craft, and unlikely to make a mistake. If the bombs did not detonate, then something else must have gone wrong. Something inside Rick's mind. And yet, the man *had* saved them, after all. He had told them another way to set the charges off.

Once he'd cleaned the filth from the missiles, he turned them over to locate the regulator levers of which Rick had spoken. He did not see them at first, and nearly despaired until he noticed a small red tab just below the cone of each missile. It was flush with the surface. He detached the blade from his jamstick and dug the tip under one of the red tabs. It popped a few centimeters, and he tore it off with his fingers. Underneath it lay a small rectangular cavity in which rested a chrome arm on a hinge. He quickly exposed the same lever on the other missile. Adoni took a deep breath and spoke the Death Plea to the Maker. Leaving nothing to chance, he pulled both levers at once.

When he let go, they began to click, running down slowly toward flush, like hands on a mechanical clock. It would only be a matter of time before they struck home. The tendrils started to grow back, and he ripped them off. Yes, he would have to stay, and see the process through. He wondered if it would hurt much. Adoni Intaba was not very afraid of the pain. Mostly, he was curious if a destruction so absolute could be felt at all. He only hoped the blast would not reach the clearing. And would Jenna wake up in time to understand, and flee? Ah, but that was beyond his control.

What have you done? What is the function of those devices?

Adoni laughed. "You will know, friend. Soon you will know."

Something burst from the wall and struck him in the back. Adoni turned in the small chamber. In the torchlight, he saw Rick Doski—the thing that had once been Rick Doski. It rushed at him like a wildcat, and clawed him across the face. He threw up his arms, but the creature slipped behind him, and wrapped its fingers around his throat. Never bested by any man, the huge miner found himself pinned to the ground and unable to move. Doski needed only one hand to choke him, for his fingers continued to lengthen as they wrapped around his throat. The other arm stretched out toward the missiles, and toward the clicking arms of the regulators. Black cords interposed themselves between the missiles and the descending regulators, while other tendrils tried to pierce the missiles' bodies. Adoni held out as long as he could, but his vision was growing dark. Once more, the voice bade him sleep. He thought of Jenna. He thought of her child. Neither thought was strong enough to move him; only to multiply his guilt at failing them.

THWACK! THWACK! THWACK!

Black and red fluid splattered the chamber wall, and Intaba felt the constricting arm go limp. He watched as the Doski-thing charged forward, only to be struck over and over again. The sound of the bolt rifle was unmistakable. It was like music. Bradley stepped into the room, crouching, and hovered over Doski's writhing body. He looked up at her, eyes pleading.

"Thank you," she said, and shot him twice in the head.

"Can you walk?" said Bradley, over her shoulder.

Intaba nodded. "Yes," he rasped.

"Then run."

Adoni rolled onto his hands and knees and watched with satisfaction as Jenna put three more rounds into the thing that had been Doski. Then she grabbed his blade from the floor and cut away the black fingers that stood between the regulator and the charges.

"I said get out of here!" cried Bradley. "Get back to the skiff! Don't worry about me. I'm no martyr."

He did as he was told, worming his way through the makeshift corridor to the darkness outside. From her brief contact with the strange un-life that was Den, Bradley had come to suspect that it did not truly *know* anything. It could only wield minds, as a virus or a fungus might wield the body of some higher organism. Its black heart could only covet; never flourish. When she was sure that Doski was truly dead, and that his knowledge of the bombs had died with him, she also turned and fled. She soon appeared behind Intaba, and they ran hand-in-hand from that vile, bloated blight at the heart of Den.

***

The skiff met the canopy just as the forest exploded behind them. It was a shame, in a way, for Jenna Bradley would have liked to watch the thing get blown to hell. As it was, she had enough work maintaining the right pitch through the dark clouds that were only briefly illuminated by the fireball below. From the perspective of this small skiff, the clouds seemed to go on forever.

Finally, they thinned, and she saw the curve of space. The last cloying fingers of thick atmosphere failed behind them, turning inward on themselves, slipping back into the misery that was Den. Beyond them lay the dark of space, and the shining slatey surface of Den's mother planet, gloriously dead, and framed by the pinprick lights of a hundred billion stars.

She set a course for the Saxon Gate. It wouldn't be a smooth voyage. Five gates lay between here and the Theonon System, and Settlement C, and Nina. The skiff had no sails, and thus no chance, unaided, of getting her through all five gates before Nina was an adult, but she'd send a tight beam—send it when they were far, far away from Den—and let Orecorp come and get them.

Adoni walked up behind her and placed his hands on her shoulders.

"I'm so sorry," he said. "For hurting you."

She reached up to touch his hand. "If you really want me to forgive you," she said, "then you're going to have to make it up to me."

"How, may I ask?"

She smiled. "Well, when we get our bonuses for exploring Den, you have to stop mining."

"Is that so?" said Adoni.

"Yes," she said, solemnly. "But that's only the first part of your penance. I can't be expected to do everything. Nina needs someone to protect her. We both need somebody. Big, strong, dangerous man like you … think you can do the job?"

Adoni smiled and began to speak, then suddenly went quiet, and turned to look behind him. He walked slowly away from her.

"Hey?" said Jenna, irritated.

Intaba did not tell her that somewhere in the skiff he'd heard a body move. It might have been his imagination, and he did not wish to alarm her. He passed quickly through the command console, searched the small medbay, and finally scoured the crew quarters. He shook his head, assuring himself that the small, shuffling noise, and the faint clink of metal, had only been his mind's inability to believe that the danger was past. *Ghosts*, he thought. *Only memories*. Perhaps he was not as fearless as he thought, now that there was something to lose, but perhaps the very fear of losing what he loved would make him all the braver in time. One thing was certain: the two of them would have to be quarantined. They'd be together for a long time. Forever, he hoped. He came back to the bridge, smiling.

"Sorry," said Adoni. "You were talking about dangerous men. I think I know just the one."

He bent down beside her and took her hand in his own. She leaned back in her chair, and without taking her eyes off the view port, kissed him on the mouth. Saxon Gate loomed before them, one small light in a gathering darkness.

UNDER THIS BLACK DOOR

Immediately upon waking, Jansen Sol set about analyzing his cell. They had brought him in drugged, and from this fact Jansen drew two related inferences: first, that they feared his escape; second, that they still feared his allies.

But for five rectangular inlets set at right angles to the circular floor and placed equidistantly along the curving walls, there was no obvious way into the circular, bone-white room. The floor was bare, excepting the black rectangular prism resting alone in its center. The prism was about man-length, like a coffin, and a slight indentation running just below its upper edge suggested a lid. To his annoyance, there was another prisoner in the cell, but Jansen ignored him for the moment aside from noting that this stranger's presence proved the inferiority of the new regime. In their kangaroo court, he'd not denied anything—admitted to it proudly—and the judge, after promising a sentence to fit his "crimes", had still agreed to give him a cell of his own. *They ought to have killed me*, he thought. *Maybe they have, and this sterile room is really my own hell.*

Certainly, they feared him. Like everyone in the court, the judge had been hooded and masked. Many of those now in power had once been willing collaborators with the Principalities and had only changed sides once the Principalities' defeat seemed inevitable. Jansen suspected the rebels were masked out of fear that he would name them to the Principalities, who might still have eyes and ears on Earth. The judge had insulted Sol by promising him a slim chance at redemption. "Yes, even you," he'd prattled. But Sol had only vowed to avenge himself.

Of course, he actually meant to escape, but he'd said it mainly to ensure they would put him in a cell of his own, without witnesses or the irritating company of lesser minds. That they couldn't keep their word on such a small matter proved the ineptitude and insincerity of the whole "Reconquista". It made Sol bitter for the loss of the Principalities.

If he was to escape, then there was the nagging matter of finding the cell's entrance. He'd been brought in somehow, as had that bearded octogenarian resting on the wall across from him. Possibly, the ceiling or floor contained some hidden opening. The black prism might be the way in, though it seemed too oddly shaped and awkwardly placed to serve as a door. He'd no intention of asking the old fellow if he remembered how he got here. The man's mere presence was an insult to Jansen inasmuch as it represented the judge's broken promise. Also, the old man's gray-green skin revealed him to be a half-breed. As much as Jansen admired the Principalities, he was still revolted by their unnatural offspring. Why was a slave sharing his cell? This was a further insult.

Still, Sol was not distressed, nor did he doubt his eventual escape. There was no mystery that couldn't be solved by reason and observation. But anything he said would surely be recorded and reported, which was another reason to avoid the other prisoner. He therefore made up his mind to keep his own counsel. Jansen Sol never asked for help.

"Been here long?" muttered the old man from across the room.

The gray, mercurial eyes held a touch of impish humor. Jansen glanced at him once, confirmed the man was a nobody, and went back to his ruminations. The enclaves set around the wall were only a meter deep, but they suggested sleeping quarters, or toilet stalls; possibly both. Or perhaps the black box was a common toilet, set in the middle of the room to maximize the prisoners' shame. *Vindictive little barbarians,* thought Jansen.

Peering into the nearest inlet, he noticed a small indentation midway up the recessed space. It must be a hinge, where the inlet's rear wall, apparently solid, folded back into space. A bed then, or at least a hard surface to sleep on. His eyes were drawn upwards toward the ceiling, and he now spotted a dozen tiny apertures that at first glance had seemed mere imperfections in the smooth ceiling.

"Do you like riddles?" asked the old man.

Jansen considered whether to strangle the half-breed for interrupting his thoughts. That might force his jailers to intervene, thus revealing the cell's entrance. On the other hand, if they were as unprincipled as he took them to be, they might leave the geezer to die at his hands, and then Jansen would have the fumes of a rotting corpse to further distract him. He tabled the consideration.

"I know a good one," said the man, "to pass the time."

"You may not speak to me," pronounced Jansen.

The other stared at him. Slowly he lowered his head as if mortified, but a small smile grew at the corners of his lips.

What are the apertures for? Jansen asked himself. He soon had his answer. There was a whooshing from above, as if a light breeze had blown into the room.

"G'night, friend," said the old man.

Jansen's head went fuzzy, his vision dark. When he came to, a third and fourth prisoner had appeared in the round room.

***

Now that there were three interlopers, Jansen saw the beginnings of a pattern. Aside from the old half-breed he couldn't place, the other two were well-known to him. The fat bishop, whom Jansen had long ago appointed Chaplain of the New Peace, lay prone on his bed slab, which indeed folded back into the recessed inlet, just as Jansen had speculated. The other inmate sat cross-legged in her enclave, brushing her hair with her fingers. She'd been known as Amelia Bel, though that wasn't her real name. Like her appearance, the name was calculated to maximize public trust. She'd played the role of Media Liaison to the People. Both functions had been Jansen's idea. He despised the brainless woman who now sat in the small toilet area below her bed slab, trying desperately to maintain her beauty without the help of makeup or preferential lighting. He disliked even more the old bishop, both because of the necessity of making use of a clergyman, and because of the man's soft education. Jansen was only pleased to have correctly deduced the functions of at least two of the five inlets. He drew no definite conclusions about the others.

He stood, and crossed the round room, stepping over the black prism in the center of the floor. The box irritated him, because of its asymmetry with the room, and because it too obviously begged investigation. A black box was a doltish metaphor for mystery. They'd expect him to try and look inside, and so he was certain it would either be locked, or else it would contain mundane items. Toiletries. More gray jumpsuits. Possibly the food came up through there. Let the others investigate. Since Jansen was going to be here a long time, he'd much rather solve mysteries his jailers didn't want solved.

Jansen crouched before Amelia's enclave, not looking at her but into the shadows behind her. They'd provided Amelia with a tiny mirror fixed to the wall. Sol glanced back at the bishop's enclave. It didn't have a mirror in its toilet area, only a copy of The People's Bible. The volume lay open by itself on the floor below the sleeping bishop, but its pages were all blank. Sol smiled at the joke, and nodded to himself, satisfied, as usual, at the pattern he'd discovered. From his wide reading, he recalled a fragment of theological mumbo jumbo to this effect: "The damned will be tormented in those senses in which they have offended." *How droll*, he thought. *And what is my punishment to be?* He turned back to Amelia.

She left off brushing her hair and looked up at him. Her face was stained red from tears, and her manicured nails showed signs of having been chewed. Yet she breathed in a slow, deliberate manner and held her cross-legged pose with purpose.

"Oh," she said. "It's you. What do *you* want?"

Ignoring her, he crouched down again and crawled past her under her bed slab. As he did so, out of the corner of his eye, he caught sight of himself in Amelia's mirror. He turned toward the mirror, alarmed, for he'd seemed to have seen a hole in the center of his forehead. However, when he looked at himself directly, there was no hole. Shaking his head, he continued crawling toward the back only to bang his knee rather painfully on a water nozzle jutting out of the wall near a small toilet area. He took care to show no signs of discomfort to the others. The mystique of command required a certain imperviousness to externals. He continued his observations. With the slab open, the enclave's full dimensions were revealed to be about four by eight by eight.

"What are you doing?" Amelia demanded. "Get out of here! Haven't you done enough?"

He placed his palms against the back of the wall and felt around for breaks or seams. Finding nothing, he backed out more carefully and investigated the space above the prone bed slab. Here, as below, there appeared to be no openings. Amelia continued to protest his invasion. He ignored her.

"Now do you want to hear it?" asked a voice.

Jansen almost turned, but remembered the old man and his riddle, and caught himself before showing any interest.

"Said I had a riddle."

Sol made his way back across the round room toward his original outpost on the wall. He slid to the ground without seeming to hear.

"A riddle?" said the bishop.

There was a rumbling and a mumbling, the sounds of a fat-bodied person struggling within a confined space. "How the Devil does this work?"

With a snap, the bishop's bed slab dropped from the front. He slid down it like a ramp and landed indelicately on his large rump. Jansen watched out of the corner of his eye as the clergyman smoothed the folds on his gray jumpsuit. It was the same prisoner's garb they all wore, though Jansen thought the bishop's must have been custom-made to accommodate his girth.

After his brief show of temper, Bishop Jubelly remembered his public face, and a serene, grandfatherly countenance leaked out across his jowls.

"*I* should like to hear a riddle," said Jubelly. "You know I was first-rate at riddles back in primary school."

"That so?" asked the old man, turning from Jansen.

Jubelly nodded, rather proud.

"What sort of riddle is it?" said Amelia.

She'd emerged from her enclave and was folding herself into a yoga pose just outside it. Her hands were pressed together in prayer, and, though still cross-legged, she posted one foot on the floor to hold her up. She looked rather like a human flower, even if the baggy jumpsuit detracted from the effect.

"Fair question," said the half-breed. "But telling you what kind would be giving a hint."

Amelia considered this, then nodded. Without taking the single foot from its position, she transposed into Warrior's Pose Number Three.

"Well go ahead," she said. "If I'm going to be thinking, I need to be comfortable."

"Yes, please let's hear it," said the bishop.

The old man smiled. His eyes flicked toward Jansen Sol, who was doing everything in his power to appear oblivious.

"Answer this question: what is found underneath this black door?"

Amelia frowned. "Underneath who's black what?"

"Door," repeated the old man. "Underneath this black door."

"Oh, you mean *that* door?" said Amelia, pointing at the black prism.

The old man tilted his head, his expression unreadable.

"I'll bet it's that," said Amelia. "I'll just go over and look."

"Wait," said Jubelly, holding up a hand. "It's not that. He said it was a riddle, and riddles don't work like that. Isn't that right, my man? What did you say your name was?"

"Didn't" said the old man. "You can call me Bartle if naming things suits you. But you're right that it wouldn't be much of a riddle if the answer was in there."

"Is the solution simple?" asked Amelia, settling back.

She lost her balance, then tried to play off her stumble as an elegant, Eastern method of reaching the Seated Pose.

Bartle shrugged. "All riddles are once you know 'em."

Jubelly smiled. "I've got it, I think."

"Do you already?" said Bartle.

Jubelly nodded, cautiously. "As I said, I excelled at this sort of thing in my youth. Verbal games are my forte."

"Then let's have it," said Amelia.

She turned to the half-breed. "You wouldn't lie, would you? You *will* tell us if we've got it?"

The old man shook his head. "I'll tell *him* if he's got it. I won't speak the rule out loud. If you name something that's found underneath this black door, I'll tell you if it is."

"Splendid," beamed the bishop. "All meaning is in the journey, anyway. Well, then, let me tell you what's found underneath this black door: a tree, a bee, and a knee."

Bartle smiled, but slowly shook his head.

"Guess again."

"It's not double vowels? Like 'door'?"

The man said nothing.

"But it's just like the riddle about the green door," protested Jubelly. "Never mind, I've got it. 'Black door.' So how about 'shark teeth.'"

Bartle shook his head.

"Chalk floor?"

"No," said Bartle. "Sorry."

The bishop pursed his lips and became silent.

"How many guesses are we allowed?" said Amelia.

The old man's eyes twinkled. "How long are you here?"

At his words, a quiet fell over room, and it seemed to constrict, as if the round enclosure was a neck being squeezed. Finally, Amelia looked up and glanced in Jansen's direction.

"Well, I think we should work together on it," she said. "Three heads are better than one."

Only, thought Jansen, *because your head has so very little in it.* He went on ignoring them.

"Why does it have to be *underneath* this black door, for example," she continued. "That's got to be part of it. What do we think about that?"

"Well, I don't think..." began the bishop, waving her off; then, "but, yes, on the other hand, perhaps you're right. Let me see. Yes. If we include 'underneath', then all five vowels are present. Perhaps it's a phrase using all the vowels."

Bartle began to shake his head, but the bishop, in deep concentration, wasn't looking at him. He snapped his fingers.

"Got it! 'Our lives and theirs.'"

"No," said Bartle.

"But it's five vowels!" complained the bishop. "It's even four words, like your original phrase."

The half-breed looked sympathetic.

"Maybe he wants three words?" offered Amelia. "Like in 'this black door.' Think of a phrase with five vowels and three words."

Jubelly scoffed. "Then it wouldn't need five vowels anymore, would it? 'Underneath' gives you *u* and *e*."

He crossed his arms and leaned back against the wall. Jansen smirked. Naturally, the bishop's one "forte" was of no use in the real world.

"Well," said Amelia. "I don't think we should give up."

"*We*," mimed the bishop, with distaste. "I don't recall your offering anything useful. Anyway, I'm just tired. I'm not going to give up so easily—wait! Now wait just a moment."

Bartle smiled. "Since you're tired," he said, glancing upwards, "perhaps we should rest."

The gentle whooshing came again from above. Jansen looked up and saw the slight distortion in the air below the pockmarks on the smooth ceiling.

"That's it!" cried the bishop, pounding the floor with his meaty hand. "Seventy-two underwater jackals. Albatross uncle cat. Just eat your food, child. Have I got it?"

He looked at Bartle with desperation and struggled to keep his eyes open.

"Tell me, man! Tell me!"

Bartle slowly nodded. He did not look happy. "Yes, I believe you've found it."

The bishop beamed and closed his puffy lids. Jansen Sol stared in irritated incredulity until his own eyes fell shut.

***

There were five of them now. Two more of the enclaves had opened, each filled by a new inmate. Jansen saw who was there and gritted his teeth. Gustov Farish was a short, thin man whose small black eyes crawled around like busy beetles behind their thick-rimmed glasses. He'd been an early collaborator with the Principalities, having seen, like Jansen Sol, the inevitability of the situation, as well as the opportunities it afforded. But Farish had crossed him once too often—they were too alike; their strengths too similar—and Jansen had maneuvered to get him reassigned to a much humbler position. And Gustov knew that.

A rude sound and a noxious smell came from the fourth enclave. Jansen realized with disgust that the other prisoner was using his personal toilet but was too stupid or too base to pull down the front of the hinged bed slab for privacy's sake. Sol recognized the man and shook his head. None other than Pongo McRea, popular musician and damned fool. Pongo could play the guitar beautifully, but he couldn't hold a note, not without certain technological enhancements unknown to his millions of adoring fans. He'd sold his soul to the Lords of Earth, to whom he owed his angelic voice. They, in turn, had used him as a mouthpiece for strange new passions that suited their purposes. Pongo smiled on his throne, perfectly oblivious to the others. Finally, he heaved a great sigh, and pushed a small button on the floor to flush his waste. Jansen looked away, disgusted, and returned his attention to Farish. Of the two new inmates, Pongo was the more obnoxious, but Gustov was dangerous.

Gustov Farish walked out of his cell holding something in his hand. He flung it at Jansen.

"This your idea?"

Jansen looked down at the item that had hit him in the chest and rolled down into his lap. It was a large wad of paper bills, balled up and soaked through. Jansen may have suggested, once upon a time, that Gustov had been laundering public money.

Sol shook his head. "I had nothing to do with that."

Gustov scowled, then scanned the room until his eyes fell on the black rectangular prism. He walked over and kicked it. It made a hollow sound, and he reached down to pull on the lid. The lid came up a hair, then caught. He yanked up and down on it, but it held solid.

"What's this?" he said, looking around.

"We don't know," said Amelia, looking to Bartle as to the resident authority.

Bartle studied the newcomer. "You don't need anything in there," he said. "Not yet."

"How do you know what I need?" said Farish.

Bartle considered. "Fair enough. Maybe it'll open if you need it to."

"A coffin's what it looks like," said Farish. "Their idea of a joke, no doubt."

He glared up at unseen watchers.

"Looks can be deceiving," said the half-breed.

Pongo McRea stumbled out of his enclave.

"He's right," said McRea. "These people are clowning us."

He held up a guitar with no strings. Jansen studied the hand gripping the dummy guitar, too distracted by whether he'd washed it to appreciate the sardonic wit behind Pongo's broken prop. Pongo looked about for sympathy and found it only with Amelia.

"Well," she said, bashfully. "You could still sing for us."

Pongo smiled a little, then glanced away, as if ashamed.

"I could write a song, at least," he mumbled. "Don't feel much like singing just now."

There was an awkward silence as the musician searched the doorless walls for a way out, while Amelia looked on, wondering if she'd offended him. She'd thought she was being rather gracious, considering the manner of his introduction. Suddenly, Pongo pointed into the bishop's enclave.

"Where'd you get that stuff?"

Bishop Jubelly looked up from where he sat on the floor. Now he had a pen to go with his blank bible, and he'd been busily scrawling away in it.

From his cheerful demeanor, one could be excused for thinking that writing his own scripture was a heretofore unfulfilled dream of the bishop's.

"I found the pen after I woke up," said Jubelly. "Maybe it was there before. I don't believe so. I choose to regard it as my reward for solving the riddle."

"What riddle?" said Pongo.

Jubelly nodded toward Bartle, who smiled in a self-deprecating way.

"Let's hear it, then," said Pongo.

"Very well," said the old man. "Answer this: what is found underneath this black door?"

Pongo looked at Gustov and smiled, rubbing his hands together as if the two were peers embarking on the same project. Farish shook his head and went over to sit in his own enclave.

"Who's guessed it already?" said the musician.

"Just the bishop," said Amelia, sweetly, then added, "Under this black door. It sounds like one of your songs. Don't you think?"

The musician bobbed his head, as if to a tune he'd already written.

"Yeah, sure does. So, what do we know already?"

"Only that it's not double letters, and it's not the number of words," said Amelia. "Was there anything else, bishop?"

"It's not vowels," said Jubelly. "In fact," he added, "it's nothing to do with letters."

"Be silent," commanded Bartle.

He hadn't raised his voice, but his tone carried an unmistakable threat. And, for a moment, that voice had sounded oddly familiar to Jansen. Looking on without seeming to, Sol wondered why the riddle was so damned important to the half-breed. Jubelly looked down, ashamed.

Sheepishly, Pongo went to sit by Amelia. She spoke with him quietly, trying to recall the bishop's solving phrases, and clearly flummoxed by her proximity to the famous McRea. She asked Jubelly for any help he could give, but the bishop, thoroughly cowed, only shook his head.

"You've got to remember something," said the musician.

She shrugged. "The solutions didn't make any sense. Something about cats underwater. And Albatrosses. I don't know, I was falling asleep."

"Well, it's probably got something to do with water then. Maybe 'this black door' is the lid of a cistern or a well."

"Or a toilet," muttered Farish, from his cell.

Pongo laughed, then looked at Bartle hopefully. The old man shook his head no.

"Do *you* remember what Jubelly said?" said Pongo to Jansen Sol.

"Yes," smiled Sol.

"Well?"

Jansen offered them nothing, not even when the two inmates begged. For one thing, he'd already solved the silly riddle, and for another, he was keeping a close watch on Gustov, hunkered down his enclave. The man would surely seek revenge on him. Jansen noticed how his eyes flitted about the room, more than once alighting on Jubelly's pen. And Farish was not the only danger. There was a clear design behind his cellmates' selection. Naturally, they'd all been associates of the Principalities, but in entirely different ways. The only person connecting them to each other was Jansen himself. These were people he'd used, either in his grand strategy, or, in Gustov's case, to advance himself. He was not afraid of any of them singly, yet assembled, they gave him a strange feeling. He was like a butcher sitting down to a surprise dinner party with the new neighbors—who happened to be cows, pigs, lambs, and a collection of sharp, smiling implements. And who was this Bartle? Where did he fit into the pattern? Without evidence, Jansen felt certain the half-breed was the sharpest knife at the table.

"I've solved your riddle," called Gustov from his tiny room.

He did not look up, only crouched in the darkness, staring at his fingers.

"Tell us then," said Amelia.

"Just the answer," admonished Bartle. "Not the rule it follows."

"Or what?" scoffed Gustov.

Bartle only looked at him. It was strange to Jansen that Gustov Farish looked away and became silent. Perhaps some half-breeds really could, like their progenitors, influence minds.

"Very well," said Farish. "Here are two answers. 'Riddles that I solve.' Also, 'kaleidoscopes' should work."

Bartle furrowed his brow and seemed to think the matter over. Gustov looked at him confidently, and then, less so.

"Come, on! I've solved it."

The old man almost nodded his head, then suddenly shook it again.

"Oh, I see. You think the answer is prime numbers."

"It *is* prime numbers, dammit!" said Gustov, kicking the wall.

"Whether you say, 'underneath this black door' or 'this black door', it's prime. Twenty-three and thirteen letters, respectively."

"Perhaps," shrugged Bartle. "But everything you said is pure coincidence."

Gustov insisted. "My answer fits your riddle!"

"And yet it fails."

"But you hesitated! You must have been counting the letters. What else could it be?"

"Be at peace," muttered Bartle.

Farish fell into a scowling silence. Amelia and Pongo looked on anxiously, their faces revealing how little hope they had of solving it. Gustov's solution had seemed brilliant, and neither of them would ever have thought of it.

"Listen," pressed Farish, after a long pause. "I've worked in cryptography, in linguistics, and in maths. I thought of the prime answer immediately, but I first applied every possible test to rule it out. I'm certain that's the one answer that fits."

"The answer is nothing like that," said Bartle.

"It has to be close! You paused too long before rejecting it."

Jubelly looked up from his scrawling and had a hearty laugh. Farish stood up quickly inside his enclave and hit his head against the bed slab. He walked out, rubbing his crown, and pointing angrily at Jubelly.

"How is it that this false bishop solved it?"

The bishop continued to laugh, now with some derision toward Farish.

"I say you're making it up, half-breed," said Farish. "You've been put here as a sort of jester, to spout infuriating nonsense."

The bishop guffawed even harder at that, but he was soon joined in his merriment by another inmate. Jansen, who'd been observing the spectacle with growing annoyance—prime numbers had been his solution as well—became aware of Pongo McRae. The musician was doubled over with laughter, and he clapped his hands from his place on the floor.

"Well done!" he said, looking at Bartle. "Well done! Now I know it! Oh, don't I ever!"

Bartle sighed. "Remember, just an answer that works. I'll tell you if you've got it."

Pongo nodded. "Now, let me see. It's not so easy to come up with an example, though, is it? Alright … here's a few. It takes a few to really make the point. Hangmen never say they're sorry. Picture books are mostly color. Backwards is my forwards. And … well why not … the number four-hundred thirty-eight."

He snickered in Gustov's direction, not waiting on Bartle's confirmation. "I'm so happy to have gotten it before these wise fools!"

Bartle's smile was almost a grimace. "That's two out of the five of you. Will there be any more?"

"Four of us," corrected Jansen, with irritation. "It's your riddle, so you don't count."

He was pleased to have gotten the old jester on something.

"Ah, so he does care after all," said the half-breed. "Very promising. Or not."

Bartle's gaze swept the ceiling, as if he consulted unseen watchers. The air rushed in again, and Jansen's head became light. As he struggled to remain conscious, a blur of motion drew Jansen's attention. Gustov Farish sprang up, snatched the pen from Jubelly, and holding it like a dagger, dashed across the room toward Jansen. Jansen tried to move but found his legs already dead. He glanced at the half-breed, seeing neither concern in his face nor any sign of fatigue from the gas pouring in. Upon reaching his victim, Farish suddenly doubled over, and collapsed against Jansen's chest. Both tumbled backwards and lay upon the bone white floor staring murder at each other.

Bartle reached out gently and removed the pen from Gustov's hand. The latter looked up at him, and said, in a slurred voice. "I … have it now."

Bartle seemed to sink into himself. Slowly, he crouched down, and put his ear to Gustov's lips, like a priest hearing a last confession. Farish swallowed, then forced out a series of numbers and words. Jansen, in twilight, saw no sense in them at all. Bartle paused, considering the answer.

"Yes," he said, looking at Farish with disgust. "I'm afraid that's it."

Something moved in the room. Many bodies were shuffling behind them. Jansen tried to turn, hoping to see who it was and how they'd entered, but he was stuck in place, all the might of his will and intellect useless before the gas flooding his brain. He heard voices that grunted and strained as if they bore some heavy object. Before he fell into darkness, he heard Bartle by his ear.

"It's five. Now go to sleep."

***

The fifth enclave was open. Each inmate stared out from his own little room at this one new occupant. Seeing it, Jansen Sol lost all interest in the black prism—and any hope for escape.

The enclave held a large transparent tank. In it, bound and fettered and pierced with many tubes, floated a Principality. The small gray body was covered in peeling scales, giving it the appearance of a slightly reptilian monkey. Its head was huge, taking up more area than the rest of its shrunken form so that only the fetters and the blue-green fluid kept the head aloft.

Outside of their pleasing bio-skins these creatures were hideous and immobile, but far from helpless. The thing was awake and looking straight at him. Jansen flattened himself against the wall, awaiting the painful mind probe. Strangely, it didn't come.

"You look surprised," said Bartle, who was now beside him.

"I thought they'd all fled the planet," muttered Jansen.

He would not admit that he was terrified. His jailers had indeed surrounded him with the vestiges of his own past, and it appeared that they meant to torment him with his own devices. Nor was it lost on Jansen Sol that of these five prisoners—excluding Bartle—he was the only one without so much as a hole in the wall to himself. He was their connection point, and the odd man out. Still, he must not show weakness. *They call me a traitor to the human race,* he thought. *But I only did what I had to.*

"What are you planning for me?" he asked.

"What are you planning for yourself?" replied Bartle, without a pause.

Jansen Sol had no response to this. The dark gaze of the Principality, though it sent no communication, made him understand that even if he could escape, he was hateful to everyone. His old masters. His fellow men.

"Why does it not tear our minds apart?" Sol asked. "Is it dead?"

Bartle shook his head. "It's quite healthy, given its age. We've given it a cross-lobotomy. It cannot project; only think."

"We," muttered Jansen. "Of course, you're not one of us. You're with them."

"But you knew that."

"I know more than that," said Jansen. "I know who you are. I think I've known all along, though it just came clear to me."

Bartle nodded. "I expected you did. But you're wrong about one thing. I *am* one of you, in a sense. I'm an inmate as long as you are."

"To torment me," said Jansen.

"To punish you," said Bartle. "In accordance with your crimes."

"Is there a difference?"

"That depends," said Bartle. "Answer my riddle."

Jansen scoffed and crossed his arms. Why should he solve the stupid riddle? The others who'd solved it—Jubelly with his blank bible, Pongo humming off-key and picking at the three strings on his now half-strung guitar, and Farish, presently writhing on the floor in a straight-jacket—were still here. They'd derived no real benefit from solving it. His eyes wandered over to Amelia. To his surprise, she now held a make-up kit. She sat before the little mirror, crying and laughing at turns, babbling to the air, and dabbing her tears with a brush to apply them more evenly. But where had Amelia gotten the makeup? *Could it be…*

"*She* solved it!" whispered Jansen. "Amelia Bel?"

Bartle opened his hands, a helpless gesture. "I know. It disappoints me too."

Jansen leapt to his feet, suddenly furious. He pointed a long finger accusingly at the half-breed.

"What is it?"

Bartle met his gaze silently.

"Tell me what it is!"

"No."

"Is it in there?" said Jansen, pointing at the black prism.

"None of them found it in there," said Bartle.

That answer was too measured. Too careful.

"But is it in there?"

Bartle took a deep breath before responding.

"You are a man of the world," said the half-breed. "A maker. A shaper. One who presumes to arrange the lives of others, whether or not they would be so arranged, and all for your own ends and purposes, as if you were a Principality. As if you were a god."

"Why shouldn't I arrange things to my liking?" said Jansen. "Life is raw material. Either one becomes a god or submits to some other. But what does it mean, 'underneath this black door'? Is that a reference to the darkness of space? Is it a reference to me, or at least your opinion of me?"

He grabbed the old man by his gray prison suit and shook him violently.

"What does it mean!"

The half-breed winced but kept his eyes on Jansen. "I thought you knew better than the whole human race, Mr. Sol."

"I want to know *this*!" spat Jansen. "I *need* to know."

"Very well," said Bartle.

He nodded at the black prism. "Everything that you want is in there. Everything you've ever wanted."

"But *what* is in there?" he said, shaking the old man again.

"Go … and … see." Bartle gasped the words out as his head snapped backward and forward.

Jansen threw him to the ground and stalked toward the black prism.

***

With two hands, he threw back the lid. Without resistance, it swung open and slammed against the floor. Jansen peered in, expecting anything but what he saw. He saw himself, broken and multiplied.

"Mirrors?" he muttered. "Is that the answer?"

Without motion, the space acquired depth. He crouched, reached his hand down, but could not touch bottom.

"Am I supposed to think this is a way out?"

Like a spider, Jansen kept a hand and leg thrown over the edge and reached farther down. Still there was no floor. But amid the ever-multiplying fractal selves, he saw one item that was not Jansen Sol. It was a slip of paper and seemed almost within reach. He let go with his leg and stretched from one hand to take hold of it. When his naked hand touched empty space, Jansen panicked. He was pulling himself back up when the lid began to close.

"What is this?" he cried.

"A place of your own," said the half-breed, looking over the edge. "Per your request."

The lid slammed down, and Jansen pulled his hand away before it could be smashed. He fell just long enough for terror to draw a scream from somewhere beneath his well-kept veneer, then landed painfully at the bottom of a long shaft. Crawling to his feet, Sol stared up into a strange abyss. His reflection stared back at him many times over. He was abstracted, refracted, and reduced to the merest accidents of his being. He moved, and the strange infinity moved as well. Feature reflected feature reflected feature, though nowhere in this nightmare could he locate his own whole form. He looked down at his hands, and could not distinguish them from the whirling, spider-like monstrosities on the floor below him. Inside the prism, he was no longer Jansen Sol, but only a complex of relations.

Panicking, he wedged himself with hands and feet between the narrow walls and tried to climb. He made it only a few feet before slipping down. When he tried again, this time leaping between walls, he slipped forward and bloodied his nose against the wall. The blood dripped into his hands, and then onto the mirror ground. The red droplets became part of the tapestry of disassembly, ever shifting as he moved. If he closed his eyes, he still saw it. When he opened them again, he became sick. Jansen vomited, and this also became part of the patternless pattern. Within this senseless maelstrom, the one persistent thought was that he'd been lied to. He was breaking up, melting. He looked up to where up should be and saw his own angry face staring back down.

"What was the solution, damn you!"

Through some strange property of the shaft, his voice echoed back to him. "Damn you," said the voice, "Damn you."

To his surprise, the prism door opened an inch. The same parchment he'd thought he'd seen below now appeared above him in the half-breed's hand. The black door shut again, and the slip of paper fluttered down through the shaft, casting white shadows, polygon sparrows that flapped their broken wings along the walls. The paper landed near Jansen's feet, though he could locate it only by feel among its dozens of twins. He picked it up and brought it close to his face. A blank sheet, roughly torn, he guessed, from the bishop's bible stared up at him. He turned it over, and read:

THE SOLUTION IS: (TURN OVER)
Jansen did, and read:
THE SOLUTION IS: (TURN OVER)

"No!"

He turned the paper over again and tried to see some meaning in the meaningless words; in the space between them; in the shape of the paper; in the color white. Perhaps in its manner of delivery? *Anything.*

But of course, there was nothing. And now he understood. The riddle was pattern without meaning. Sound and fury, signifying nothing. Any structured pattern to life was pure fancy, coincidence, imposed by the mind. Was that not the very fruit of all his learning? Meaninglessness *was* the solution. That was why the false bishop and the false musician had understood and had laughed. Why the cryptographer and the pseudo-journalist had lost their minds. They'd seen the terrible anti-truth, and they'd believed it.

Jansen buried his face in his hands. "It cannot be. It cannot be."

"Be-Not-Be-Not-Be," said the echo.

He pressed his eyes shut, but the colors of the world still slurred behind his lids. *Am I dead after all?* he wondered. *Is this hell?* Though his cell was deep, he made himself smaller than a man in a coffin, the better to avoid hearing his own voice, and seeing himself stripped down to bundles and tropes.

And it was there, in the darkness of his self, that he considered the light. If the prism door was shut, if the walls were all mirrors, by what were they illuminated?

Jansel Sol opened his eyes. He rolled up onto his knees and looked for the source of light. It seeped in like a mist; seemed to come from everywhere and nowhere. Now turning slow in circles, he searched for some point on the wall that did not shift and fade as he did. At length, he found it, a humble, solitary beam no bigger than a needle's eye. He crept toward it, stealthy, like a hunter. With every small step he had to find it again. When he reached it, he tried to touch it, and his hand passed through space.

Too quick, he thought. *Too greedy*. He crouched down and looked again. That was when he saw that the wall of the shaft wasn't solid here. A smaller shaft, also mirrored, grew out perpendicular to the floor. The light came in from there. He would have to lie prostrate to enter, and his progress through it would be slow. The thought of being so confined horrified him. What if he got stuck?

Yet the light was there. As he squeezed inside the smaller shaft, he saw that his reflection within it was whole. He wormed forward till he was fully encased. Though frightfully hemmed in, within this narrow shaft Jansen felt less a prisoner. The certainty of light, and the comfort of forward motion, made up for the loss of space. The very closeness of the walls seemed to hold his being together.

Sol lost all sense of time. As he crawled, the light grew steadily brighter until its brightness was a sort of reward. The shaft was steadily widening too. Sometimes he thought he could feel the space around him growing, though he dare not test it. A thought came to him—he no longer cared if it was rational—that he did not deserve to stand. Were he to try, his back might hit the ceiling, and then he would lose the sense of growing space, the slow and steady joy of progress towards the light. Yes, it was better to stay very small, and be satisfied with the light he had.

Sometimes he would sleep, and upon waking, find bread and drink resting on the floor before him. He went on like this for time out of mind. He'd passed a lifetime—though perhaps only a few hours—inside that narrow way when he came to a place where the light seemed to dim.

Jansen wormed forward, not yet panicking. Where there was still some light, there was hope. It dimmed further until his reflections became only shadows around him. Still, he crawled, for he remembered from which direction the light had come, even if he could not now see it. Ages passed in total darkness. The air around him was no longer clean. He smelled only his own fetid breath in that small space. Yet he drove forward, for Sol remembered the light. Though its absence tore at his heart, turning back now was senseless. The darker the way, the more resolutely he crawled. He would not be fooled again by darkness, for it was only absence, and absence was not a thing.

One day Sol came to a place where the darkness was absolute and seemed poised to devour him. He put his face in his hands and wept. It was possible, at that moment, that Jansen Sol would have given up, but then he remembered the riddle. He hadn't solved it. He hadn't believed in meaninglessness, as the others had. He'd lacked the courage of conviction. Thank God. He clawed forward.

Presently, he came up against a solid object. He reached out, and his shaking fingers brushed the ankles of someone standing in his path. *Standing!* A hand reached down and took his. The light crept in, but softly. The air became cool and open, and it danced over him, ruffling his hair, caressing his skin. Summoning all his courage, Jansen climbed to his knees and then looked up at a blue-black sky filled with stars. Framed within these stars stood the hooded judge, who towered like a mountain peak under an infinite sky. With his left hand, he removed the hood and tossed it to the ground. The face revealed was smiling, and full of warmth.

"Jansen Sol," said the half-breed. "Stand."

THE ALIEN AND THE JEWELER

Illana Greystoke was the name the twenty-nine-year-old behind the counter had given herself. The name on her birth certificate was less grand, but, like everything in *Greystoke Originals*, this name was shiny, hand-made, and a matter of her customers' perception.

"That is the price," she said.

The man on the other side of the glass countertop frowned. He was in his late fifties, stocky, with slicked-back thinning hair, almost unnaturally black but for the give-away gray at its roots. A recently retired stockbroker, she guessed, but not the fantastically successful kind. Illana could read his story in all the things he tried not to show. He'd been here earlier haggling over the same piece. He'd taken the wife on a nice trip upstate to Hudson. They'd gone shopping, like always. She'd taken a liking to one of the most expensive pieces in Illana's shop. He was supposed to be treating her to a fine getaway, but she didn't yet understand that their income level was now fixed. He needed to get her this keepsake just to keep up appearances. That was Illana's read, anyway.

"I saw earrings just like this," he paused as one of Illana's cats leaped onto the counter and tiptoed between them like a referee, "online, at a fraction of the cost."

Illana smiled patiently, gathering her response while she stroked the Russian Blue's head. "Not *just* like this," she finally said. "Because this set is handmade."

The broker bit his lip in consternation. "I don't think that's particularly relevant. You see, in business, if a machine can do the same job at a lower price, then the machine wins. You're going to have to adapt to the market."

He offered a fatherly look to go with this free counsel and reached for the earrings. She pulled them back, slightly.

"These are handmade," she explained, in the same patient voice.

He shrugged. "You know, machines are hand-made too. I met a real machinist, once. Talk about a *truly* indispensable job! Those guys are the real craftsmen of our age if you want my opinion."

Illana didn't. But she did want his money, and he must have known it. Illana's time in sales had taught her that if the customer found the product desirable, and had the necessary funds, he'd usually buy. It was just a question of time and creating the right context. She was pretty sure he had the money, in a technical sense. The haggling wasn't about affording *this piece*, it was about all the other expensive things that Mrs. Retired Stockbroker would be wanting in the years to come. And maybe it was about proving to himself that he still had it; not money, but *it*. But she couldn't back down on price.

The elements were all in place for a sale. Illana knew the man's wife really wanted these blue-stone fringes that had taken her the better part of fifteen hours to fashion. He didn't know—and Illana couldn't let him suspect—that she'd need to sell all three remaining sets, or the equivalent in scores of smaller pieces, by the end of the week, if she were to make the mortgage payment on the picturesque little house-shop on Warren Street. Otherwise, Illana would have to take another bite out of her savings. And how much longer could she sustain that kind of thing?

"As you said," tried Illana, "we live in an age of machines. That's why this piece has the value that it does. When people see these fringes dangling from your wife's ears, catching and scattering the light, they'll ask her where they can get the same earrings. And that's when your wife gets to say, 'These? Oh, *thank* you, but, you know, they're *hand made*. They're the only pair like them in the whole world. My husband bought them for me on our little trip upstate.' That's what you're paying for, sir."

It was her best argument, and she tried to deliver it with the serene confidence of some Couture luminary, and not like someone who had to dig into savings every month to keep her dream afloat. He smiled. But it was a triumphant smile, as if he knew everything going on inside her head. The man looked around the store slowly, emphasizing its emptiness.

"I'll give you fifteen hundred cash," he said, almost casually. "Final offer. Looks like you need it."

She almost wavered. If he'd guessed she needed the money, then she was already defeated. But if she took his money and let him burst the bubble of perception that separated a high-price luxury item from almost the same thing made in a factory, then she really *was* defeated. It would be the first in a long series of small compromises whose end was mediocrity, the loss of the veil of veneration whose invisible presence made one material thing priceless, and another, plain.

"Twenty-three fifty is the price," she repeated.

He shrugged. "Not worth that."

"It's actually quite competitive," she tried again, "given the sort of piece it is. Elsa Peretti—"

"Yeah? But you're not her."

He turned to go. It took everything in her not to call out after him. The door chimed as he closed it behind him, none too gently.

Though it was fifteen minutes before closing time, Illana found herself locking the door, and turning the sign around. In a kind of daze, she floated toward the back room. Three long, collapsible tables covered in white tablecloth took up half of the re-purposed living room that was her workshop. Beads, gold and silver beadlets, and tiny colored gemstones formed a functional mosaic that would be chaos to anyone else but her. Three kinds of pliers lay where she'd left them. Illana sat down, intending to finish the piece she'd started that morning, then pushed it all aside and put her head on the table.

Outside, the day was failing. She knew she must put in two more hours before bed, or else get up at four and finish the same piece before opening. She scraped herself off the table, and stared, bleary eyed, at the complicated, many-colored device, trying to remember where she'd left off. Frustration welled upside in her, moving about her insides slowly, like the browned leaves of late November that turned and fell, churned and disappeared, into the Hudson River. Disappeared. They died there; though, like her dreams, they'd so recently been striking and vibrant. She gritted her teeth. Two hours now, and rise a little later, or sleep now, and face this complicated thing with half a brain. Every day, the same. Rinse. Repeat. Rinse. Repeat.

She forced her fingers to move, and kept at it until a third and unconsidered option imposed itself at 10:36 p.m. That was when Illana fell asleep at her workbench. She would have lain like that until the cats' scratching woke her, except that something else jolted her awake.

She'd been dreaming about being sentenced to a debtors' prison from the old days, and, in the retroactive logic of dreams, her mind had interpreted the loud bang in her back lot as a heavy iron cell door being slammed shut by a stocky guard with black, slicked-back hair, frosty at the roots. The cats' frantic whining proved the sound real, and she was suddenly afraid. Illana stood cautiously, brushing away the golden beadlets that had lodged themselves into her forearms and chin. When she slipped on her coat and opened the door to the hallway that stretched darkly toward her back door, the four cats she'd barricaded there shot past her, ignoring the coveted and forbidden workshop, and making directly for the stairs.

Illana had no weapons in the quaint little house-shop; a fact that hadn't, until now, struck her as inconvenient. Red, smoky light glared through the back window, and by it she saw that she'd fallen asleep without threading the door chain. Even the deadbolt was open. Crouching, she moved toward the door, staying below the plane of its window, and turned the bolt. Quickly and without looking through the glass, she threaded the door chain. Back on her haunches, she stared up at the smoky red light floating in above her through the absurdly large and insecure portal that, it now occurred to her, anybody could simply break. She was all alone and should have been afraid. But she was also curious.

Illana rose to her knees and peeked through the window. Her back lot was a narrow rectangle, fenced-in, and sparsely covered by dormant November grass. In its center was a smaller rectangle, the now-abandoned herb garden she'd attempted last spring. In the middle of that, like a bullseye, a smoking red crater marked the end of her modest agricultural dreams.

She should have been upset but felt only relief. After all, a smoldering fireball in her backyard was significantly better than a bearded man with a knife or a demon from hell. At least she wouldn't have to bother with that garden anymore.

"Well, what do you think?" she said, by instinct consulting the ever-lurking cats.

But her six little companions were nowhere to be found. Four had run away, she now remembered. The others were busy sleeping or pissing on her furniture. Useless. Maybe it was time for a dog. Illana took a deep breath and stood. She slowly undid the bolt and the sliding chain and opened the door. Wondering if she had a secret death-wish—if she were dead, there'd be no mortgage payment—she crept toward the red crater.

Bits of what seemed to be hot scrap metal lay scattered around the indentation. In its center sat a cracked, lozenge-shaped cylinder no larger than a cinder block. The lozenge wobbled.

Illana shrieked, but she had the presence of mind to run to the outdoor shed and grab her metal rake. It was the kind with heavy iron teeth that made it almost useless for leaf-removal because the leaves got caught in the tines. She raised it above her head, fueled by adrenaline, and prepared to bring all its force to bear on whatever wobbled inside the metal lozenge.

The lozenge cracked apart. Inside, its small mouth opening and closing like a fish out of water, lay a little man. Well, not a man. He had large red eyes, a tiny, helpless mouth, and skin the color of dead leaves.

***

After Illana had recovered her wits enough to scramble back inside, she got to thinking about the tiny man. He was frightening, certainly. But he was small, apparently alone, and it was cold outside. If she looked past the large fire engine-red eyes, their image still imprinted in her brain, and the tiny claws on his tiny hands and feet, what remained was almost cute. A lonely little monster. A spaceman, though he was more brown than green.

"Why am I calling it 'he'?" she said to Chekov, the AWOL Russian Blue.

Because it had eyes. Because those eyes had seen her, and seen into her, showing awareness. That made him more than a thing. And she'd left him there, naked, in the cold dark.

Illana took a deep breath, then darted upstairs. From a chest in her room, she retrieved a fuzzy blanket. A relic of her childhood, it was too small now to be used on her bed, and too special to risk some accident with the cats. Just right for him, though. She walked down the stairs with it. Five of her cats were still in hiding, but Chekov followed her down, purring in what seemed a threatening way; warning her, as if he knew only too well what his mistress was thinking.

Illana ignored him and marched toward the back door. Chekov scratched desperately at her ankle.

"Stop it," she said, kicking him back inside as she opened the door.

The red smoke from before had dissipated. Now there was a black space in the center of the garden, illuminated only by stars, since the porch light, like the light for the basement stairs, and the one in her guest room, was out. Illana cursed her own negligence.

The moon had not yet risen. Everything was coated in a soft blue. For a moment she feared that the tiny man had run away, but a brief exploration found him huddling against the fence, balled up for warmth.

"Oh, you poor thing," said Illana.

She crouched and spread the blanket. The creature flinched, then fixed her with a hard stare. Once more, reason told her to be wary, but her heart said otherwise.

"It's not a net or anything," she said, fluffing the blanket with her hand. "You must be so cold."

The creature stood on shaky legs. It took two steps toward her, then tentatively extended a tiny, clawed hand. It touched the blanket, recoiled, then touched it again. One of its claws seemed to grow longer, and, with a sudden swiping motion, it sliced through the material. Then, with what Illana could have sworn was a nod, it walked its little body into the warm blanket, and looked up at her.

"My goodness," she said. "Look at your eyes!"

The eyes grew narrower, as if the little man were warning her not to try any funny business. She giggled, wrapped him slowly in the blanket, and lifted him into her arms like a baby.

"Let's get you inside," she said.

A minute later, they were upstairs. The creature allowed itself to be cradled, and she felt it pulling the blanket more closely around its chilled limbs. Everything was going well, until she got to the bedroom. All six of her cats sat rigid on her bed, their back hair straight. Chekov was at the front, like a town magistrate. Though the little man couldn't see them from inside the blanket, he stiffened, and she felt his tiny claws pop through the material.

"It's alright, it's alright!" she said. Then, to the cats, "Get out of here. Sleep somewhere else tonight."

She shooed them out with her feet, ignoring their protests, then shut the door behind her. The creature in her arms instantly relaxed.

"There, now," she said. "They're all gone. Now, hold on just a second."

Illana placed the bundle on her bed and opened the closet door. She had the old plastic carrying case she used to bring her cats to the vet. She'd need to reassemble it. She separated the pieces, took the small bolts from the sandwich bag taped against the bottom, and quickly rebuilt the carrier. When she looked up, the creature was standing on her bed, its fingers splayed out. Extended, its claws were as long as its fingers.

"Um..." she began, "I'll ... I'll leave the door off, okay? I just thought, maybe, you'd want a little space of your own."

She took it apart again and removed the door, which she waved at him before tossing it into the closet.

"See," she said, indicating the open portal. "In and out whenever you want."

The creature seemed to relax again, its claws visibly retracting. Outside in the hall, the cats whined loudly.

"Jealous little stinkers," she said, glaring at the bedroom door.

When she looked back, the tiny man was facing away from her, staring at the opposite wall. There she had a poster of Brandon Lee. The image, found at an Oakland thrift store on a college road trip long ago, was a still shot from *The Crow.* Beneath it sat a small end table bearing several scented candles. Brandon lounged in an ancient chair, elbows propped up on the chair's Gothic arms, wearing an expression that promised death to men and seduction to women. The candles under the image gave that corner of the room the appearance of a shrine. Silly, perhaps, but it was her own damn room after all, and she could hang anything she wanted.

"That's ... impossible to explain," she laughed. "Don't worry, though. It's just a picture."

The tiny man turned back to her, and now its expression was almost thoughtful. She set the pet carrier on the floor, not far from the heater, and placed the blanket inside, neatly folded. Outside, the cats whined more insistently. Illana thought she recognized and could pick out Chekov's particular note. She sighed.

"Well," she said. "Those are cats. I can't promise they'll ever *love* you. Hell, I'm not sure they really love *me.* But I feed them, so ... wait a second. What on earth do you eat?"

Then she laughed at the irony of the expression and laughed again when she saw the little man's confusion at her laughter.

"They don't laugh on Mars ... or ... whatever?" she asked.

The tiny man cocked his head.

"Well, I have lunch meat and lettuce in the fridge. Maybe some crackers, too. Eat whatever you can, I guess. I'll bring it up in a second. I ...

uh … I don't know what to do for you in terms of a bathroom. Guess we'll play that one by ear."

The creature startled her by dropping into a lotus position. She couldn't tell whether it was resting, meditating, or seething with anger.

"Man, what *are* you?" said Illana.

She wasn't really expecting any reply.

"Do you have a name?"

No answer, only a narrowing of the eyes. She wondered if it—he—could even hear her. Did he have ears? Well, he'd sensed the cats. Yes, and he'd reacted to her laughter.

"I'm going to give you a name. Let's call you Victor. Don't ask me why. It just fits."

Victor seemed to shrug, and that made her giggle all over again.

***

[Translated from Xtolchetznhautlz]

Ship's Log, LD 5,736

We have been taken captive. The quantum storm that disrupted riftspace and laid waste one third of our comrades in the Forty-Second Wave did not destroy our own pod, only pulled it into lower space. The coincidence is so great, we'd be inclined to suspect it was intentional, were it not for the primitive technological level of this planet. We should have died honorably, either with our comrades in the rift calamity, or with those who passed through to wreak havoc on the Phlegmatarian cowards. We have been most unfortunate.

Yet all is not lost. Our mental link to the pod is still intact, obviously, for we sense the imprinting of this record as we make it. The ship's core is still alive, and through it we also sense that the field configurer has survived impact. It lies somewhere in the surrounding countryside. Still, we were wise to eject, as the hull was breached, and the sub-light engines smashed to powder. Our plan must therefore be to recover the configurer and reassemble the ship's components bit-by-bit, however long this may take. This done, we shall attempt to find a rift pore in local space, and, at some distant moment, claw our way back to Phlegmatar. We burn with envy, for many of our comrades must already have died gloriously, slaying the putrescent, cowardly Phlegmatarians without us.

There is, apparently, no danger of the local apex species finding and making use of the configurer, though even their simple defense array must have detected the pod ship's entry. We must soon recover the config unit, lest it be spirited away to become an item of local worship. Speaking of this, our captor is a female of the brontian type, varieties of which have long been cataloged in the Index. She maintains a large icon of one of the local deities, has pierced her body through with many small bits of shaped metal, and lines her limbs and digits with still more pieces of metal and stone, and with various tribal etchings. She employs half a dozen warcats as guards, but evidently has little control over them. We shall have to make an example of the lead guard, and, in any event, will soon require sustenance if we are to convert to a more practical form.

Regarding the latter, we have so far detected no conversion capacity among the local faunae. Our captor's living quarters, the implements she makes use of, or which decorate her limbs, even the dead matter which she both consumes and offers us for sustenance, imply a static morphology, one which cannot dynamically re-purpose living matter. If this is so, then we have a great advantage, for she cannot suspect what she cannot conceive.

On the other hand, our captor is far from harmless. Thrice we have fixed her in the death stare, and thrice she has broken free of its grip with hardly an effort. When locked in the stare, her upper body and mouth begin convulsing—an adaptation that greatly resembles the hoovering of burbleslurbs—and the stare is broken. If this adaptation were, as it initially seemed to us, a well-developed defense mechanism against mental attack, we'd be forced to infer a long co-evolutionary arms race. Yet she shows no other signs of mental agility. Our captor relies on her limbs and digits for virtually all manipulation, even when directing her warcats. From this we must draw one of two conclusions: either she is a top level mentaxic, choosing to conceal the full breadth of her acumen except when breaking the stare, or—and this seems more likely—her species lacks sufficient mental acuity even to *feel* the impact of a mental touch. In short, they are too stupid to be manipulated.

We must wait and gather evidence before making a direct move against our captor. We do not fear her. All that we fear is a meaningless death among primitives. Our heart burns to return to battle, to hear the warscream as it radiates through the infinite darkness of the Core Mind, to feel, to see, and to taste the hopeless suffering of the cursed Phlegmatarians, our slavers of old, as they burn in our fires and die in our jaws, their pups crying out helplessly as their sires are consumed by fang or by fire. O, Death! O Glorious Vengeance! How we long for thy sweet kiss!

***

When Illana woke up, the cold air that had bitten her nose and cheeks while she slept became more than an inconvenience. As the confusion of sleep lost its hold on her, she began to panic. She was under several thick blankets. The space heater was on; she could hear it running. Yet the weatherman had warned of a coming deep freeze, and, somehow, that freeze had gotten into her room, where it had no business being.

She leapt from the bed and wrapped herself in blankets. In her anxiety about what the cold implied, she forgot to check on her small visitor, and made straight down the hallway for the thermostat. Her heart sank as she read it. It was set to seventy-degrees, but the temperature inside the house was forty-one.

"Okay," she said, "I probably just left a window open."

This was what she told herself in the moment, though it could hardly explain the cold. Illana looked anyway, hoping for some cause other than the one her panicking hindbrain had already suggested. She moved diligently from window to window and checked every door. Almost to her surprise, the back hallway door was slightly open—she was certain that she'd locked it—though not wide enough to have let in all that cold. She shut it hard again and bolted it. And while this development carried its own causes for concern, Illana had only the emotional bandwidth for one potential crisis.

Bracing the blankets against herself, she opened the basement door, tried to turn on the lonely light that lit the stairwell, remembered that she'd been too lazy to replace it, and headed in a huff down the dark stairway. When she stepped from the stairs to the unfinished concrete floor, the cold went right through her fuzzy socks.

"It's okay," she said, wishing there were a few more lamps in the place. "This has happened before. It's just the pilot light. I can do this."

It occurred to her, as she thought out loud, that none of her cats had made an appearance.

The basement was too dark, and Illana was too distracted with worry, to notice the little man hiding in the darkness as she passed through the unfinished space. She stepped into the utility room, flipped on the overhead light that was mercifully still working, and opened the heavy door to the furnace room. She propped it open with a cinder block, crouched down, and removed the top access panel. The pilot light stared back at her, unlit.

She pressed the igniter switch. Nothing happened. After checking to ensure the gas valve was open, she tried again, with the same result. A third attempt, this time with the grill lighter, produced only a fleeting flame. It quickly died.

Groaning within, Illana removed the bottom access panel. A mess of wires greeted her. Though she was already past the limits of her H-Vacial powers, Illana risked a look with the flashlight on her phone. Plastered to the control board, rigid in exquisite death agony, was the largest, deadest rodent she'd ever seen.

Four hours later, wearing three layers, Illana opened the store. Her weather app promised a coming freeze, and she'd left every faucet in the house running. The HVAC repairman, busier than usual this time of year, would not be there for a day and a half. When she'd informed him about the rat on the panel, he'd suggested she just replace the old Goodman unit. "Easier, faster, and probably even cheaper than trying to repair that old thing," he'd said.

Illana, with little enough money, now faced the prospect of having even less. She'd told him that she would just have to find somebody who could repair the unit without trying to make her buy a new one. He'd said, "Good luck," before hanging up on her.

Then there was Chekov. The other cats she'd found huddling together in the guest bedroom, but the Russian Blue was gone. Had he run out? Illana wondered how she'd been foolish enough to leave the back door open. And yet it was strange that the willful, short-haired cat would choose such a cold night for its escape.

The door chime sounded only a few times that morning. It was cold. People were not in a shopping mood. By 4 p.m., she'd made only five sales, each of them small items under one hundred dollars. The braided cuff bracelets in mermaid colors were at least consistent sellers, but only at a price that hardly justified the time it took to make them. Meanwhile, her high-grade pieces stayed behind the display glass, gathering dust.

Illana was already well-past the point where tears of frustration usually overwhelmed her, when the door chime rang, and the black-haired broker entered. He'd brought his wife.

Silently, Illana rejoiced. No longer thinking of the mortgage, content now simply to keep her pipes from freezing, she beamed at Mrs. Stockbroker and her conquered husband.

"Well, hello!" she said, breath fogging up in the air. "This is a pleasant surprise."

Mrs. Stockbroker returned her smile, but there was something in it that felt wrong. Something cunning.

"Mizz Greystoke," said the stockbroker's wife. "We were hoping you'd be open."

"Let me get that tassel set out for you," said Illana.

She opened the display case and set the earrings on the counter. Normally, when making a big sale, Illana had to control her movements lest her excitement became too obvious, but her hands were so cold that she could only move slowly. The stockbroker looked around, frowning, and pulled his jacket tighter.

"Furnace broken?" he said.

Illana smiled wanly. "The repairman said he'd be here already," she lied. "Sorry for the inconvenience."

He looked at her, and then at his wife. That same cunning smile.

"I see," said the man. "Better keep a faucet running. It'll be cold enough soon to burst pipes."

Illana nodded. "Thanks."

She lifted one of the tasseled earrings and placed it gently across the woman's gloved palm.

"Would you like to try it on again?" asked Illana.

Mrs. Stockbroker smiled. "That won't be necessary," she said. "We're ready to purchase."

Illana moderated the smile that threatened to take over her face.

"I'm so pleased," she said, modestly.

Mrs. Stockbroker smiled. "We'll give you sixteen hundred for it."

Illana reeled. For a moment, she wondered if she'd misheard.

"S-sixteen hundred?" she said, unable to suppress a frown. "No. The price is twenty-two fifty."

She looked at the man. "I thought … sir, we'd already established that. Remember—"

"Yes, I remember you said that," he said, laconically. "But the temperature is dropping. The best part of fall is over. You know as well as I do that your sales are going to *fall* off a cliff until Christmas. Pardon the pun."

She stared at him, stunned at his temerity. He smiled, and leaned in.

"And, let's be frank, young lady. Your shop isn't doing so well. I've been here four times, and not once have I seen another customer."

"I … I don't think you understand," she stammered.

"And," he said, with finality, "you can't even keep the heat on here. So, this is what we're going to do. We're going to give you sixteen hundred. Cash. Straight up. And you're *going* to sell at that price because we both know you need the money. You don't spend thirty years on Wall Street and miss a detail like that."

Illana gaped at him, unable to conceal her disgust. The black-haired man looked neither surprised nor terribly offended by what he saw. If her anger was obvious, so now was her desperation. He dropped a stack of hundreds on the display case, and slowly counted it out before her. With each bill placed, her will evaporated. As in a dream, her hand released its hold on the tasseled earrings, and fell shakily on cold hard cash. Mrs. Stockbroker smiled triumphantly, and swiftly removed the prized items from the counter.

"We won't make her give us a box, will we?" she said to her husband.

He chuckled. "No, no. After all, she gave us a deal."

He nodded at Illana, injecting a little sympathy into the movement, as if to say, "We won this time, but that's the game."

They turned to go. Illana groped for the chair behind the counter as the door chime rang with her customers' departure. They'd beaten her. He had known; had pierced the veil of value. She collapsed into the chair, cheapened.

Illana didn't move from the spot for the better part of an hour. She grew colder, becoming a human icicle in the frigid room. When the door chime sounded again, she did not even look up.

"Ahem," said a male voice.

She raised her head. Two men stood at the counter in black suits. One was tall and thin, the other shorter, with a bulldog face. He stared not at her, but at her hands, and Illana realized that she was still cradling the filthy lucre from an hour before. Embarrassed, she quickly opened the cash drop below the register, and stuffed the bills in. Standing slowly, she smoothed her gown, and tried to find the face she used for customers.

"What can I do for you gentlemen?"

They were an unlikely pair.

"We're here to talk about your visitor," said the first man.

She stared blankly. "Visitor?"

In all that had happened, Illana had almost forgotten about the little spaceman. Understanding gradually dawned. She tried to make her face an empty sheet of paper.

"What visitor?" she said.

The scarecrow frowned. "Come on. You're not fooling anybody."

The other man walked over, locked her front door, and turned the sign over.

"I don't know what you're—"

"—Save it, miss. We know where it landed. We know you have it. Turn it over now, and there'll be no trouble for you."

Illana's mind raced. An instinct warned her not to give the creature up, told her that it would be wrong, somehow, to betray her tiny refugee. But she couldn't think. There hadn't been time to invent plausible stories, and, anyway, she was a terrible liar. Obviously.

"Before you say anything else," said the bull-faced man, wagging a finger at her. "Understand this: we *will* get it. Anyone you think you can call, any plan you may have, it's not going to work. Cooperate, and it'll go well for you. There's a reward involved with this kind of thing. A considerable finder's fee … along with an expectation of absolute and perpetual silence on the matter. As for the alternative … well, you might call that the opposite of a reward."

Illana backed up, knocking into a rack of hanging bracelets. She hardly noticed the pain as the rack's metal arm poked into her shoulder bone.

"You're threatening me?" she said. "Who are you, anyway? What agency do you work for?"

The scarecrow man took a deep breath before responding. "We don't make threats," he said, calmly. "We're just couriers. We state facts. And, if you knew who we were, trust me, it wouldn't help your situation. Be glad you're talking to us, and not the other guys."

Illana felt the room spinning around her. She had no particular reason to protect the tiny man from space, but Illana was a sensitive soul, and their bad intentions were as obvious to her as the cold in the room. Her heart seemed to scream, "DO NOT HELP THEM!"

"No," she said, after a long pause.

"No, what?" said the bull-faced man.

She looked up at him. "I don't know what you're talking about. There's no one here, but me and the cats."

She trembled as she lied, but it hardly mattered. The scarecrow chuckled at the lie.

"Like I said, we're only couriers."

He nodded at the stocky man, who shrugged, and shook his head.

"It's a shame, though," continued the scarecrow. "You were a pretty girl. Tomorrow, you won't be."

Without another word, the two men turned, and left the little shop on Warren Street.

Illana locked the door behind them. Freezing, and now terrified, she wanted nothing more than her own bed. She stumbled up the stairs, groped her way down the hallway, and fell into her blankets. The little man was sitting in a lotus position atop his carrying case. He seemed larger than before, though the detail meant nothing to her. Seeing him there, red eyes fixed upon her like angry fireballs, she was overcome by a sense of cosmic absurdity. Illana put her face in her pillow and began to sob. The creature she'd named Victor watched her for a while, fascinated. Then, with a sort of nod, he hopped down and slipped from the bedroom.

***

[Translated from Xtolchetznhautlz]
Ship's Log, LD 5,737

Hail to the Cosmic Chaos, the Death Pulse of the Universe, which fuels our brethren in arms! But woe to those who languish in exile while others achieve the peace of immortality!

The previous day brought many small victories, along with unforeseen complications. Of these, we shall, perhaps, speak a little.

Our initiatives to recover the configurer and to humble the enemy guard were successful—perhaps too much. As our captor slumbered, trusting foolishly in her pack of warcats, we slipped our cell and began our initiatives.

(It bears noting that these brontians cannot convert forms, just as we suspected. One final example proves the point: our captor closed the hinged portal that secures her berth and made no further efforts to secure it, on the apparent belief that our present stature was fixed; that we could not reach the control lever! But we digress.)

Descending to the ground level, we were confronted by the lead beast, which, unrestrained by its brontian mistress, engaged in various intimidation displays, and attempted to smite us with its claws. Unlike the brontian female, the warcat was quite susceptible to the death stare, and we had the pleasure of watching it tremble and of listening to its pathetic whimpers, as we consumed it limb-by-furry-limb. This provided us sufficient energy stores to attempt the cold temperatures, and we soon located the configurer and the ship's core mind in the surrounding hills. Upon our return, we left the rear external portal open, thinking it wise to provide our captor some plausible explanation for her guard-captain's sudden absence. However, this bit of cleverness on our part had an unintended effect, which we shall now relate.

Escaping the frigid temperatures without, a small furry creature entered the structure and made its way down to the building's subterranean level where we had established camp. It skittered around noisily whilst we set to work fabricating, and we had half a mind to consume it as well. We ought to have done so, for it made its way into the heating apparatus, where it proceeded to chew through cables, and eventually shock itself to death. This was more than an inconvenience to us, for the resulting cold drew our captor's notice, and our workshop was at risk of being discovered.

Now begins a series of events which have proved both inconvenient and perplexing. Rather than simply repair the heating apparatus, our captor became distressed, and her anxiety only increased throughout the day. To explain that distress, it is first necessary to describe, in some detail, the primitive economy here. Our captor has no practical skills. Instead, she assembles wampum by hand, then trades the wampum to other brontians for small bits of combustible green fuel. (We assume it to be fuel, for it could have no other utility.) She seems to have a diminished supply of the latter and is in such straits that she was forced to part with a valued piece of wampum at an unfavorable rate.

Reading her from afar—not an easy task with female brontians—we determined she is in a desperate state of mind. Nevertheless—and here is the oddest detail—when planetary magistrates later confronted her about our presence, she did not give us up. This, even after the magistrates threatened her life. Now, we cannot, even for a moment, pretend to understand the politics of this planet. It seems that our captor is a sort of local baroness, and that she had hoped, by our capture, to improve her standing in the global power structure. Evidently, she considers us too valuable a prisoner to surrender, and is willing to risk her bodily health in a gamble to keep us from the planetary overlords.

A bizarre calculus, indeed, but can one expect reason from creatures that trade carefully assembled wampum for useless fire strips? Still, it's in our interest to remain under her imagined confinement until we've reconfigured the ship. For that reason, we began to consider how we might stabilize her political situation, buying ourselves the time needed. This brings us to the final perplexity:

As we sat ruminating on these matters, joining ourselves to the Core Mind, and sharing, albeit vicariously, in the victories of our comrades under far-distant stars, our captor re-entered her berth. As we looked on, she displayed an adaptation with which we have no prior experience. Salivary glands in her eyes produced gobs of fluid, which were then excreted over her skin. She began to heave and tremble, like one already defeated. In short, the creature's distress was sufficient to initiate some form of chemical self-immolation!

This will not do. Our situation must remain stable if we are to join the mighty Chorus of Death on Phlegmatar. We cannot have the brontian dissolving herself from the outside in, however amusing that might be to watch. Consequently, we have resolved to eliminate the sources of her anxiety. An irritation, but a necessary one, if we are to rejoin the Brethren, and find peace in the red and thirsty jaws of Blessed Death. We have therefore resolved to divide our fabrication time between shipbuilding and wampum production. The configurer can certainly handle the latter, menial task.

***

When she woke in a hot sweat, the latest of three nocturnal wakings, Illana realized that her dreams about being baked to death inside an oven had an external source. The house was warm and toasty. She threw off her comforter and peeled the sweat-soaked sheets from her body. Victor was fast asleep in his carrying case. *So he did sleep.* The cats were whining in the hallway, informing her of their feeding schedule, and lodging official complaints in the tongue of their ancestors.

She looked out the window, and saw the deep frost over everything, the creeping early glow of a cold morning, the water frozen solid in the bird bath. Was she dreaming all of this? She darted from the room and padded quickly down the steps. She passed through her workshop, noticing but not fully processing some small incongruity in the darkened room. In her urgency, she pressed on to the basement stairs. She reached for the light switch and found to her consternation that the bulb she'd finally replaced was out again. *God,* she thought, *I hope it's not the wiring.*

It was very dark, but her excitement over the house's unexpected warmth overcame her fear. She descended quickly and crossed the dark space without looking around. She could hear the furnace now. Entering the utility room in a state of wonder, she flicked on the overhead light. Wondering if she were dreaming the subtle groan and hum of the furnace, she failed to notice the shapes that protruded from under a tarp, tucked away in the darkened corner of her unfinished basement. She rarely looked at the piles of assorted junk down there.

Cautiously, Illana pulled back they heavy door, propping it open with the cinderblock. The old furnace was indeed running. But how? She began to work off its lower panel, then stopped. What if opening it would jostle the innards, and undo whatever accident had caused it to start up again? Last night, she'd prayed through tears that everything would be alright. What if touching the thing stopped that magic? She'd be Moses, striking the stone twice.

She decided to let it be, and so never saw the alien arrangement of jury-rigged, custom-fabricated tubing, now wrapped like octopus arms around and through the fried control panel.

An image came back to her. She stood, suddenly rigid, her hindbrain now informing her of what she'd seen only in passing. She ran back upstairs. After she shut the basement door behind her, a translucent floating orb that had been hiding in plain sight swam out into the dark basement and began to hum. Fluids within it turned green and crackled with an enigmatic power she'd have called "electricity", had she witnessed it. Upstairs, Illana's gaze settled upon the workshop tables. She rubbed her eyes, but it was all still there.

On the white tablecloth, arranged neatly in rows, rested a dozen mermaid bracelets, two chokers, three gorgeous brooches, and two large statement earing sets, of which one pair were tasseled fringes of the most elaborate and unique design. It was like her work. No two pieces were the same; each was the sort of thing she would have made, if only she'd had the energy to make it. But she hadn't. Not unless she were a sleepwalking Michaelangelo. She'd heard of things like this, but—

The cats whined at the workshop door. She slapped herself, hard, but the jewelry remained stubbornly tangible. The whining grew more insistent.

The clock on the wall read 7:02. Had she really slept through her alarm?

"Impossible," she whispered, shaking her head.

In a kind of haze, Illana fished the cats' food out of the downstairs closet, and proceeded to fill the various bowls, hidden around the house to give the ever-fattening creatures some exercise. She recalled that there was one less cat to feed now but was too perplexed to be sad.

All that day, the shop door opened and closed, chiming. Illana didn't know why so many more people came in than usual, and she didn't ask. It was like with the heater. Fortune kept its secrets, and she didn't dare pry.

By four in the afternoon, Illana had sold nine of the twelve mermaid bracelets, one of the chokers, and all three brooches. The fringed earring set that the magic had made looked so good to her that she'd priced it boldly at thirty-two hundred. After all, it looked better than the Elsa Peretti set she admired. She wondered if that was *too* much; if greed would somehow break the magic, but two couples entered the store around six-thirty. Both wanted the set, bid for it, fought over it like sharks in a feeding frenzy, and in the end, she got thirty-five hundred. When the last customer left, Illana wondered again if she were dreaming. She began periodically poking herself with the needle-clasp from one of the cheaper brooches in the bargain bin. Little beads of blood were all she got for her efforts.

She decided it had all been real, and that magic and good fortune had finally found their way into her life. And hadn't she struggled, and sacrificed? Maybe it was just her time. Crying in a different way now, she went to close up for the night. When she got to the door, dark shapes stood behind the glass. The door was shoved hard against her, and she fell backwards.

The men who entered the store were not the same men who'd come the day before. Their bodies were of a different cut, tall and thick. Like ogres. Once, she'd served on jury duty, and, on the last day, when the verdict was being given, the small and non-threatening court officers were swapped out for huge men, the guys they sent to drag you to prison and throw away the key. These men were built just like that. Violence radiated from them. Their eyes were dead and stared out coldly from behind ski masks. One of the men held her down, while the other took out a roll of sticky black paper and ran it along the inside of the large glass storefront window. Illana would have screamed, but the first man pinched her mouth open, thumb and forefinger squeezing her cheeks, bruising them, and stuffed a rag past her teeth. They rolled the chair from behind the front counter and tied her arms and legs to it.

She looked up from a seated position. One of the men took out a black metal baton. He thumbed a button, and the baton crackled and hummed. He brought it close to her face. She could feel the tiny hairs on her neck dancing in painful anticipation.

"You're not going to make it through the night," said the man with the baton. "But if you tell us where it is, I'll make it quick."

He took the gag from her mouth. "Don't scream. Just talk."

She was too scared to talk. He stuffed the rag back in and tapped her shoulder with the baton. She screamed into the rag.

"That was just a taste," said the man. "I can make it take a long time, or a short time. I can make it clean or very, very ugly. Talk."

He pulled the rag out, but Illana still felt like she was choking.

"You can't do this, can you?" she said, in tiny voice. "If I've broken the law, arrest me. Take me to jail."

He chuckled.

"Free country, and all that?" he said.

She nodded, warily.

"Free to sell and breed in. That's all. Laws don't keep the planet safe, girly."

He twirled the baton in his fingers. "A state's just like nature. Under all the pretty colors, 'neath the fur, the fuzz, the mask, there's only this one thing."

He touched the baton to her thigh, pressing it down into the muscle there. Somewhere in the house, the cats whined for her, but of course they didn't help. Illana was drooling and foaming at the mouth now. The man with the baton draped his heavy arms over her knees and leveled his head with hers.

"Is it dangerous? Did it threaten to hurt you if you told us? Trust me, you're getting hurt either way."

She cried, but there seemed to be no moisture available for her face.

"How is it communicating with you? What kinds of weapons does it have?"

She didn't answer. She couldn't think. He slapped her thigh hard, this time using only the force of the baton.

"Where is it?"

"I don't know," she whimpered.

While the first man was interrogating her, the second had been searching the house. He came back into the front room now holding the empty pet carrier. He showed it to his partner, very casual. The baton man nodded and turned back to Illana.

"You think it's a pet, don't you? Like one of your cats."

She didn't answer.

"There are a bunch of different kinds, you know," he said, indicating, with the sweep of his baton, the great empty ocean of space. "Grays, greens, and other things. Things that you wouldn't even recognize as living. That's the problem."

She shivered and stared down into the pattern of her gown. Its beauty, the craft of it, was somehow preposterous now. The world was a cold edge.

"We're like children beside them," he continued. "Every living thing keeps its head down in the universe because the universe ain't friendly. No, sister. First one to show his hand, dies. That's the game. Only rule that matters. Compared to that, laws are just fur and feathers and fakery. You should have told the truth before. They might have let you in on the game. Now you're part of the problem. People like you—naive people—can't be allowed to tell what they know. You put everyone else at risk, see? That's why I don't feel sorry for you. I have no problem hurting you. Do you understand? You're helping my enemy."

"This one is … not an enemy," she said, trembling. "Please, it's just a little thing."

"That landed here," he said.

"I think it was an accident," she said, struggling to form the words. "I-I think it didn't mean to come."

The man paused, then looked thoughtful.

"That's good," he finally said, to the other man, not to her. "Maybe they won't miss it. Think we should give the labs a heads up?"

"Why do you have to capture it?" she cut in, feeling a sudden flash of anger. "If you hurt it now, you'll just make enemies with its kind."

He slapped her.

"No one asked you," he said. Then, more thoughtfully. "We're already enemies. Everybody's enemies with everybody else. That's the truth people like you never understand. In the desert of space, every little oasis is an outpost. Expensive real estate, that's all. You think I'm cruel? The universe is much crueler."

"I think the universe is magic," she said, looking up at him with a defiance that surprised even her.

He shocked her again with the baton. There was no reason for it this time but spite.

"Check the basement," he said to the other one. "This one's useless."

Illana heard the basement door open, and the light switch flick on and off futilely. It occurred to her that if Victor wasn't upstairs, he might be hiding in the dark down there. The stairs creaked slowly under the other man's weight. She could see him in her mind's eye, gun drawn, creeping like a cat. *Poor little Victor*, she thought. Then it hit her like a shock from her captor's baton; how her heater must have been fixed, and where the jewelry must have come from. She should have realized it had been Victor. Behind those frightening crimson eyes was a beating red heart. A little helper. It couldn't be allowed!

"Please!" she begged. "You have to let him live! You don't underst—Aagh!"

He rammed the baton into her stomach and twisted. Illana foamed at the mouth until she finally lost consciousness. She didn't hear the sudden cry of alarm from the basement, or the brief sounds of struggle. She didn't hear the long silence after, the sounds of squelching and squeezing, and then the long heavy tramp up the stairs.

The second man lumbered into the storefront room. His partner stared at him and held the baton defensively with one hand. The other hand reached for his gun.

"Why did you take your clothes off?" he asked.

The second man did not respond, only stumbled awkwardly forward.

"Where is it?" hissed the baton man. "Why … why are you naked?"

The naked man inched toward him, skin hanging in loose folds. The other dropped his baton and leveled the gun.

"Don't come any closer!"

The naked man came closer anyway. His skin was wet, oily, covered in strange perspiration. His face wore no expression. It hadn't yet learned expressions. The first man pulled the trigger, emptying eight silenced rounds into the other's body before the shuffling naked man twitched, then closed the distance in the twinkle of an eye. He had the first man pinned on the floor by his arms, and he stared down at him with red, hungry eyes.

"Get off me! Brian! What are you do—"

The naked man with the hanging skin opened his mouth wide, and then still wider. It was very wide now; as big as a dinner plate, like a cartoon hole from Acme Supply, only stretched between thin red lips. It swooped down, engulfing the head of its screaming partner—the man was still screaming, even inside the huge mouth—and then worked its way down past the chin. Over the neck. Over the chest. The second man had really stopped looking like a man at all. He was more like a giant, white slug. When he finished engulfing his partner, he lay on the floor as a fat cocoon. The skin-cocoon wriggled violently. There were sounds like belching, and other, squishy sounds, and the dull crack of bones, now being ground to powder, now entirely dissolved.

Illana saw none of this. Her head hung limply against her chest. She didn't see the skin-cocoon change color, then contract into itself. Certainly, she would have screamed if she'd witnessed the slow-but-steady metamorphosis from fleshy cocoon to dark brown, shriveled prune-thing, finally resolving to a shape more familiar, if larger than before. Victor emerged from the fleshy pile, knitting himself together from what he'd consumed. He was taller now, though not as tall as commonsense physics would suggest. Most of the matter he'd hyper-compacted and stored in his interior sacks for later nourishment or future conversions.

He leaned in towards her. She was asleep in one of her elaborate gowns. Beautiful, if vile, brontian primitives could be that. The females from his planet were far less ornate; more functional. One long claw brushed the dark hair from her face. She wore some scent and smelled even now like flowers or fruit. He allowed himself a moment's admiration at her warrior-courage in the face of death and wondered why her instinct had been to protect him, even when she no longer stood to gain any advantage. This was an odd thing and would perhaps have to be investigated. With his claws, he sliced her bonds, and lowered her gently to the ground, intending to return to his repairs. Then, following some whim he couldn't analyze, he scooped her up, brought her to her quarters, and laid her on her sleep rack. When she awoke, hours later, the house was still warm. Her would-be killers were nowhere to be found. Victor worked steadily in the darkness below the house.

***

[Translated from Xtolchetznhautlz]

Ship's Log, LD 5,746

How we long for thee, Death, thou sweet Kiss, thou simple End to life and drudgery! And speaking of drudgery, our Work progresses steadily, but with more complications. Some five local cycles after the brontians' failed assault, we completed—or thought we had—the sub-light pod, which, Death willing, will allow us to search out a tear into the rift, and make our long-delayed rendezvous with Phlegmatar (curse its vile name!) Alas, we've sensed through the Core Mind that there is little work left to be done. If Death permits, we shall, perhaps, find some suitable lingering target on the surface and fly directly into it. But what terrible fortune is this: another obstacle has arisen, which will further delay us from tasting that sweet fire whose name is Destruction.

The sub-light pod must now be expanded, because the brontian female must be brought to Xtolchetznhaultzig for examination. Loathe as we are to admit it, there are matters here which the Thought Caste would find strategically interesting. Duty requires we delay our own long-desired end—glorious, fiery Death—in order to reconfigure the sub-light pod for prisoner transport. It is now beyond certain that these creatures cannot be compacted without losing their functionality, and a larger pod requires a greater fuel-load. As the Sage said, "Complication breeds complication, until Death brings release." But we see no way of avoiding it.

Let us elaborate. Our initial desire to create stability for our captor, luring her into that false security which is the god of all females the universe over, worked too well. Domestic concerns having been easily allayed through our superior technology, brontian cretins having easily been drawn hither through the rewired entrapment orb, ship repairs having proceeded without issue, we foresaw a quick return to action. However, while dispatching these cretins who foolishly thought to take us into custody, circumstances revealed our brontian captor's rare, and decidedly un-female qualities. Qualities that left us perplexed. Qualities rarely seen in our own females, save—so we're told—in the birthing process. To wit, courage in the face of Death!

Now it is well-known that our species' only weakness lays within its accursed females. Left to their own devices, they'd fritter away their days in gem-digging, star-staring, and in useless conversations about their own fuzzy impulses. Was it not precisely these qualities that left our ancestors' slaves of the cursed Phlegmatarians, and was it not the overthrow of the vile matriarchy that led to our current dominance of the Xigflig Sector? And yet the problem remains, seemingly written into their soft natures, always threatening to drag us back into obscurity and impotence. Who would have surmised that an accidental gravity-storm resulting in our temporary exile on this primitive planet, would lead to the discovery of this most extraordinary of things: a female with grit!

The more we reflect upon this, the more are we loathe to leave her behind. True, the brontians are so dull and undeveloped a type as to be beneath contempt. Beneath even conquest. And yet, this female is—we hesitate to admit it—a rare gem. We must bring her to the home planet, where she can be properly turned-over, and her qualities extracted, reproduced, and—if this is feasible—injected into our females. Imagine the prowess of our people if, alone among all star-faring peoples, our females could be induced to drink Death like our males!

We hasten to add that we are not, in any way, smitten by this brontian hag! It is purely a matter of science and strategy, and, of course, war. Still, those very qualities of grit and strength that make her useful also suggest that an outright capture might prove counterproductive. Better to lure her into compliance; not a difficult prospect, considering her species' low intelligence. We have already decided on the ideal means of persuasion, though its execution will involve a small violation of Code 4326.14 of the Xytruthian Treaty. If this violation is discovered, we'll happily offer ourselves up for execution, for that will be but another means of glorious Death for the sake of our people. In the meantime, we expect at least one further assault from the brontian cretins. Indeed, we eagerly anticipate it. Such an assault will play directly into our hands.

***

Rising from her bed the morning after the attack, Illana would have preferred almost anything to opening her store. Her body ached; her mind was in tatters. When her eyes had last been open, they'd stared into those of a killer, a man for whom she had no value. He'd hated her, and she'd never really been hated. The pain had followed, and then the darkness. She'd thought it was the darkness of death, then realized that if she really were dead, she'd perhaps not have thought so. Or, if consciousness continued after death, it ought not be accompanied by pain in those same places in her body where she'd been tormented. She opened her eyes in silence and saw no vicious killer staring back. Only the image of Brandon Lee watching from the wall like some dark guardian angel.

But open the store she did. For one, the workshop table was again covered in the finest pieces she'd ever seen. For another, the next attack would not come while the store was open and filled with witnesses. And there were many, many witnesses.

After she peeled the dark covering from her storefront windows, Illana saw that despite the frigid temperatures, the sidewalk on Warren Street was lined with men, women, and children. They stood, looking anxiously in, twitching in the cold like zombies. Victor had done it. She didn't know how. He'd saved her business, and then her life. And she was sure he was somehow drawing them all here. Victor was watching over her.

For the next week, hardly a minute passed without a customer in the store. Overnight, she'd gone from a woman on the brink of financial defeat to a woman who could hardly afford to visit the bathroom or feed her cats. Already she was thinking of hiring help. Even with Victor making the jewelry, she was far too busy for comfort.

She wanted to thank him, but the little man stayed always out of view. From time to time, she'd hear him down in the basement, tinkering away on some great project. Something warned her not to go down there; not to pry. When fate gave you a magic helper, it wasn't right to look it in the mouth. But she longed to do something for him. Make him clothes, brew him tea; anything! But what gift could you offer a being of such power and pure benevolence? Perhaps only gratitude. Perhaps only love. Gradually, Illana became fixated on this question of what she could give him. So much so, that she failed to wonder what he might want in return.

On Tuesday evening of the second week since the attack, and of the windfall, two hours after she'd closed the doors, and while she sat sipping tea in quiet security and the warmth of a working heater, they came again. The assault happened all at once. The front windows shattered, and smoke bombs hit the ground all around her. She tried to run, but heard the windows break upstairs, the back door bursting open, and tens of boots on the ground. She coughed from the smoke, and crawled along the floor, unable to breathe. The cats screamed and ran past her in the fog like ghosts. Her hand was on her mouth when another closed over it, dragging her to her feet. A gun's hard barrel was placed against her temple. She struggled, swatting the arm down, only to cry out as something hard bit her ribs. Illana sank to the floor. She touched the wound, and seemed not to register the muted gunshot until after her hand came away bloodied. A figure in a gas mask bent down and leveled his pistol on her face. There'd be no discussion this time. But then his head flipped off his shoulders, sideways, like it was doing a cartwheel. It landed in her lap.

Illana did not even scream as a dark figure flew through the smoke. She did and did not recognize him. The figure was too big to be Victor; too quick to be human. And yet, she'd seen him before. As dying men dropped, falling in scores throughout the house, attacked on all sides at once, Illana hearkened to the plaintiff timber of their screams. In a contemplative haze, brought on, perhaps, by the surreal circumstances, Illana thought to herself, *Death makes us hypocrites.* What right had a killer to protest his own end? Death, after all, was the currency in which he traded. But there it was.

The smoke began to clear. One dark form stood over her, its face still partially obscured.

"Close your eyes," he said. "Lay back, and bite down on this."

She obeyed, opened her mouth, and closed it on what felt like the bone of his wrist.

"You won't damage us," he said, "and we've made friends with pain."

He tore her gown to the waist, and something sharp—a blade, a claw—probed at her wounded side. She bit down, even though she feared hurting him. She felt him find and pluck the bullet from her body. He tore another strip of her gown, and, taking his arm back from her mouth, tied the strip tightly around her wound. She cried from the pain. He glared at her.

"Do you now fear death?"

She sensed uncertainty in his voice. Perhaps the hint of a threat.

"No," she said, by instinct. "Only … it hurts."

He brought his face close to hers. For the first time, she really saw him.

"You'll heal inside the pod—" he began to say, but her cry of surprise cut him off.

The face was handsome and gaunt. It was painted white. Shoulder-length dark hair framed dark eyes, themselves circled in black mascara. Or was it war paint? Dark strips, like black raindrops ran down his high cheekbones.

"You're … him!"

He nodded.

"We are. We've heard your prayers. We have come to take you to … the heavens."

"We? I don't understand."

He frowned.

"I," he said, almost reluctantly. "*I* have seen your valor in the face of death. I have heard your cries in the darkness, at night. Verily, I have come to liberate you from this primitive prison. There are, of course, certain conditions—"

Victor's carefully prepared speech, cleverly worded to lure her forth from the planet without explicitly violating certain cumbersome interstellar laws that forbade impersonating deities, was suddenly cut short by a new, and unexpected brontian ritual. Her lips on his. Her hands, trembling, soft strong fingers pressing into the shoulders of his assumed body. He permitted the gesture. Allowed it, in fact, for longer than was strictly necessary to secure her agreement. His mind, filled just moments prior with visions of fire, and Death; the hopeless pain of his enemies, the sweet lamentation of females, and of pups left fatherless in ash and fire, was suddenly fuzzy. Death-heat gave way to an odd warmth whose existence he hadn't known, nor, until that moment, even suspected. It *was* strategically interesting. It *would*, he admitted, have to be investigated. For science.

"Do you..." he stuttered, "consent to ... eh ... capture, and transportation?"

Illana Greystoke looked around only once, gathering in a glance the beads and baubles, the work and worry, her dreams behind display glass—and laughed.

"Take me away," she said.

BEE, ON THE LAST DAY

I.

Dulcet-blue flower, thistle-like in the distance, narrow grasping stalk. The neck is still green, hardy in the ash-strewn plain. Well, something like ash. Bee sees it, and flies straight.

Alights there gently, stalk slight-swaying from her weight, for there is no wind. Bee probes for nectar, and, finding, doesn't wonder how roots still reach water. A bee, she never ponders, only bees. In these times, limitations are gifts.

She feeds her aching stores, flits from bud to blue bud, sharp mercy seat, one lonely living cluster in a graying world. Full, finding no more, bee turns homeward.

The hive has gone quiet. Drone nor maiden manning combs. Yet something waits. Watcher from the dark. Hidden form and hidden ends. Learning, to unmake. Bee's belly work through, she pours out her sweet raw gift. Nothing receives it.

Mathematic eye, an empty hex cell stares up, cradling no young. Bee must beat her wings dutifully, and then lie down. Unmarked moments pass. Gash-cloud sky churns overhead many slow times, as if seething.

She rises to dance. Tells of scarce blue gems for others' sake. There are no others. Only It watches, connives. Pouncing now would be premature. Still, nothing without can be left alive.

It cannot find all life. Lacks that looking knack of life. Self-moving being, challenging the twitching It, which brooks no challenge. Does not share power. But transeunt stirrings, that incalculable inner spark, submits not to Its analysis. And so mustn't be allowed.

II.

No being still marks time. While the bee slept, rains that are not rains fell where she had been. Found sustenance, found out. And when the ash comes, there'll no more be a there there; a rose will not be left a rose.

Bee takes flight. Cheerful hustle over meadows, hills, houses. Houses in which no man moves. Inside them, lights turn on and off. Doors remain locked, from the inside, though no hand pushes, flicks. The hand made long-unneeded, switches go it alone.

Houses, which are meanings, have no meaning for Bee. Sometimes, though, they hoard flowers behind glass rooms. Untouched by It, inaccessible to Bee. Rolling on, past the man-hives, she finds again her blue bachelors. Well-named flowers, those. Lone stand in field of ash, and unmoving grass. Grass monument. Still. Blue faces glisten, strangling, strangely wet, though not watered. Held captive now in glass that is not glass, that is not water, that does not quench. Douses, rather. Fixes things forever.

Bee searches on without ken. Only knows the stand is spent. Still, there might be others, somewhere in the life-circle of these growers, finding the true waters these found before false rains claimed them. Ever-seeking life. Nature's clean logic, sensed by a bee, but never apprehended.

Bee circles back round, toward the clockwork town. Far off, encroaching mountains, stripped to mesas, buttes like fissured teeth, ogle down, lense-eyed, seeing naught, yet surveying all, as through a darkly glass. The Thing upon the world does not see, does not see out, espies but a mirror-thought, correcting what departs from It. Peppers the ground with ash and rain that are not what they are.

Gray-white granules, creeping weightless tasseling, skuttle the shaped land. Skitter secretly, resolute, dissolute, mindless, under Bee's true flight.

Oh, how she swims and bounces, through the antiseptic air, without fright. Without worry. Lacking the reason that gives it rise.

Bee swings, arcs—*zip zuh, zip-sip, zuh*—meanders mumbling over strips called streets, were there any left to call them that, o'er man-hives lacking men, and she, a striped yellow comet, singing careless and gay her mono-tune melody.

One hive differs from the rest. A door stands open. Without knowing 'door', she knows 'open', and plunges down.

The air within is close and dark. Flowers in a frame on the wall. She touches, and finds them flat, like a stretch of stone or dry-packed earth.

Tired, she alights on a soft, billowed expanse beneath the flowers that are not. A boy is curled up there, shivering, shuddering, cheek-flesh stained red. Not of roses but some other red. Bee does not know 'boy', only 'body', other-kind. Not one of her own. But 'lone', 'one-only'—she knows that. Boy like bee without hive.

Are you real asks the boy, stirring. Am I dreaming?

His fright-voice sends tremors through the air, which Bee can feel. She takes flight.

Back in the meadow, hungry, she wanders a long, long time. Then, at length, finds and lands on a red-faced bud. It glistens. She knows or senses better. Hunger makes fools of all beings. Her knobbed legs touch down. False, glistening water sticks, strikes, creeps up furry feet toward yellow body. Bee darts away.

Heavy now. Left side weighted down. Dead heft of it pulling her toward ash-strewn earth. Musn't land on the ash. Nor on grass that once was grass. Back to the hive.

Bee plummets; does not land. Crashes into darkness, dead hex eyes stare on solipsistically. Though exhausted, she cleans furiously, trying to strip the glistening stuff. Like a man on fire, clothes burning up. She cannot get it off. And the gray thing watches from the darkness.

It is time. No more use in this one. The incalculable thing within Bee, that spark of transeunt causality—only a threat to the It that must be All. It strikes.

Gray, gaunt form on fuzzy, fleshy body. Bee flails. Tries to sting. Better to die than to accede. Such is its telos. Sting, covered in fixing water, cannot escape its sheave. Not even death is left its dignity. But something—perhaps Something—more incalculable than life, intercedes.

Lightning flashes in the valley. Hex eyes stare on, patrician-like, thumbs jutting out at every angle. In that light, Bee escapes. Takes flight. Rushes back toward lonely other-hive.

III.

Gray, insectile demon in pursuit. Jaws open. Eyes gone white, painted with machine indifference that is hate. Equivalent to hate. Heaven, not It, sent a bolt, and burnt the sky. It thought It owned the airs.

Bee finds again the open door. Topples down onto kitchen counter, like some fallen star. The boy at the table.

You came back! I knew you would! They all walked toward the mountains. But I plugged my ears. I wouldn't go. My heart told me no. We're the only ones left, you know.

The bee shudders on island counter. Boy reaches as if to touch. Pulls back. Oils in his skin might harm small creatures. Mother once said.

I have something for you. Do you eat honey? You can live in our greenhouse, if you want. I can live there too, with you. My name's Cormac. We're alike. The only living things.

Bee struggles. Tries to scrape away the glistening glaze. How it clings and cloys. No one leaves this world alive. The It that clutches, flattens, distorts has been growing since before gardens. Now, full-grown, incarnate in aped life.

The boy spoons honey on the counter. Places warm water beside Bee in a shallow dish. Reaches for the bee, again, then withdraws. His fingers, too big to help.

Bee inches toward the honey drop. Tastes tentatively, then gulps. Buzzes in place, breaking it down. Taps its honey stomach. Strength returns.

Mom has little pincers, somewhere, boys says. For pulling out ticks. Wash your legs in there; I'll try and find the—

Bee takes flight. Wobbles like a drunken man through open door. Boy stands at threshold calling.

Don't touch the ash!

Weighted down, dragging the world behind her, bee again makes for the hive. Must share this windfall with little lives. She has a memory for places, for tastes, but not for facts. There are no little lives in the hex cell eyes. But bee can't believe in that. And the threatening thing, because it matched no nature she knew, fades in memory to a gray impression.

Boy stares after her. Is lonely, later death indoors better? He's sure she will not make it far. But fly she does.

Bee soldiers homeward, leaving nothing for the return. She's no planner. Head down, eyes forward, on goal. God's little worker. Task follows task follows task. Produce. Give. Spend body. That is the way. There is no future, nor past; only now. Happiness is motion. And, if bees could fear, she wouldn't fear the heartless thing that watches and descends.

Unnatural sky, cloven and split like desert, begins to seep. A thunderclap, then a sound like a ship's foghorn, or the deep dread throb of trumpets of war.

GROMMMMMB!

The rains are coming. No cover between her and the hive, only plains of false grass. Frozen flowers, encased in glass. No tree left untouched. She won't make it. Bee hovers, recalls tall straight light-sticks lining stretches of flat black stone. Turns back once more, toward the man-hives. She sees them, now illuminated, and spreading soft light. Tops like mushroom caps, where she can hide.

The rain comes. *Pitta patta, pitta patta, throosh pitta* on the meadows and plains. Bee reaches the streetlamp—metal mushroom, in her mind—just in time. Crawls into the grate on its spreading underside.

Bee rests. Falls asleep. Careless honey dreams, and visions of a teeming hive. Rain pelts the metal ceiling of her refuge, but cannot make her mind. There is peace in good work.

She does not stir. Does not look down through the grating to see the boy out in the rain. He is wrapped in cloth and plastic, taped-up to stop the flood, creeping like an upright glowworm, under a yellow umbrella.

Not afraid, says the voice from the make-shift mass. The earth is mine. No more hiding. If bee can fly, then so can I.

GROMMMMMB!

Sounds the terrible voice. Dark summoning voice that brought them all to black, bent mountains.

Alright, I'm coming. For them, not for you.

GROMMMMMB!

Fills the earth again. Trembling, yet he stands his ground. Fixes feet in swirling flood, not to be moved but by his will. Not cowed, nor kept in lonely house. He trudges forward, toward the black mountains, like a hunter, at whatever waits. Through the ash heaps, dragging clefts and furrows in the drifts. Gouges of black in the sopping ground mark his history. Marching now, making his own time, the boy tastes a pure defiance, the might of good will, and looks not on the twisted mountains whence It summons, but on everlasting hills.

Squesh, skuk. Squesh, skuk.

It is hard going. Ash flakes under false rain cement the land, coating, laminating what was. What was taken for granted. The ground sucks at his feet, and skeins of black in the ash he dragged fill in, leaving no monument. One boot comes off, stuck in the muck. He reaches down with two hands, and tries to pull it out, balancing the yellow umbrella. It slips. He tries to right it, before the rains cover him. And trips. Sinks in the ash mud. It sticks. Sucks on the blankets wrapped around him, dragging him in.

The bee sleeps through all of this. When she wakes, the rains have stopped. It is day, though the proof is but a shade of gray. The sky is a closing hand. The earth shows no signs of having ever put up a fight. Ash and water have done their work. The world is a toy landscape under the gaze of watching crags, and strange dull lights within. Trees are fixed forever according to their last breath; last bend in the last wind.

Silence. Only the buzz of bee, hungry, making her way toward the ash-topped man hives. Cheerful, recalling the taste of honey, she sails through the open door. Lights are on inside. The little house, a zombie now, will never die; only grow into the new Thing growing. Bee lands on the kitchen island and finds the pool of honey where she left it. Bends down to lap it up.

The house lights flicker. Something is here. Very near. Watching.

The lights go out, and still she drinks. Under this diminutive form, It creeps along the marble slab, watching the last thing living outside Its metal belly, savoring—if unlife can savor—the end of old ways, ending of the spark that does not draw from It, the energy, self-moving, that defies Its regime.

It moves with serpent speed. A gray tassel of its ashen vessel, a finger, a claw, presses bee down into the honey pool.

You like to drink? It thinks, Drink. Drink.

Bee buzzes madly, enmeshing itself more deeply in the sticky life food. Compound eyes coated, blinded. Little legs becoming heavy. In a dark house, a yellow bee is black, like everything else. Everything the same. No more defiant life sparks, going their own way.

Bee twitches, near the end of its struggle. Its wings are soaked in sweet amber. A rude black extremity grips it round the thorax, drags it free with a dull *plup*. Flies toward the open door, in the dark house, toward the gray light of the world. Drop it in the ash. Let it become grass. Plastimoss. Useful, fixed, trash. The earth does not need skin, only flooring. Skin feels, and feeling is outside of It.

Violating Thing ferries bee body over the dead ground, twenty yards, toward a soft spot where ash and false water still mix and settle, making the soil consistent. Same. Surfacing.

The Thing let's go. Bee drops like a sticky stone. Lands on sticky ground. Begins to sink. If unlife could feel triumph, It does now.

I, *I* slayed the last living thing!

But then, darkness. The lights go out for this node of It. Two hands smash Its form to bits. A gray beast, naked, on two legs. Ash-covered monkey with feral, living eyes. Boy reaches down, no longer minding the ash, which covers him, which will claim him, and scoops up the gray soil. Picks it off, tears it, twine by twine. The bee twitches, still alive.

A lumbering giant, a gray child, marches toward the man-hive. Does not go in, but walks behind. Glass dome in the fixed lawn behind. Like a snow globe in the ash. Things still grow inside. Flowers. Weeds. Things It could not claim, and left to rot.

The boy grips the handle. He'd like to say a word to the bee, though it wouldn't grasp his words. Boy's mouth is stuck closed. The ash, working steadily to fix him in the vacancy that It calls silence, permits no human voices. Only screams. Screams, which sound to It like the whining of engines, the whirring of functional things.

He turns the handle quickly—the ash swirls toward him in the air—and drops bee gently to the still-brown soil in there. Behind the glass, in the house of green.

Boy swiftly shuts the door. Leans his head against the glass to watch the bee. He smiles a little as it cleans. Picking its tiny limbs of ash and rain. There are true waters behind the glass. Drawn from a well. As long it lasts. Till the Thing on the world plugs the deepest wells. Which it will. But not yet. Not today.

Boy is being drawn away. Darkling cliffs, like jutting teeth, like jagged eyes, call, and he can't resist. He looks upon the bee once more, and thinks, because he cannot speak:

I saved the last living thing. One bee alone can't make a hive. But stay awhile. Buzz, while you're alive.

He turns away, and stumbles toward the waiting buttes. Dark eyes upon the world. Teeth of something lifeless that never sleeps. A wheel turning, turning Itself, in envy of Self, ensnaring, preserving lives as fleshy batteries.

You are not God, thinks the boy. Someday you'll run out. And on that day, I'll run free.

THE WAR GOES ON

Seven hours. Kael sat up in the dark and remembered the pack of cigarettes in his thigh pocket. He fished one out, and half the tobacco spilled onto his tactical pants. He tried vainly to pinch the dry leaf back inside the paper tube, then gave it up, and twisted the paper down to keep what he had. He blew smoke toward the closet door, propped open with his boot. If they hadn't located him by now, then he'd probably gotten away clean.

There were alleys on either side of the building, and this room abutted a utility room with a ladder that went up to the roof, and down into the basement. The basement connected to the storm drains. Lots of ways out. He knew the Replacers wouldn't easily forget. This time, he'd hurt them.

Four, maybe five, of his best men were dead. Nathaniel had at least made it out. They'd failed to free the originals, but Kael's team had breached the cube and seen the captives with their own eyes. Seven hours earlier, the sapper army around the world had flooded the public servers from a thousand different terminals with visual proof. That was too much data to catch, and too damning for even the Repos to obfuscate.

Once upon a time, Kael believed that truth had a way of coming out. Grim experience taught him otherwise. A million private people with a million personal experiences could never unseat a powerful lie. Plenty *believed* that the Restorers were really Replacers, but people were a simple, cowardly lot. They needed to both see the truth, and to know that others had seen it too.

He finished and lit another. Kael thought he'd smoke one for every member of his team, even Crumb, whose mistakes had gotten them caught before the job was done. Maybe Crumb just lost his nerve when he saw his own wife in the cube, or maybe the Crumb on his strike team was a replacement. Kael had known for a while that the Restorers had been swapping out perfectly healthy people too in order to infiltrate the Sapper Zone. They lied about everything else, so why would they keep the treaty promise never to "heal" anyone without consent? The frustrating thing was not being able to prove a swap had occurred; not unless the original was deformed, or chronically ill. The Repos were way ahead of them there. Their detectors meant they could recognize their own.

He cracked the closet door again to let the smoke out and heard something. It was an atonal creaking, a frustrated back-and-forth sound, like someone trying to sharpen a pencil with one hand. The noise came from the alley on the east side of the building. It went on for a few minutes, retreating into the distance until he couldn't hear it anymore. Kael relaxed, but he kept the door cracked.

"Raef," he said, taking a long drag, "this one's yours."

He closed his eyes, and let the tears fall free. You couldn't lose men without asking yourself some ugly questions. He'd asked them back when it had all started. He did it again now. Was he willing to be killed? Yes. To be caught, and swapped out? Yes. Was he willing to risk other men dying or being captured? Yes, because he'd pay that price himself. The hardest question of all: would he sacrifice others without proof that he was right? Same answer, because that was the kind of war they were in. And he could toss that last question now.

The terrible secret was finally out. The beings who called themselves Restorers were *not* taking the sick and deformed and healing them. They were replacing them and locking away the originals. Everyone should have known this. Hell, why else would they use detectors in the Repo Zone, or make cooperators carry passes? But some people just didn't want to believe, and the Repos were always ready with a slick explanation, so he had to remind himself that the proof they'd found was worth losing men over. He took another drag.

"Sorry, brother. Wish it'd been me. You know I do."

In the smoke, he could almost see Raef's face; hear his voice.

Better slopped than swapped, said the ghost.

He had a way with words, did Raef. The creaking, squeaking noise came back down the alley. It could have been someone pulling a trashcan to the street or bringing one back. Not that anybody'd do that over and over. The noise faded away in the other direction.

Kael wondered why cracking the cube didn't make him happier. It had only cost a few good men. There'd be more bloodshed, but that was alright. A good war was better than a bad peace. God knew he'd probably be following the others soon enough. But there was one question he'd never really asked himself: what did victory look like?

It was worth it to punch a bully in the mouth even if you knew he'd kill you for it later. Better than pretending things were right when you knew they weren't. But what if, even with the truth out, the Replacers wouldn't leave, or people wouldn't make the effort to make them leave? What if things just went on the same forever, with the Replaced and the Sapient living parallel lives, staring at each other across the borders for years and years, forced by circumstances to engage in commerce until one day every sapper was replaced anyway, or worse, nobody cared anymore who was real and who wasn't? What if sapper *victory* was unachievable, not because it was too hard, but because there simply wasn't any concrete scenario that corresponded to the word?

That was a terrible question, and Kael instantly regretted posing it. But maybe it had always been there, at the back of his consciousness, taunting him.

The squeaking sound again. Not threatening, but concerning, because he couldn't identify it. He stood, stamped out Raef's memorial smoke, and crept over to the window with his rifle at the ready. He was inside sapper territory, but it would be naive to think he was safe. Surely, they'd be trying to scan every inch of the Sapient Zone from space, and he was only just inside the border. From the shadows, he looked down into the alleyway.

A little girl, maybe seven or eight, was riding back and forth on a tricycle. The ground was strewn with loose garbage, broken appliances, and even a few winos leaning around a trashcan fire. The girl weaved around these obstacles as she travelled the alleyway. She was pretty, dark haired, and of Asian descent. Korean, he guessed. He thought she was a little old for a tricycle, and that the vehicle was over-sized anyway. He soon understood. The girl had only one good arm and leg. Her left hand was a doughy, misshapen thing, like a claw. A shoe was mounted absurdly a few inches below her knee. As she picked up speed, dodging obstructions, her bad leg would sometimes slip off the left pedal, or her claw would lose its tenuous grip. The trike would pull hard to the right, and she'd scramble to correct just in time to avoid hitting something. Despite this, the girl beamed at every little victory. She smiled to spite the spiteful world.

Kael leaned against the window trim, watching the girl play. She knew something about life that he'd forgotten. He saw that it was so without knowing what it was he'd lost. Maybe it was enough that people like her still had it.

And what was his next play? Seven hours since the upload. Enough time had passed for the news to get out. Yet he could look down the alleyway, and see the Restored territory just across the border road, where three women—real, swapped, who knew?—were walking down the sidewalk holding shopping bags. Truth didn't glitter, or feed bellies. What would he do if it came to this: that everybody knew, and nobody cared?

He looked back at the little girl, now wobbling toward the northern end of the alleyway. A police car marked neutral came up parallel with the alley and slowed as the girl approached. She waved, showing her flesh-claw without shame, but she turned the trike around and started back the other way. Good girl. Mama trained her well. That street was the only thing standing between being herself and being swapped out with something that only looked like her. Kael watched her zip southwards, this time dodging barriers without having to stop and correct. She was learning. He could see the pride swelling in her mangled frame. Kael sighed. If she could fight her little battle, then so could he.

She made a circle and started the whole thing over again. There was something wholesome, maybe even holy, in that childish repetition of the simple and the good. After a few minutes, the girl returned to the northern end. Once more, a police car slowed down along the border road, and now stopped in her path. Was it the same car? Kael's eyes narrowed.

"Shit, if I have to…"

He opened the window and saw a fire escape thirty feet to his right. He tore out of the room, and down the hallway, then went left at the intersecting corridor. He climbed out the window, and quickly scrambled down a metal ladder to the alley floor. The girl was almost to the police car. Again, she waved. Kael saw the officers wave back. One of them rolled down a window. The girl stopped. The officer in the passenger seat was engaging her in conversation and beckoning her forward. The driver opened his door and slowly circled around behind the car.

"That's low," muttered Kael.

He could try shooting them from here, but he'd be hard-pressed to drop them both before they got her across the border. Kael's bike was parked in the west alley, and he cursed himself for coming out on this side, wasting precious time to be sure of their intentions instead of acting on his gut. He ran back into the building through the ground floor entrance. The motorcycle was where he'd left it. He hid his rifle in a shallow gutter, opened his chest holsters, and drove the bike toward the building's entrance, shooting out the glass as he passed through. He re-entered the east alley just in time to see the squad car turn casually into Restorer territory, leaving an empty tricycle behind.

Kael revved the engine. It only took three seconds to cross the border road and enter the enemy's world. Three seconds, and no signs, or lights, or gates to separate the City of Man from the City of New Gods. He quickly caught up to the squad car, which seemed in no rush. Dressed for war, with two guns on his chest and a cannon mounted on his bike, there was no question of concealing his intentions. Some on the streets pointed and gesticulated; the smart ones ran for cover. He drove his bike up on the sidewalk, just beside the squad car. The girl was not in the back seat, but he could hear her kicking and screaming in the trunk.

Just then, the driver looked up at him. Casual. Mystified. Why were tyrants always so surprised at resistance? Kael shot him in the head. The other cop reached for his sidearm, but got two bullets in the chest, and one more in the throat for good measure. The squad car pulled lazily to the left and struck a wall. Kael parked his bike and reached around the officer's body to grab the car keys.

By now there were sirens from every direction, and he heard the telltale *CLIP CLOP* of the robot sentinels. People stared out shop windows or leaned down from apartment buildings. Everyone so outraged. He'd violated their precious tranquility.

He pulled the little girl out of the trunk, and promised he wouldn't hurt her. As if nature weren't cruel enough, the olive-brown skin of her face was marred by a white skin blotch that looked vaguely like a hammer. Maybe God had decided to hit her on the way out of the womb.

The girl fought, and tried to bite him, and he let her do it. He told her his name and lifted her up to show her what he'd done.

"You're one of them?" she said, sobbing. "The men who fight?"

He nodded. "Let's get you home."

He wedged her behind him and turned the bike around. You could see the Sapper Zone from where they were. He was sure he'd make it and couldn't resist a parting shot at the cooperators looking down from their safe windows.

"What's the matter?" he said. "Don't like to be reminded of what you're serving?"

Screams and boos from above. He revved the engine.

"Hold on tight, sweetheart," said Kael, and took off for the border road.

Someone shouted, "You won't get away!"

Kael grinned. Let them try to follow him into sapper territory, where even the hobos had guns. He was within fifty feet of freedom, feeling pleased, when he saw his error. Two Repo float-tanks dropped down from the sky and hovered in the center of the border road. At that moment, armed bodies appeared on the rooftops to either side of him. This hadn't been some casual Repo kidnapping. It looked like the Replacers had known all along where he was hiding, and they'd waited for the right moment to lure him over to their side.

Behind him the little girl screamed pitifully. If she hadn't been there, he might have had a chance to get away, but with the child at his mercy, he couldn't take risks. The cynical bastards probably knew that too.

"Listen to me!" he shouted. "Are you listening?"

He felt her little head nodding against his back.

"I'm going straight at those tanks. I'll fire my cannon through the center. Their shields'll shove them off to either side, and then they'll come after me. I let you off, and you run. Understand?"

Another nod.

"Tell me the plan!" he shouted.

"You shoot! I run!" said the girl.

"Good! Ready? Now!"

He fired the cannon twice, then came to a screeching halt only ten feet from the border road. The float-tanks spun sideways through the air, their shields crackling with blue energy. The girl almost flew off the bike, but Kael caught her, and set her down.

"Run!"

She froze and turned around. "What about you, sir?"

"Run! Run!"

She scuttled forward pitifully on her cruel appendages. One of the float tanks came back into view, and Kael fired past the girl to knock it out of the way. The second tank jumped over the girl, letting her pass underneath, and turned its long gun on Kael. He didn't budge from the spot. They wouldn't shoot him. He was too useful alive. Kael waited until he saw the girl cross the border, then made a break for it.

Stun cartridges sizzled through the air, hitting the asphalt all around him. No way they shot that badly. They were corralling him deeper into Repo territory, keeping him from side roads and alleys, sealing the border behind him. Once he was contained, they'd drop him for real. Then they'd swap him out with another Kael Konstantius. He could only imagine what they had in mind for the real one.

He approached an intersection, hoping to turn hard right and loop back around toward the border. Squad cars rolled in from either side, and three more float tanks appeared above the rooftops. In the distance, the lift bridge was already being raised. No way forward; no way back. But one of the vehicles that had been forced to stop in front of the bridge gave him an idea. Kael scanned the buildings around him. Mostly residences, and a few shops. He fired wildly into the air, and the people looking out scrambled back inside their houses. That was good. He didn't want witnesses.

Kael drove hard for the lift bridge. The squad cars were hot on his tail, and the float tanks, about ten of them now, dropped down to intercept him. There were two ways this could go. One gave him a chance in hell to slip away, and the other ended up with him in an inferno. Either was acceptable. *Try questioning a piece of charcoal*, he thought. He fixed his cannon on the fuel truck, fired, and leapt from the bike.

The explosion was instantaneous. Kael skidded along the asphalt, felt his arm break, and then felt the heat. A fireball rushed toward him, and he clenched his jaw, bracing for the end.

The smoke was choking him. He swallowed burnt air with no oxygen in it. Strong hands suddenly gripped him beneath his armpits and pulled him backwards. He couldn't see who it was, couldn't see anything at all in the fire and smoke. Again, he tried to breathe, but there was nothing for his lungs to gather. Somebody was coughing and wheezing. Kael was set down for an instant, then gathered up more forcefully, and dragged.

"Get it open!" said a muffled voice.

"I can't see," a woman replied.

"It's right behind you!"

There was noise of heavy doors being lifted, and then dropped. Kael was pulled backwards, and down. It was a hole then; maybe a cellar. He looked up into a square of light and smoke and fire. A woman was descending, something wrapped around her face, but he saw only her silhouette, and the fire burning in her long black hair. She slammed the cellar doors, then screamed, and slapped at her head. The man set him down on a gravelly floor and climbed up to slip a beam of wood between the handles before attending to the girl.

"Are you alright?" he said.

"Yes, it's out, I think—" she looked at Kael, "—is he dead?"

"Give him oxygen," said the man.

The young woman darted off, and soon returned with a tank and mask. Kael opened his eyes and drew long, deep breaths. The oxygen rushing in made him almost giddy, even though his left arm throbbed, and both his legs were beginning to burn as if they were on fire.

"Sedative," said the man.

"No!" growled Kael.

He knew the stories about what happened to sappers captured in Repo territory. These people were probably after the reward. He struggled, but struggling only multiplied his agonies. The girl approached with a long needle and tried to peel his jacket back. He fought her, and felt the sting in his neck instead, before slipping into darkness.

***

Kael woke up to hard gravel, and a rifle in his face. A bright light shone down on him, and a dog that looked at least half wolf hovered close to his head. The dog's tongue lolled out, and its wet breath wafted over his nose and mouth. Rifle Girl was pretty, despite the charred ends of her hair. An old man sat on his haunches, surveying his legs. They hurt like hell, but his forearm was in a cast.

"You gonna shoot me?" he asked the girl.

"Maybe?" she said, with a shrug. "Probably."

The old man had what was maybe a stud finder sticking out of his vest pocket. He turned it on, and it beeped for a second before going quiet. The girl glanced at the dog and moved the gun closer to his head.

"Watch him, Chuck," she said.

Instantly the dog's demeanor went from pleasant to downright evil.

The old man waved the stud finder over Kael's body, starting with his head, and moving towards his feet. His knee bumped against Kael's leg, which sent pain knifing through him.

"Sorry about that," said the man, absently.

He turned his face away and began coughing into his arm.

"I thought you people weren't allowed to have guns?" said Kael to the girl.

She narrowed her eyes. "Oh, so you're taking notes on us?"

His coughing fit over, the old man continued scanning Kael. The funny-looking stud finder made a harsh buzzing noise, and turned red. The old man looked up at the young woman meaningfully. They had the same eyes.

Kael sighed. "Looks like I failed your test."

"Yes," said the old man, with another grating cough. "Lucky you."

He looked again at the girl, but she shook her head and kept the gun on Kael.

"Let him explain himself first," she said.

"He isn't one of them," said the old man.

She looked hard at Kael, then blew an ashy strand of hair from her face. Slowly, she moved the gun until it pointed at the floor. The safety, Kael noted, was still off, and her neck and hands were taut as cables. He addressed himself to the man.

"You splinted my arm."

The other nodded.

"Thank you."

"Zara helped," he said, nodding at the girl. "I'm teaching her."

"Don't tell him my name!" she snapped.

The man shrugged. "Why wait? He passed the test. If you aren't going to trust him now, you might as well shoot him and be done with it."

Zara looked like she was considering just that.

"I thought you said I failed," said Kael.

"You did fail, therefore you passed."

Zara rolled her eyes, and then surprised Kael with a sideways glance that was almost a smile. "You'll be hearing a lot of *that* if you stick around."

The flash of her smile lasted only an instant, but it was a good smile. The old man looked wryly back and forth between them. "Are you a praying man, stranger?"

Kael paused. "No atheists in foxholes," he offered, with a judicious nod.

"Well, even if you're not," said the man, "you are a damned lucky one. Some stunt you pulled off, going after that girl, and then trying to hide in an explosion."

Kael shrugged, then winced as the motion made his arm bump on the gravel.

"My duty, that's all. Thought I'd probably just burn up."

"Ah. The man of war," said the old man, sighing. "Hardened by it. Probably can't imagine any life besides one spent fighting."

Kael considered the comment, which was so obvious as to be nonsensical. "Live or die," he said, "the war goes on."

The old man rubbed his chin.

"Some say so. Let's get you upstairs, and then we'll talk."

***

They helped Kael into a comfortable chair in a small sitting room that shared the same four walls with a rather large kitchen. The pain in his legs had become almost unbearable, and Zara and the old man had practically needed to carry him up the stairs. The old man reclined Kael's chair and studied him with obvious concern. That kind face was suddenly contorted by another fit of coughing. He pounded his chest to get the cough under control.

"Sorry about that," said the old man. "Cold keeps hanging around. Anyway, we'll need to get those pants off. Unfortunately, you woke up before we finished, and that was the last sedative we had on hand. I do have some strong liquor to help with the pain."

Kael thought about it, and shook his head no. He'd need all his wits about him.

"As you like then. We'll tend to your burns, and then talk about some things. My name is Apollo Wright, by the way."

Kael nodded but did not share his own name. The old man gently prodded the black tactical pants. Kael grimaced.

"I think, to be on the safe side," said Apollo, "we'll just cut these off."

Apollo looked up at Zara, who stared back at him with exaggerated puzzlement.

"What? *I'm* not going to do it."

"Well, he can't," said the man. "And you need to practice burn care. These old hands get shaky, and I'm afraid I might poke him with the scissors."

"I have a few burns of my own, Dad," said Zara, taking a chunk of hair, and wagging it at him.

"That can wait."

She stood rooted in place for a moment, then stormed over to Kael.

"Look," Kael said, "you don't have to—"

"Oh, shut up," she said. "Just get that ammo belt off and undo any clasps. That is if you're not *too* crippled to move your other arm."

Kael did as she asked, and helped her as much as he could, bracing himself as she took a pair of medical sheers and began to cut through the material. It was an awful process that seemed to take hours, though it might have lasted fifteen minutes. He had friction burns from the crash, but his skin was also scorched from the explosion. Some of the cloth stuck to his wounds. It was all he could do to grit his teeth and drive his head back into the chair, trying not to scream, regretting his decision to refuse the liquor. When she'd fully exposed his legs, Zara gasped, and wrinkled her nose.

"You really need a bath."

"Zara!" said her father.

Kael stared at the ceiling, pain and embarrassment giving way to a growing anger at being so confined. Grateful though he was for the help, he wasn't used to being cared for, nor could he shake his constitutional suspicion of anyone in the Repo Zone. If these were good people, not replacements or cooperators, then why were they here? When he finally looked back, Zara seemed to have softened.

"Sorry," she said. "That wasn't kind."

The girl and her father began cleaning his legs. Both were swollen and red, and a great deal of the hair was burnt off from his ankles to about halfway up his thighs. Zara's wound care was considerably gentler than her talk. Though less knowledgeable than her father, she did the work with more grace, and less pain to him. Apollo seemed to have a medical background and would often stop to give her pointers until the job was finished.

"There," said the old man, finally. "Not as bad as it looks, and it should heal well. The burns are extensive, but only superficial. We got you out just in time. You won't need grafts."

He left the room, then returned with a bed sheet, which he drew over Kael's bandaged legs.

"I have some clothes and a robe that you can borrow for tonight.

Tomorrow I'll go out and buy you something more your size. We'll also need more sedatives and painkillers. Antibiotics wouldn't hurt either, to prevent infection."

Kael frowned. "Go out and buy something?"

"Well … yes? You don't think we grow supplies in here, do you?"

Kael glanced casually at his two chest holsters. Both were empty. He might have lost one gun in the accident, but two? He was suddenly wary again, and his eyes darted back and forth between his two rescuers, and then stopped on the large dog, which now lay on the carpet only four feet from him.

"Is something wrong?" said Apollo.

"You're not saps," said Kael, coldly. "And you're not in hiding here, if you can just go to the store without being detected."

Apollo shook his head. "You don't understand. We still have to talk."

Kael kept his eyes on the man, but felt around inside his tactical vest, probing for the hidden dagger. He palmed it, then rested his hand on the chair arm. He was too wounded to be subtle, and the old man followed his hand to where he'd placed it.

"I've set your gun aside for you. You are perfectly safe here, son."

Kael smiled. "Sure, pal."

His arm shot out like a viper, and he pulled Apollo over the chair arm, and pressed the dagger against his throat.

"No!" cried Zara.

The wolfdog barked loudly and rushed at Kael.

"Tell it to back off!" he hissed.

"I … I can't breathe!" wheezed Apollo.

"Tell it!" Kael shouted to Zara, lifting Apollo's chin with the dagger.

"Heel, Chuck! Heel!" shouted the girl.

The dog froze, but leaned toward Kael, bristling with violence.

"Get it out of my face!" spat Kael.

Zara nodded, and dragged the dog across the kitchen floor, shutting it inside a small room. She quickly returned, the anger of betrayal on her face, tears running down her cheeks.

"Why are you doing this? We helped you! We saved your life!"

"You saved my body!" spat Kael. "For them. I'm sure I'm worth a lot to them, healthy."

"No!" pleaded Zara. "Please, Daddy can't breathe!"

Kael relaxed the blade enough for the old man to cough loudly and take several more labored breaths.

"You're going to drive me out of here," said Kael. "Or I'm going to kill him."

She shook her head. "Fine! If that's what you want, fine! Just don't hurt him, please!"

Zara began to cry pitifully, and she sank to the ground with her face in her hands. Kael felt almost guilty, though he didn't doubt his guess about their true intentions. He looked down briefly to adjust his headlock enough to leave the man's windpipe free, and then turned the point of the blade against his jugular, daring Apollo to escape. When Kael looked up, Zara stood with her feet planted squarely. The rifle from before was pointed at his chest.

"Let him go," she said.

The tears were gone. Zara's tone was flat, her eyes emotionless. Kael was more stunned by the transformation, than by the gun. He'd seen killing eyes before. He decided she would shoot him either way. *Fine, then,* he thought, *better slopped than swapped.* But killing the old man would make no difference now. Kael released Apollo, who slumped to the floor, wheezing and coughing.

"Ungrateful monster," spat Zara, pulling the trigger.

"No!" cried Apollo.

The blast tore into his jacket, driving the air out of his body. Kael groaned and clutched his chest. Zara swore, seeing that the round hadn't penetrated his body armor, and she put the rifle to his temple. Kael looked up at her, offering no resistance. Swapped and tortured for information? No thank you. Dead? Well, he could deal with that. But Zara's hands shook.

"Don't kill him!" said Apollo. "I beg you. He doesn't know."

"He was going to kill *you*!"

"He was only trying to protect himself," wheezed the old man. "Can you blame him?"

Zara glared down at Kael. Slowly, she drew the gun away, and handed it to her father. All the hard edges of a moment before melted in a second, and she covered her face with a trembling hand. That same transformation, but in reverse. Apollo displayed the weapon before Kael. He cleared the chamber and made a show of tossing the gun away.

"Now will you listen?" he said.

Kael nodded.

"The knife," said Apollo, holding out his hand. "Please."

With a great effort, Kael turned the blade hilt-forward, and placed it on Apollo's open palm. Apollo took it with a great sigh. He righted his chair, and sat beside Kael, gesturing for Zara to do the same. The girl came back over but watched Kael with wary contempt. Kael met her gaze with respect, but without apology. Apollo reached out and took Kael's hand in his own.

"We are not replacements," he began. "But neither are we cooperators. Not anymore. We live here, in occupied territory, hiding in plain sight. And in this, we are not alone."

Kael shook his head. "How can that be? They'd catch you."

"They'd catch us," said Apollo, "if they could detect us. But they cannot. They think we're replacements. That's the key."

Kael balked. "But the detectors—"

"—Are everywhere?"

"Yes," said Kael.

"Yes," repeated Apollo. "Not just in shops, and government buildings, but in bridges, and under the very streets. The enemy has total control."

Kael stared, waiting for an explanation.

"And that is their weakness," continued Apollo. "Overconfidence. If we were cooperators, we would have to show a pass, and go to them to have it checked and renewed. But replacements have full freedom of movement. That's the incentive, you see. So, the question is, how do we do it? Why do they mistake us for their own?"

Kael shrugged, still waiting.

"I'm a biologist by training," said Apollo. "And the problem is essentially biological. If a replacement is a clone—albeit one without any of the sicknesses or deformities of the original—then how can it be distinguished from an original? How would the detectors or the Repo sentinels know? It can't be a matter of genes, or fingerprints, because the replacements are exact copies, minus imperfections. There had to be something else, and it had to be a simple mechanism. As a biologist, and, at the time, a cooperator, the problem intrigued me."

Kael adjusted his recliner to a sitting position. He saw Zara flinch at the movement.

"You've got my attention," he said. "You're telling me you figured out how to trick the bastards?"

Apollo nodded. Kael whistled low.

"That's the one thing we could never crack" he said. "It changes everything. We could walk right into their citadels, and kill them all before they even—"

"—Stop, please," said Apollo, putting up a hand. "Hear me out entirely before you start making plans to go out and get more people killed fighting a war that can't be won with bullets."

Kael looked at him incredulously, but the old man continued.

"When the Replacers swap a clone for a man, they also introduce a novel mechanism into the clone's cellular machinery. It's a simple thing, really. Just instructions for a harmless cocktail of amino acids, which are then folded into a very basic protein. Call it the ID protein. It does nothing but sit there, and it's the same protein in every replacement."

"And you're a biologist," said Kael, drawing out the implications.

Apollo nodded. "Synthesizing complex proteins is difficult. If that had been the way of it, my theory would have been hopeless, even if proved. However, I conjectured that to be practicable, this ID protein would need a relatively basic structure. Something that could be produced quickly yet could be easily recognized by any number of detection systems. Once I understood this theoretically, I only needed the chance to verify the matter … experimentally."

Kael noticed a shadow pass over Zara's face. Was that sadness? Shame?

"You … got inside one of them, and looked?"

Apollo nodded.

"Was it someone you knew?" said Kael.

"My wife," sighed Apollo. "Zara's mother. Although not really. Her real mother had cerebral palsy. We tried to keep her hidden from them, but her own cousin reported her. Out of *love*, you know. This was before the treaty, so…"

"And you experimented on the replacement," finished Kael, looking at the old man with new respect. "That's cold. Must have been damn satisfying, too."

Apollo's face became hard. He took a deep breath and held it. Zara put a hand on her father's shoulder.

"It was not like that," said the old man. "*I* am not like that."

"Then how?" said Kael.

"I loved my own Genevieve. So, like many people, I could never bring myself to hate this new Genevieve. That, of course, is the greatest weapon they wield against us. Our sympathies, not to mention our fear of conflict. But for my own reasons, I chose to love this new Genevieve. I wouldn't touch her as if she were my own wife, but I chose to treat her with kindness and respect. She has a soul, you know. The Replacers can't create those. And the truth is the replacements themselves know deep down that they're only loved *as replacements*. Therefore, I chose to love her as a person. I never thought anything would come of this love. My theories were only a sort of desperate hobby. However, it was she who stumbled upon my notes one day, and, out of love, offered to help us."

A tear traced its way down Zara's cheek.

"A replacement helped *you*?" said Kael. "Did she let you … kill her?"

"No," said Apollo. "That I could never do. But I ran many tests on her blood, and eventually found the hidden identifier. In time, I was able to synthesize it here, in my laboratory."

He indicated the kitchen.

"So, you inject it?" said Kael, flabbergasted. "And then walk about as you please?"

"Sometimes," said Apollo, "if there's a need for haste. Otherwise, we drink it in a mixture, and wait half an hour. To go out for extended periods, one must continue sipping it intermittently."

Kael stared at him, finding it difficult to believe he'd pulled this off.

"What happened to this woman?"

Apollo sighed. "She left. Only a day after my greatest triumph. The very night that I first synthesized the protein … she … you see, she asked me if now I could love her as I had my wife. I told her that I *did* love her, but not as my Genevieve. I remember that moment like it was yesterday. She must have been hoping all along … but what could I say? The next morning, she was gone."

"She could have gone to the Repos, and told them everything," said Kael.

"I feared that she would," said Apollo. "We waited for a year, expecting any day to be raided. In that time, I tested out my formula. I left my pass at home and found that I could walk among them without detection. Not only did the formula work, but my wife—the second Genevieve, rather—had not reported me, for my face never triggered a response from the sentinels."

Kael became silent. "Where did she go?" he asked, softly.

"Far away, we think," said Apollo, looking at Zara. "Perhaps to the Sapper Zone. No one there would know what she was. Perhaps someone could love her. I like to think that she found love, though sometimes I fear that she took her own—"

"Daddy!" said Zara, her eyes pleading.

He shrugged. "I feel a certain guilt, but I simply couldn't give her what she wanted."

"Daddy," insisted Zara, "Stop it! You did nothing wrong. Everyone is proud of you."

Kael considered the two of them. He couldn't detect a lie. Still, it seemed too good to be true.

"You mentioned that you're not the only ones?" said Kael.

Apollo straightened up, seemingly relieved at the change of subject.

"There are seven-hundred forty-three of us," he said. "And growing."

"Right here?" said Kael. "In the Repo Zone?"

Apollo nodded. Zara squeezed her father's shoulder.

"Daddy is at the center of it," she said. "He's the one man who's really given us a chance."

Apollo waved off her praise, and then her protests. He looked hard at Kael, as if knowing what must be going through the other's mind. Kael was thinking of his own men killed or captured over the years. Of the friends only recently lost. They'd paid the ultimate price to expose the truth. They'd paid in blood, and struggle, and years of going without. Could victory mean something as cheap as hiding? He wasn't even sure he *wanted* to believe that.

"Daughters are wonderful," offered Apollo. "It's in their nature to take pride in their fathers, but mine is only one small success. Others have done as much or more. For example," he looked at Kael, "those men who just died to prove the truth about the cubes. You knew those men, perhaps?"

Kael debated for a long time, but finally realized that his silence had already given him away. He nodded.

"We're sorry for your loss," said Zara. "And I wasn't trying to say that you sappers aren't fighting bravely."

"Forget it," said Kael. "I just … it's hard for me to believe you're telling the truth. And if you *are* telling the truth, then it's hard for me to see how this all ends in victory."

Apollo rested a hand on Kael's good arm.

"As far as its being true, I can show you. After things have settled down out there, you can watch me from the window whenever I go to work. Oh yes! I'm able to work among them without detection. But, as for how it ends, consider this: the Repos believe in genetic purity, and they have the weapons and the technology to enforce their vision. Over time, by force of arms, they're bound to win. Your friends may have exposed them, but in dying, they also proved how utterly incapable we are of—"

He broke out coughing again. Zara looked at her father with concern.

"Are you sure it's only a cold, Dad? It seems like it's getting worse."

"It'll pass," he said, smiling. "Don't worry."

He squeezed Kael's arm, as if to convince him too.

"I'm under the weather," he continued. "I'll need to calm this cough before I go out for supplies."

"I'll go, Dad," said Zara.

"Well, we'll see. Anyway, let me finish. The Repos know that *we* know they could destroy us if that became their goal. They also know how weak we are; how fickle and given to comfort. They aim to replace us all, for what ultimate purpose the Devil only knows. Maybe they believe their own propaganda. Maybe there's a later stage, where all the clones become slaves. Whatever the case, the path to victory lies in reverse infiltration. We cannot outfight them, but we can outbreed them. You see, we can live among them, right under their noses, until there are more of us than of them. Others, men like you, will still fight them in the traditional way. A necessary fight. A good one. But tyrants rule by force. It's their language, and they speak it infinitely better than we do. We shall defeat them through meekness. In this quiet way, we'll inherit the Earth."

He coughed again, three long, hoarse sounds. The dog barked loudly from across the room, and those noises blended with Apollo's so that the two were almost indistinguishable.

"Daddy?" said Zara.

"I'm fine, girl. The smoke from before seared my lungs a bit. What I need is rest. I suppose you should go to the store after all."

She nodded, looking anxious, and turned to Kael.

"I'm going to set a room up for you," she said. "You can stay here however long you need until your body heals. Then, if you want, I'll take you back."

Kael thanked her. Zara and her father got up and walked toward the small room across the kitchen, their whispers drowned out by the barking of the dog.

***

It was the first chilly day in autumn. Kael sat by the window in the small room that Zara had made up into a bedroom. It was the same place she'd stashed Chuck almost two weeks before to keep him from tearing out Kael's throat. Until a few days ago, Chuck was still padding after him wherever he rolled in the motor chair, or else sitting statue-still on the floor, watching him. Now the hound lay across the foot of his cot. Not that the animal trusted him. Kael was sure that Chuck would never forget what he'd done, but the dog seemed to grasp that its masters regarded Kael as part of the pack. Kael wondered if he'd stick around long enough for that to become true. He'd already stayed much longer than he'd intended.

The window curtain was closed, and he pulled it back just a sliver, waiting for Apollo to return from work. Chuck raised his head from his paws and opened one eye to let him know his every motion was accounted for. Master had said, "Be nice," but that didn't mean the hound should let his guard down.

Kael smiled grimly at the dog. "I think you and I have a lot in common."

The wolfdog chuffed, as if he found the possibility remote, and rested his head back on his paws. Kael looked back through the curtain slit and spied Apollo in the distance. The sentinel presence in that part of town had increased, despite the Repos' public announcement that the "reactionary terrorist" from two weeks before had ended his own life in the explosion. Kael wondered if the Repos really believed that. Hadn't they checked for his body? Or had they confused it with the burnt corpses of other drivers near the lift bridge? The whole escape had seemed far too easy.

Down below, the old man walked slowly and deliberately past three hulking sentinels that loitered on the near side of the intersection. They hardly paid him any mind, though one side-stepped to let him pass by. Apollo greeted the sentient machines in a neighborly way, and seemed entirely untroubled when they summarily scanned him. Kael shook his head. Magic formula or not, it'd be a while before he'd be willing to walk up to one of those things without something in his pocket that went "bang".

He let the drape swing closed. Thanks largely to his tactical pants' fire-resistance, his burns would fully heal in a few more weeks. His arm would take longer. At least he could walk with a lot less pain now, when he tired of the motor chair, but he doubted he'd be fit for any serious combat action for another eight weeks. He did what he could to keep his muscles from atrophying, but his skin was covered in scabs, which cracked and oozed when he moved too quickly.

The greater agony was that he'd missed his window to strike. Were there to have been a sapper uprising, it ought to have begun already. He'd even made himself watch the Repo-cultivated feeds a few times, hoping to infer the situation in the Sapper Zone from what the feeds *didn't* say, but the reports offered only vague allusions to "increased reactionary unrest." Given how they spun facts, that could mean anything from more full-scale raids on the cubes, to a half-dozen sappers throwing eggs at the sentinels from across the border road. People everywhere must have viewed the cube footage, but you wouldn't know it from looking out the window. That there'd apparently been no official comment on his cube raid seemed even more ominous.

Kael heard the wall screen go on in the living room, another news report turned down low so he couldn't hear it. Zara knew how angry they made him. He wondered why she even bothered. After a few moments, there was a knock at his door.

"Come in," he said.

Zara entered and walked over near the cot. Chuck whined and flopped on his side. Zara smiled a little, seeing the dog on Kael's cot, and began rubbing his belly. The smile faded, and she looked at Kael with a troubled expression.

"There's something on the screen you should see."

He nodded at his wall. "I have one in here. I could watch it if I wanted to. I've seen enough."

He turned away from her. Zara sat down on the cot. He had to allow that she treated him with far more patience than he would have treated himself.

"Please," she said, touching his hand.

Kael looked at her. Though a woman, he sometimes saw in her only a girl; pretty, hopeful, and incredibly naive. But on that first day he'd witnessed another Zara: the cold, pragmatic creature, dangerous under her pretty costume. Maybe she was more like him than he wanted to believe, or maybe he sensed in her a slight attraction for him. If so, he didn't want to get her hopes up. But he could be imagining it all. Zara was that rare thing, a good person, and maybe he was confusing her kindness with a growing tenderness. It had been a long time since he'd encountered either, and he didn't really know how to tell.

"They only spew lies," said Kael, controlling his temper.

She shrugged. "Some lies are more revealing than others."

He took a deep breath. She was still touching his hand. This would be the time to pull it away if he was going to do it.

"Fine," he said, nodding at the wall.

She turned but left her hand where it was. "On. Current Reports."

A section of white wall faded out. In its place stood a reporter, flanked by perhaps a dozen sentinels. They were standing before a large gray cube. It appeared to be the same cube his team had cracked open, and he even recognized the burns from the shaped charges. Whether it really was their cube or only a clever facsimile hardly mattered now. By the end of the reporter's first sentence, Kael knew what the spin would be.

"...continuing shock and hurt at the actions of a few violent reactionaries against a Restoration Power Grid ... members from both the Sapient and Restorer leadership of the Harmony Council came together today to denounce the attacks, and to reaffirm the Treaty of ... and perhaps most disturbing of all, a carefully doctored recording of the attack in which the grid's internal structure appeared to be comprised of row after row of captives ... while experts note that the window of time between the initial attack and the subsequent mass uploading of the doctored film was just enough to ... officials now believe that the terror-suicide attack in the thirty-ninth quarter of Ash City's Restoration district involved a member of the same group that targeted the grid ... our thoughts and prayers remain with the victims of the attack, and with the families of the two Neutral Force border officers who witnesses say were gunned down while trying to rescue a young girl from..."

"Shut it off!"

"Okay," said Zara.

She gave the command, and the wall turned white. Zara squeezed his hand. "I just wanted you to see that—"

"—What?" he snarled, pulling his hand away. "That my men died for nothing? And not just those men. Hundreds. Thousands of men and women! Doctored film? How can anyone believe that shit!"

Chuck raised his head and growled at Kael.

"It's alright," said Zara, stroking the dog. "Kael's just growling in his own way."

Chuck put his head back down but kept his eyes open. Zara folded her hands together in her lap and closed her eyes as if in prayer. Kael heard the creak of the front door, and Apollo's heavy footsteps on the stairs. The old man began to cough, then loudly cleared his throat. Grocery bags were dropped onto the counter.

"Zara?" called Apollo.

He poked his head around the door.

"Everything alright?" he said.

Apollo surveyed the scene and nodded to himself. "So, you heard?"

Kael gritted his teeth and stared at the wall. At that moment, he wished nothing more than that he really had died in the fire. Raef had had it right, but maybe not right enough. It was better to be dead than to be replaced, sure, but worse than either was seeing that nothing would change. Not for him. Not for the children of Man.

"Dad," said Zarah, softly. "Let me … talk to Kael a little."

The old man nodded and let himself out. Amid his despair, it struck Kael that Apollo trusted him to be alone with his only daughter. Trusted his story—and not the well-spun lies. That was something. One spark in an abyss, but something.

"Look," began Zara, "I wanted you to see it because of what Dad said. About force. How useless—no, not *useless*—how it can sometimes play into their hands. Not that anything you did wasn't perfectly justified, and heroic. I don't believe that any good act is wasted."

Kael scoffed. "Nice sentiment. If only sentiments changed reality."

"Goodness does," she said. "Love does. Love means fighting, sometimes. But sometimes love means building, not fighting fire with fire, especially when the other guy's fire is infinitely more destructive than your own. And do you really want to beat them at their own game? What would that mean for you? What would you have to become?"

"I want the truth to be known! I want…"

She waited, but Kael had no follow-up.

"Right now," she said, "they control the avenues of truth. You heard the report: even your own politicians won't admit facts that shake things up. Because they're comfortable. They've got security, and position. You know who else does? All the well-to-do people in the Sapient Zone. All the businessmen. All the people you'd need to win over to have a chance in hell of replacing the Replacers."

Kael shook his head in firm denial, but she pressed on.

"This uprising you're hoping for? Kael, it's *never* going to happen."

"Not if I quit, it won't."

"But not everybody's like you! You're brave! You're committed! Most people just scrape by. And if they do make progress, they hold on for all they're worth. I know you think we're all cowards, and maybe we are. But there's plenty of it to go around. At least our *cowardice* comes at the Repos' expense, instead of giving them more ammunition!"

"You want me to give up!" said Kael. "If I was the Repos, I'd want me to give up too."

"No," she said. "No. Listen. I just want you to consider fighting them another way."

Kael looked at her thoughtfully, and his lips stretched into a grim smile. "You know, I think you're right."

"I am?" she said.

"With your father's formula, if we can find a way to mass-produce it, we can come in under their noses and—"

"No! No!" she said, slapping her hand down on his cot, and barely missing his broken arm.

She stood up and turned her face away. He knew she was starting to cry, and that she didn't want him to see that he affected her.

"You'll never get it," she said, staring at the door. "You'll never understand because you don't want to. And you'll never get the formula either if that's what you want it for."

She rushed out of the room, and slammed the door so hard that it bounced off the frame and swung back open. The dog looked up again, chuffed at Kael with evident disapproval, and followed Zara out.

***

Outside the sitting room windows, a cold wind blew through Ash City, stripping the last leaves from the street trees to send them skipping along sidewalks and into gutters. Zara sat on the couch beside Kael, waiting for him to make his move at the castella board. His left arm newly free of the cast, Kael pulled periodically on a tension band, trying to recover the strength in it. He found the exercise very distracting, and even the castella board chimed at him as if it too had become impatient. Kael glanced at Zara and noticed she was sitting closer now than when they'd started the game. He asked himself, for the hundredth time, if he should do more to push her away.

"Better make a move soon," said Zara, "or the game might get tired of this campaign and just come after you personally."

He shrugged and spent twelve counters to arm two gate-busters. He moved them forward to fire, and watched as both tanks exploded, then disappeared from the board.

"Hey, I thought you dealt with the mines."

"Not all of them," admitted Zara. "I needed the distraction—" she tapped the board, sending a twist-missile through the smoke, "—for this."

The missile struck the fortress wall, a section of which fell away. The castella board made a sad sound.

She beamed at him. "Now we're ahead!"

Kael frowned, and forgot to pull on the tension band. "You used my failure to launch your own attack," he said.

"But … I did it for the team," said Zara.

"Ah, yes," he sighed. "The 'greater good.'"

"Well, this way we both win," she shrugged.

Kael nodded. For the space of one heartbeat, their eyes met. Kael looked away, suddenly very interested in the tension band. The old stairway creaked. Kael knew by the tread that the old man was carrying something moderately heavy. He appeared at the doorway with a bulky gray bag.

"Hello, you two," said Apollo.

"Oh!" said Zara, "today?"

Evidently the bag meant something, but all Kael heard was "you two." Apollo set the bag down on the kitchen counter and opened it. He removed several small plastic bottles, followed by the homemade device he'd once used to scan Kael, and finally a large metal cask. Apollo needed both arms to get it out and set it on the counter.

"Who's coming?" asked Zara, standing up to help.

"Sit down, sit down," said Apollo, waving her back.

He slid the metal cylinder to the end of the counter and fixed a spigot to a hole near its base.

"Johanna Ched," said Apollo. "And her children. And the baby."

He placed one of the clear bottles under the spigot and began filling it with amber liquid. Kael knew what it was, because he'd watched both

Apollo and Zara drink the stuff before heading out on the town. Did this mean he would finally get to meet some of the others? The door chime buzzed.

"View," said Apollo, and a square of wall-screen revealed a small family on the doorstep.

"Open," said Apollo.

There was a buzz, followed by the disordered tramp of feet coming up the stairs, and the fading noises of a sibling argument that had evidently been carried over the threshold.

"Hush, hush, now," a woman said. "On your best behavior!"

The four of them soon entered the house at the second level. The woman held a baby in her arms, and she fixed her two older children, a boy and girl of similar age, with a glance whose dreadful import couldn't be missed. Their mouths zipped shut, and the two wandered away from their mother toward a corner of the sitting room.

"Johanna!" said Apollo, embracing her and the baby.

"Thanks for seeing me on such short notice," started the woman. "Forgive the intrusion. I just didn't want to take the risk that—"

She stopped, seeing Kael on the couch. Apollo nodded, inviting her to continue.

"Well…" she began, "he's just not getting a lot of it through feeding. We had a scare a few days ago. Luckily, I was able to whisk him away into the bathroom and inject it before the sentinels came by, but it really spooked me. The baby started screaming and it looked terribly suspicious, and…"

Apollo put a comforting hand on her shoulder.

"It will be alright, I promise."

The woman nodded, but she was obviously doing her best to hold back tears. Apollo leaned in, whispering to her. Kael caught a word or two. He gathered the baby was still nursing and wasn't getting enough of the amber formula through the woman's breast milk.

Apollo proceeded to show her how it could be heated, and mixed with pumped milk, so that the child could ingest it himself through a bottle.

"Thank you," said Johanna, wiping away a tear. "I just can't stand to see him crying from the shots. Every time I do it, he looks up at me like I'm trying to hurt him. I'll still have to ween him, but I suppose…"

She droned on, giving voice to a thousand concerns. The old man nodded, letting her talk. He took the scanner from the counter and waved it over the child. Kael found it odd that the woman would have such an intimate conversation in front of a stranger like him, but evidently, she'd judged that any friend of Apollo's could do her no harm. *Imagine trusting that much*, he thought. The scanner in Apollo's hand buzzed red, then beeped green. It floated back and forth between these two states, while Apollo's thumb moved along the buttons. Kael watched the process, wondering how such a clunky, and evidently jury-rigged device could defeat Replacer technology. Presumably, Repo science was several millennia advanced beyond that of Earth. Was it also so simple that it could be cracked by a common biologist? The only plausible explanation was that the Repos were utterly complacent in their superiority, so disdaining of the human race that they couldn't conceive of an effective human resistance. Unless there was some other explanation.

"Hi!" said a cheerful voice to Kael's right.

The two children had come out of their corner, and now stood by the coffee table. The girl stood nearer, while the boy's back-leaning stance suggested compulsion.

"I'm Marian," continued the girl. "This is my brother Aaron. He's eight, but I'm nine."

"So nice to see you again," said Zara.

The boy looked at her, confused.

"We've met before," said Zara, smiling, "but it was a few years ago."

"*See*!" said Marian, glaring at her brother. "I *told* you that we knew her, and you said you didn't remember."

Aaron shrugged. Marian shook her head at him.

"Aaron thinks he's *so* smart, but he doesn't remember anybody."

"That's bull," said the eight-year-old.

"Oh!" replied his sister, apparently shocked beyond words. "I'm telling Mom you said that."

"Not if you're smart, you won't," said Aaron, with a vengeful twinkle in his eye.

"*Any*way," continued Marian, "I see you're playing castella. Are you any good?"

Kael smiled. "She is. I haven't had much practice."

"Oh, well, my brother says he won't play with me because he says I'm terrible, but I'm actually just kind of unlucky."

Kael nodded magnanimously. "Aren't we all."

Zara elbowed him. The motion caught Marian's eye.

"*So* … how long have *you* two known each other?"

Kael froze. He looked at the castella board. "Well—"

"Are you gonna have any kids, you think?" asked Marian.

The boy suddenly glanced heavenward, his face twisted in horror. "Come *on*, Mare! Mind your own business!"

Zara broke out laughing and covered her face. Kael felt his own flush with blood. He looked at Zara, and the shared blush was more than either of them could take. He started laughing too, and felt her arm slip around his. Then, to Kael's consternation, Zara tilted her head to the side, as if waiting for his answer.

"Well," he stammered. "Well, first of all, we're not…"

Marian leaned in. Aaron shook his head, offering Kael what sympathy he could.

"Who knows what the future holds," Kael finally managed.

He looked down at Zara's arm, knotted with his own, and felt troubled.

"Well, *I* think you make a beautiful couple," said Marian.

"But nobody cares what you think about anything," added Aaron.

"Mom!" shouted the girl.

Mercifully, Johanna intervened, calling the children over to her. She was making her goodbyes, having evidently finished her conference with Apollo. Marian pointed accusingly. Her brother glared, and blew air out the side of his mouth, a victim of terrible circumstances. Johanna silenced them with an icy glance, said goodbye once more to Apollo, and smiled politely at Kael and Zara. Soon they were tramping back down the stairs, the children punctuating the clamor of their departure with appeals to mother's justice, and meticulous and mutually contradicting accounts of the origins of the conflict.

Kael was left on the couch beside Zara. She leaned into him. Their game of strategy was abandoned, no longer of pressing interest. Apollo, seeming not to notice the two of them, walked cheerfully upstairs.

***

Zara leaned over the message in the table. She swiped it away, and wood grain appeared in its place.

"Dad says he'll be here soon, and to start eating."

Kael wasted little time. The steak was lab grown, but it was salty and red, and it tasted almost real.

"How is it?" said Zara, watching him chew.

He shrugged. "Better than it has any right to be."

Zarah's frowned.

"I mean it's good," he said. "It tastes just like beef."

She favored him with a little corkscrew smile.

"I don't mean it's bad," he said, with his mouth full.

"I know," said Zara. "I just can't believe you can tell the difference."

"Maybe I can't," he said, taking a sip of wine, "but I still *know* it."

The front door opened, and they heard Apollo walking up toward the kitchen. While Zara was turned, Kael excised a small square of steak, and waved it under the table toward Chuck. The dog gobbled the meat from his hand, then waited patiently by his knees.

Apollo greeted them and took his seat. Kael watched him pray quietly before unfolding his napkin and spreading it over his lap. He started in on the asparagus.

"How was class?" asked Zara.

Apollo finished chewing. "Good, good. Most of the students are thinking more about break than biochemistry, except for the serious ones."

He took a sip from his glass. "And what fun are they?"

He chuckled at his own joke, and the chuckle became a raking cough, which he dispatched with a thump on his chest, and several large gulps of water.

"Almost choked there," he said. "How are you two?"

"I'm well," said Zara, pensively.

She looked at Kael, who had just slipped another hunk of steak into the dog's mouth.

"Hey! He's got his own food. And I thought you said you liked it!"

"I do," said Kael. "But if this dog is ever going to trust me, it'll be through smuggled steak."

Apollo smiled, then glanced intently at Zara. She seemed to plead with her eyes, and she shook her head emphatically. Apollo looked past her.

"So … does this canine diplomacy mean you're planning to stay?" he asked.

Zara pressed her eyes shut, but Kael saw her tense, waiting for his answer. He took a deep breath.

"Maybe," Kael finally said. "I can't seem to decide. One thing's for sure, I can't stay couped up all day anymore. I'm all healed up—"

"—Well, not quite," said Apollo. "But you're getting there."

Kael frowned at the interruption. "I can move," he said. "I need to get outside and walk around."

"Eventually, yes," said Apollo, cutting him off again. "That can … be arranged."

Kael set his fork down and frowned at Apollo across the table. "Arranged? It's a simple matter of drinking your formula, isn't it?"

Apollo glanced away, then at Zara. She smiled and placed her hand on Kael's.

"What my dad is trying to say is … of course the formula works, but your face is still in the system, and we want them to go on thinking you died, until…"

She trailed off, and Kael opened his hands, waiting for her to continue.

"—until things have died down a little more," finished Apollo.

Kael shook his head. "I've seen you walk past the sentinels. They don't even notice you're there half the time. I don't see why I couldn't do the same thing."

"Sure," said the old man, "but they're used to me."

"I'll wear a disguise," shrugged Kael. "I've already grown my beard out."

Apollo shook his head, smiling, but he seemed to stumble for a response.

"Sometimes they stop to scan retinas, or check for passes," he finally said, "and you're not in the registry."

"Neither are you."

"What do you mean?" said the old man.

"I mean that you told me that you were cooperators before you stumbled upon the right protein marker," said Kael. "Well, if there's also a registry for replacements, how is it that you're in it?"

Apollo went silent. Zara twirled a bit of steak on her fork and didn't look up. For a moment, the only sound was Chuck's panting under the table.

"I didn't know how to tell you this," began Apollo, measuring his words, "because I didn't want you to leave before there was time to … to … well, to fully integrate you."

He paused. Something in the old man's silence made Kael wonder if he was framing his words carefully or just making up a lie.

"Even after inventing the formula," continued Apollo, "in order to *really* pass as replacements, we needed someone on the inside."

Now Zara nodded. Quickly. Too quickly?

"The long and short of it is, this inside man entered us into the ALR—the Augmented Life Registry—and removed us from the cooperator registry. For that reason, we're able to survive even a retina scan without detection. It's why I'm able to work at the university and pass as one of them."

Apollo looked at Zara again. She dropped her chin and seemed to relax. Kael studied the two of them in silence.

"So how is it that this man had access to the registry?" pressed Kael. "Wouldn't he need to be a replacement himself?"

"Yes," said Zara. "That's correct. But he's a sympathizer, so—"

"Another Repo secretly on our side," said Kael, deadpan. "Like your mother's double."

Apollo shrugged. "There *are* a few of them," he said. "Every organization has its turncoats. Without them, we'd never have been able to—"

"—So put me in the system," said Kael. "You're the leader, right? Tell him to add me in under a false name."

"It's not that simple," said Zara.

"Why is it not that simple?"

"Because … because," said Apollo, "this man is in a very vulnerable position. He can't, he *won't*, take unnecessary risks. With you being a terrorist—in their eyes, of course—it'll be more difficult to integrate you."

"So, what? I have to stay in your house forever?"

"No," said Apollo. "It'll just take more time. Before our friend will add you to the registry, he wants to be sure that you've really given up your old, more aggressive tactics. One slip-up could give the whole community away. That's why it's important that you not go out yet, even with the formula. Not at this time."

"You asked this Repo man about me specifically?" said Kael.

"I've raised the subject in general terms," said Apollo. "More importantly, I know him. He's deeply embedded. As far as he's concerned, discretion is paramount."

"I thought you were in charge of this … resistance movement," said Kael.

"I never said that I was," said Apollo.

Chuck whined and dug his head between Kael's knees.

"See what you've done to my poor dog?" laughed Zara.

Kael didn't smile, but quickly tore off half his steak, and tossed it on the ground under the table.

"What's his name, this mystery man?"

Apollo shrugged.

"I don't think we should say," said Zara. "Not yet."

"Not yet," mimed Kael, "but later. Always later."

"Yes," she repeated, "definitely later."

Kael smiled. "Later, when all memory of what's in the cubes has disappeared? When the Repos have had time to root out the entire sapper army around the world, and rewrite history too?"

Zara's eyes went dagger thin.

"What are you saying?" she said. "What are you insinuating?"

"I'm saying," said Kael, through gritted teeth. "That you two have done a pretty good job of taking me out of the fight. And, all of a sudden, your magic formula won't work if I use it. Makes a person wonder."

Zara's face went as white as the wall behind her, then quickly shifted to scarlet. The change from Sweet Zara to Ferocious Zara was as swift as it was unsettling.

"We've ... taken care of you!" she spat. "Nursed you back to health! We've tried our best to l-love you and show you a different way of living. *How* can you *dare* to..."

She threw her napkin down on the table, and fled the room, knocking her chair over in the process. Kael sat staring at the wall, an ugly feeling in his gut. The dog, no longer eating the steak, growled suspiciously at him. Apollo looked across at Kael, defeated. He opened his mouth to speak, then swallowed another cough. At length, he seemed to gather himself.

"I don't know how to make you trust us," said Apollo, very quietly. "Trust is a choice."

"You want me to trust you?" said Kael. "Let me go outside! Let me leave!"

Apollo shook his head. "I've never tried to stop you," he said. "Indeed, it would be easier for you to leave now. Before it becomes..." he glanced in the direction Zara had departed, "...too difficult."

The old man took a deep breath and seemed to decide on something. "Yes, it would be easier than your distrust. And probably, nothing would happen. But if it did, and if they scrutinized you, then not only would you put Zara and me at risk, but you'd risk exposing all of those we've freed."

Kael pinched at his thick red beard, considering. There was no way to be sure of anyone, or anything. Life always seemed to offer two competing, and equally plausible narratives.

"If I'm wrong to be suspicious, then forgive me," said Kael. "For your sake, for Zara's sake, I'll set my suspicions aside. For now. I owe you my life; that I can't deny. But hear me, old man. I'm a dangerous person. If I ever find out that you've deceived me, then God help you."

Kael sat back in his chair and crossed his arms. Apollo looked across the table with a mournful expression. He stood abruptly, placed his daughter's dish and silverware upon his own, and left without a word.

***

Three nights later, Kael woke suddenly from a deep sleep. They said one didn't dream in deepest sleep, but every night Kael drank a sleeping draught, and every night he dreamed of men—his men—screaming, and dying in front of him, or he saw them stretched out on a table in a Repo interrogation chamber, their senses dialed up to eleven, their pain exquisite. He never tried to escape these dreams, even when he became aware of them. The dreams were Nature's just punishment for his failures.

Mere noise hadn't woken him this time. He kept the window cracked at night, in part to let the night sounds in from the street. The cries of birds, the chirping of insects, the infrequent, melodic zoom of a car approaching and passing in the night, made him feel human; reminded him that the world, at least, was real. Kael opened his eyes in bed, and tried to put his finger on what was wrong with this sound beyond his door. In the kitchen, feet stepped quietly at long, irregular intervals, a pattern that spoke of concealment, not consideration. Kael was out of his bed and across the room in one continuous motion. He opened his dresser drawer in perfect synchronicity with the next footfall, pulled on trousers, and grabbed his old sidearm from beneath the folded underclothes. Gun in hand, he stood by the door, listening.

One of the kitchen cabinets opened. The near imperceptible shift in the shadows under the door suggested a small flashlight. Quiet as he was, the creeper couldn't hide the deep, thick draw of his breath, or the edge of panic in it. Small containers were being shifted around in a tight space. Seasonings? No, pills. A druggie then?

A shuddering cough rent the air, then was swallowed. Apollo. The man sped across the kitchen floor toward the stairwell. The footsteps went down, down, past the front door, and still further. Kael frowned, wondering what Apollo could be needing in the basement this hour of night.

He opened his door, glanced once at the medicine cabinet, which was still ajar, and made for the stairs. As he descended, he set his feet only on the bend of each step lest it creak and give him away. Small scabs, still not entirely gone from his legs, caught and rubbed against his trousers.

He reached the front door, then continued on toward the unfinished basement. A light was moving around in there, not the bright overhead beam he remembered shining into his face the day they'd pulled him into the cellar, but the soft, erratic glow of a flashlight. He waited at the threshold. The flashlight beam ceased its dance. Something heavy was being pushed across the rough basement floor. He peeked around the corner and saw Apollo on the far side of the room fumbling with his keys before a crawlspace door that had been hiding behind a stack of boxes. The old man trembled, as if holding back a flood, and dropped the keys several times before finally getting it open. He stumbled forward into the dark space and shut the door behind him.

Kael considered the pistol in his hand, then stashed it in the small of his back, and crossed the room. He tried the door, and found it unlocked. Beyond it, a brick-walled alleyway lined a small chamber with yet another hatch at the far end, but Apollo was on the gravel floor of this passage, his hands and knees gripping the tiny stones. The old man's back arched like a cat's, and his elbows were bent out sideways. Kael watched him retch and noisily struggle to clear his throat. A long string of red phlegm trailed from his bottom lip to where it pooled on the gravel before sinking into it. His eyes and cheeks were wet with tears.

"Aghhh! Aaaaagkkkkhhhhhhh!" moaned Apollo.

It sounded like an old truck engine trying and failing to turn over. Kael crouched beside him. Apollo fell to his elbows and retched again without looking up. His torso whipped about mechanically, as if his body were trying to reach inside itself and tear something out. Gradually, over the next few minutes, the struggle ebbed. Apollo wiped his mouth, then rolled to a sitting position against the wall. The pool of blood and bile kept seeping under the rocks, and, when Apollo kicked more gravel and dust over it, Kael couldn't help but think of a cat, secret yet tidy in its private litter box. After a few clear breaths, the old man opened his eyes on Kael.

"Now you know," he said.

Kael studied him. "Cancer?"

Apollo nodded and placed a palm over his chest. His lungs, then.

"How long?" said Kael.

"I mean how long has this been going on," he quickly amended.

"Longer than I … *aagkkhh* … could have expected," said Apollo. "Almost two years."

Kael nodded. A pill bottle lay open on its side, and several small blue tabs had spilled out. Kael picked it up, and carefully replaced the tablets before shutting the lid.

"These help?" he said.

Apollo shrugged. "Only the symptoms. I need them for when I'm at work."

He took the pills from Kael and slipped them into the pocket of his robe.

"Ironic … isn't it?" said Apollo, gathering strength. "We live in an age of … wonders. The Repos could certainly cure cancer if they wanted to. But for them it's the hand of God. *Their* God. Which is to say … the Devil."

He gasped and took several deep breaths. There was relief in the old man's face.

"Does she know?" said Kael.

Apollo shook his head.

"What are you going to do?" said Kael.

Apollo laughed, and laughing made him cough all over again. He took his time before answering.

"I had a sort of plan," he finally said. "But now that I say it out loud, it doesn't … doesn't sound very good. Very just."

Kael waited for him to go on.

"Remember, I asked if you were a praying man? Well, I'm a praying man. At least a *hoping* man. For a while, I've been hoping that … that someone would come along. Someone strong, and decent. For Zara, I mean."

Kael kept the emotion out of his face. Apollo smiled grimly.

"You see what I mean?" said the old man. "Not very fair. You have your own life. Even if you did want to give it up, and stay here, there's no guarantee that you two would…"

Apollo looked down, embarrassed. Kael sat on the gravel and pondered the matter. Only a few months before, to give up his struggle and settle down in any capacity would have seemed treason. But perhaps things were different now. The revelations about the cubes had had virtually no impact on the general population, and that fact had knocked the wind out of his soul. The whole set of assumptions upon which he'd built his life of war had been proved false. And here was this other life, ready-made. Perhaps it was providence. He'd always thought 'providence' was only a word that weak men said when they were ready to give up, surrender to circumstances they might have changed, and blame the whole thing on a god.

Kael sighed. "I can't promise I'll stay here forever."

Apollo nodded. "It was only a hope. But when you came along, I thought, perhaps, it was a sign."

He smiled, but his shoulders slumped. Kael sat by him, wishing that he could promise the man that his daughter would be looked after.

"Look, no matter what I do," said Kael, "I'll keep in contact with her. If I leave, I'll come back to help if she's in danger. Though I'm pretty sure she can protect herself."

Apollo looked up at him, a twinkle in his eye that could have been tears, or amusement. "You think that I don't know that she can handle herself? I *do* know it. Only too well."

"Then what?"

Apollo shook his head. "I don't want her to become fully that other woman, the hard one lurking beneath. You've seen it."

Kael nodded. Apollo continued.

"You're a hard man, Kael. It's too late for you. Too late for me, too. Neither of us have had the luxury of being what they call 'well-rounded'. How can our hearts stay fleshy and warm when the enemy is cold, and calculating? But Zara ... she still has a chance. Yes, when I'm gone, she'll survive, but it'll be that *other* Zara. It's not her *life* I'm trying to protect, Kael. It's her heart. It's her soul."

Kael looked away from him, his gaze alighting on the brick wall, fixating on the staggered pattern of the bricks and mortar, as if in that pattern lay some hidden truth about life. After a time, he got up and dusted off his trousers. He extended a hand. Apollo took it, and Kael pulled him to his haunches.

"Look at me," said Kael, not relinquishing his grip.

Apollo met his gaze, and braced, as if he knew what was coming.

"You need to tell your daughter," said Kael. "Do it, or I will."

The old man bit his lip, then slowly nodded. Kael released his hand. He helped him replace the box barrier in front of the door, and the two crept up the stairs and parted ways without saying another word.

Kael stood by his bedroom door without opening it. He listened to Apollo's sad tramp up the stairs, and to the creaking of the floorboards as the old man passed above him toward a troubled sleep. Somewhere down the hall, Zara slept alone, too young to be fully jaded, too old to be happy alone. He imagined her soft face resting on a pillow under moonlight, troubled, perhaps, but mostly content. Ignorant of what she'd soon face. Zara had lost her mother, twice. Apollo would follow soon enough, before her twenty-first birthday, by the looks of it. Triply orphaned, then forced to bear the full weight of her father's little mission? And the father, at least, had had her to lean on. The Zara he'd come to love, the gentle-hearted woman, would not survive the ordeal.

If he left, she would only endure. She'd live moment to moment, just as Kael had before coming here and finding something that felt like home.

He opened his door, buried his gun in the depths of his sock drawer, and peeled off his trousers. Only a little scab came with them, and he plopped heavily onto his cot, not bothering to dab up the trickle of blood. Kael lay awake a long time, staring up at the ceiling, imagining the sorrow on Apollo's face, and the soft curve of Zara's shoulder as she swam in an ocean of naive peace. By the time his eyes closed that night, Kael Konstantius had made his choice.

***

Zara pulled the door almost closed, leaving it cracked so that she could hear the slow beep of the vitals machine from down the hall. She'd fallen asleep in Apollo's room, and in the haze of waking thought, Apollo's heart was a fleshy clock winding down. She had no plan but to stumble into her own bed, and cry into her pillow until sleep took her again. Outside, rain was pounding on their old roof, plunking noisily against the sagging gutters. That was just as well. Rain made her sleepy. If only she could wake up later and find that this had all been a bad dream.

Things had been progressing so well between Kael and her for the last few months. She'd hoped to be planning a wedding by now. Instead, she'd have to go to Central in search of a work assignment, since Apollo could not plausibly return to teaching. She needed income to keep their little project going. Others would help, but the responsibility still fell squarely on her shoulders. She had to keep up appearances because others were watching. Above all, she had to keep Kael with her.

Upon reaching her bedroom, Zara noticed the light on in Apollo's study. She opened the study door, and found Kael seated on the ground. Apollo had a number of storage bins for his supplies and his scientific implements, and half a dozen of these had been pulled out from the wall. Kael sat in their midst, turning Apollo's detector over in his hand.

"What are you doing?" said Zara.

"Oh," he said, looking up sheepishly. Then, after a long pause, "Just … trying to understand how this works."

She took a deep breath before responding. "My father is lying on his deathbed, and you're going through his things? Without asking him—or me?"

Kael looked at the detector thoughtfully. He returned it to one of the bins, then looked around rather hopelessly at the mess he'd made.

"I'll put all this … look, I'm sorry," he said. "I didn't mean to be disrespectful."

"What *did* you mean?" she said.

Kael stood up and dusted himself off.

"It's just … I was thinking that if your father should pass, we'd need to be able to reproduce these items in the future. The detector. The formula. So, I thought I should start familiarizing myself."

"Is that the truth?" she said.

Kael didn't answer.

Zara crossed her arms. "Thanks. But I have his blueprints, and I've helped him mix the formula."

"I see," he said. "That's good."

"You could have asked," she said.

"I should have," he agreed.

Zara considered whether to cry in front of him. Kael walked over, and put his arms around her, and she leaned her head against his chest. The tears began as a slow patter, and grew into a torrent to match the storm outside. Far away, the vitals machine tolled in its sinister way, and she flinched a little with every mechanical beat.

"I'm sorry," she said. "It's just like he was already dead, and you were going through his belongings."

"That isn't what I meant."

"I know. It just felt that way."

She kissed him. Black mascara came off on his cheek.

"I'm afraid you're going to leave," she whispered. "And I'll be here. Alone in this house."

"Leave?"

He pulled back, meeting her eyes. "I promised your father I would stay."

"Promise *me*," she said.

He pulled her close. "I'm not going to leave you alone."

"Because you promised Dad," she said, wiping her face.

"No, not just because of that. I love you, Zara."

She shrugged. "Why do you always have to poke around? How can you love me if you don't trust me?"

He sighed and closed his eyes. "It's not you," he said, at length. "It's just that I've never had the luxury of trusting people. It's like … pulling your hand back from a fire. My instincts tell me one thing—not to get too close to anybody—but my choice is what matters. I don't know how to change the feeling. Always watching my back. But it doesn't mean I'd abandon you."

"Alright," she said. "That's enough. That's all I needed to hear."

They both became quiet. Down the hallway, the rhythmic beeping of the vitals machine slowed. Zara gripped Kael's arms tightly. Her fingers dug into his skin.

"No!" she whispered. "Not now."

"Let's go to him," said Kael.

But she stood rigid as a statue, a child afraid of monsters.

"Zara!"

She shook her head. "No, this isn't happening. This can't be happening."

The machine sounded one final, continuous note.

***

Winter overstayed its welcome. A cheerless, bitter air held on through March like a junkyard dog with its teeth in the Sun. The wedding was set for May, but nature dragged its feet till mid-April. Finally, the stubborn cold broke, and the stillborn leaves spread their new green wings. Dandelions popped up on grassy patches that Kael could see from the windows, and the killdeer and the blackbird arrived to aid the stalwart robin.

People, mostly women, tramped in and out of the house, consulting with Zara, and helping her to plan. Kael complained once that he hadn't spoken to another man since Apollo passed away, and, shortly after that, a man named Jake began coming to the house to play him at chess and castella. Kael didn't much like Jake, whose saccharin demeanor reminded him of missionaries that knock on doors, but he appreciated Zara's attempt to quell his loneliness. Still, it was difficult not to punch a guy who began every sentence with "Hey, buddy."

The wedding was to take place at the cathedral in Ash City, just beyond the lift bridge, less than a mile from the place where Kael's old life had ended in fire. There was, to him, a kind of symbolism in this turn of events. As he stood in the basement, surveying the unfinished floor, Kael found himself thinking of the mythical phoenix. But unlike that bird, which died and was born again, Kael had been spared, the necessary death having been borne by another.

Kael glanced behind him at the door to the little crawlspace where he'd found Apollo and had learned of his cancer. He guessed now where the man had been heading that night. At the other end of the crawlspace was a second door that led into a small room in which sat a small marble altar with two urns. One held Apollo's remains. The other was filled with smooth white stones, because the real Genevieve Wright had disappeared into the bowels of a Replacer cube. In this brave new world, death, and even sickness, were kept out of sight, lest the Repos take notice. Therefore, when Apollo had passed on, members of the movement had come immediately to whisk the body away, only to return with his ashes.

It still troubled Kael that he hadn't been allowed to attend the old man's funeral in the crypt chapel of the cathedral. But that would have meant leaving the house. Zara promised Kael that their Repo ally would soon add him to the registry. For now, he was content to stay inside the house, passing the time with the irritating Jake, or pursuing his own projects.

There was a lot to do. Long ago, before he'd joined the sapper army, Kael had trained as a carpenter. Now he meant to make a living from it. This rough basement would have to be finished if it were to become his workshop. He intended to add outlets, and plumbing, and lay a floor over the concrete and loose gravel. He'd forgotten a lot, but it would all come back to him, he was sure. He set about with a tape measure taking down the room's dimensions and making notes in a journal. The simple act of starting put a smile on his face. To build and no longer to break, to forge a human world under the Replacers' noses—this was the novel form of revolution that Apollo had preached. As long as Kael kept moving, he could almost believe in it.

He heard footfalls on the steps, and groaned, hoping that it wasn't Jake. The man would only talk his ear off and get in his way. He looked up to see Zara instead. She glanced around, then spied him crouching in the dust.

"You've begun!" she said, cheerily.

He shrugged. "No point in waiting till the wedding. Anyway, I might be less motivated to come downstairs after that."

Zara blushed. There was no trace now of that other Zara, the hard woman threatening to swallow up the beautiful girl. It really did seem that they'd come into each other's lives at just the right moment. She offered him youth and hope, things he'd long given up for lost. He offered her a sturdy bulwark to hide behind, and so keep her heart untrammeled.

"What are you going to do first?" she asked.

He shrugged. "I think the floor, but I have to do a little research. Just measuring right now."

She smiled. "You should make a project notebook."

"I have a notebook," he said, pointing.

"Oh, I see that. But Daddy had a whole system."

He gently set down the tape measure, following an instinct that it was always good to let her speak about her father as much as she wanted.

"How did it work?" he said.

Zara plucked his notebook from the ground. She opened it and paged to the middle.

"First, he would divide the notebook into two parts," she said, flapping the journal to emphasize the two sections. "The front half was just for research. He turned the back half into a planner, like this."

She unclipped the mechanical pencil from his notebook and drew a table with sections cordoned off by hour, step, materials, estimated time, and so on. Kael made sure to lean in and look very interested. Mostly he was paying attention to the way she came to life thinking about Apollo. He wondered if his frayed personality was enough to fill some of that gap.

"Same thing," she said, "page after page. Daddy wouldn't even start a project until he'd researched it so well that he could portion it out to the day. That's why the Movement is so well-organized. Dad always said that if you wanted to be sure you were going to do something, you had to map it out in inches. 'Entropy eats the legless,' he used to say."

Kael thought about it a moment. He took her hand, and squeezed it gently.

"What?" she said. "You don't agree?"

"Sure," he said, cautiously. "If I had a mind like Apollo's. But I can't work like that. I have to get started, then feel my way through. Planning's good, but no plan survives first contact with the enemy."

"Oh," said Zara.

She looked displeased, but quickly smiled to hide it. "Sorry. I suppose I'm being pushy."

"No," he said. "It's good advice, and I'll really try it. I just won't do it as well as Apollo. Not yet."

That seemed to satisfy her. Zara smiled and leaned over to kiss him on the cheek.

"Make sure to build the floor sturdy. Someday, we might need to turn this into a playroom."

"Eh? Yeah. Part of it, maybe."

She grinned mischievously. "Oh, don't worry. I won't try to take over. Men just love their fortresses."

He shrugged. "We do."

Then something occurred to him. "Why didn't Apollo ever finish this room?"

He didn't mention the gutters, or the roof, or the upstairs light fixtures that were long due for replacement.

She shrugged. "Dad wasn't much of a fix-it man. Not really his strength."

Kael frowned. "That's odd. I mean, he built his own detector from what looks like spare parts."

"He was old!" she said, a little sharply. "And he was busy with his work."

Some deep instinct he couldn't analyze warned him to let the matter be, but the question spilled out anyway. "Too busy to repair the overhead light fixture in his den? The lamps in there aren't as useful as an overhead light would be."

"Are you … are you criticizing my dad?" she said.

"No, no," he said, "It's just that … I'm confused. Your father was a brilliant inventor. These things just usually go together."

There was a padding of feet on the stairs. Chuck sauntered into the room and trotted over to Zara. The dog slipped its muzzle under her hand. Zara stared at Kael, and absently stroked Chuck's head.

"I see," she said. "I'm talking to the suspicious Kael. The one who can't take anything at face value."

He braced himself, sensing a storm.

She shook her head, disappointed. "You know Kael, for such a great observer, you miss a lot."

"I'm sure I do," he said, quietly. "But I haven't missed what good people you and your father are. I'm just asking because I'm confused."

"Oh, *confused*," she said, unbelieving. "Okay, Kael. You're right. Daddy didn't build the detector himself. He discovered the marker protein and developed the concept, but he had help from the Movement. Is that what you wanted to know?"

He nodded. "Yes. Sorry. It's just, you said before that they were *his* blueprints."

"No, I said, '*the* blueprints.'"

"No, I'm sure it was 'his'."

"Fine! I misspoke! Maybe I fibbed a little bit, to give him all the credit. Is that what you wanted—for me to admit that Dad wasn't amazing in every way? What, are you jealous of him?"

"No!" said Kael, smothering indignation that would only make things worse.

"Zara," he said, beginning again, "It was just an incongruity that I noticed, but it's not important. I didn't say it for any other reason than that. Please."

He reached for her. She flinched, but relented, allowing him to touch her.

"Okay," she said, suddenly rueful. "God knows we're going to have a lot of these stupid fights over the years."

He forced himself to chuckle, then kissed her. She kissed him back. Not to be left out, Chuck wormed his head into the small gap between the two lovers.

"You're probably right about the stupid fights," sighed Kael, redeploying one free hand to scratch the short hair on Chuck's skull. "We're both stubborn."

Zara smiled dreamily and settled into his embrace. But Kael, in silence, stared off into the space behind her, pondering incongruities.

***

Two weeks later, the basement floor was half-finished. Kael looked up distractedly from where he crouched, laying finished hardwood planks over the newly cemented floor. Chuck was a few feet away, observing the process with great interest.

Zara smiled. "Sorry to interrupt, Mr. Fix-it. I said I'm going on some errands."

Kael nodded slowly. "Will you be long?"

"A few hours," said Zara. "You gonna miss me or something?"

"Always. Anything you want me to do around here?"

"Yeah," said Zara, gesturing at the saw. "Be careful with that thing."

Kael picked up the saw and gawked at it with exaggerated wonder. He brought it up level with his neck and made as if he were about to cut his head off.

"Stop!" she laughed.

"How dis works?" asked Kael, in a stupefied, sing-song voice.

She glared at him mockingly. "Bye, then."

She turned to leave.

"By the way," he called after her, "when do I become official?"

Zara stopped on the stairs and stepped back into the basement.

"What's that?"

"When do I get added?" repeated Kael.

"Added?"

"To the Augmented Life Registry? Remember?"

"Oh, yes," said Zara. "Um … well, I'll talk to him today! While I'm out."

Kael smiled. "Great. Don't you need something from me? A blood sample? A pound of flesh?"

She shook her head. "No, no. He'll come here and get whatever he needs."

"Of course," said Kael. "That makes sense."

"Well," he shrugged, "back to it."

He didn't look up again until he heard her leave by the front door. Kael stood and headed toward the stairs. The dog yawned and stretched its limbs straight, then began to follow him. Kael passed the middle floor and kept climbing until he reached the upstairs hallway. He went over to Apollo's den and tried the door. It was locked, as he assumed it would be. He produced the pick that he'd fashioned earlier that week out of a pair of metal tweezers. Minutes later, the tumblers popped. He turned the handle, and the door swung open.

Kael surveyed the room, paying special attention to the bins against the wall, memorizing their positions. Finally satisfied, he began pulling them out one-by-one. He quickly found a tub of Apollo's formula. After ten minutes, he still hadn't located Apollo's detector. Kael set the vat of formula on a bookshelf, then returned everything else to where it had been.

He went through a chest of drawers and looked under it. He rummaged through the closet and reached up to run his hand along the top of the bookshelf. Why would she have moved it? Chuck stared at him as he searched, muffing occasionally as if he didn't quite approve. Kael made his way to Zara's room.

It was a cozy space, and Zara's large, four-post bed took up a third of it. He'd never been inside. Perhaps out of deference to Apollo, they'd silently agreed to keep something back for the wedding day. Now, as his suspicions grew, he found himself grateful for that physical detachment.

He began searching her room, taking even greater care than before to leave things as they were. There was a small chest on the dresser, some boxes under the bed, and the closet, the vanity, and the desk drawer to explore. After five minutes of looking, the detector was in none of these places. He stood in the middle of the room and closed his eyes. The thought suddenly came to him to look under her mattress. Kael walked around to the bedside facing the wall and lifted it.

The detector was there, nestled down into the gap between the bed's support beams. He counted the beams, memorizing its placement and position. Chuck whined again. Kael turned the detector over in his hands and looked down at the dog.

"Let's just see," he said.

He fumbled with the switches, and managed to turn the thing on. Kael thought back to the times he'd seen Apollo use it. He could hardly remember all the details of his own rescue, but he'd paid close attention when the old man used it on the baby. In hindsight, that entire episode struck him as a kind of theater, and he recalled how Apollo's thumb had moved back and forth along the switches as he'd waved it over the child.

"Chuck," said Kael. "Come over here."

With one hand, Kael stroked the dog's head, while with the other, he waved the detector over Chuck's body. It flashed red. Kael sighed. The Repos had no interest in cloning or replacing dogs, so of course the animal *should* fail the test. It wouldn't have the identifying protein in its blood. *Still*, he thought, *what if...*

There were three unlabeled switches on the side of the detector. He flipped one and tried again. Still red. He did it again with the second switch and got the same result. He tried the last. The detector chimed pleasantly, then flashed green.

Kael's heart sank into his stomach. He muttered something obscene. Chuck whined and pulled away from him. Trembling, Kael turned off the detector, and replaced it under the mattress.

He sat down on the floor and put his face in his hands. The whole thing could be—looked like—a ruse! The old, improbable suspicion, that they were trapping him here to keep him out of the fight returned with sudden plausibility. Now that he thought about it, he'd never actually seen Apollo's body. Could they be playing him? Was Zara the Calypso to his Odysseus?

But if it was a trick, it had worked. He wanted nothing more than to settle down with her. *But surely*, said his gut *it would be better to be miserable—even dead—than to live a comfortable lie*. He'd always thought so.

Perhaps he just didn't understand how the detector worked. There was still one final, definitive test. The test was the formula itself.

He stood robotically, not giving himself time to reconsider, and marched back into Apollo's workshop. Struggling against a sense of vertigo, he crouched down and began sifting through the bins. He found the spigot attachment he'd seen Apollo use when the woman visited. With shaking fingers, he connected it to the vat of formula, bent his face underneath it, and pressed the button. The liquid dribbled down into his open mouth. It was slightly viscous, but the taste reminded him of soup broth, were it sweet instead of salty. He gulped down a few cups' worth, then cut the stream. Slowly and methodically, Kael went about setting the room in order. He pressed the button on the inside doorknob, and pulled it shut behind him.

Kael sat in the living room, watching the clock. The half-hour passed slowly. When the time was up, he marched toward the front door. He remembered his gun upstairs in the sock drawer. But there was no point. If the test failed, a single handgun would be of little help against sentinels. Anyway, he wouldn't feel like fighting them. The betrayal, if it was a betrayal, would run too deep.

Kael left the front door unlocked, and circled cautiously around the building toward the side that faced the crossroads and the lift bridge. There were plenty of people out, but, as luck would have it, no sentinels. The lift-bridge was about a quarter mile off, and he walked toward it with the general idea of crossing on foot. He remembered that there were detectors embedded in the ground, and he could see several mounted against the blue metal framing of the bridge. There'd be no alarm if he set them off, but the sentinels wouldn't keep him in suspense.

Ambling along the sidewalk, he was calmer than he had any right to be. The air was warm, and a friendly breeze kissed his nose and cheeks. Kael hadn't felt the wind on his face in many months. He made it to the lift bridge, and ascended the metal lattice stairs of the walkway that spanned the river. There were lots of people around, most choosing, like him, to walk rather than drive on such a nice day. No one seemed to recognize him, or to notice him at all, except to smile politely if their eyes happened to meet. He passed eight or nine obvious detectors, and estimated he'd walked over a half-dozen invisible ones. If they were coming for him, it would be soon. He was nearly across the bridge when the crowd thinned out just enough to reveal what awaited him on the other side of the walkway.

Three sentinels lurked near the bottom of the steps. Even from this distance, they were as large as brown bears on hind legs. He considered running, then discarded the thought. If he ran, he'd never know. If, by some chance, the metal men were *not* waiting there for him, then he could put his suspicions aside, and allow himself to live that happy life, which, deep down, he didn't feel he deserved.

There was no point in being casual. The sentinels weren't taken in by such things. He reached the end of the walkway, and stepped down slowly, passing between the monsters without any hurry.

Nothing happened. Kael glanced over his shoulders to see if they'd made any move. The sentinels glanced around, apparently scrutinizing every person, place, and inch of ground, but they didn't give Kael a second look. But maybe they'd missed him. He turned on his heel and walked back in their direction. Now, standing directly beneath one of the robot soldiers, he planted his feet, and loudly cleared his throat. The monster looked down and fixed Kael in the cyclopean gaze of its single red eye.

"Hello," said Kael. "Fine day, isn't it?"

The eye fluttered, and Kael knew he was being scanned. For a moment, he was sure it had recognized him. After a time, the thing swiveled its head away from Kael, and went back to patrolling the environment. It had no quarrel with him.

"On your way, sir," said the mouthless head. "Must keep traffic flowing."

Kael shivered, feeling a mixture of profound relief and joy, and headed back across the bridge. He seemed to float the whole way. Never had he been so happy to be wrong. Already his mind was making up excuses for him not being allowed to see Apollo's body, and for Zara hiding the detector. Indeed, he was beginning to feel guilty over the whole affair, and he doubled his pace to make sure he'd return before Zara did. How could he explain to her that he'd risked his life—and potentially hers—to prove that she wasn't lying to him?

He reached the other side of the bridge, and stopped. No less than ten sentinels stood arrayed on either side of the intersection, their hands retracted, and replaced with wide-barreled guns. He wasn't the only one frozen in his tracks. Dozens of pedestrians stood around gawking at the metal men. Mothers were gripping their children by the wrists and dragging them away from the road. Something was very wrong.

A sentinel with its guns trained on the intersection swiveled its head around to face him.

"Clear the area, sir."

"What's going on?" said Kael.

It didn't answer, but its head snapped back around toward the street, and its thick legs moved into a wider stance. Echoes of the same order sounded all around the street. Some people began to run, while others moved very slowly, their curiosity greater than their sense. What happened next felt like a dream.

There was a screech of tires and a blaring of horns. The sound of gunfire cascaded in from the streets leading to the border road. People turned and screamed at something Kael couldn't see. Three large military-style trucks plowed into the crossroads, their windshields blown out, their cabins and trailers twisted, and on fire. One swerved directly toward the sidewalk where Kael stood with a dozen other people. The sentinel nearest him raised its gun to fire, then quickly abandoned the attempt and started charging toward the truck. The vehicle hopped the sidewalk.

Kael stared in horror as a family of five was swallowed up beneath the truck's grill. Two sentinels clung to its bumper, clawing the pavement to slow it down, but with little success. Finally, the sentinel that had first warned him to flee closed upon the truck. It made its arms spikes, screwed its legs into the pavement, and plunged the upper half of its body into the barreling truck. In a movement as deft as it was beautiful, the metal man forced the truck up its bent thighs, then bridged backward, flipping the vehicle upside down, and slamming it on the pavement behind. The truck's momentum kept it skidding forward, half on the pavement and half on asphalt, until it came to a stop less than a foot from Kael.

The sentinel snapped up, and turned toward him. Mangled from its struggle, it now looked like a giant piece of aluminum foil. Kael actually pitied it.

"Rekurn to gur ghome!" said its broken voice box.

Kael took off running toward the townhouse. Behind him was pandemonium. The air was filled with human cries, and the noise of metal-on-metal, the sounds of human terror and of tearing metal blending to become one anxious, unnatural racket. He dared not turn around to see what was happening. Twenty yards from the house, a loud boom sounded behind him. He was lifted from his feet and tossed into a stand of trash bins waiting by a metal fence. The bins cushioned his fall, and he landed harmlessly on a patch of grass. He stood and turned, like Lot's wife, to stare at the destruction behind him. There were no longer three trucks, but one. Two had detonated, tearing huge craters in the intersection from which he'd just escaped. The ground was covered in metal, and fire, and in broken human bodies.

As he stared, unbelieving, a single item floated down upon the heated air. It was black, and frayed, and it opened just long enough for him to recognize the crimson "S" behind a crossed sword and gun. The flag of the Sapient Resistance. His people. It fluttered down to the broken asphalt, landing by chance over the face of some anonymous Repo woman whose hand still gripped the wrist of a small, bodiless arm.

"Dear God!" stuttered Kael.

His head swam, and he fell to his knees. The gentle breeze blew away more of the black smoke, revealing black and red splatters that dotted the fractured sidewalks. Kael clutched his heart and bent over to vomit.

***

A voice came through the door. "Buddy? You about done in there?"

Kael looked up, irritated. "Yep."

He was in the little room getting dressed for a wedding. His own, as it happened. Nine months was a long time; enough to grow a new life, or reconfigure an old one. Jake was waiting to drive him to the cathedral.

Everything Kael had on had been donated. Someone had come over to the house to take his measurements the day after someone else had come over to take his blood and scan his retina so they could put him in the Repos' system. That was only a few days before Jake shared the good news with him: his role as Kael's best man. Like so many other things pertaining to the wedding, this decision had been made without input from Kael. He went along with it. After all, his real "best men" were probably all dead. Jake was a decent enough fellow—a turncoat cop working for the Movement—but he hung around too much, and tried too hard to be Kael's friend, and Kael couldn't help but notice that he'd never really left his side since Kael had come back from that explosive little outing. Maybe it was coincidence.

When he finished putting his suit on, his big toe popped out through a hole in one of his socks. Kael bent down to pull it off, then cursed, because he could barely move in the monkey suit. The lack of mobility made him nervous. There was a ding on the wall, and he heard the com open.

"Hey, lover," said Zara's voice.

"You're not supposed to see me before the wedding," he said, without looking up. "Or is it the other way around?"

"I'm off-screen," she said. "Everyone's here. Will you be soon?"

"Ten minutes, tops," he said.

She sighed. "Okay. I love you."

"I love you too," said Kael.

She closed the connection. Kael took his suit jacket off so he could move. He tossed it on the cot next to Chuck and pulled off the offending sock. Even without the coat, he felt like a puppet on strings. There was no reason to think anything would go wrong, but if it did, he'd be moving in molasses. He pulled out a drawer and dug around for a black sock that matched the one he was wearing. His fingers brushed something hard.

Kael pulled out his old sidearm. On a whim, he checked the clip. Six rounds. Not that six rounds would do him much good if anything went down. Chuck picked his head up and whimpered.

"Bad idea?" asked Kael.

The dog chuffed at him. Kael considered the gun again. If he did bring it along, he'd just have to get rid of it sometime between saying "I do" and boarding the lev train. But anything could happen out there on the street.

"Buddy!" called Jake. "We gotta go!"

Kael sighed and set the gun on the cot beside him as he pulled on the new sock. He put his shoes on, then picked up the gun with the intention of returning it to the drawer. Instead, he slipped it into the small of his back, not realizing what he was doing until it was done. He shrugged and covered the gun with the jacket. Paranoid, maybe, but maybe his instincts were smarter than his head. He could always ditch the thing later.

"Alright," he said, stroking the dog's head. "But next time you see me, I'll be a better man."

Kael took a deep breath and headed for the door.

***

The wedding seemed to happen underwater. From the sacristy, there were far-off sounds of people shuffling into pews, and the smell of roses that lined the chancel. There was organ music practiced in fits and starts before the main event. The cheerful chirping of whispered conversation floated up from the nave. Children cried, and were silenced. Once, Kael got up from his chair in the little room near the altar and peered around the corner at the ancient interior, more than half-filled with faces he didn't recognize. All seven-hundred-odd citizens of Apollo's secret flock must have been in attendance. It made him think of being in a cult.

The music started in earnest, and a thousand-plus knees straightened.

"Let's go, buddy," said Jake.

They came out of the sacristy, and Kael found himself alone at the bottom of the steps to await his fiancée. The bridesmaids filed in. Kael didn't know how to stand. His eyes instinctively scanned for one old, familiar face, though he knew Apollo wasn't there. He looked through the congregation for some of the people who'd stopped by the house, and that was like trying to find a few cornstalks in a field. Every face he passed over smiled at him. They might have been mannequins, or film extras; there was that much between them and him. Finally, she came.

The old man escorting her bore a passing resemblance to Apollo, and was probably an uncle of hers. Zara floated up the center of the nave on a cloud of white lace, painting the hundreds of onlookers in commonplace obscurity. When her eyes met his, Kael forgot everything else.

The Mass was a strange ritual, but its ebb and flow were somehow meaningful, a sort of microcosm of the pattern of death and rebirth in which he found himself embedded. The vows came sooner than he thought they would, in the middle, not at the end. Probably, someone had told him the agenda, but it still came as a surprise. He spoke the words at the priest's prompting, feeling their weight as they left his lips. Just like that, the two of them were seated together, their love on display for the company of secret strangers. Kael held Zara's hand, and leaned slightly forward, because the gun dug into the small of his back. He deeply regretted bringing it, not least because the thought of how to get rid of it as soon as possible distracted him from the moment. When it came time for communion, he did not receive, for he knew only the gods of death found behind barricades and in violent, desperate oaths uttered in firefights. He did not yet know or trust this God of Bread, Hearth, and Home, phenomena he'd heretofore seen as mere luxuries, or as smiles on the faces of drowsing dogs.

The organ music played. It was over. Everyone stood and filed out toward the narthex, to the stairway that led from there down to the reception hall beneath the church. Zara clung to him and kept trying to wrap her arm around his back. He would catch her hands and hug her awkwardly with her hands in front of her. The crowd was pressing in. He had to get rid of the gun. How could he have imagined there would be any need for it here?

The stairs gave him a reprieve. They held hands descending, and everyone gave them space. Downstairs, past the basement chapel where a small service had once been held for Apollo, was a large, stone-tiled room set with many tables in white tablecloths. He tried to separate himself from her to visit the restroom so he could ditch the gun there, perhaps in the ceiling panels, if there were any. There was so much noise. Everyone was looking their way. By the time he made her understand that he needed a moment, the restroom line was already ten men deep. Someone escorted them to the front for their first dance.

A soft song played, and Zara draped her arms around his neck. Kael clutched her very close, the better to keep his elbows short, and prevent the bulge of the handgun from showing through his jacket. So positioned, he relaxed a little. Zara leaned up and whispered in his ear.

"I love you."

"I love you too."

"Is everything alright?" she said. "Are you just reeling from the experience?"

She'd sensed his anxiety.

"I was … just wondering how it was for you," he said. "Not having your dad here. But I didn't want to bring it up."

He winced at this first married lie, hoping it would be the last, but Zara stared at him blankly for several seconds before she seemed to process what he'd said. The shift in her expression toward sadness was strange, he thought. Almost mechanical.

"Sorry for mentioning it," he added.

"No, no," she said. "That's very considerate of you."

Zara stroked the back of his neck gently with her nails. "I'll be okay. This is a happy day. Dad is looking down on us, very pleased with both of us."

He nodded, and kissed her, and they danced some more.

There was food, and a speech by Jake. It consisted of the sort of generalities you'd expect from a best man who hardly knew you. The most authentic-sounding parts were anecdotes about Zara, or Apollo. Kael found himself thinking of Raef, and Crumb, and Nathaniel, and a dozen other men—most of them probably dead now—who'd have given a better one. The artificiality of the whole situation, the sense of being a foreigner for whom everyone was playing host—or playing a role—got under his skin. He held more tightly to Zara's hand, and lamented all the more the absence of Apollo. He was Robinson Crusoe in reverse, a dangerous savage shipwrecked on a desert island with a tribe of happy civilians. Kael suddenly smiled at his fear that one of these people would look at his jacket and know that he was carrying. Not one of them would recognize the outline of a gun, even if he were staring right at it.

Someone got on the microphone and announced that it was time for the bride to give away her bouquet. The bridesmaids, and every young female who could walk, poured like a river onto the dance floor.

Zara squeezed his hand. "Be right back!"

Kael and all the other men got up and shuffled over to the side to watch the event. Zara turned her back on the crowd and covered her eyes with one hand. The women surged forward, then backward, trying to anticipate the pattern of flight before the flowers even left her hand. A clutch of young girls, including Marian, who'd visited the house with her brother a million years before, moved desperately behind the grown women. The girls were bound together like a life raft, hoping to increase their chances. But for the bouquet to make it over that sea of outstretched adult hands, it would probably require a wedding miracle. Kael watched the young girls, and quietly rooted for Marian. But not far behind Marian, in the center of the girls, he saw something. What he saw was impossible. It took the smile from his face.

An Asian girl about eight years old hopped up and down with the others. He got a clear glimpse of two arms—perfectly normal, not deformed—waving and reaching above her head. He saw the tell-tale patch of unpigmented skin on her face. Why was she here? Where was the fleshy claw that had been her hand? When the bouquet flew through the air, and was tipped and sent spinning so that it actually did clear the crowd of taller women before sailing down toward the girls, this one surged forward with her peers. He saw two hands close upon the green stem bundle, and snatch it back. In that instant, she looked up at him through the sea of bodies, a tiger in the reeds. Their eyes met. The girl grinned, and faded into cover.

"Hey! Hey! Stop!" shouted Kael.

In all the noise, only a few people heard him. Jake noticed, and looked at Kael warily.

"Hey, buddy, what's wrong?"

The best man put a restraining hand on his Kael's shoulder. Kael shrugged it off and ran into the crowd.

"Grab her! Stop her!" he cried.

The gaggle of women closed together, moving in strange unison to bar his path, but roughly, as if by happenstance. He plunged into their midst and started pulling them apart, digging his way backward through the crowd.

"Hey, there, buddy!" said Jake, close behind him. "What are you doing?"

Kael, who was almost through the women, grabbed a frightened bridesmaid by the hair and tossed her out of his way. He towered over the gathering of small girls.

"Where is she?" he roared, scanning the room.

The girls closed ranks, a terrified little platoon. The Asian girl was suddenly nowhere to be seen.

"Did she run?"

No response. They must have been hiding her in the middle. Kael grabbed their little arms and began pulling the girls out one by one. They cried piteously for their mothers, but Kael knew better now than to be moved by such impostures. In the center of them he found not the girl, but

Marian. She was crouched down in a squat, arms locked around the bouquet, lips trembling.

"Where is she?" snarled Kael. "The girl who caught it!"

Marian burst into tears. "It was me," she said. "I caught the bouquet. Why are you doing this?"

He grabbed her by the shoulders and shook her.

"Liar! Where did she go? She was just here!"

"Please! I don't know what you mean!"

Jake caught up with him and tried to pull Kael away from Marian.

"Hey buddy—"

Kael swung an elbow into his head. There was an audible crack, and Jake crumpled to the floor like a sack of bricks. By now the crowd of women had begun to scatter, disappearing behind the circle of wedding guests which, like the Red Sea, parted into a standing wall. Kael dropped Marian with disgust. The girl ran off, crying, but still clutching the bouquet.

Only one person remained in the center with Kael. Zara stepped cautiously toward him. In her cloudy dress, makeup running down her face, she looked like an angel who had taken her death-hurt. Or maybe just a clown.

"What have you done?" she said. "Why are you doing this?"

He stalked toward her, pulsing with energy. She shrank from him, but did not flee.

"You did it so carefully," he said. "You all think you're so clever, but you made a mistake."

Zara shook her head, uncomprehending. Kael looked her up and down thoughtfully and smiled. The grim smile seemed to frighten Zara more than his approach.

"Or was it a mistake?" he mused aloud. "They say the Devil can't resist one final boast. But you people showed your cards too early."

She held her snow-white hands out toward him. They were perfect. Soft. How he would have loved to have disappeared into the soft perfection of her body—and how well *They* had known it!

"All I have for you," she whispered, "is love. Even now. But I don't understand."

He laughed. She shrank from his laughter as if it were shards of glass spilling forth from his mouth.

"Where is Apollo?" said Kael.

He searched the crowd. *'Looking down on us,' indeed!* He now suspected the old man was hiding in a corner somewhere, taking in the show. Zara only covered her mouth with her hand, and quietly wept. Kael was amazed that she did it so well. Even knowing better, he still wanted to believe her. Comfort her. Then, considering the depths of her manipulation, and the depths of the feelings that she'd kindled in him—a false love; a love based on lies—he lifted the back of his jacket, cycled a round into the chamber of his gun, and aimed it at her.

If Zara was afraid, her face did not give it away. On the contrary, the sight of the gun seemed to awaken understanding. She folded her hands in front of her waist, and stared at him with something like amazement.

"You're going … to kill me," she said.

It wasn't a question.

"Probably," he said. "For what you did, you deserve it. God knows I won't get any other satisfaction. I'm sure you've got this place surrounded. I won't get far."

She took a deep breath. "And what … have I done?"

He scowled. "Ask me that again, and I'll pull the trigger. Seduce me. Betray me. Make me fall in love with a pretty illusion. But don't insult my intelligence. That's been you people's downfall all along. You think we're stupid, and it's why you'll lose in the end."

She nodded, slowly, as if now she understood. *Such wonderful acting,* Kael thought. *How can they all be such talented liars?*

"I think I see," said Zara, sadly. "You believe this was all some kind of trick."

He took two steps toward her, placing the barrel of the handgun against her chest. It sank into the delicate flesh there, of which he'd deprived himself out of respect for Apollo, flesh which now he would never touch. She glanced down at the gun, then up at him. Her breath was sweet, and she smelled of roses. Women's beauty was, thought Kael, a weapon more effective than any devised by man or machine. No wonder They'd made use of it.

"Darling," she said, "I've done everything I could to show you love. If you don't trust me now, you might as well just shoot me and be done with it."

Kael looked into her eyes, and tried, in their brightness, to find the truth. But facts were hard, cold things—like bullets—and beauty only a battleground where gods and demons fought for human hearts. He pressed the muzzle of the gun until it touched hers. He could feel her heart pulsing through the metal.

"Why don't you know?" she pleaded. "Why don't you know what love is?"

Kael Konstantius considered her, then sighed, and shook his head.

"All I know," he said, pressing the barrel in, like a dagger, "is that I'd rather be slopped than swapped."

***

Kael stood naked in front of a full-length mirror. He pulled back the hair under his armpit, wondering if that smaller mole had always been there. Probably it had. He went over to the table and stripped his sidearm, the one he'd had in the Repo Zone, down to its component parts. He scoured those parts for anything that shouldn't have been there, and found nothing. You could drive yourself crazy thinking of such things.

He threw on a t-shirt and sweatpants, and reassembled the weapon. Despite—or because of—the relative ease of his flight from the Repo side of Ash City two weeks prior, he still didn't feel safe. Even after last night's successful raid on another cube, Kael couldn't shake the feeling that They knew his every step. There was a knock at the door.

He frowned, and glanced at the sonar camera mounted on the lead-lined wall. Gray paint flaked off it, and some of the flakes littered the rust-colored floor. The sophisticated device looked out of place here. On the screen he saw the three-dimensional image of a man, as well as the outline of the ornate personal sigil he wore on a chain beneath his clothes. It was the sort of identifying mark Kael insisted on now. He touched the com.

"Nathaniel," said Kael.

"The same," said the voice.

"What do you want? We have an early day tomorrow. I was going to get some sleep."

"There's someone outside the gates asking to see you," said Nathaniel.

Kael frowned. "Outside the fortress? Have you checked them out?"

The ghostly three-dimensional image smiled sardonically. "Definitely our people," it said.

Kael took a deep breath. He shouldn't be surprised that his triumphant return had garnered him a few fans among the plebes, the sort of people who gave them money and offered prayers but didn't lift a finger to fight on their own behalf. Still, it made him nervous. Ever since he'd burst forth from that cathedral and had practically sprinted the three miles back with his gun still hot and not a single sentinel to bar his way, he'd been waiting for someone to find him, and put a bullet in his head.

He touched the com again. "Man or woman?"

"Woman and a girl," said Nathaniel.

So, admirers, not assassins. But they'd come all the way here to talk to him. He might as well greet them. Maybe they'd donate to the cause.

"Have the guards put 'em in the one of the empty warehouses and wait. The gray building, a hundred paces from the gate."

"Okay, but..."

"What?"

"Never mind, boss. I'll tell them."

Nathaniel walked away. Kael took off the sweatpants, and quickly put on tactical pants, a long-sleeve shirt, and the gun vest that was never far away from him. He probably didn't need to be armed, since they'd cover him from the wall, but he never took chances anymore.

A few minutes later, Kael was outside the gate, walking toward one of the abandoned warehouses that surrounded their makeshift fortress, and which acted like the curtain walls around a keep. The warehouses had kill-holes punched through their outside walls, with many pieces of artillery mounted behind. He meant to enter the gray building through an open doorway at the ground level. The door hung by one hinge, and he pushed it aside, and stepped in.

A woman stood in the center of the floor. She looked Korean. Very pretty, and probably not as old as suggested by the lines that a hard life had traced upon her face. Someone small was standing behind her, out of sight, a little arm wrapped around her waist. Kael smiled.

"It's okay, miss. You can come out."

The woman smiled. "She is very shy."

Kael nodded, understanding.

"But, when we heard about your return," said the mother, "she wanted to come and thank you personally."

Kael frowned. "Thank me?"

"For what you did," said the woman.

He chuckled. "So, we've got a future freedom fighter on our hands, huh?"

He crouched down to his haunches and beckoned.

"Come on out, young lady. I don't bite."

There was a pause, and the little hand slid off the woman's waist. The girl appeared beside her mother. She was about seven or eight years old. One hand was perfectly normal; the other, a hideous claw. Her legs didn't match. She suddenly smiled, threw her hands open wide, and hobbled toward him.

Kael jumped up and scuttled away. The girl looked at her mother, confused.

"You!" gasped Kael.

He reeled with sudden understanding. "So now they're doubling freaks as well, huh? Anything to get at me!"

The mother looked at him, aghast. "How … how can you say such things to my daughter?"

Kael spat upon the ground. Were there no limits to the Replacers' depravity?

"I know what you are!" he shouted. "I know what's going on here!"

The woman and her daughter stared at him, uncomprehending.

***

A few minutes later, Kael was back inside the fortress heading for his quarters. He reached the heavy metal door of his berth, and keyed in the code. Nathaniel ran up beside him.

"You okay?" he said.

Kael looked at him. "Why shouldn't I be?"

Nathaniel frowned. He sniffed at the air and glanced at the gun mounted on Kael's chest.

"The guards reported shots from the vicinity of the warehouses. I thought…"

Kael shrugged, and chuckled grimly. He turned behind him, looking through the dark window in his berth toward a moonless sky.

"I'm still alive," said Kael. "So I can't complain. The war goes on."

MANY HORIZONS

Harley drew the lines thin so they wouldn't overwhelm the picture. He'd already done the rocky fissure that looked like someone was pulling apart the earth at the seams. He'd put in a viperfish, a black dragonfish, and a sea tadpole. He added a humpback anglerfish and a few sea walnuts. With a white pencil, he began outlining the monstrous entity that lived at the bottom of the Trench. He liked the idea that real sea monsters existed, but were just hiding, and maybe that was why scientists hadn't found them. He left the outline simple because Grandpa said less was more. Grandpa said a lot of things. Some of them were true.

He smiled. Now came the fun part, drawing the monster darker than anything else in the dark trench. Harley used a Midnight Black pastel for that. He grinned, because he could already see that the plan was working. The white pencil he'd used to outline the creature barely showed up, yet it did the job of helping to offset one dark from another. His monster was to be darkness-in-darkness, an inky eel crouching at the bottom of the world. If, somewhere, there was a planet where even the daytime sun was dark as coal, then his monster was the color of that world's night.

"What are you drawing *now*?"

Harley pressed his eyelids closed. That was what he did when a good thing was suddenly interrupted by one of life's annoyances: in this case, his sister Macy.

"A picture," he said.

"I know, *weirdo*," said Macy. "Why do you always draw pictures of the ocean. You're not a fish."

He was glad he'd finished the dark just inside the white outline before Macy had found him. Now he could fill-in the body without worrying that he'd get strokes of Midnight Black inside the Midnight Blue. Foundations were always difficult. You had to earn the easy part.

"I like the ocean," he said, absently.

Nothing so simple would make her go away.

"Why is that part super black?" she said.

He was mad that she had to ask. Harley knew that this time the picture really looked like what he imagined. If she couldn't see the creature, then she was stupid.

"It's a sea monster," he snapped.

He kept filling it in.

"There aren't any sea monsters," said Macy. "You know that, right?"

At eight, she was two years younger than he, almost to the day, and entirely dedicated to annoying him. If there was a constellation Irritatio, Macy was born under it.

"Right?" she repeated.

"I'm trying to concentrate," he said.

"You don't need to concentrate," she shot back. "Because you're making it up. The details don't matter."

"Please … go away," he said absently. "Go talk to Mom."

"I don't want to," she said. "She and Dad are fighting about Grandpa Moore."

He stopped coloring. Her voice had creaked a little.

"They're not really fighting," he said, more softly. "Just having a discussion."

She crossed her arms and leaned her shoulder against his. It was harder to draw when she did that. Harley sighed. He wrapped his arm around her and gave a little squeeze.

"Sorry you're upset," he said. "It'll be okay."

He found it difficult to stay mad at her. Sisters were impossible to understand, but sometimes they needed things. And he couldn't blame her for being upset. Harley had known that this old argument would break out again, just like it had the last two times they'd come to Grandpa's ranch. Grandpa Moore had always been a little odd, even more after Grandma died, but now that his hounds were gone too, he seemed to have taken a turn. The things he'd always whispered to Harley—stories about other worlds; strange warnings about unseen dangers—he now told to anyone who would listen. Harley sighed, put the sketchpad on the ground, and began returning pastels to their slots in his art case.

"I said it's going to be fine. They just want to make sure he's okay."

She shook her head. "Dad wants to let him be, and Mom wants to put him in a place for old people."

"How do you know that?"

"I listen."

He wanted to say, "You spy."

"They both love him," was all he said.

"Yes, but they don't *agree*!"

All of Macy's anxiety came to a head in that last word.

"You should go talk to Grandpa," said Macy. "Before they do it."

He frowned. "What can I do? I'm a kid."

She considered her words before answering. "Grandpa … likes you the most."

Harley looked at her, thinking that it must have cost Macy a lot to say that out loud.

"So, what do you think I should say to him?" he asked.

She brushed a tear away with the back of her fist. "If you can make him stop talking about the things he sees, then maybe Mom won't be as worried."

Harley nodded. He had, in fact, been considering this very course of action, ever since the incident of the night before. Grandpa had been offering yet another, contradictory account of his mysteriously wounded hand, when he'd suddenly excused himself from the table, claiming that he'd needed to "finish something important." Mom had silently waved them over, and they'd watched him through the window, rocking in his chair, yelling at the air, and generally behaving like a madman. Harley had thought then that he ought to take his grandfather aside and tell him how much his actions were worrying Mom and Dad. Now that Macy was making the same suggestion, it felt like a sign.

"Okay," he said. "I'll go talk to him."

***

It was the right sort of porch for a grandfather. It wrapped around the whole house, and there were double doors at either end. The front porch overlooked farmland and an old brown road. The rear view offered hills that rolled down, down, down into a great valley, with a few painted farms and blue mountains in the distance. Because of that wraparound porch, a person could stand at any point and take in a different horizon.

It was late afternoon. Grandpa was nestled in his rocking chair, a quilt over his thighs, though it wasn't even cold. His hands lay together in his lap. The fingers of his right hand were more gnarled than ever, but the left was wrapped in cloth bandaging. Harley dragged a wicker chair alongside of the rocking chair, threw his sketchbook under the seat, and plopped himself down.

They were quiet for a while. That was their ritual. Grandpa's reading glasses were hanging by a lanyard. Harley noticed the notebook beneath the sun-browned fingers. *So,* thought Harley, *he's at it again.* Presently, the old man put his glasses on, and scrawled a few things in illegible black script, holding the notebook open with the mysteriously bandaged hand. He closed it, placed the same hand over his heart, and shut his eyes. Then he rocked. Once. Twice. A third time. There was no momentum to it. Each forward-back slide was a distinct event from the one preceding it. The old man kept his watch for a long time before again donning his glasses and scribbling in the pad.

This visit to Grandpa's house had an odd flavor. Normally, Harley would pat the hounds, and talk to them during Grandpa's long silences. But the hounds were gone; run off, apparently, though Grandpa couldn't say how, or why. That was another reason why Mom didn't think he was safe on the ranch anymore; that, and the wounded left hand. Grandpa said he'd nicked it slicing potatoes, but you could see the blackened skin where the bandage overlapped his wrist. As with his other stories, it was hard to say whether Grandpa was lying or deluded. And Harley had always been the one to believe him. But he was older now.

The boy tried to convince himself that it didn't matter what he believed. All that mattered was what had to be done and said to keep the old man out of an old people's home. Life wasn't fair. It just *was.*

"You troubled?"

Grandpa didn't look over at him. Harley shrugged his hands.

"Just thinking," he said.

Grandpa nodded.

"Used to put a lot of stock in that, myself," he said. "Now it's more about looking than thinking. Thinking too much keeps a man locked inside his own head. All the really interesting stuff's outside of it."

"But I guess you do a lot of thinking anyway," said Harley, pointing at the notebook.

"My extra memory cache," said Grandpa, tapping the leather pad with his good hand.

It was a pleasant sound, those sandpapered digits thumping against the thick journal.

"I just can't keep it all in here anymore," he said, pressing one bony finger to his skull. "And I don't want them getting lost when I go."

Harley flinched. He hated it when Grandpa spoke of 'going'.

"So … you're losing your memory?"

Grandpa shook his head. "No, no. The things I've seen out there. And my strategies. Someone's got to know about them."

Harley frowned. Grandpa finally looked over at him. "You got something to say, boy?"

Harley pulled one knee against his chest and crossed his arms around it, tying himself up in a knot.

"Just that I wouldn't let anyone throw away your journal," he mumbled.

Grandpa smiled. He reached over, and punched Harley's knee.

"I know you don't like to think about me passing on. Boys never do. But the worlds'll keep going when I'm gone."

Harley looked over. It was the opening he'd been waiting for.

"*Worlds*, Grandpa?"

"You know," said Grandpa. "Out there. Like I've told you."

He nodded his chin towards the deep valley. The blue mountains framed it all like frozen waves lurking over a misty green sea.

"I only see this world," said the boy, carefully. "So do Mom and Dad."

Grandpa nodded, like he'd expected the comment.

"Well, maybe they can't see everything there is. Maybe they don't want to."

Harley shook his head. "They say you need help. They say you're all alone out here. Seeing things. Losing things."

Grandpa laughed. "Well, they're right about that."

Harley drew himself into a tighter ball. Grandpa looked him up and down.

"You doing some coal mining today?"

Harley glanced at his blackened fingers and smiled.

"What were you drawing, Harl?"

"The Mariana Trench," said the boy. "The deepest place in the ocean."

"Bet there's life even there," said Grandpa.

Harley nodded.

"Life is fecund," continued Grandpa. "No matter where you look. Show me your picture."

Harley reached under the wicker chair for his drawing pad. Grandpa put his reading glasses on. The boy held up the unfinished picture, and Grandpa smiled appreciatively.

"Nice sea monster," said Grandpa.

Harley smiled. Of course, Grandpa would know what it was.

"It's not a real animal like the others in the picture," said the boy, cautiously. "I wish there *were* sea monsters, but they don't actually exist. And speaking of—"

"—Don't exist?" exclaimed Grandpa. "Well, now, let's just take a look."

"Grandpa," said Harley. "Wait—"

But Grandpa was already taking off his glasses. Again, he covered his heart with his bandaged left hand, muttered mysterious words, and began to rock. Each rocking movement was separate and intentional, like a man on his couch flipping channels.

"There," he said at last. "I found a world with sea monsters. Real big ones. Should I tell you about it?"

Harley heard himself mutter "yes". Maybe he just didn't have the courage to say what needed saying. Grandpa beamed out, glassy-eyed.

"It's an ocean world. Huge. Maybe three times as big as Earth. There's hardly any land on it. Just a few islands in the north where all the people live, and one continent in the southern hemisphere. You can't get there easily. There's a wall of darkness and storms over the equator, and a sea of green vines that'll catch any ship that makes it through that darkness. But in the southern ocean, in the deep water just beyond the shores of the lonely continent, mighty sea serpents dwell. It's a good thing nobody can get down there to visit. These creatures hunt whales as easily as a lizard hunts ants. They make a cyclone in the waters, and suck everything down to the ocean floor. Sometimes they come up and sun themselves on a vast white beach. My goodness, what a world! The struggle's on there, let me tell you. The serpents ain't even the real threat."

Harley bit his lip. "Sounds amazing," he finally said.

Grandpa glanced at him.

"You want me to find another? You don't seem too pleased with this one."

"Grandpa," said Harley. "It's a wonderful story. You know I love your stories."

The old man closed his eyes. His face went slack, and sad. "You too, huh?"

The boy, suddenly panicked, shook his head.

"I'm not saying I don't believe you…"

"And you're not saying you do."

"Mom and Dad—"

"—Want to put me away. I know. Well, your mother does. Your dad can't forget; not entirely. No, don't shake your head like that, trying to deny it. I guess they mean well."

"If you could just … just stop saying these kinds of things out loud, Grandpa."

Grandpa's expression soured. "I'll admit it'd serve me to keep this old trap shut. But it wouldn't feel right. And, anyway, I gotta find a seer."

"A seer?"

Grandpa nodded. "Somebody who'll keep the watch when I'm gone. Someone with a heart that looks."

Harley didn't know what to say to that. Grandpa lived all alone. It wasn't like a crowd of people were swinging by his old rancher house, out in the country.

"I didn't always see the worlds," said the old man. "It's a gift, but it can be trained. You gotta open up your eyes first."

Harley stood up suddenly. He walked over to the railing and looked out over the green and blue vista. He stared hard.

"They're open, Grandpa. There's nothing but grass and mountains."

"There's more, but only if you want there to be."

Harley sighed. "That isn't how seeing works."

"Oh?" said the old man. "What makes you so sure?"

Harley shrugged. "Isn't it obvious? You see things with your eyes, and maybe touch them with your hands, and that's how you know they're real."

"Harley," said Grandpa. "We've always been straight with each other. Do you think I'm crazy?"

"No," said Harley, looking down at his feet.

"Belief is a choice, Harley. Seeing is wanting to see."

"Grandpa, if that was true, you could believe anything you wanted."

"Believe one and one makes three," said Grandpa.

"I can't, of course."

Grandpa nodded. "Exactly."

The boy looked at him, perplexed. "But that's my point. That's just what I was saying."

Grandpa smiled. "Look, have you ever got in real big trouble with your folks, and got punished? Something that really stung?"

Harley didn't have to think that one over long.

"One time I got in trouble at school, and my parents kept me out of a trip to Terror Forest" he said. "They knew I was looking forward to it."

"Well, did they do that out of love or because they wanted to hurt you?"

Harley sighed. "Out of love," he mumbled.

"Are you sure? Maybe they wanted to pay you back for embarrassing them."

"But I know they love me," said Harley.

Grandpa chuckled. "Sounds to me like belief has a lot to do with seeing."

He tapped his eyeglasses. "It frames our horizons. It helps decide what we notice inside that frame."

"I guess," shrugged Harley.

"I know," said Grandpa.

Harley looked at his grandfather. Bright eyes. Frail body. Gnarled old fingers. Did it really matter if he was a little insane so long as he could feed himself and move about the house?

"You still don't see it," said Grandpa.

The boy kept a poker face.

"Maybe I can prove I'm telling the truth," said Grandpa. "But you got to be willing to believe. Come back and sit by me. Please."

Harley wiped a hot tear that had somehow snuck into his eye. He coughed, composing himself, and returned to the wicker chair.

"That's right," said Grandpa. "Now I'm going to try and show you."

Grandpa craned his neck forward, scanning the deep valley. Harley gave up all the hope he'd earlier entertained of making his grandfather see reason and practicality. He groaned internally, imagining the look on

Grandpa's face when the old man tried to show him something, and Harley couldn't see it. Could he lie *that* much?

"There!" said Grandpa Moore, pointing. "Yes, that'll do nicely. Look out there."

Harley looked where Grandpa pointed. Far down the valley, past winding roads hardly visible, lay a few small homesteads and family farms. The people who lived there looked up every day at vast blue mountains. It was very pretty, but he'd seen it all before.

"What am I looking at?" he said.

"The cows," said Grandpa. "In the east there. See 'em?"

Harley squinted. The cows were so far away, they looked like brown and white mice.

"I see them," said the boy.

"Do you?" said Grandpa. "Look more carefully. Look at what they're doing."

Harley looked.

"They're just standing," he said.

Grandpa nodded.

"Well?" said Harley, after a pause.

"Are you really looking, Harl?"

"What is it you want me to see? They're just standing there."

"Exactly," said the old man. "In all that beautiful green grass. Bales of hay all around. But there they stand, still as statues."

Harley looked again. Grandpa was right. They didn't move, not at all, as if the valley were a canvas, and they'd been painted on.

"Huh," he said. "Maybe they're just too far away for us to…"

But that didn't make sense. After all, you could spot a turkey vulture gliding over the blue mountains. The cows were stock still, not wandering about or grazing, as cows were wont to do. He didn't know what to make of it.

"They look like a picture," Harley said.

"But they're not," said the old man. "They're alive."

"What could make a cow stand totally still like that?" mused Harley, out loud.

"Something *they* can see," said the old man. "Something that scares 'em."

Harley frowned at that, but he could think of no good reason for cows to freeze in place. A spooked cow would run. These were, well, petrified.

"I can see what's frightening them," said the old man. "And so can you. If you look. If you want to see it."

"Grandpa, don't—"

"—Look!" insisted Grandpa, his voice husky. "Look with your other eyes. With the light inside your eyes."

Harley tried. Slowly, something happened in the vista before him. The change was subtle, not unlike a book he had at home with stereoscopic pictures. When you stared into the senseless, colored blotches and let your eyes sort of blend, something would come out of the page in three dimensions. The change was just like that. From the top of the sky to the valley's deep bottom, things were taking shape. They were smoky, near-transparent columns that reminded him of serpents or eels. Only colossal. The off-gray titans hovered vertically in the air, rising perpendicular to the horizon. Then he saw that wherever they touched the world, the world twisted just a little.

"What?" he whispered.

Now, as he watched, the left-most of the titan columns floated toward the petrified cows. Some finally broke and ran, but the nearest beast remained frozen. Even at this distance, Harley could almost feel its terror at the approaching, unnameable thing. "Get away from it!" he wanted to shout. Soon the serpentine column enveloped the space in which the cow stood. The animal tipped over. It seemed to be shaking in the grass. In his heart, Harley knew it was suffering.

"Enough," growled Grandpa, through clenched teeth. "I have seen you. Begone!"

The column's eastward drift was suddenly arrested. It began to dissipate, like smoke, as did the other columns. In a moment, the horizon was clear, just as if the things had never been there. The cows wandered about normally, though they kept their distance from the one that had fallen. It lay dead in the grass.

"What was that?" said Harley.

"What did you see?" asked his grandfather. "Describe it."

"They were like … like giant snakes with their heads in the sky, and their tails touching the ground."

Grandpa relaxed his grip and seemed to sigh. He squeezed his eyelids shut, but Harley saw a few tears escape, and roll down to dampen his cheeks.

"You saw," murmured the old man. "I knew you would."

They were quiet for a long time. For a few minutes, everything looked different to Harley. More fragile. The distant cries of birds, the solid mountains, the gentle *fwoosh* of a westerly wind—all of it seemed highly debatable.

"What were those things?" he finally asked.

"I call them the Unmade," said Grandpa.

Harley waited for some further explanation, but none was forthcoming. He swallowed. "How did you … make them leave?"

"I looked at them. Cast light on them. They don't like the light."

"They're evil?" Harley asked, but it was more of a statement.

Grandpa nodded. "Those kind like to take the eyes. The tongue. Other organs, too. They can't create anything, but they can stitch things together. But that's only them playing—if you can call it playing. I shouldn't have let them go that far, but you needed to see."

Harley shivered. It was a hot day, the kind of muggy heat that foretold a summer storm. Still, he felt cold all over.

"I … I wish they didn't look like that," he said.

His grandfather turned to him. "Why not?"

"I like snakes. And eels."

Grandpa smiled. The smile seemed out of place, too soon, given what they'd just witnessed.

"That's cause you're a good soul," said Grandpa. "You appreciate all of God's creatures. The thing is, the Unmade don't really *look* like anything. They never settle on one form, because the truth is not in them. But they seem to enjoy imitating dark good things. Because they're shallow."

"Dark good things, Grandpa?"

The old man nodded. "It's what I call snakes, and spiders and the like. Creatures that have their place in the world, but scare us, sometimes for good reason. A snake is like a swirling dagger with teeth at the end. A spider's like a hairy hand, prowling the night, cold and calculating, and driven by dark appetites. They're not at all evil; just sort of dark. But the Unmade are a different kind of dark. You could say they're creatures of anti-light."

Harley got up again and walked around the deck. His skin had broken out in gooseflesh. Part of him was already trying to explain away the things he'd just seen.

"They don't always look evil," continued Grandpa. "Sometimes, when they think they're being clever, they'll manifest as something bright and sweet. Setting traps, you see. But they don't really understand 'bright' and 'sweet' any more than they understand creatures of the night. Their bright is too bright. Their sweet is sickly. *Garish*, yes, that's the word for their style."

Grandpa cleared his throat, then continued in the most matter-of-fact way, as if he were discussing the weather.

"It feels good, doesn't it Harley, to find the right word for something?"

Still dazed, the boy went over and leaned against one of the white columns holding up the porch roof. It was cool against his shoulder. He felt very small.

"And you," he stammered, "you sit out here, and fight them?"

"You could say that," said Grandpa, behind him. "When they come here in the valley. Or other places I'm permitted to see. I'm not the only one, either. But ... well I can't keep it up any longer, son."

Harley turned around and looked at him. "You fight them in other places too?"

Grandpa nodded. "Take a seat. I'll try to show you."

The boy looked past him, toward the safety of the house. He felt sure that whatever Grandpa wanted to show him would make the world even more dangerous. He could walk through those doors, to his parents, and leave this thing behind. He sat down anyway.

"Take my hand," said Grandpa. "It'll help."

He extended a mess of long fingers, bent at the ends by arthritis, the skin mottled like the bark of sycamores. Harley took the hand.

"Now," said Grandpa quietly. "Look out. Like you did before."

Harley lay back in the chair and relaxed his vision. Grandpa pressed his wounded hand against his heart. He rocked once. Then the old man spoke in slow, sing-song tones. At first nothing seemed to happen. Then, very gradually, the scene before them changed, not as in a movie or a show, but as one image laid over top of another until the first almost melted away. Harley thought he was staring at a flat landscape. Strange silver spires rose thousands of feet into the air. In the distance, a great city lay quiet. Everything was silent, abandoned, overgrown, but there was a subtle, ominous thumping from within the great chrome structures.

"That's a world," whispered Grandpa, "where Machine has conquered Man. See it."

He rocked his chair again and spoke in that same hypnotic voice. The spires turned brown, becoming the trunks of mighty trees. Pine-like, but not quite pines, their boles rose up to the sky as pillars of heaven. What before had been clouds were now but the underside of a vast green canopy. Now the trees shook, and a mighty humanoid form stepped between them. It stopped, as if resting from a hard day's work, and took a swig from a huge animal skin that had been hanging from its leather belt. Harley heard many small voices lifted in praise. Presently, he noticed the tiny beings that danced around the giant's feet. Some welcomed him home. Others taunted him. The giant smiled paternally.

"And that's a world," said Grandpa, "where the balance between big and small is the heart of the Struggle. It's not too bad, yet. It's much better off than the first we saw."

He rocked again. "Oh, not this place. Listen, listen, if you can."

Now Harley saw an ash-covered world. The air was filled with terrible, mocking howls. Harley wanted to plug his ears. A few lonely metal buildings jutted out from the ashen landscape, and a dark mass swirled about them, forming itself into frightening, aggressive shapes. The swirling mass was trying to get inside. The cloud reminded him, vaguely, of the entities he'd seen in the valley, because its forms were also suggestive, but indefinite.

"That's another place where people do battle against the things they've made," said Grandpa. "Because when Man makes idols, the idols eventually try to eat him. Remember that. That's a principle."

The howling from the black cloud worked its way inside Harley's mind. He had sudden, terrible thoughts. It would be good to leap off those mountains in the distance. It would be good to take a long nail and drive it through his skull. It would be good to cut himself, to cut shapes out of his skin.

"Make it stop!" he cried.

Grandpa rocked again, and the world became a vast pink sea. Harley gasped in relief. There didn't seem to be any people in this world, only strange blue blobs in the pink water, floating, splitting in two, or coalescing into larger blobs.

"This is one we really can't understand," said Grandpa. "But the Struggle's on there too."

"Struggle?"

"The battle with the Unmade. It's happening all over."

Harley was quiet for a while. He had so many questions, and hardly knew which to ask first.

"Are these ... are these different planets, Grandpa? Or different universes?"

The old man chewed his lip. Harley knew that meant he was unsure.

"They're connected, in any event," said Grandpa. "How is not my business, or yours."

Harley hesitated. "What is our business?"

"The business of a seer," said Grandpa, "is to see and to name. Everybody has light in his eyes. For some, that light is darkness. For others, it's what you might call common-place light. The way the world looks when you live on the surface. But for us, it's *the* light. Part of the true light that made the worlds. A little speck of it, anyway. Our job is to scour the worlds for the Unmade. Find them. Force them out in the open. Look at them. Name them. They don't like to be named. They don't like to be seen for what they are."

"And what are they?" muttered Harley. "What are they made out of?"

Grandpa looked at him, hard. "Don't be too curious about details. They're the Unmade. They're the ones who could have seen things in the greatest of all lights but chose to see the worst. Long, long ago, deep back in time. And they go on choosing it. That's why they unmake. Like I said, Harley, we all choose what we believe. That's what makes it so important. Belief decides what we become."

In the pink water, the floating blue blobs began to shudder and move aside. Something was coming up from below. A circle in the water darkened, first to red, and then to a sickly hue that was like what happened when Harley tried to blend red and green pastels. A sort of funnel appeared. The blue blobs, many of which had been floating away, turned slowly and began swimming toward the dark funnel. They went up to its edge and craned over it, as if staring into an abyss. Some threw themselves in. This was unnatural. This was wrong.

Grandpa muttered under his breath.

"What's happening?" said Harley.

"I've seen this place before," said Grandpa, sighing. "Only once or twice. This is a world—or maybe a planet—where creatures that look to us like cells or amoebas have the gift of reason. They don't reason the way we do. For them, everything's about unity. They think clearly only as they become one. But when creatures like that go bad … well, I once saw a whole planet that became a predator. A single, wicked mind. Maybe this is like that world, or maybe it's the same world at an earlier stage. When you're seeing the worlds, time works funny."

Harley wanted to look away. Even without understanding, the vision disturbed him.

"Can't you help?"

"Yes," sighed Grandpa, "but I don't know how. I know I wouldn't be seeing if I couldn't do something, but I don't always know what I'm supposed to do. Some worlds are too strange to even learn the rules. Or, by the time you do, too much damage has been done in some other place where you could have made a difference."

Grandpa lowered his voice. "Or you … you try to do too much, and then they get a bead on you."

He moved the rocking chair, and the pink ocean melted away. They were looking out at the familiar valley again. Grandpa stopped rocking but kept hold of Harley's hand. Though thin and frail of body, Grandpa seemed to weigh down the chair. Harley noticed he was breathing hard. Grandpa Moore looked tired; even worried.

The sun was in the west now, blocked by the porch's ceiling, but Harley could tell it was inching lower in the sky. The August air, still warm, felt precarious, as if it tasted autumn, and feared the stalking beast called Time.

"Harley," said the old man, squeezing his hand. "Listen."

Harley looked over at him. His grandfather's face was stone.

"In a few moments, your mother will open the door. She'll call to you in that sing-song voice that mothers use when they want to tell you something that isn't meant for all ears. Namely, mine. She's gonna call you in, and she and your father are gonna sit you and Macy down."

"How do you know?"

"Hush!" said Grandpa. "Listen. They're gonna tell you that they've had to make some difficult choices. That they love me so much, and so on and so forth, and that they're going to have to put me in a home."

"No!" cried Harley. "I won't let them!"

Grandpa shook his head. "You won't have a say in it. Don't quarrel, now. I've gotta tell you something while there's time, and I don't want to say it too loud."

Harley clenched his teeth. He couldn't stop the tears anymore and didn't really try.

"It isn't as bad as you think," continued Grandpa. "You might even get to see me more often. If I make it."

"If you make it?"

"If I live long enough, boy."

"But you're fine!" said Harley. "Why do you have to talk like that? Like Mom and Dad are right?"

The old man shook his head. "They're not right, but they're right. My body still works, but that doesn't mean I'm safe."

Harley felt a cold dread creep up his chest. He looked out at the valley, then back at Grandpa.

"What do you mean?"

Grandpa grimaced. "I've pushed my luck too far. Looked too long, sometimes. Even when the light in me was running low, I needed to go back to the Source. It's possible to be too ambitious, even for the Good, if you depend too much on yourself. Then they have the right to come after you. Don't make the same mistake, Harley."

Harley felt cold all over.

"But can't you just … look at them, and make them go away?"

Grandpa nodded. "True, but they've got other weapons. Emissaries. Things they can make. Things they can send. Not living, maybe, but material. They fill them with their un-life. The dogs managed to save me last time. But I've been carrying this burden far too long. It's best I lay it down, and then lay quiet for a while. I got a dark wound now. A splinter in the eye and in the heart. Next time … well … any time could be the last time."

He looked hard at Harley to be sure he understood.

"But you stopped that one today," whispered the boy, unbelieving.

Grandpa sighed. "True. But that's like telling a drunk, 'You took one drink, and nothing bad happened.' I'm on the downswing now. Playing roulette. They may not be able to see me, but they can find me. All because I played their game. I acted just like them. I forgot once too many times that the light in me is not *from* me. Now I'm marked, and I've got to lay it down. I don't want to, but I've got to."

Harley looked at him with dread.

"Don't worry," said Grandpa. "Worry never helped anyone."

Grandpa pulled his hand away and began once more to massage the wounded one. When he did, all the striking images of a moment before, all the worlds Harley thought he'd seen, began to fade from his memory. Like dreams. Just like that, he wondered if any of it had happened.

Grandpa glanced at him, then smiled. It was a sad, knowing smile. Harley felt exposed. He was wondering what to say, when one of the doors to the back porch swung out from the house.

"Sweety," said Harley's mother, smiling politely at Grandpa; not really looking at him. "Please come inside. We need to have a little talk."

***

Harley and Macy had spent the morning walking the grounds, exploring the unused barn, and rebuilding Harley's old fort inside the small but thickly grown stand of trees that he called Green Island. Everything looked a bit smaller to him now. For once, he was glad to have Macy tagging along. To her, the ranch was still a place of wonder.

"Are there ticks in here?" said Macy, as they crawled through Green Island's dense and tunnel-like underbrush, preparing to head back toward the ranch house.

"Maybe," said Harley. "Mom can check you and pull them off. It's not a big deal."

"Oh," said Macy, with a puzzled expression.

She'd been expecting him to say something like, "Yes, and they'll dig tunnels into your brain." But Harley wasn't in the mood.

He found a path through the dark bushes, and the two of them soon emerged from under the shadow of Green Island and climbed to their feet in the tall grass. Macy dusted her knees off and slapped her hands together. She looked at her brother. He seemed far away this morning.

"I think Grandpa will be happier in the retirement community," she offered.

"Why?" said Harley, distractedly.

He wiped dirt from his hips and began striding away from her, as if he thought more distance would let him escape the situation with Grandpa.

"'Cause he won't be by himself," said Macy, skipping after him. "I wouldn't want to be by myself."

Harley didn't say anything. He'd spotted his father standing on the porch on the east side of the house. Mr. Moore caught sight of his children and waved. They waved back, and Macy doubled her pace toward the house just as Harley began to slow his. He could tell from his father's expression that he wanted to talk about Grandpa. By the time Harley reached the house, Macy had run ahead of him. Dad gave Macy a hug and told her to go inside. She left slowly, glancing back-and-forth between the two of them, unhappy at being excluded. Mr. Moore waited for her to go inside before speaking.

"Harley, do you have a second?"

The boy nodded. Mr. Moore smiled, and started walking away from the ranch house, gesturing for Harley to follow.

"Nice day, isn't it?" said Dad, when they'd gone a ways.

Harley shrugged. By now he was hot and itchy from the underbrush. He slapped at a place on his arm where it felt like a bug was crawling. Dad put another twenty paces between them and the house.

"Son, I wanted to talk to you about your grandfather."

"Okay," said Harley.

"I know that you're feeling upset."

Harley shrugged again.

"Maybe you think that what we're doing isn't fair."

Harley bit his lip. He hadn't been planning to say anything, mainly because he didn't think they would listen. Anyway, Grandpa seemed resigned to his fate; even a little relieved. Yet he'd hardly left his room in the two days since they'd told him. The rocking chair sat lonely on the back porch.

"I just don't think you should have called it a family conference," Harley finally said, referring to the way his parents had broken the news to Grandpa. "Mom is the one who decided. The rest of us had nothing to do with it."

"Don't put the blame on your mom. She and I decided together."

"But he's your dad," said Harley, struggling to contain his emotions.

Harley's father nodded. "Yes, and I've known him a lot longer than you."

"Grandpa's not crazy," said Harley.

Mr. Moore sighed. "But he's not well. He hasn't been since I can remember."

Then he grimaced, as if he were about to say something especially painful. Mr. Moore's voice went lower, but also softer. "Even when I was your age, my dad was … very imaginative. He told stories. Made-up ones, but in a way that made you think he believed them. Until I was around ten, I believed them too. They were great stories."

"Are you saying he's a liar?" said Harley,

Harley's father looked troubled. "I don't quite know how to answer that. I don't think it's *lying*—not from his point of view. More like a kind of wishful thinking. Do you know what that is?"

Harley nodded.

"But he makes them seem so real," the boy said. "And … and his stories match up with each other, sometimes. Not like a crazy person's."

His father sighed again. "I know."

Harley wanted to tell his father what he'd seen on the porch, but he worried that he'd be betraying Grandpa's secrets. Anyway, it was all faded now so that he couldn't really be sure he'd seen anything. And what if his father thought he was crazy too? But if he said nothing, then that might also be a kind of betrayal.

"I know he's telling the truth," mumbled Harley, "because … because he showed me."

Mr. Moore looked at him, and his sad expression didn't change, nor did the man seem surprised.

"When I was your age," he muttered, "I thought I saw things too. My dad has a powerful effect on a person. Like a hypnotist. He starts talking, and, well, your own imagination starts filling in the gaps. Did he tell you you had the gift?"

Harley hesitated, then nodded.

"But I'll bet you haven't seen a thing since then."

Harley's silence was equal to consent. His father sighed and wrapped an arm around his shoulder. Harley thought about the other worlds he'd seen while Grandpa spoke of them. Could a person wishfully think in such detail? Those scenes had been vivid at the time, but now they were all vague, like half-remembered dreams. Perhaps that was because they *were* a kind of dream. And hadn't Grandpa asked him leading questions, and partly told him what he was seeing? Harley began to feel like a fool, but he suddenly remembered the cow, and the serpentine columns.

"No, wait!" he said. "I saw the Unmade, right down in the valley! They killed a cow. I saw them do it."

Harley's father shook his head.

"I saw it, Dad!"

"I'm sure you did," said his father. "And did this cow stand very rigid and then drop to the ground like a statue?"

Harley stopped walking and stared up at his father. "How did you know that?"

Dad shook his head, very sadly. "It's on the local news. There's a disease hitting the cows, Harley. And I know your Grandpa knows about it, because he mentioned it to me on the phone not three weeks ago. I guess he forgot to tell you that?"

Harley's expression began to run like half-wet plaster.

"What you saw down in the valley," Mr. Moore continued, with great gentleness, "was what he wanted you to see."

Harley's face was burning. He couldn't stop the tears now. He forgot where he was. He didn't care where they were going. He wanted to run. To run straight into those blue mountains.

"I'm sorry, Harl," said his father. "Your grandfather really loves you, but sometimes sick people can be very self-centered. They can hurt the ones who love them without trying to do it. And now that his memory is starting to go … well, it's better that he be someplace where others can look after him."

"I don't want to talk about this anymore," said Harley.

"Okay," said his father.

"I want to go home."

"Okay."

Harley brushed his father's hand off his shoulder as nicely as he could, and turned and ran back toward the house.

***

It was dinner, and Grandpa had finally come down from his room. The old man sat there the whole meal, picking at his food and saying nothing, while awkward, stilted conversation flew about him. His silence spoke more loudly than their words. Mrs. Moore periodically attempted to engage her father-in-law, but to little effect. It did not help any of their moods that the sky had gone dark early. A summer storm flailed the valley, and the hanging lights over the dinner table flickered, while many large raindrops pelted the porch and windows. At intervals that seemed mere punctuation to the silence of the table, or the raging of the skies, they could hear the disembodied creaking of grandpa's chair, rocking in the wind.

"Hank," said Mrs. Moore, trying again to bring the old man out of himself. "That chair of yours has a life of its own."

Grandpa looked up at her. Through her.

"How long have you had it?" she said.

His eyes returned to his uneaten meatloaf. Halfheartedly, the old man began to dismember the loaf with his fork.

"Please toss the chair," he finally said. "I won't be using it anymore."

Harley's father shot a quick look at his wife. "Are you sure, Dad? We'd be happy to bring it to Mayberry Farms. The house we're looking at there has a porch."

A savage look, almost a smile, crossed Grandpa Moore's face, then faded. Harley knew his grandfather well enough to guess that the old man had just stifled some sharp comment.

"Throw it out, please," said Grandpa.

He mumbled a word excusing himself and pushed his chair back loudly from the table. Grandpa hobbled away, leaving his food uneaten. As he creaked up the stairs, Macy looked over at her brother and shook her head.

"Well," said Mrs. Moore, pitching her voice to make it audible several rooms away. "*That* wasn't manipulative."

"Cindy, please," muttered Mr. Moore.

But Harley thought his mother was right. Grandpa in his rocking chair was Grandpa as they knew him. The chair was part of him. To throw it away was to throw away their shared past. And why such pettiness? Hadn't Grandpa already told him that he wanted to get away from the dark powers with which he was supposedly contending here at the ranch? But perhaps when one told as many stories as Grandpa did it was too difficult to keep them all straight. After the dinner cleanup, when things had settled down, he walked up the stairs and knocked on his grandfather's door.

"Harley?" said the muffled voice from behind the door. "Come in."

Upon entering, Harley found his grandfather in a chair by the window, watching the storm. For just a moment, out of the corner of his eye, Harley thought he saw a shadowy figure standing in the room. It gave him a start, but when he turned to look, he saw only the general shadowiness of the room.

"Grandpa—"

Grandpa Moore waved for him to be silent and pointed at the storm. Thick black clouds snaked through the sky like thousand-mile ropes, blotting out the blue mountains, imposing an ominous weight on everything below them. Grandpa gestured for Harley to sit, but the boy remained standing. The storm winds howled and carried upon them the distant sounds of police sirens. Grandpa shook his head.

"They're having their way now," he said. "They're off the leash. Well, it can't be helped."

"Grandpa," Harley tried again.

His grandfather finally turned from the storm. He saw Harley's face and frowned.

"What's that look mean?" said the old man.

Harley couldn't come out and say all that he'd meant to say. Not all at once.

"I think you should keep your rocking chair," said Harley. "I think you should let my parents do that for you."

Grandpa Moore turned back to the storm. "You do, do you?"

Harley nodded.

"And I guess you think I was being rude to your mother?" said Grandpa, still watching the horizon.

Harley shrugged.

"Well, good," said the old man, "That's what you were supposed to think."

Harley groaned within himself. It was just like Grandpa to use a shocking statement to grab his attention. To spin everything that happened as if it were part of a plan. He felt another tale coming on, and, when he didn't ask, "Why, what do you mean, Grandpa?", like usual, it did not surprise Harley to see the old man suddenly frown.

"I told you I'm a seer," said Grandpa. "And that I bit off more than I could chew."

Harley took a breath. "You told me that," he said.

"That chair's my totem," said Grandpa. "And that's why it has to go. 'Course I can't explain that to your mom and dad."

"Okay," sighed Harley. "What's a totem?"

Grandpa Moore looked surprised. "Don't you read books, Harley? At least you watch movies. Hell, I'll bet they've got totems even in video games."

He shook his head, then continued.

"A totem's like a crack in the wall between the worlds. It's your magic lamp. Your ruby slippers. It's one of the things you need to be a seer. And it's different for everybody."

Harley frowned. "But you said being a seer was a gift that ran in families."

Grandpa nodded. "Oh, sure. It is."

"But now you're saying—"

"The *potential* for seeing's a gift," explained the old man. "The capacity. If you didn't have the gift, then you wouldn't have been able to see all the things I showed you. But you also needed my help. And I needed my totem."

"Grandpa," sighed Harley. "I'm not really sure I saw anything out there."

Grandpa gave him a sharp look, and shook his head. "Got to you, didn't he?"

"What? Who?"

"Your father, that's who. He's blind, you know. That's what happens when a man rejects his gift."

Harley gritted his teeth. "Grandpa, I know about the cows."

Grandpa Moore seemed confused for a moment, then slowly nodded. "I see. Well-played, son."

"Dad told me you already knew they were sick," said Harley.

"I said something was killing them," said Grandpa, "but of course, I couldn't tell your father the whole truth. The media people *say* it's just a disease, but they're blind too."

Harley shrugged. "That just seems kind of convenient, is all. You didn't tell me about any cow disease."

Grandpa straightened up in his chair. The lines in his face became hard. "So, what's the accusation, boy? Crazy old man, or liar? What do you say I am?"

Harley looked down at his feet. "I love you, Grandpa. I don't know what's true."

"You know *me*!" snapped Grandpa. "And you know what you saw. The worlds. Remember?"

Still fixated on his own shoelaces, Harley chewed his lip. "But maybe you sort of … hypnotized me."

"Ha! And put all those images in your brain?"

Harley shrugged.

"So then," said Grandpa, chuckling, "I don't have the powers of a seer, but I *do* have the power to make other people see things. That make sense to you?"

Harley let out a breath he'd been holding. He finally met his grandfather's eyes.

"I guess not," he said.

"Course not. Now grab that chair, and that notebook on the desk. We have important matters to discuss."

Harley saw his grandfather's leather-bound journal sitting on the desk. He picked up the journal and pulled the desk chair over.

"Here," he said, handing over the notebook.

Grandpa shook his head. "You keep that. I made it for the next seer. Which is you."

Harley looked down at the journal, feeling the weight of it in his hands. He ran them along the leather, touching with his fingertips the little imperfections that gave it character. The journal was bound with a leather cord, which Harley began, absently, to undo.

"Don't read it now," said Grandpa. "Use it later, when you're ready to take up the sword."

Harley looked at him warily. Suddenly, the notebook felt ponderous and full of peril, like some radioactive stone, or a wizard's book of spells.

"Just now you said a totem was 'one of the things' you need to be a seer," said Harley, carefully. "Is this the other?"

"That's just a sort of log book," said Grandpa. "Sometimes the gift'll show you world's you've already seen, but you don't remember 'em too well. Like trying to remember a dream. It's good to keep track of how the Unmade look and act in different places, and what's worked against 'em in the past. The Struggle's the same everywhere, mind you. Them flattening things. Twisting things. But it always shows up different."

"Oh," said Harley, because he didn't know what else to say. "So, what else would I need?"

Grandpa pressed his hand to his chest as Harley had seen him do in the rocking chair. Then he reached two bony fingers under his collar and began to fish something out. It was a length of chain, thicker than that on a typical necklace. Having only one unbandaged hand, and an arthritic one at that, it took him a moment to get to the necklace. He pulled it over his head and held it up. From the chain, like an amulet, hung a narrow golden cylinder. The cylinder was perhaps three inches long and a centimeter in diameter. The gold caught all the light in the dark room and seemed to amplify it. As gravity spun the object back and forth, Harley noticed the ovular window in its center. Something was inside.

"What is it?" he said.

"Never seen one of these before?"

Harley shook his head.

"It's a reliquary, boy. A powerful thing."

Grandpa took one last long, shuddering look, then handed the strange necklace to Harley.

"Slip it over your head now," he commanded. "Keep it under your shirt, and out of sight."

Harley slipped it over his head. The chain was cold, and a little heavy, but the golden cylinder felt warm against his skin.

"What's inside?" he said.

"The power you'll need," said Grandpa. "Or a line to it, anyway. That vial holds a fragment of the arm of St. George. If you believe, then you can draw on it. But only if you believe."

"But what am I supposed to believe *in*? A piece of bone?"

Grandpa frowned. "Not in the bone itself. In what made it holy. The source of all the worlds."

"God?" said Harley, uncertainly.

"Naturally," said Grandpa. "Or, supernaturally, I suppose."

He chuckled, and the lines of his face stretched themselves into little streams and rivulets, dry watercourses bearing old sorrows from a sea of memory.

"Draw on it when you do battle," muttered Grandpa, "but respect the power. It ain't from you. It'll never be from you. If you don't remember that, and try to go further than the portion you're allowed..."

He looked away, and his face darkened. The old man suddenly reminded Harley of a small child, caught stealing cookies, and ashamed of its actions.

"I'm marked now," he said, displaying his bandaged left hand. "It took a bite out of me, after it killed my poor dogs."

"What did?" said Harley.

Grandpa didn't seem to hear him. "Thing is, even knowing what danger I'm in, it's still so hard. So hard."

Harley shook his head, uncomprehending.

"Passing on the power," explained Grandpa. "It's everything I am. Now I gotta go on without it. Without even *looking*. Those worlds have kept me company these long years. I'm lonely without 'em. I don't feel like me."

Harley puzzled over that. "But you used your ... power ... a couple of days ago, when you showed me."

Grandpa shook his head. "That was different. My intentions were pure. I showed you only because I meant to pass the power on. And not a moment too soon, boy."

"Why?" said Harley. "What are you afraid is going to happen?"

Grandpa looked out into the storm and shuddered. "Don't ask me that, Harley. Just you heed my warning, and never go beyond the power you're allowed. You're not the savior of every world. Just of the little slices you're shown. You lean too much on *you*, and you'll be starting to act like Them."

He clutched his bandaged hand, massaging it unconsciously with his right. Harley wondered again if he were speaking to a madman. But surely it was better for Grandpa to be a madman than a liar. And either scenario seemed preferable to one in which Grandpa was telling the truth. Some things were just too terrible to be true, weren't they? Nightmares. Horror movie monsters. A mature person comforted himself by remembering that truly dangerous and extraordinary things were all imaginary. As he was thinking this, another siren sounded in the distance, carried on the wind. Somebody, somewhere, was in the middle of a real-life nightmare. And if Grandpa Moore was telling the truth, it raised an obvious question for Harley.

"If it's so dangerous," Harley stammered, "aren't you … putting me in danger too?"

Grandpa studied him quietly. The storm behind framed his white head like a halo of chaos. The old chair down on his porch rocked sporadically of its own accord, habituated to battling the wind, but now masterless; impotent. Still, its disembodied rocking was like a grim commentary uttered, through puppetry, by the mindless forces that yet moved it.

"You're in no *real* danger," said Grandpa in a low voice, "provided you stay little. Believe in the power. Receive the power. But go no further. Trust me, boy, the power is frightening enough on its own. It'll be many years before you even think to take it for yourself. I remember when I first got started. Early on, wielding it by my own lights would have been like grabbing a live wire, and plugging it into my heart. I should have kept that fear in front of me always. But you'll have what I did not: a guidebook—" he pointed at the journal, "—and a clear warning."

Grandpa held up his bandaged left hand. Bracing himself, he removed the metal clasp that held the bandage in place and began slowly to unwrap it. Harley was already expecting something awful. Still, he gasped and pushed himself away when he saw his grandfather's left hand.

It was difficult even to name what he was looking at. The hand was a misshapen mass. There were several deep puncture marks from his wrist to his back knuckles. The left thumb and pointer finger had shriveled to twisted, root-like tumors. The ring and middle fingers were wrapped around each other, crudely braided, then fused at their tips so that the bones and fingernails grew against each other, splitting into shards. Grandpa's pinky had become a wet, fat, red thing, like a cartoon sausage. This was no wound. This thing on the end of his blackened wrist was a sculpture; one crafted by something that detested the human form.

Grandpa sighed, then hurriedly re-wrapped the hand. "Ain't been to a doctor about it yet," he chuckled. "Suppose I'll have to at Mayberry *Farms.*"

He said the last word with a sneer. "Wonder what nonsense they'll say when they see it."

"Does it hurt?" whispered Harley.

"Thank God, yes," said the old man. "Else I could almost forget and go looking again. Just to scratch the itch. But I'd be a damned fool to do so now. You have my relic."

Harley pulled up the golden cylinder by the chain. The reliquary fit neatly inside his fist, being about the same size as one of the pastel crayons from his set.

"So, you used this for protection?" said the boy.

Grandpa Moore nodded. "It's a line to the Word that speaks things true. Makes things be. With it, you can speak them back. They hate words, you know. They hate naming things true."

Harley was quiet for a long time. He did not want to believe any of it. He felt that, so long as he refused to consent to believe, these things wouldn't be real for him. But the wound was real enough. His grandfather's hand, like a dark miracle, testified to the reality of some pressing, potent wrongness. To things that should not be.

"Well?" said the old man.

"I don't want it to be true. I don't want there to be real monsters."

"That's funny," said Grandpa. "I thought you said you did."

Harley thought back to their earlier conversation.

"I guess I didn't think it through," he said. "If things like this exist, then the world isn't a good place anymore."

Grandpa Moore slapped the arm of his chair.

"That's nonsense!" he said, with such vehemence that Harley winced, and threw up his hands defensively.

His mother called for him from downstairs. The anxiety in her voice meant she'd heard Grandpa's outburst.

"That's the very lie the Unmade live to tell," continued Grandpa, lowering his voice to an angry hiss. "Listen, boy, evil don't get to veto what's good. After all, a bad thing is just a twisted thing that was once good. A shadow ain't equal to the light. It's just absence. A dead branch, a diseased limb, a vicious lie—all of 'em are back-handed complements to the things they deny."

Harley put his head in his hands. "But I don't *want* to believe these things," he said, through tears. "Even if they do exist, they won't for me, unless I look."

"Then you'll be blind," said his grandfather, coldly. "Like your father."

"My dad is a good man!" snapped Harley.

It was the first time he'd felt real anger toward his grandfather, and the feeling scared him. Grandpa Moore pursed his lips. Harley's mother called for him again, and then, after a pause, for his father.

"Your dad is only a nice man," continued Grandpa, ignoring the sounds from below. "And nice men pose no danger to the Unmade."

Harley rose from his chair. The boy could not look at his grandfather. Without any particular vehemence, he placed the old man's journal back onto his desk and walked toward the door.

"No, keep it," said Grandpa.

Harley shook his head. Then, thinking, he began to remove the necklace.

"At least keep that!" Grandpa said. "I know you're angry at me, but at least wear it to remember me."

"Remember you?" said Harley.

Then Harley was sad. Framed by the window, the old man looked thinner, and less substantial than ever. He wondered how long Grandpa had left on this earth. Harley tucked the necklace back in place, then wiped a tear that had been hanging in the corner of his eye. Part of him kept waiting for his grandfather to relent, and to say it was all just a story, and that he didn't have to believe it if he didn't want to. Other adults said that sort of thing when the stories they told frightened children. Why couldn't Grandpa be like them? Harley put his hand on the doorknob, then stopped. The wisp of a plan came into his mind. If Grandpa would not give up his delusions, then maybe he could make the most of them.

"Aren't there any worlds where the Unmade haven't come? Worlds they can't touch, where you can be happy?"

Grandpa shook his head. Then, seeing Harley's disappointment, he heaved a great sigh.

"I saw a place like that once," said the old man. "Only a glimpse, to keep up my hope, I think. But seeing's one thing. You can't go there on your own power. Someone from there has to … to take you."

He cradled his left hand, that bandaged abomination, in his right. Some unspoken fear still hung like a storm cloud above the old man.

"I hope…" whispered Grandpa, his eyes flicking here and there about the shadowy room, like a cornered rabbit. Those dark eyes, haunted windows in a haunted house, fixed suddenly upon Harley with desperate purpose.

"You were meant to be a *protector*," pleaded Grandpa. "And would you hold onto your unbelief even at the cost of a human soul?"

Harley heard his father's footsteps on the stairs. Dad called to him from the hallway just outside the door. The boy turned the knob and left his grandfather alone in the storm-dark room.

***

Harley had been playing at the feet of the distant blue mountains, which towered over him like big brothers, and, in the un-logic of dreams, it hadn't occurred to him that if they were so near, they wouldn't have been so blue. The dream had been pleasant, and Harley was no light sleeper. The white, awesome noise of the pouring rain, its *pumble-drumble* on the house and porch, its *piddle-tink* on the basement window glass, ought to have kept him under. The light on his wristwatch revealed 3:13. Something had plucked him from a heavenly sleep, and then had dropped him onto the gray plains of mere reality.

Harley sat up on the sleeper couch in Grandpa's basement. He flipped his pillow to the cool side and lay back for a while. But it was useless. Something lurked like a stone angel over the arches of his mind and kept him from returning to those pleasant blue hills. He felt unease without cause, reaction without clear stimulus, and this very inversion made him wary. Then he thought of Macy, asleep in the guest room on the other side of the basement. Perhaps she was in trouble.

Harley threw the blankets off. His naked feet were glad of the shaggy carpet. As he crossed the room, some sound that he had heard quite recently came back to him. Outside. It was on the rain, or under it. He stopped and tried to listen. Nothing stood out from the general *drum-pumble* of rain on wood and tile and siding. He tried Macy's knob, and found the door unlocked. It swung inward without a sound. The unicorn nightlight she'd brought from home cast a dull ochre pall over part of the room. Harley walked over to her bed. It was empty.

The comforter had been pulled off, but Macy's pillows were still on the bed. A stab of panic brought him fully awake. Had someone taken his sister? Though he felt his heart and brain seizing up with fear and an unnamable certainty that something was wrong, Harley forced his eyes to search the dark spaces hardly touched by the nightlight's dim halo. On the floor, in the gap between the bed and the wall, Harley saw a little foot. He gasped and clambered over the bed to look down at it.

But Macy was there, sleeping soundly, the captive comforter draped over her like a tent. It was like her to fall off the bed and pull the blanket down to her rather than climb back up. He started breathing again and didn't know why he'd been so frightened. The worst that could happen to her now is that she'd move too quickly, bump her head against the bed's leg, and wake up with a bruise. Harley carefully exited the room, and pulled the door shut.

He sat down on the sleeper. The more he thought about it, the more it seemed likely that what had woken him had only been the sound of Macy falling off the bed. Perhaps she'd cried out before sleep reconquered her. Yet, as he lay back, pulling the comforter over his head, the aura of unease lingered still. Harley felt distinctly that he was *needed* somewhere.

Nevertheless, he shut his eyes, and made sure he was entirely covered in blankets, but for a small gap in the comforter to let in the coolness from the air-conditioned room. And, while his floating anxiety kept him from sleep, he at least achieved a certain calm. Presently, he was quiet enough, still enough, to hear again that sound he'd heard while far away, playing under the blue mountains. It was this sound that had first drawn him up from sleep, the very one which now, as it penetrated his consciousness, made him stiffen with alarm: the slow creaking of a rocking chair.

It did not move as things move on the wind. It slid forward, into the position of greatest tension, then held, before sliding back. Harley had seen it do that a hundred times. Therefore, he understood that at this moment, as the storm raged, his grandfather sat by himself on the porch, peering into the darkness. The boy felt the weight of the chain around his neck and remembered his grandfather's words. He touched the bulge near his sternum where the golden cylinder hung warm against his flesh. Harley leapt up from the sleeper and raced for the basement door.

***

The rain fell in slant lines and soaked the porch. The water formed little pools on the old, warped planks. A fog blurred the valley, and a scent like sulfur or the hint of spoilage hung in the air. On the porch, in the rocking chair, a creature in faded green pajamas sat stuck like a moth to a mounting board. It was soaked through, its lips pulled back in a hideous grimace, its eyes wide and bulging, the sclerae red and weeping and unblinking. The bony fingers of this creature's right hand dug hook-like into the chair arm, but its left extremity was pressed up against its thin chest as if it were pledging allegiance to the storm. The bandages that had covered that hand were nowhere to be seen. Black skeins threaded their way up the wrist and had begun to corrupt the forearm. Grandpa shivered like a man in the electric chair. Guilt and terror, despair and self-destruction, were all written in his face in fleshy hieroglyph.

Harley tried to go to his grandfather. Something held him in place, but whether it was the fear flooding his veins or some power external to him, the boy could not say. He looked out into the valley, following his grandfather's haunted gaze. There was little to see. The miles of hills and grass and patches of trees were partly hidden by a black fog. Yet, if this were not impossible, given the rain, he would have sworn that the valley was burning. There was an unpleasant heat on the air, and it smelled not of ozone but of cooking rot. Such heavy rains ought to have pierced the fog, but seemed to flee this one, the raindrops sprinting through the mist to take refuge on the porch.

Grandpa suddenly hissed and threw up his hands as if to ward off a blow. Harley's attention was drawn to the man's left arm. That diseased limb now looked preposterous. A rationalizing instinct, a part of Harley's mind that lived to explain away what it did not wish to see, recalled a detail from Grandpa's old western novels—he'd read them in this very house, when stuck inside on stormy days—that an untreated wound could become gangrenous. Yes, a long infection could even breed madness. *Come to think of it,* offered the pacifying voice, hadn't grandfather's recent turn coincided, more or less, with the dogs going missing? Perhaps, in his advancing dementia, he'd mistaken them for enemies, and had attacked them, or had just forgotten to feed them. Maybe one had turned on him, and had bitten his hand, and then, maybe, he'd shot the dogs, and some combination of guilt, untreated infection, and his already fragile hold on reality had finally driven him over the edge. Harley was just witnessing the final stages of that process.

It was not a plausible story. Harley knew that, but he used the thought to get himself moving. The atmosphere of terror that his grandfather cast about was keeping Harley from helping the man. When he did manage to move, it was like trying to walk in a bog with a sucking bottom. The boy was surprised that another man's fear could infect him so. Croaks and hisses and little guttural pleadings fumbled from the toothy, grimacing face. Grandpa was caught like some faulty spider in a web of its own making, and these cries were the last protestations of prey before predator, that predator being the dark corners of Grandpa's own mind. Harley reached his grandfather and took him by the shoulders.

"Grandpa," he said, shaking him. "You're wet and cold. Come inside!"

Grandpa Moore's head whipped up to face him. His pupils were so large that the irises had disappeared. They were ink-black planets floating in red fire.

"Harley?" said the old man "Run!"

The voice was high and creaking, and utterly defeated. Harley swallowed his terror. Stepping in front of the chair, he bent his knees, and made his hands scoops, digging an arm under each of his grandfather's armpits. He popped his hips hard, pulling his grandfather out of the chair. The thin old man came up easily. Harley re-secured him in a bear hug and was just taking the first steps toward the porch doors, when his grandfather cried out, as if in agony. Thinking that he had hurt him, Harley relaxed his grip, but no sooner had he done so than the old man was yanked incomprehensibly out of his grasp. Grandpa struck the porch with a wet slap. Harley stumbled and fell, landing in a large puddle that had pooled on the porch. He shook his head in confusion, unsure how the frail man had managed to propel himself in the opposite direction. Back on his feet, Harley scrambled over to where his grandfather lay sprawled.

"Please," he said. "You need to let me help you. You're having some kind of nightmare."

He reached, but Grandpa Moore slapped his hand away. The violence of the blow, the anger in it, was even worse than the sudden pain. Harley clutched his throbbing hand against his belly.

"Please," he whispered.

He looked down at his hand, seeing blood where the flesh beneath his knuckles had split. When he looked up, Grandpa had slid further away from him.

"Leave, boy!" hissed Grandpa.

Harley bit back tears.

"This is my own doing," whined the old man.

Grandpa Moore laid his head on the porch and began to weep. He struck the wood pitifully with both fists, exactly like a child throwing a tantrum. The blackened deformity that was his left hand oozed and squished as it struck the hardwood, leaving splotches of gray and yellow pus. Harley swallowed back vomit.

"You're sick," he pleaded. "You have an infection."

As he was speaking, Grandpa shot down the porch stairs. His head thudded sickeningly against each step. Harley stared on, dumbfounded. Now ten feet away, the old man lifted his face from the muddied soil and forced himself up on his good right arm.

"Ruuuuun!"

Now he slid in jerks and starts across the sopping lawn, hopping backwards into darkness as if someone had a rope around him, and was periodically giving it a hard yank. Harley collapsed to his knees, gaping at the nonsensical. As Grandpa moaned and beat at the air, Harley surveyed his cut hand. The cut, he now realized, must have been made by the spiny growth of Grandpa's fused fingers. The pain in his own hand, the preternatural deformity of Grandpa's, and, especially, the old man's terror—all of it argued for the reality of something very tangible, very real. Something monstrous. But Harley did not want it to be real. With his wounded hand cradled against him, Harley grazed the metal lump beneath his shirt. Grandpa's relic. A choice lay before him, terrible; unavoidable.

He drew the golden phial from under his shirt, and, by some instinct, gripped it tightly in the hand that Grandpa Moore had bloodied. Warmth crept into his veins. The warmth was not quite strength, but felt like an invitation to it, like something tapping at the back of his soul, soft as rain on a windowpane. He closed his eyes, and opened them, and saw for an instant that which he did not wish to see.

There was a tear in the air. Behind the tear lay a hole in space. It floated ten yards away, six feet off the ground, black, and red, and infinitely dense. Slices of the world hung like drapes to either side of the opening. Then he saw the awful thing that was dragging his grandfather toward the gash. The thing was bony, and brown, and many-legged; most like a spider, but with furry flesh pulled taut over segmented legs. Cow-flesh, maybe. Its limbs were not all covered with skin, and seemed to be made of pipes, and trash, and bits of dirty plastic. The tall sharp legs were not all the same length, and it struggled to move them in tandem, otherwise it would already have succeeded in carrying off his grandfather. The thing looked thrown together and seemed destined to be torn apart and ground back down at the earliest opportunity. And yet, the more Harley tried to look at it, the more he couldn't believe that such a thing could ever be. And, perhaps more strangely, the more he couldn't believe it, the more it ceased to be fully visible.

The thing that wasn't there dragged his grandfather along the wet ground anyway, toward the place where the gash in space had been, though now even the gash seemed but a trick of the mist. A voice in his soul cried out to him: *Strike it! Use the power!* But both spider and dark doorway were too horrible for Harley to accept, and he did not *want* to see them anymore. They faded, like shadows, into the pouring rain, and out of Harley's sight. Yet Grandpa Moore still whined and clutched his own face as nothing dragged him away. Rain still pounded down on the nothing that dragged him, so that if Harley looked closely, he could still make out its sprawling, gangly outline in the fall of the water. But he did not wish to see it. If he saw it, then there would be terrible things in the world. There would be terrible stakes in life. Harley did not wish to live in a world with such stakes, and so he resolved in that moment to attempt his grandfather's rescue without admitting them.

He got down on his knees by his grandfather and wrapped his arms around the man's chest. A stink came off the old man that was different from the stink in the air. Locking his hands together behind Grandpa's back, he dug his feet into the ground and arched backwards in the direction of the house. He managed to roll-through several times, making reasonable progress, but Grandpa Moore began to scream. There was a smell of burning. The old man shook violently against Harley's grip, and then clawed at his shoulders. When Harley wouldn't let go, Grandpa Moore pressed the bony protuberance of his fused fingers into his ribs. The boy recoiled in pain, and finally released him.

"Why are you fighting me?" said Harley, holding back tears.

But he soon understood. The golden reliquary hanging from his neck, where it had been pressed between the two of them, had burned a hole through Grandpa's shirt. There was a black scorch mark on the exposed flesh beneath, though Harley's was undamaged. The frail old man now looked down at the smoking spot, which burned hot despite the pouring rain. He began to weep, a pitiful, burbling sound. It was not the pain, Harley understood, that drew these tears. As the fight went out of Grandpa, he slid the more rapidly in the opposite direction, until Harley was forced to witness what even the sternest denial could not unsee: Grandpa Moore, lifted from the ground feet-first, and dragged kicking and screaming, up and over into empty space, like a sack full of rocks. Then he was gone.

Face bloodied, heart in knots, Harley stared into the tempest. They would ask him in the morning what had happened to Grandpa. They would never blame him, because they would never believe him. But he would know. Know what he had seen and had not wanted to see; what he had not believed, and so had not fought. He hadn't dared to strike, because striking would have made it real.

The rain whipped about Harley's small frame. Winds in the valley howled, now in dolorous lament at the soul lost, now in frenzied glee at the death gained. Wind vied with wind, rain with rain, eternal day with eternal night. He could almost see it now. It was too late, but he could just grasp it. That endless struggle. The battle beyond time, encompassing all worlds, of which Grandpa had spoken. And, as if carried to him on the wind, Grandpa's words came back, now spoken by some other, surer voice: *Belief decides what we see.*

But it was too late. He'd let it take his grandfather. There was no hope.

Is that what you choose to believe? said the voice. It spoke not in words but in singular, pure meaning, meaning that was before words and rendered them only after, like ripples from a single pebble dropped gently in the oceans of his heart. The voice was warm but strong; meek, but painfully earnest. Something burned near his heart. Harley put his hand to it again. His fingers wrapped once more around the reliquary, making a fist, as if fingers understood what minds, retarded and restricted by rationalization, could easily forget. He drew the reliquary over his head and held it out before him like the pommel of a sword. The heavy chain hanging down from the bottom of his fist swung like a pendulum. Now the dark skies seemed to whirl about and glance down, as if only just noticing him over their immense black shoulders.

Harley cried into the night, "You cannot have him!"

Silence. Whining of the winds. Harley called out again. "I love him. You will not take him. I see you, and I bind you."

Harley's voice echoed back at him, small and twisted. A mockery.

"Give me strength," he whispered. "Though I do not deserve it."

Gripping the golden phial, he marched toward the place where the gash in space had been.

"If you can come to me," he growled, "then I can come at you."

The dark, sulfurous vapor rushed at him, driving him backwards. Harley punched his fist to the sky and held it aloft. The power that he held grew out straight, and true, and sharp as a blade. Had anyone, even Mrs. Moore, looked out the window at just that moment, they would have beheld not a boy, but a warrior in golden armor wielding a golden sword. They would have seen him take the blade and plunge it into empty air. They would have watched as he cut a doorway between here and Nowhere. They'd have heard the harsh howls, the ghoulish groans, and the desperate skitterings of dark things fleeing as Harley steeled himself and stepped through the gap.

***

Macy slid back the porch door and called for Harley. The air out there felt like hot rags rendered down into gaseous form, then spread over skin. She he went back to grab a sports bottle and fill it at the fridge. A gentle chime sounded, and her mother called for her to shut the back door so as not to let the AC out.

"Okay!" said Macy.

Water bottle in hand, she stepped onto the back deck and slid the door closed behind her. Her brother had to be outside, somewhere. He was such a private person, always going off by himself to draw or to think. Macy was not at all like that. She needed to be around people. Summer was nearly over, and a part of Macy wanted to be back at school where at least she could speak to her friends. In the meantime, there was only Harley.

She circled the house's exterior first. Harley's bike was in the garage, so she figured he hadn't gone far. The air was too hot and clammy for long explorations. When she didn't find Harley immediately, Macy turned her attentions to their old tree house. She climbed the ladder, found the trapdoor unlocked, and poked her head through. No Harley. It was surprisingly cool in the small structure, and she climbed the rest of the way inside to drink some of her water.

Sitting in the corner, in the shadows, she pondered the situation with Harley. Her brother had become even more quiet, even more reserved, since coming home from Grandpa's. It was not that he seemed sad or angry. If anything, he was kinder to her now than he'd been before. But he was also more serious; more mature. If before he'd been a shallow green pond, now he was a deep blue lake. And, even though she knew he'd run off to sit somewhere where he could be quiet and deep and mysterious, Macy couldn't stop herself from seeking out his company. Their backyard wasn't that big, yet it abutted a stretch of woods with a nice wide creek, and deer trails that ran downhill towards it. They had a couple spots by the creek where nobody else went.

Ten minutes later, having picked her way through the half-overgrown trails, Macy found him. Harley sat in the place they called the Throne, a sort of chair formed by the exposed roots of a leaning sycamore tree. The creek had carved away the shore, and the sun had bleached the roots, which now hovered over the moving waters. It was hard for Macy to get onto the Throne without first wading across the creek and climbing up. Harley could leap to the roots from the shore without getting wet.

She hopped down into the creek. Harley did not look up. He did not seem to have registered the splashes she was making. She watched him as she crossed. He stared straight ahead, then at his drawing pad, then ahead, as if he were sketching a landscape. She reached the roots of the Throne where they pierced the water, and, with some difficulty, scrambled up beside him.

"Harley."

He seemed to shiver but did not glance over. The image on the page did not look anything like the landscape in front of him.

"Harley, what are you doing?" Macy said.

"Shush," he mumbled. Then, more gently. "Please."

She huffed and blew at a strand of hair in her face. It stuck stubbornly to her forehead, so she brushed it aside with irritation, making sure to hold onto the roots with her other hand. Knowing that her brother was off in his mind, being weird, Macy watched the moving water, and listened to its bubbling, gurgling music. She tried to be contemplative, like Harley, but it was not easy. You could only stare at water and trees for so long, after all. Yet in that silence, she finally did notice something: Harley was not drawing. He didn't even have a pen or pencil to draw with. He just stared, and turned pages. Sometimes he stopped to press his hand against his chest, looking just like their father when he ate too much meat and got heartburn.

"Harley," she said.

He sighed and shook his head at her.

"Har*ley*!" she snapped. "I want to talk."

"Macy, please," slurred Harley.

"But why are you acting so weird?" she said.

He made a gesture like brushing away a fly, only she was the fly.

"That's not rude or anything," said Macy. "It's not like I'm your own sister."

He didn't answer. Macy felt her blood begin to boil.

"Are you acting like this because of what happened to Grandpa? 'Cause the doctors had to amputate his freaky arm?"

Harley didn't answer, so she grabbed a root to secure herself, punched him in the shoulder, and repeated her question more loudly.

"Better an arm than all of him," muttered Harley, finally.

But he did not look up at her as he said it. Talking to Harley when he was like this was like talking to a person you've just woken up, who's still halfway inside a dream. Whatever you said just became part of the dream they were having. No wonder Harley got along so well with Grandpa. They were both weirdos.

"Well, I don't even know why I bother trying to talk to you," she said.

Harley sort of twitched but kept at his vigil.

"There are other people in the world besides you, you know," said Macy.

Harley's fingers turned a page.

"And some of those people are your own family," said Macy.

Harley did the heartburn thing again.

"And if you don't show love to your own sister, who else do you think is going to put up with you?"

Harley's back went rigid, and he looked in her direction with wild, distant eyes.

"Silence, fiend! I see you, and I bind you in the Name of the True Word!"

"Exc*use* me?" said Macy.

This time she slapped him. Harley blinked rapidly, and then looked at her, very confused.

"Oh, hello Macy," he said, very pleasantly. "When did you get here?"

Macy gawked at him. "When did I … are you serious?"

He made a sort of awkward grimace, then smiled in a way that reminded her of a guilty puppy that was trying to make amends. Macy huffed and shook her head.

"Just … never mind," she said.

She plopped down into the creek, and began wading back across, leaving her brother to his own devices. When she'd exited on the other side, preparing to brave tangled creepers and thorny bushes, she could not resist a parting shot.

"Why does my brother have to be such a *weirdo*?" she said, just loud enough for him to hear.

Macy started off into the woods and glanced back only once to make sure her insult had found its mark. But Harley was back in his own world, gazing out upon some hidden horizon.

* * *

ABOUT THE AUTHOR

Joseph Breslin lives in the great state of Maryland where the roads are generally well-maintained and the Old Bay mélange (produced, so they say, by colossal crabs that lurk beneath Baltimore) continues to flow, miraculously lengthening the lives of those lucky enough to get it. The author's beautiful wife, the space princess Elizabeth (whom he kidnapped from a Frazetta painting), their three swashbuckling sons, and their now *two* cats are all doing well, despite Maryland's high taxes and its alien overlords. Since the publication of *Other Minds*, Frodo the cat has switched his allegiance, and now prefers the author to his wife. Meanwhile, Luthien, the Russian Blue, subscribes to the X-Files mantra, "Trust No One." You can find more of Joseph's stories and thoughts at joeybreslinwrites.com.

A HUMBLE REQUEST

Dear Reader,

Thank you so much for spending time with these stories. The only thing more difficult than crafting engaging tales is helping potential readers to find them. The world is a big place run partly by large corporations and mindless algorithms, and our collective attention spans are getting shorter. If you loved *Hearts Uncanny* and want other readers to discover it, please spread the word, and please (*please*) rate and review wherever you purchase or discuss books. No review is too short, and your brief, honest sentiments trump purple prose and complicated verbiage.

Gratefully,

Joey

Scan me to rate and review!

Milton Keynes UK
Ingram Content Group UK Ltd.
UKHW032330041024
449133UK00017B/209/J